Emily Giffin is the international bestselling author of *Something Borrowed* and *Something Blue*. She lives in Atlanta with her husband and twin sons. Visit her website at www.emilygiffin.com.

By the same author

Something Borrowed
Something Blue

Baby Proof

Emily Giffin

An Orion paperback

First published in Great Britain in 2006
by Orion
This paperback edition published in 2007
by Orion Books Ltd,
Orion House, 5 Upper St Martin's Lane,
London WC2H 9EA

An Hachette Livre UK company

3 5 7 9 10 8 6 4 2

A CIP catalogue record for this book
is available from the British Library.

ISBN 978-0-7528-8159-1

Printed in Great Britain by Clays Ltd, St Ives plc

The Orion Publishing Group's policy is to use papers that
are natural, renewable and recyclable products and made
from wood grown in sustainable forests. The logging and
manufacturing processes are expected to conform to the
environmental regulations of the country of origin.

www.orionbooks.co.uk

For my father, with gratitude

acknowledgments

Many thanks to my family and friends for their love and support over the past year. I am especially grateful to Mary Ann Elgin, Sarah Giffin, and Nancy LeCroy Mohler, who, as always, were there from the very beginning of this story with their invaluable input. I couldn't ask for a better mother, sister and friend.

Special thanks also to Lisa Reed, Julie Portera, Allyson Wenig Jacoutot, Jennifer New, Eric Kiefer, Brian Spainhour, Selina Cicogna, Stephen Lee, and Carrie Minton, for their friendship and generous contributions to this manuscript.

Abiding appreciation to Jane Wood and Orion, and to my agents, Lorella Belli and Stephany Evans.

A warm thank you to readers everywhere who took the time to send me such kind and inspiring e-mails.

And finally, I thank my husband, Buddy Blaha, and our sons, Edward and George, for giving all of this meaning.

Baby Proof

one

I never wanted to be a mother. Even when I was a little girl, playing dolls with my two sisters, I assumed the role of the good Aunt Claudia. I would bathe and diaper and cradle their plastic babies and then be on my way, on to more exciting pursuits in the backyard or basement. Grown-ups called my position on motherhood "cute"—flashing me that same knowing smile they give little boys who insist that all girls have cooties. To them, I was just a spunky tomboy who would someday fall in love and fall in line.

Those grown-ups turned out to be partially right. I *did* outgrow my tomboy stage and I *did* fall in love—several times, in fact—beginning with my high school boyfriend, Charlie. But when Charlie gazed into my eyes after our senior prom and asked me how many children I wanted, I reported a firm "zero."

"None?" Charlie looked startled, as if I had just confessed to him a terrible, dark secret. "Why not?"

I had a lot of reasons, which I laid out that night, but none that satisfied him. Charlie wasn't alone. Of the many boyfriends who followed him, none seemed to understand or accept my feelings. And although my relationships ended for a variety of reasons, I always had the sense that babies were a factor. Still, I truly believed that I would someday find my guy, that one person who would love me as is, without condition, without the promise of children. I was willing to wait for him.

But around the time I turned thirty, I came to terms with the fact that I might wind up alone. That I might never have that gut feeling when you know you've found *the One*. Instead of feeling sorry for myself or settling for something less than extraordinary, I focused my energy on things I could more easily control—my career as an editor at a big publishing company, fascinating trips, great times with good friends and interesting writers, evenings of fine wine and sparkling conversation. Overall, I was content with my life, and I told myself that I didn't need a husband to feel complete and fulfilled.

Then I met Ben. Beautiful, kind, funny Ben who seemed way too good to be true, especially after I learned that he actually *shared* my feelings on children. The subject came up the night we met, on a blind date orchestrated by our mutual friends, Ray and Annie. We were at Nobu, making small talk over yellowtail sashimi and rock shrimp tempura, when we became distracted by a young boy, no older than six, seated at the table next to us. The boy was ultratrendy, wearing a little black Kangol hat and a Lacoste polo with the collar turned up. His posture was ramrod straight, and he was proudly ordering his sushi, proper pronunciation and all, with no input from his parents. Clearly this was not his first trip to Nobu. In fact, I'd have guessed that he had eaten sushi more often than grilled-cheese sandwiches.

Ben and I watched him, smiling in the way people often smile at children and puppies, when I blurted out, "If you have to have kids, that's certainly the kind to have."

Ben leaned across the table and whispered, "You mean one with a bowl cut and a hip wardrobe?"

"No. The kind that you can take to Nobu on a school night," I said matter-of-factly. "I'm not interested in eating chicken fingers at T.G.I. Friday's. Ever."

Ben cleared his throat and smirked. "So you don't want to live in the suburbs and eat at Friday's or you don't want kids?" he asked, as I noticed his slight, sexy underbite.

"Neither. Both. All of the above," I said. Then, just in case I hadn't been clear enough, I added for good measure, "I don't want to eat at Friday's, I don't want to live in the suburbs, *and* I don't want kids."

It was a lot to put out there so soon, particularly at our age. Ben and I were both thirty-one—old enough to place the issue of kids firmly on most men's list of taboo topics for first dates. Taboo assuming you *want* kids, that is. If you don't want them, then raising the topic is akin to announcing that you are close friends with Anna Kournikova and that you and she enjoy three-ways, particularly *first-date* three-ways. In other words, your date probably won't view you as marriage material, but he'll certainly be enthusiastic about *dating* you. Because a thirty-one-year-old woman who does not want children equals a nonpressure situation, and most bachelors relish nonpressure situations—which is why they target women in their twenties. It gives them a cushion, some breathing room.

On the flip side, I knew I could be automatically disqualified for long-term consideration as I had with so many guys in my recent past. After all, most people—women *and* men— view not wanting kids as a deal breaker. At the very least, I risked coming across as cold and selfish, two traits that don't top the list of "what every man wants."

But in the messy world of dating, I had grown to favor candor at the expense of positioning and posturing. It was a nice advantage of not wanting kids. I wasn't up against that infamous clock. Nor was I about checking the boxes on a blueprint of life. As a result, I could afford total honesty. Full disclosure even on first dates.

So after I floated the kid issue out there with Ben, I held my breath, fearing that familiar, critical look. But Ben was all smiles as he exclaimed, "Neither do I!" in that jubilant and marveling tone people adopt when they've just stumbled upon a staggering coincidence. Like the time I ran into my third-grade teacher at a pub in London. Maybe the chances of being on a first date and discovering that neither party wants children aren't quite as slim as sitting on a barstool on the other side of the ocean, sipping a pint, and glancing up to see a teacher you haven't run across in two decades. But it's certainly not every day that you can find someone who wants to have a monogamous, meaningful relationship but also opt out of the seemingly automatic choice to experience the magical world of parenthood. Ben's expression seemed to register an understanding of all of this.

"Have you ever noticed how couples discuss the merits of having children early versus late?" he asked me earnestly.

I nodded as I tried to pinpoint his eye color—a pleasant combination of pale green and gray outlined with a dark ring. He was handsome, but beyond his fine nose, thick hair, and broad, muscular build was that incandescent intangible my best friend, Jess, calls the "sparkle factor." His face was alive and bright. He was the kind of man you see on the subway and wish you knew, your eyes uncontrollably darting to his left ring finger.

Ben continued, "And how the main feature of each scenario is freedom? The freedom that either comes early in life or late in life?"

I nodded again.

"Well," he said, pausing to sip his wine. "If the best part of having kids early is getting it over with, and the best part about having kids late is putting off the drudgery, doesn't it follow that *not* having kids *at all* is the best of both worlds?"

"I couldn't agree more," I said, raising my glass to toast his philosophy. I envisioned us defying the forces of nature together (the stuff about man wanting to sow his seed and woman wanting to grow life inside of her) and bucking the rules of society that so many of my friends were blindly following. I knew I was getting way ahead of myself, imagining all of this with a man I had just met, but by the time you reach thirty-one, you know immediately if a guy has potential or not. And Ben had potential.

Sure enough, the rest of our dinner went exceptionally well. No awkward lulls in the conversation, no red flags or annoying mannerisms. He asked thoughtful questions, gave good answers, and sent interested but not eager signals. So I invited him back to my apartment for a drink—something I never do on a first date. Ben and I did not kiss that night, but our arms touched as he flipped through a photo album on my coffee table. His skin felt electric against mine, and I had to catch my breath every time he turned a page.

The next day Ben called me just as he said he would. I was giddy when his name lit up my caller ID, and even more so when he announced, "I just wanted to tell you that that was far and away the best first date I've ever been on."

I laughed and said, "I agree. In fact, it was better than most of my second, third, and fourth dates."

We ended up talking for nearly two hours, and when we finally said good-bye, Ben said what I had just been thinking—

that the call felt more like five minutes. That he could talk to me forever. *One can hope,* I remember thinking.

Then came the sex. We only waited two weeks, which went against all the standard advice from friends, family, and magazine articles. It wasn't so much that I *had* to be with him in any urgent, lustful sense (although that was certainly part of it). It was more that I saw no reason to squander a single night together. When I know something is right, I believe in going for it, head-on. Sure enough, our first time was neither quick nor awkward nor tentative, the usual hallmarks of first times. Instead, our bodies fit together just right, and Ben knew what I liked without having to ask. It was the kind of sex that makes you wish you were a songwriter or poet. Or at least a woman who keeps a journal, something I hadn't done since I was a kid, but a practice I promptly began the day after we made love.

Ben and I quickly discovered that we had a lot more in common than our view on children, and a lot more binding us together than our crazy chemistry. We had a similar background. We both grew up in New York with two older sisters and parents who divorced late in the game. We were both hard-working, high achievers who were passionate about our careers. Ben was an architect and loved buildings as much as I loved books. We enjoyed traveling to obscure places, eating exotic food, and drinking a little too much. We loved movies and bands that were slightly offbeat without straining to be intellectual. We relished sleeping in on the weekends, reading the paper in bed, and drinking coffee into the evening hours. We were the same combination of clean freak and messy, of sentimental and pragmatic. We both had come to believe that short of something magical, relationships weren't worth the trouble.

In short, we fell in love, everything clicking in place. And it wasn't the one-sided delusional happiness that comes when a woman wants desperately to believe that she's found her guy. Our relationship was so satisfying and honest and real that at some point I started to believe that Ben was my soul mate, the one person I was *supposed* to be with. It was a concept I had never believed in before Ben.

I remember the day when all of this hit me. It was relatively early on, but well after we had exchanged our first *I love you*s. Ben and I were having a picnic in Central Park. People were all around us, sunning, reading, throwing Frisbees, laughing, yet it felt like we were completely alone. Whenever I was with Ben, it felt like the rest of the world fell away. We had just finished our lunch of cold fried chicken and potato salad and were lying on our backs, looking up at a very blue summer sky and holding hands, when we began that earnest but careful conversation about past loves. About the people and experiences that had brought us to the moment we were in.

Fleeting references to our history had been made up to that point, and I was well aware that we were both silently making those inevitable comparisons, putting our relationship in context. *She is more this and less of that. He is better or worse in these ways*. It is human nature to do this—unless it's your first relationship, which might be the very reason that your first relationship feels special and remains forever sacred. But the older you get, the more cynical you become, and the more complicated and convoluted the exercise is. You begin to realize that nothing is perfect, that there are trade-offs and sacrifices. The worst is when someone in your past trumps the person in your present, and you think to yourself: if I'd known *this*, then maybe I wouldn't have let him go. I had been feeling that way for a long time with respect to my college boyfriend, Paul. My relationship with Paul was far from flawless, and yet I hadn't found anyone in a decade who could squelch the more than occasional longing for what we had shared.

But with Ben, something was different. I was happier than I had ever been. I told him this, and I remember him asking me *why* it was different, *why* I was happier. I thought for a long time, wanting my answer to be accurate and complete. I began to awkwardly detail what made my relationship with Paul fail and spent much time ticking off Paul's specific attributes and qualities. I then listed for Ben the ways in which he was better—and more important, better *for* me.

I said, "You are a better kisser. You are more even-tempered. You are more generous. You are smarter. You are more fair-minded."

Ben nodded and looked so serious that I remember saying, "*And* you recycle" just to be funny. (Although it was true that Paul never recycled, which I thought said a lot about him.) As I talked, I had the distinct sense that I wasn't really capturing the essence of the way I was feeling. It was frustrating because I wanted Ben to know how special he was to me.

So I sort of gave up and asked Ben the same question about his ex-girlfriend, Nicole. I had begun to piece together a pretty decent picture of her based on snippets of conversation. I knew she was half Vietnamese and looked like a porcelain doll. (I *might* have snooped through his drawers once and come up with a photo or two.) She was an interior designer and had met Ben on a big museum project in Brooklyn. Her favorite book was *One Hundred Years of Solitude,* which was also Ben's favorite book (a fact that irrationally annoyed me). She smoked—they smoked together for a long time until he quit. They lived together for three years and dated for nearly six. Their relationship was intense—high highs and miserable lows. They had only broken up the winter before. I still hadn't heard exactly why. So of course the word *rebound* haunted me. The name Nicole filled me with crazy jealousy.

"Why is this relationship different?" I asked Ben, and then worried that I was presuming a bit much. "Or *is* it . . . different?"

I will never forget the way Ben looked at me, his pale eyes wide and almost glassy. He bit his bottom lip, one of his sexier habits, before he said, "That's actually not a difficult question at all. I just love you more. That's it. And I'm not saying that because she's in the past and you're in the present. I just *do*. In absolute terms. I mean, I loved her. I did. But I love you more. And it's really not even close."

It was the best thing anyone had ever said to me, and it was the best for one reason: I felt *exactly* the same way. The person who loved me like this was the person I loved back—which can feel like an absolute miracle. It *is* an absolute miracle.

So it came as no surprise when Ben proposed a few weeks later. And then, seven months later, on the anniversary of our first date, we eloped, tying the knot on an idyllic white crescent beach in St. John. It was not a popular move with our families, but we wanted the day to be only about us. Right after we exchanged our vows, I remember looking out across the sea and thinking that it was just the two of us, our lifetime together stretching endlessly ahead. Nothing would ever change, except the addition of wrinkles and gray hair and sweet, satisfying memories.

Of course the subject of children surfaced often during our newlywed days, but only when responding to rude inquiries regarding our plans to procreate from everyone and anyone:

Ben's family, my family, friends, random mothers in the park, even our dry cleaner.

"We're not going to have children," one of us would matter-of-factly reply, and then we would tolerate the inevitable chatter that followed about how much children enrich your lives.

Once, at a book party, an editor came right out and told me that if I didn't have kids at some point, then my life "would be devoid of meaning." Now *that*'s a pretty extreme statement. I think I said something like, "Well, gee, I might as well off myself now then, huh?" She pretended not to hear me and kept going on about her children.

Another common response was the sympathetic nod from people who believed that we were actually concealing a painful truth: our inability to conceive. Like the time a friend of Ben's from college slipped me a business card with her fertility clinic information scrawled on the back. I handed it to Ben who promptly announced to his friend that he had had a vasectomy several months into our marriage. This wasn't true—I was on the pill—but there was something about his statement that both shamed her and shut her up.

And the final recurrent motif was the whole, "Who is going to take care of you when you're old?" query. Ben and I would say, "Each other." They'd (unbelievably) respond, "But what about when one of you dies?" At which point, things would *really* become cheery. Occasionally I'd point out that nursing homes are filled with people whose children never visit. That children are no guarantee of anything. You could have a kid who becomes a poor, struggling artist. Or a kid who grows into a selfish, ne'er-do-well adult. Or a kid who has special needs that render him unable to care for himself, let alone his elderly parents. Bottom line, Ben and I agreed that worrying about your care is a stupid, selfish reason to procreate anyway. We preferred to work hard and save our money, rather than burden a future generation.

But over time, we learned to keep quiet on the subject. It was so much easier that way. We would simply exchange a knowing glance and then discuss it all later. We were annoyed by the narrow-minded assumption that children were a given, but at the same time, we enjoyed the underlying smugness that came from being part of a child-free union. Our relationship was about freedom and possibility and exploration. We were together because we *wanted* to be together. Not because we needed a partner in parenthood or because children were keeping us together, caging us with eighteen years of obligation.

Then, about two years into our marriage, something changed.

It was subtle at first, as changes in relationships typically are, so it is hard to pinpoint the genesis. But, looking back, I think it all began when Ben and I went on a ski trip with Annie and Ray, the couple who had set us up on our first date. I had known Annie since our bingeing college days, so I noticed right away that she was sticking with Perrier. At first she claimed to be on antibiotics for a sinus infection, but the whole antibiotic excuse had never slowed her in the past so I dragged the truth out of her. She was eight weeks pregnant.

"Was it planned?" I blurted out, thinking surely it had been an accident. Annie adored her career as a documentary filmmaker and had a million different causes on the side. She had never expressed an interest in having children, and I couldn't fathom her making time for motherhood.

Annie and Ray clasped hands and nodded in unison.

11

"But I thought you didn't want kids," I said.

"We didn't want kids right *away*," Annie said. "But we feel ready now. Although I guess you're never completely ready!" She laughed in a high-pitched, schoolgirlish way, her cheeks flushing pink.

"Hmm," I said.

Ben kicked me under the table and said, "Well, congratulations, guys! This is awesome news." Then he shot me a stern look and said, "Isn't that wonderful news, Claudia?"

"Yes. Wonderful," I said, but I couldn't help feeling betrayed. Ben and I were going to lose our favorite traveling companions, our only close friends who were as unfettered as we were by babies and all their endless accoutrements.

We finished dinner, our conversation dominated by talk of children and Westchester real estate.

Later, when Ben and I were alone in our room, he chastised me for being so transparently unsupportive. "You could have at least *pretended* to be happy for them," he said. "Instead of grilling them about birth control."

"I was just so shocked," I said. "Did you have any idea?"

Ben shook his head and with a fleeting expression of envy said, "No. But I think it's great."

"Don't tell me you want them now, too?" I asked him, mostly joking.

Ben answered quickly, but his words registered flat and false. "Of course not," he said. "Don't be ridiculous."

Over the next few months, things only got more troubling. Ben became all too interested in the progress of Annie's pregnancy. He admired the ultrasound photos, even taping one to our refrigerator. I told him that we were not a "tape things to the refrigerator" kind of family.

"Jeez, Claudia. Lighten up," Ben said, appearing agitated as he pulled down the murky black-and-white image and slapped it into a drawer. "You really should be happier for them. They're our *best* friends, for chrissake."

A short time after that, right before Annie and Ray had their baby, Ben and I planned a last-minute weekend getaway to the resort where we had been married. It was early January when the abrupt disappearance of Christmas decorations and tourists always makes Manhattan seem so naked and bleak, and Ben said he couldn't wait until early March for our tentatively planned trip to Belize. I remember tossing some shorts and a new red bikini into my leather duffel and remarking how nice it was to have spontaneity in our relationship, the freedom to fly off at a moment's notice.

Ben said, "Yes. There are some wonderful things about our life together."

This sentence struck me as melancholy—even ominous—but I didn't press him on it. I didn't even pressure him to talk when he was uncharacteristically taciturn on our flight down to the Caribbean.

I didn't really worry until later that night when we were settling into our room, unpacking our clothes and toiletries. I momentarily stopped to inspect the view of the sea outside our room, and as I turned back toward my suitcase, I caught a glimpse of Ben in the mirror. His mouth was curled into a remorseful frown. I panicked, remembering what my sister, Maura, once said about men who cheat. She is an expert on the topic as her husband, Scott, had been unfaithful with at least two women she knew of. "Look out if they're really mean or really nice. Like if they start giving you flowers and jewelry for no reason," she had said. "Or taking you away on a romantic getaway. It's the guilt. They're trying to make up for something." I tried to calm down, telling myself that I was being paranoid. Ben and I always took spontaneous trips together; we never needed a reason.

Still, I wanted to dispel the lingering images of Ben pressed against a sweaty bohemian lover, so I sat on the bed, kicked off my flip-flops, and said, "Ben. Talk to me. What's on your mind?"

He swallowed hard and sat next to me. The bed bounced slightly under his weight and the motion made me feel even more nervous.

"I don't know how to say this," Ben said, his voice cracking. "So I'll just come out with it."

I nodded, feeling queasy. "Go ahead."

"I think I might want kids after all."

I felt a rush of relief and even laughed out loud. "You scared me." I laughed again, louder, and then opened a Red Stripe from the minibar.

"I'm serious, Claudia."

"Where is all of this coming from? Annie and Ray?"

"Maybe. I don't know. It's just . . . it's just this *feeling* I have," Ben said, making a fist over his heart.

At least he hasn't cheated on me, I thought. A betrayal of that magnitude could never be erased or forgotten. His fleeting wish for a child would surely go away. But as Ben continued to spout off his list of reasons why a baby might be a good thing—stuff about showing children the world, doing things better than our parents had done—my relief gave way to something else. It was a sense of losing control. A sense that something was slipping away.

I tried to stay calm as I delivered a rather eloquent speech. I told him that all of that parenthood stuff wasn't who we were. I said that our relationship was built upon our unique twoness, the concept that three or more is a crowd. I pointed out that we couldn't have taken this last-minute trip. We'd be anchored to home all the time.

"But we'd have *other* things," Ben said. "And what if we really are missing out on something great? I've never heard a single person say they regret having a child."

"Would they admit it if they did?" I said.

"Maybe not," Ben said. "But the point is, I don't think they ever would."

"I *totally* disagree . . . I mean, why are there boarding schools? The mere existence of boarding schools proves something, right?" I asked. I was partly kidding about the boarding schools, but Ben didn't laugh.

I sighed and then decided to change the subject altogether, focus on having fun. Show Ben what we'd be missing with children.

"Let's get changed and go to dinner," I said, turning up "One Love" on our portable CD player and thinking that there's nothing like a little Bob Marley to put you in a child-free, unencumbered state of mind.

But despite my best efforts to have a good time, the rest of our weekend passed with an increasing tension. Things felt forced between us, and Ben's mood went from quiet to lugubrious. On our third and final night on the island, we took a cab to Asolare, a restaurant with incredible views of Cruz Bay. We ate in virtual silence, commenting only on the sunset and our perfectly prepared lobster tail. Just as our waitress brought us our coffee and sorbet, I looked at Ben and said, "You know what? We had a *deal*."

As soon as the words came out, I knew how utterly ridiculous I sounded. Marriage is never a done deal. Not even when you have children together, although that certainly helps your case. And the irony of that seemed overwhelmingly sad.

Ben tugged on his earlobe and said, "I want to be a father."

"Fine. Fine," I said. "But do you want a baby more than you want to be my husband?"

He reached out and put one hand over mine. "I want *both*," he said as he squeezed my fingers.

"Well. You can't have both," I said, trying to keep the angry edge out of my voice.

I waited for him to say that of course he'd always pick me. That it was the only thing in the world he was really sure of. "So? Which is it?" I said.

It wasn't supposed to be a test, but it suddenly felt like one. Ben stared down at his cappuccino for a long time. Then he moved his hand from mine and slowly stirred three cubes of sugar into his mug.

When he finally looked up at me, there was guilt and grief in his gray-green eyes, and I knew I had my answer.

two

When we return home from St. John, Ben and I decide to take some time and think things over. Actually, Ben decides that's what we should do—those are his exact words. I have to bite my tongue to keep from telling him that I have absolutely nothing to think over. He is the one who has radically changed his mind about something so fundamental in our relationship. So he's the one who needs to do the thinking.

I fall into my normal routine, going to work and returning home to Ben at night, where I read and he sketches until we go to bed. Meanwhile, I try to convince myself that my husband is only going through a phase, a kind of reverse midlife crisis. Some men regret settling down and having kids early; Ben is simply questioning our decision not to have them at all. I tell myself that it is normal—maybe even healthy—to reevaluate your life. Ben will take some time and do all of that, and then surely he will come to his senses and reaffirm our choices.

I resist the urge to discuss the situation with my family or friends because I somehow believe that talking about it will solidify our rift. Instead I ignore it, hoping it will all go away.

It doesn't.

One Saturday afternoon Ben points to a fair-skinned, blue-eyed girl with strawberry-blond hair on the street and says, "She looks like you." Then, in case I missed his point, he says,

"If we had a daughter, she'd look like that."

I just give him a look.

A few days later, as he watches a Knicks game on television, he says he wants a son because otherwise what is the point of all the useless sports trivia he's memorized since he was a little boy. "Not that I wouldn't teach our daughter about sports, too," Ben adds.

Again, I say nothing.

The following week he announces that having an only child could be a compromise of sorts.

"How do you figure?" I say.

"Because I'd like to have two and you think you don't want any," he says, as if we are six years old and deciding how many doughnuts to buy.

"I *know* I don't want any," I say, and then open my birth control packet at the bathroom sink.

Ben furrows his brow and says, "How about you stop taking those things? Can't we just see what happens? See if it's meant to be?"

I tell him that this plan of his sounds akin to the Christian Scientist approach to modern medicine.

He gives me a blank stare.

"I have a better idea," I say. "Let's hold hands and jump out the window and see if we're meant to die."

Then I take my pill.

The most egregious of Ben's remarks comes one Sunday when we are having brunch in Rye with Ben's mother, Lucinda, his two sisters, Rebecca and Megan, and their husbands and children. As we finish eating and move into the family room of the home Ben grew up in, I am thinking what I always think when we get together with his family: could our

18

families—and specifically our mothers—be more different? My family is volatile; Ben's family is placid. My mother is unmaternal and quirky; Ben's mother is nurturing and vanilla. I watch Lucinda now, sipping her tea from a china cup, and think to myself that she is a complete throwback to the fifties, the kind of mother who had homemade cookies waiting when the kids came home from school. She *lived* for her children—so much so that Ben once pointed to that as a possible cause for his parents' divorce. It was a classic case of empty nesters realizing that they had nothing holding them together but the kids.

So, as it often happens, Ben's father found a new life with a much younger woman while Lucinda *continues* to live for her children—and now grandchildren (Ben's sisters each have two daughters). Ben is her clear favorite, though, perhaps because he's the only boy. As such, she is desperate for us to change our minds about having a baby, but way too polite to come right out and criticize our choices. Instead, she is full of seemingly breezy comments on the matter. Like the time when we bought our car, and she slid into the backseat, remarking, "Plenty of room for a car seat back here!"

I always have the feeling that she is directing her comments at me and that she blames *me* for our decision. Ben used to say I was paranoid, but now, of course, I'm actually right.

Rebecca and Megan are both stay-at-home mothers and don't help matters for me. They show genuine interest in my publishing world, and frequently select my novels for their book clubs, but I know they wish that I would put my career on hold and give their baby brother a baby of his own.

So although Ben's family is perfectly pleasant and utterly easy to get along with, I dread spending time with them because they inevitably make me feel defensive. Of course, I feel even more defensive now that Ben and I are no longer a united front. And I have a gnawing feeling that they will sniff the situation out and seek to divide and conquer.

Sure enough, as the adults talk and watch Ben's nieces play with their Barbies, Rebecca says something about how nice a boy cousin would be to break things up a little. I make a quick preemptive strike by looking at Megan and saying, "Well, Meg, you'd better get busy!"

Megan's husband, Rob, shakes his head and says, "Heck, no! We're done!" and Megan chimes in with, "Two children is enough. Two is *perfect*. Besides . . . I wouldn't know what to do with a boy!"

Lucinda smooths her skirt and shoots Ben and me a demure, hopeful look. "So I guess it's up to you two to have a boy," she chirps innocently. "Besides, that's the only way to carry on the family name!"

I can feel myself tense up as I marvel at how she can care so much about a name that belongs to her ex-husband. But I just say, "I wouldn't know what to do with a boy, either . . . Or a girl for that matter!" Then I laugh as if I've just made a very clever joke.

Everyone joins in with a polite chuckle.

Except Ben, who squeezes my knee and says, "You'd figure it out, Claudia. *We* would figure it out."

The joy in the room is palpable. His family practically applauds, they are made so giddy by this comment from their only brother and son.

Lucinda leans forward and says, "Do you have something to tell us?"

Ben smiles and says, "Not yet."

I restrain myself until we're in the car alone, driving home. "Not *yet*?" I shout. Then I tell him that I've never felt so betrayed.

Ben tells me not to be so dramatic, that it was just a turn of phrase.

"A turn of phrase?" I say indignantly.

"Yeah," he says. "Jeez, Claudia. Chill out, would you?"

I decide right then that it's time to talk to one of my loyal triumvirate—either my two older sisters, Daphne and Maura, or my best friend, Jess. After some consideration, I rule out my sisters, at least preliminarily. Although they always have my best interest at heart, I am pretty sure they won't stand by me on this one.

Maura's motivation will have more to do with not wanting me to lose Ben than thinking I should have a baby. She respects my decision not to have a baby. She has three children whom she loves dearly—and whom *I* love dearly—but I think in some very quiet, introspective moments, she might nearly regret her decision to have them. Or at least have them with Scott. I have often heard her say that the biggest decision a woman can make in life is not who to marry but who should be the father of her children. "You can't undo it," she says. "It bonds you for life." Although the truth is, I think Maura made a bad decision on both fronts. She is a good example of someone caring too much about passion and excitement and surface appeal rather than being with a solid, good, honest man. I call it the "high school girl phenomenon." Most girls in high school discount the nice, quiet, slightly nerdish boy and instead seek out the flashy, popular jock. If they somehow land the latter, they truly believe themselves to be the luckiest creatures on the planet. They got the big prize. Yet when they return to their twenty-year reunion, they see the error of their ways. The nice, quiet, slightly nerdish boy has bloomed into the perfect husband, wholesome father, and loyal caretaker while the flashy, popular jock is off in the corner playing grabass with Misty, the slutty ex-cheerleader.

This is, more or less, the Cliff's Notes version of Maura's misguided relationship history. She dated a guy named Niles throughout her late twenties, and came very close to marrying him. But when Niles started asking her about rings, she freaked out and decided that he was "too boring and predictable." She said she couldn't marry someone who didn't give her heart palpitations on a daily basis. At the time I was very supportive of her decision. I was all about finding true love and not settling—which is something I still believe in wholeheartedly. But with hindsight, I really think Maura was confusing love with lust—and nice with boring. Niles treated her well and was eager to make a lasting commitment. Thus, she assumed he was somehow unworthy—or at least wholly uninteresting. Frankly, I also think Niles's looks factored into her decision, although she would never admit it. Maura was attracted to Niles, but he wasn't the sort of guy who other women took note of in a bar. And Maura wanted hot. Maura wanted to impress. So it wasn't surprising when her first boyfriend after Niles was tall, gorgeous, life-of-the-party Scott. And although I'm sure there are plenty of tall, gorgeous, life-of-the-party guys who are also true to their wives, I happen to believe that a disproportionate number of them are cheaters.

In any event, *Scott* is a cheater, and I think Maura's views on my relationship will be colored by the fact that she picked wrong. That, in Daphne's words, she went with "Suave Scott" over "Nice Niles." To this point, Maura has spent years being envious of my relationship with Ben, a relationship that is pretty ideal on the inside, and thus looks even more perfect from the outside. She is never begrudging of my happiness, but Ben is still a constant reminder of what she could have had—and what she desperately wants me to appreciate and protect. So I am certain that she will tell me that I should have a baby in order to keep Ben. That I should do *anything* to keep him. And that is something I *really* don't want to hear.

Daphne's reasons for telling me to stay with Ben will have less to do with my relationship and everything to do with her baby obsession. It is the filter through which she observes the world around her. She and her husband, Tony, have been trying to get pregnant for nearly two years. They tried for a year the old-fashioned way: drink a bottle of wine, hop in the sack, pray for a missed period. After that, they progressed to buying fertility monitors, making ovulation charts, and bickering about peak times in the month. She is now taking Clomid and researching fertility clinics.

It pains me to watch my sister's monthly heartbreak, to see the way the struggle has changed her, how she has become increasingly bitter as her friends, one by one, all have babies. She is particularly resentful when other people have an easy time of it, and she went so far as to write off her girlfriend Kelly altogether when Kelly got knocked up on her honeymoon with boy-girl twins. When Maura told Daphne she should be happy for Kelly (which might be true but was certainly an unnecessary comment), my sisters got in a huge argument. Daphne hung up on Maura and promptly phoned me, trying to enlist me to her side. Then as Maura beeped in on my other line, eager to share her version of the spat,

Daphne yelled, "Don't you dare answer call-waiting!" and then frantically argued her point. She insisted that the fallout with Kelly had nothing to do with her blessing of twins, and everything to do with Kelly's proclamation that she was naming her daughter Stella. "That's *my* name," Daphne must have said ten times. I resisted the urge to crack myself up with a, "No, your name is actually Daphne," and instead assured my sister that I wasn't a big fan of alliteration in naming anyway (Daphne's last name is Sacco). I told her Stella Sacco sounded like a stripper—and that if I received a "Stella Sacco" résumé at work, I would instantly toss it aside and never even see that she was a Fulbright scholar. A long conversation about baby naming ensued, a topic I find to be ridiculous and tiresome unless you have a nine-month deadline in the works. Discussing baby names when you're not even pregnant is almost as ridiculous as laying claim to a name. Of course, I shared these observations with Maura when I finally called her back, but told her that we should nonetheless try to support Daphne. I am very accustomed to brokering a delicate peace between my sisters, although they might say the same. Perhaps that's just the natural dynamic of three sisters. We are all very close, but we are frequently two against one and the alliances constantly form and re-form.

So, anyway, the mere thought that my sisters might side with Ben, and try to talk me into having a baby, is just too much to bear. I need an unconditional, unwavering supporter. Someone who will put aside her own bias. That's where my best friend, Jess, always comes in.

Jess and I met our freshman year at Princeton when we bonded in our distaste for our respective roommates, both strident theater majors named Tracy. One night right before

Thanksgiving break, Jess plied the Tracys with vodka and cranberry juice and talked them into a roommate swap. She was so effective that she made the Tracys think it was *their* idea. My Tracy even wrote me a note of apology—in *calligraphy*. The next day Jess schlepped her clothing, books, and comforter across the hall in plastic crates and garbage bags, and we ended up living together for the next *fourteen* years (nearly as long as we lived at home), throughout college and then into our first crummy Manhattan apartment on Ninety-second and York.

We upgraded several times over the years, until we nabbed our spacious, sunny loft on Park Avenue South that, due to Jess's kitschy style, drew many comparisons to the apartment on *Friends*. We each had a few boyfriends along the way, but none that we considered ditching the other for.

Until Ben came along.

Jess and I were both teary the day I moved in with Ben, and then joked that our separation felt like a divorce. We continued to talk every day, sometimes several times a day, but there was a definite change in our friendship. In part, it was just that we saw each other less. We no longer had those late-night and early-morning chats that can't really be duplicated over the phone. In part, it was an inevitable shift of loyalty. Ben became the person I talked to the most, the one I turned to first in crisis or celebration. I've seen married women put their girlfriends over their husbands, and although I admire this brand of female fidelity, I also believe that it can be a dangerous dynamic. Certain things should stay sacred in a marriage. Jess and I never discussed the changes in our relationship, but I could tell she understood. I think she also pulled back a little herself, out of respect for my relationship and perhaps as a point of pride. She cultivated a new circle of friends—all single women in their thirties, all searching for love.

There are times when I have a nostalgic pang when Jess is meeting the girls out for sangria in the Village—or doing all the things we used to do together. But for the most part, I do not envy her position. We turn thirty-five this year, and I can tell the benchmark birthday stresses her out. She's not desperate to marry, but she does want children someday. And she's all too aware that her eggs have a sell-by date (her words, not mine).

Which makes it all the more frustrating when I watch my best friend repeatedly star in what would make the perfect Jackie Collins novel. She consistently gravitates to unavailable types—shameless players, married men, or West Coasters who refuse to even *consider* living in Manhattan. In fact, she is currently embroiled in a two-*year* relationship with a guy named Trey, who is all of the above. I know, it's tough to be a shameless *married* player, but Trey accomplishes the feat with great flourish. In Jess's defense, Trey didn't tell her he was married until *after* she developed feelings for him, but she's had at least a year to digest the news and move on.

Bottom line, Jess has abhorrent taste in men and always has. Even in college she'd go for the frat boy with attitude, the kind of guy you can totally see being brought before honor council on date rape charges. It's odd, because in all other facets of her life, Jess is completely in control. She is confident, funny, and the smartest woman I know. She graduated summa cum laude from Princeton without studying much at all and then got her M.B.A. at Columbia. Now she's an investment banker with Lehman Brothers, kicking ass in a male-dominated world and making money I thought only professional athletes and movie stars could make. On top of this, she looks like a model. With short, blond hair and a tall, willowy build, she is more runway model than underwear model, which my sister Maura highlights as Jess's problem. "Men don't like the runway look," she says. "Women do." (Maura has a whole collection of superficial relationship theories. Some of her gems: the more attractive one in a couple always has the power; women should marry men at least seven years older than they to close the aging gap; short, bald men had better be well endowed.)

In any event, I decide it's time to confide in Jess.

So the next day we meet for lunch at a deli halfway between our respective offices. We order sandwiches at the counter, then pick up bags of Baked Lay's and bottles of Evian and sit at an open table by a window. There are five construction workers sitting behind us, and after one gets up to go, Jess remarks that he has "the perfect ass." She reminds me of a guy in her unabashed commentary on body parts of the opposite sex. I check out his Levi's-clad backside, agree with her that it is a mighty nice one, and then tentatively launch into my dilemma.

Jess listens intently, her expression sympathetic. It has been a long time since I have needed any real relationship counseling from her. I can tell she welcomes the distraction from Trey's latest angst-causing stunt as she says in her Alabama accent she has not shed despite years in the Northeast, "You and Ben will work this out. Do *not* panic."

"I'm not panicking yet," I say. "Well . . . maybe I am just a little bit . . . After all, having kids isn't really something you can compromise on, you know?"

Jess nods and recrosses her long legs. "Good point."

"So I'm hoping it's just a phase," I say.

Jess lifts the bun of her chicken salad sandwich and tucks a few chips inside. "I'm *sure* it's just a phase," she says. "A little something he's going through."

"Yeah," I say, staring at my turkey sandwich. I haven't had much of an appetite since our return from the Caribbean.

"Remember his guitar?" she asks, rolling her eyes. Jess loves to make fun of Ben, and he does the same to her, which I only take as a sign of their fondness for each other. She laughs and says, "Ol' Benny Van Halen was hot to trot for a few months, wasn't he?"

I laugh, recalling the day that Ben and I wandered past a little shop in the Village called the Guitar Salon. It was tucked inside a charming brownstone, all lit up and inviting on a rainy day. So we went inside and looked around, and after a few minutes, Ben decided that he just *had* to own a vintage guitar. It was literally the first time he had shown the slightest interest in any musical instrument, but by this time, I was used to Ben's sudden interest in a wide range of topics. Ben is one of those people who manages to be an enthusiast for many, many things—astronomy, films, collecting old watches, you name it. So I watched him fondly and waited patiently as he asked the owner a slew of questions. Then he took his time sampling guitars, running his fingers over the strings and even attempting to play. An hour later, he was spending a small fortune on a 1956 Spanish guitar made of spruce rosewood, along with a package of lessons taught by someone of moderate fame in the New York classical guitar world.

For months, Ben practiced with an endearing fervor, quickly mastering the basics and acquiring impressive calluses. On my birthday he serenaded me with a perfect rendition of "I Can't

Help Falling in Love With You"—a song that, I sheepishly confess, makes me melt, especially because I've always maintained that Ben looks a little bit like a young, sandy-haired version of Elvis.

But a short time later, Ben lost interest in his new hobby and retired his guitar to a dusty corner under our bed. Recently, he posted it for sale on eBay. Jess reassures me now that his current fixation on fatherhood will be just as short-lived.

"Only problem is," I say, "Ben actually *owned* a guitar before abandoning the idea of becoming an accomplished musician."

"That's true," she says, scrolling through e-mail on her BlackBerry. Jess is a masterful multitasker. She furiously types a reply with her thumbs as she says, "And there's no way to temporarily own a child, is there?"

"That's where Ray and Annie's baby could come in handy," I say, thinking of the week-long stays at my sister Maura's house after she had each of her three babies. All three visits were initially thrilling as there is nothing quite as meaningful or special as meeting a new member of your family. I also loved spending such quiet, intimate time with my sister, who is usually so frenetically busy with her many Bronxville social obligations. Maura and I have had some of our best talks in that cozy new-baby aftermath, both of us in our robes and slippers with our teeth unbrushed. Still, the nighttime feeding duties I would volunteer for were always brutal, and I would leave her house with a bone-tired weariness that verged on actual *pain*. I honestly don't know how so many women keep that up for weeks and months at a time.

"Was the kid born yet or what?" Jess asks.

29

I smile at her wording. For someone desperate to be a mother, she's going to have to soften up her vocabulary.

"Any day now," I say. "So let's hope that this is nothing that a few hours with a real, live infant can't cure."

As if on cue, Raymond Gage Jr. arrives the following afternoon, following fourteen hours of labor and a last-minute emergency C-section. Ben calls me at work with the news.

"Annie and Ray want us to come right over," he says excitedly.

The hospital invite surprises me. Annie and Ray are our close friends, but I didn't think we were *that* close. I thought we were more "Come see the baby as soon as we take him home" level friends. Still, the current controversy notwithstanding, I am looking forward to meeting their baby.

So after work I take the subway to Roosevelt Hospital where I meet up with Ben in the hospital gift shop. He has already picked up a couple of Mylar balloons and a card that we sign on the elevator ride up to the baby wing. We make our way to Room 1231. The door is adorned with a big, pastel blue stork holding an IT'S A BOY! banner, as are approximately half of the doors on the corridor.

Given Annie's rough delivery, I am expecting a subdued gathering, but there is a full-on, raucous party inside. The room is filled with flowers, gifts, and at least a dozen friends and relatives who are snapping photos of the baby and clamoring to hold him. There are even a few bottles of champagne that Ray hides behind his back whenever a nurse stops by.

Ray and Annie beam as they retell the details of Annie's water breaking, the cab ride to the hospital, and their fight right before Annie got her epidural when Ray admitted he had left the video camera at home. We laugh and listen and admire Raymond Jr., who looks exactly like his father (and I'm not one who can normally see such resemblances).

It is a good time for all, but I am very aware of the effect the celebration is having on Ben. He is swept up in emotion and clearly thrilled for our friends, but I can tell that he is also uneasy and wistful. Not quite sad, but as close as you can get to being sad without actually being sad. His expression reminds me of a single bridesmaid at a wedding as she listens to the twentieth toast of the night.

Just as we are about to take turns holding Raymond Jr., a lactation consultant stops in, and Ray asks politely if everyone would please leave. I'm surprised that Annie, who would have been burning bras had she been born a few years earlier, cares a lick about her privacy, but then again, don't they say a baby changes everything? We give Annie and Ray our final con-gratulations and tell them we'll be in touch soon.

As we ride the subway home, I am hoping that Ben under-stands that the party only lasts so long. That once you bring the baby home from the hospital and a few weeks pass, the champagne-and-casserole flow stops, and you're on your own in the middle of the night.

In case this point is lost on him, I let a few weeks pass and then call Ben and innocently suggest that we offer to babysit for Annie and Ray. Give them a chance to go out alone. Ben thinks it's a great idea. We conference call our friends who gra-ciously accept.

So the following Friday night, Ben and I take a cab over to Annie and Ray's and climb the stairs to their third-floor walk-up (as I comment on how hard it will be to drag a stroller up and down the steps). I am hoping for a set of haggard parents, a messy house, the stench of sour milk commingling with the odor of dirty diapers. But Ray comes to the door clean-shaven and chipper, and I notice with dismay that their apartment is spotless. Neil Young's "Good to See You" is playing a bit louder than you'd expect in a home with a new baby, who is sleeping angelically in his car seat.

"Where are you all going tonight?" I ask, eager to move them on their way. Leave the baby with Ben and me. Shine a light on our grand incompetence.

"Change of plans," Annie says briskly. I note that she looks beautiful. Her hair is pulled back in a sleek chignon, and she still has that pregnant glow.

"What? Too tired to go out?" I prod.

"No. We're *all* going out. Table for four at Pastis awaits us!" Ray says.

I silently curse my choice of nice jeans, a basic black top, and flats. I can't very well protest on the grounds that I'm wearing babysitting garb. Not that my friends would likely accept an "I'm wearing sneakers" sort of excuse.

"Are you sure?" I say. "We wanted you to have some time alone."

"No! We miss you guys!" Annie says, hugging me.

"So who is watching Ray junior?" Ben asks.

"He's coming along," Annie chirps.

"Seriously?" I ask.

Annie nods.

"He sleeps all the time. He'll be fine!" Ray says, lifting his son's car seat up as if to prove the point. "Hey—you guys wanna hold him before we take off? We have a few minutes . . . It won't wake him up."

"Sure. Let me wash my hands first," I say, remembering

my sister's obsession with germs after her first baby was born.

I walk over to the kitchen sink and scrub in, considering my strategy. Should I jostle him a little and try to wake him? Should I feign an awkward cradle, proving that babies aren't my thing? I dry my hands and decide that such stunts might be too obvious. So I gently take the baby from Ray's outstretched arms. I cradle his tiny head with my free hand and sit on the couch next to Ben. We both gaze down at Raymond Jr., who is wearing a white cashmere onesie and matching cap. He remains sound asleep, and I can tell right away that he is going to screw me and play the role of perfect baby.

After a few minutes of conversation, Ben says, "May I?"

Annie beams. "Of course."

Ben is a natural, completing my handoff with ease. Raymond Jr. opens one eye and peers up at Ben. Then he yawns, tucks his knees up against his chest, and falls back asleep. Ben looks smitten.

"Don't they look *precious* together?" Annie says.

I nod, feeling annoyed by my friend's use of the word *precious*. It is the first sign that she has changed. The old Annie would never have used a word like *precious*—unless doing so disparagingly.

Ben runs one finger gently over Raymond Jr.'s cheek. "I can't believe how *soft* his skin is."

Of *course* he can't have a little eczema or baby acne, I think.

Ben keeps gushing. "Look, Claudia. Look how *tiny* his fingers are."

Raymond Jr. clutches Ben's thumb, and I wonder how I'm supposed to compete with a stunt like that. The kid is *good*.

"Does he ever cry?" Ben says.

Annie says, not too much, he's a very easy baby.

Naturally.

"We're really lucky," Ray says. "In fact, we have to wake *him* up at night for his feedings."

"That's highly unusual," I say, glancing nervously at Ben.

Everyone ignores my comment as Ray whisks his son up, bundles him back into his car seat, and leads the charge down to the street where he flags a cab almost instantly. I am hoping that the baby counts as a fifth person—over the legal limit in a cab—but our driver doesn't protest.

The rest of the evening continues smoothly, with Raymond Jr. snoozing peacefully in the noisy restaurant. Our conversation is normal and fun, and I almost forget that there is an infant sleeping under the table. When all else fails, I find myself rooting for an unsavory boob out on the table, but Annie produces a discreet bottle of formula, explaining that she's decided breast-feeding isn't her thing.

So short of the word *precious*, I have nothing on Annie or Ray or the baby.

On our way home that night, Ben asks what I thought of Raymond Jr.

I say he is really cute, very sweet.

"But?" Ben says, because my tone suggests a *but*.

I start rambling about how rare it is for a baby to sleep so much. I remind Ben that my sister's kids all had colic, and that even short of colic, most babies fuss a lot more than Raymond Jr. My monologue is not exactly subtle, but neither is Ben's rebuttal: a sales pitch centered on lofty and impractical offers to take "full, nighttime responsibility" for our baby should we somehow produce the difficult kind. It is as if he believes that the only thing keeping me from having children is my desire for a full eight hours of slumber. He follows that up with a speech about his firm's liberal paternity-leave policies and the appeal of being a stay-at-home dad.

"A stay-at-home dad?" I say. "You love your career."

Ben shrugs. "I'd love our baby, too . . . The point is, *you* wouldn't have to change your schedule at *all*, Claudia," he says. Then he repeats the statement, with the same emphasis on *you* and *all*.

"I heard you the first time," I say.

That night, around three A.M., I find myself wide awake and worrying. I strongly consider shaking Ben and saying, "Your turn to get the baby, honey." After all, it's one thing to talk about getting up in the middle of the night. It's a very different thing to do it when all you really feel like doing is sleeping.

But I decide against this tactic. After all, the way things have been going for me lately, Ben would likely get up, whistling and brainstorming baby names.

three

Ben's baby comments verge on bribery and continue rapid-fire over the next few days. I tell myself to hang in there, don't blow up, ride it out. I tell myself that I should give him at *least* as long as his guitar-playing days lasted on the off chance that babies are just Ben's current fixation. Or maybe he's just a little restless or bored or looking for something to fill a void. This would fit with one of my theories of why some couples— even the ones so ill-suited to be parents—have children. The theory is that part of the baby allure might have to do with our society's focus on "firsts." With benchmarks and rites of passage. We have our first kiss, first relationship, high school graduation, college, college graduation, first job, wedding, first home. Having a child just seems to be the next thing remaining in the progression of life, the only momentous step left to take. Or maybe couples just want to vicariously experience all those great firsts again through their children. Relive the highs and erase their mistakes. I'm not saying all couples have a baby for these reasons—most truly *want* to be parents—but I think some do.

In case Ben falls into this category, I make a point to work a little less and see to it that our life together is as full and fun as possible. I see to it that we do all the things we have always done together, but with greater intensity and frequency. I make reservations at new restaurants and take us to hear great music and see fabulous art. I plan weekend getaways to the Berkshires and the Hamptons.

Most important, I follow Jess's advice and keep our sex life strong. Jess is a huge believer in sex as a panacea to any problem—which is why she is so convinced that Trey is going to leave his wife any day now (she claims to be *that* good).

One night in particular, I wear my best lingerie and initiate the sort of lovemaking that is worthy of a lifetime highlight reel. All the while, I am feeling our crazy chemical connection, the part of our relationship that has felt lacking since our trip to St. John. I am sure that this effort will turn the tide back in my favor.

Afterward, my mind is blissfully blank. Then it drifts back to babies. I resist the urge to point out the obvious—that a child might jeopardize our love life. That we'd have little time or energy for sex. That we wouldn't be able to put each other first anymore. Surely Ben must be thinking the same thing when he kisses the top of my head and mumbles, "I love you, Claudia . . . Sweet dreams."

"You, too," I say, feeling myself drift off.

That's when Ben rolls toward me and says, "Claudia, if we have this baby, I promise you will be the first woman in the history of the world not to lose a wink of sleep."

It is very unlike Ben to talk at all after we make love, so I'm especially irritated that he is breaking his typical male pattern with this gem. I can feel all my muscles tense as I say, "For heaven's sake, Ben. This isn't a *puppy* we're talking about."

"What's *that* supposed to mean?" he says.

"You act as if you're offering to walk a damn *beagle* in the middle of the night! We're talking about a baby here!"

"I know that," Ben says.

"A baby that will *completely* change my life. *Our* life."

"I know that," Ben says again. "But our life will change for the better. I promise you that."

"You can't *promise* something like that," I say. "It's a ludicrous, impossible promise to make. You have no idea what having a child will do to us. Besides, there are many, *many* other reasons I don't want kids—aside from my love of sleep."

"Okay. Like what?" Ben says.

"We've been over them before," I say, not wanting to rehash my reasons or hold them up to scrutiny. "Many times."

But he presses me so I start out with an easy, albeit shallow one. I tell him that I don't want to be pregnant.

"Pregnant women are beautiful," he says.

I roll my eyes.

"Besides, you'll only be pregnant for *nine* months. A blip on the radar of life."

"Easy for you to say. I don't want to be *invaded* like that, no matter how short the time frame . . . And I like working out," I say. I know this reason is a bit on the lame side, especially considering the fact that I haven't even been to the gym in weeks.

"You can work out when you're pregnant, ya know," he says.

"Yeah, right. I've seen those women, laboring at a fast walk on the treadmill. They look miserable . . . And you know I'm thinking of running the New York marathon. Maybe next year. It's something I've always wanted to do," I say, which is true in theory. Running a marathon *is* one of my lifetime goals. But to date, I've never made it past four miles. I'm not very naturally athletic, unlike Ben, who runs and swims effortlessly. Still, when I see elderly and disabled people crossing the finish line every year, I figure I can do it, too. Someday.

"Well, we could always adopt a baby," he says.

"That's not the point, and you know it. The pregnancy is the *least* of it."

"Okay," he says. "So we don't have to have a baby immediately. I mean, we can wait a few years to do this. I don't need to have one *now.* I just want you to tell me that you're open to the *idea* of it."

I see a loophole and am tempted to buy myself some time. I could "think about it" for years and then just *say* that I'm off the pill. I could get us to forty and hope for infertility to kick in. Solve the problem naturally. But I refuse to be dishonest. We *have* no relationship without honesty. So I tell him the truth—that I'm not going to change my mind.

Ben seems to ignore this statement altogether and instead asks me for another reason.

I humor him and say, "Okay. I like living in the city."

He sits up in bed and says, "We can have a baby in the city."

I admire the silhouette of his shoulders as I say, "Not very easily. We'd need to get a bigger place, and we can't really afford to do that."

"Well, don't you ever feel like you're sort of *over* living in Manhattan? We both grew up in the suburbs, after all. Wouldn't it be nice to return to our roots? Have a yard again? Trees and squirrels and some peace and quiet?"

"Okay, now you're talking crazy," I say. "We *love* living in the city."

"I know, but—"

"I don't want to move," I say, feeling panicked just thinking about it. I have visions of Volvos and PTA meetings and camcorders at soccer games and family dinners at the Olive Garden. Now I am sitting up, too. "I'm not going to move to the *suburbs*."

"Fine," Ben says, nodding. "We could have a baby in Manhattan. People do it all the time. We would just find a bigger apartment and make it work financially. So that's not a valid reason. Name another."

I exhale loudly and say, "Okay. My career."

I have saved the big guns for last. I have worked way, *way* too hard to jeopardize everything for children. I've seen it happen many times, even to the editors who are determined to stay on the fast track. They have to leave work early, they can't sacrifice their weekends, and they inevitably seem to lose their edge, their hunger. It just happens that way. I don't know why that is—whether they've reprioritized or simply don't have the energy to do better. But I don't want to find out . . . and I certainly don't want to join the ranks of seemingly miserable working mothers who strive to have it all and end up frustrated, exhausted, and guilt-ridden.

"What about your career?" he says, all innocence.

"A baby would impact it," I say.

"I told you—I can stay at home for a while. Or we can hire a nanny. You don't have to quit your job. You don't even have to go part-time. There are lots of working moms out there. You can have *both*."

"But I don't want both. See? That's the thing you don't seem to get. Having both means doing nothing very well."

"But you'd be an awesome mother, Claude," he says.

"I don't *want* to be a mother," I say with as much conviction as I can muster. "I'm sorry if that makes me selfish. But what I think is way worse—way *more* selfish—is having a child when you're not fully committed to the idea of it. And I'm just not on board with this plan of yours, Ben."

"Not now?" he says, reclining again.

"Not now," I say. "And not ever."

Ben shoots me a frosty look. Then he shakes his head, rolls away from me, and says into his pillow, "Fine, Claudia. I think I'm all clear now."

The following morning we get ready for work in silence. Ben departs first, without kissing me good-bye. Then he refuses to return any of my messages during the day. I'm so distraught that I cancel an important lunch with a high-profile agent, and then I'm short with one of my sweetest, most diligent authors on the phone for being late delivering a manuscript.

"You do realize that if you don't get this to us soon, there will be absolutely no way we'll be able to get bound galleys out to reviewers, right?" I say, hating the strident tone in my voice.

One of the things I pride myself on at work is that I *never* take things out on people—not my assistant, nor authors. I hate people who let their personal life bleed into their profession, and I think to myself that if even the mere *conversation* about children impacts my job, I can't imagine the carryover if I actually had one.

That night, I reread a manuscript and realize I don't adore it as much as I did when I first bought it. It is a quirky love story—and I can't help but wonder if my change of heart has to do with what's happening in my marriage. I panic to think that this is the case. I desperately don't want to change. I don't want my life to change. I fall asleep on the couch, worrying and waiting for Ben to come home. At some point, I hear him stumble into our apartment and can feel him standing over the couch. I open my eyes and look at him. His hair is mussed, and he smells of bourbon and cigarettes, but he still looks hot. I have a sudden, crazy urge to just pull him down on top of me and make out with him. Cigarette breath and all.

"Hi," he says, somehow managing to slur a two-letter word.

"Where have you been?" I say softly.

"Out."

"What time is it?"

"Two-somethin'."

Then he makes some crack. Something about wanting to reap the benefits of a childless life. I notice that he used the word *childless* and not our old term—*childfree*. I am suddenly angry again.

"Real mature, Ben," I say as I get up and walk toward the bathroom. "Get wasted when the chips are down. Solid move for someone who thinks he'd make a swell dad."

It is a harsh, unfair thing to say. Ben is anything but irresponsible. But I don't take anything back. I just let the words hang in the air between us.

Ben's eyes narrow. Then he clears his throat and says, "Fuck you, Claudia."

"No, fuck *you*, Ben," I say, moving past him and slamming the bathroom door behind me. My hands shake as I unscrew the toothpaste cap.

As I brush my teeth, I replay our exchange. It is a first. We never say things like that to each other. Although we've had heated arguments, we never resort to name-calling or swearing. We've always felt superior to couples who engage in that sort of battle. So our *fuck you*s become an instant symbol of our impasse—and of our impending split. It may sound

42

melodramatic to hinge a breakup on a couple of harsh words, but I can't help feeling that this is our point of no return.

I spit out a mouthful of toothpaste, wondering what I should do next. It must be something significant, something more significant than sleeping on the couch. I have to mention the word *divorce* or leave our home altogether. I round the corner to our bedroom, fumbling in the closet for my largest suitcase. I can feel Ben watching me as I haphazardly shove clothing into it. T-shirts, underwear, jeans, and a couple of work outfits. As I frantically pack, I feel as if I am watching myself in the role of angry wife.

At some point, I change my mind. I don't want to leave my apartment in the middle of the night. But I have too much pride to reverse direction. It feels utterly foolish to pack up a bag and then stay. It's like hanging up on someone in a self-righteous huff and then being the one to instantly call back. You just can't do that. So I calmly walk to the door, suitcase in hand, hoping Ben will try to stop me. I bend down, holding my breath as I put on my sneakers, double-knotting my laces, stalling to give him a few more seconds, time to formulate an apology. I want him to kneel before me, take everything back, tell me how much he loves me. Just as I am.

Instead, he says, cold as ice, "Good-bye, Claudia."

I look into his eyes and know that the end has come. So I have no real choice but to stand up, open the door, and leave.

four

The sole benefit of leaving your husband in the small hours of the morning is that it only takes a nanosecond to get a cab. In fact, I have my choice of two, both converging upon me at the corner of Seventy-third and Columbus. The cabbies undoubtedly spot my suitcase and think that they're getting a good airport fare, so as I climb into one, I say, "Hi, there. Sorry. I'm only going to lower Fifth." Then I blurt out, "I just had a big fight with my husband. I think we're getting a divorce."

It has always amused Ben how much I chat with cab drivers. He says it is a very touristy thing to do, and that it is unlike me to be so candid with strangers. He's right on both counts, but for some reason, I can't help myself in a taxi.

My driver glances at me in the rearview mirror. I can only see his eyes, which is unfortunate, because I have always thought a person's mouth reveals more of what he's thinking. The driver either doesn't have a firm grasp of English or he is colossally deficient in the empathy department, because he says nothing except, "Where on Fifth?"

"Twelfth. East side," I say, as my eyes drift down to read his name on the seatback. It is Mohammed Muhammed. I have to fight back tears as I think of how Ben once told me, on about our fourth date, that getting a cabbie named Mohammed or Muhammed, whether as a first or last name, is akin to a coin toss, a fifty-fifty proposition. Obviously it was a gross exaggeration, but ever since that night, we always check the medallion, and smile when we get a hit. It seems to happen at least once a week, but this is my first-ever double. I suddenly have the strongest urge to turn around and go home. Touch Ben's face, kiss his cheekbones and eyelids, and tell him that surely this man's medallion is a sign that we must fix things, somehow move forward together.

Instead, I rifle through my purse for my phone so that I can let Jess know that I'm on my way over. I remember that I left it in its charger in the kitchen. I whisper *shit*, realizing that she might not hear her doorman buzzing her. This could be a problem because Jess is a very sound sleeper. I fleetingly consider heading straight for a midtown hotel, but I'm afraid I'll completely fall apart if I'm alone. So I stay on course.

Fortunately, Jess hears her buzzer, and within minutes of being dropped off, I am curled up on her couch, rehashing my fight with Ben while she makes us cinnamon toast and a big pot of coffee—the extent of her expertise (and mine) in the kitchen. She brings us each a cup, mine black, hers loaded with sugar, and says that it is time for a serious talk.

Then she hesitates before adding, "And the topic of this conversation is 'Why Claudia doesn't want kids'?" She shoots me a sheepish look.

"Aw, c'mon. Not *you, too*," I say.

She nods like a stern schoolteacher and says, "I just want to review your reasons."

"You already *know* my reasons."

"Well, I want to hear them again. Pretend I'm your therapist." She sits up straight, crosses her legs, and holds her mug with pinky and thumb out, Kelly Ripa-style. "And this is our first session."

"So now I need to see a therapist just because I don't want kids?" I feel myself slipping into my defensive mode, an all too familiar emotion lately.

Jess shakes her head. "No. Not because you don't want kids. But because your marriage is in trouble. Now. Let's go. Your reasons, ma'am?"

"Why do I need to have *reasons*? When someone decides to have a baby, people don't go around asking what her *reasons* are."

"True," Jess says. "But that is a *whole* nother topic about women's role in society."

In my mind, I hear Ben ranting about people saying *a whole nother* instead of *another whole*. "*C'mon, people! Nother is not a word!*" And just like I did when I saw Mohammed Muhammed's name in the cab, I feel myself tearing up, thinking how much I am going to miss him and his quirky observations.

"Don't cry, hon," Jess says, patting my leg.

I blink back my tears, take a deep breath, and then say, "I'm just so *sick* of everyone assuming that you have to have kids to be happy. I thought Ben was different, but he's just like everyone else. He totally bait and switched me."

"It must feel like that."

I notice that Jess is not exactly agreeing with me, so I say, "You're on his side, aren't you? You think I should just suck it up and have a baby."

"I'm not . . . *judging* your feelings about not wanting kids. I'm the last one who should be judging anyone's life choices, right?"

I shrug and she continues, "I think your decision on this is a perfectly legitimate choice. It's the right choice for a lot of women . . . I think, in many ways, it's a very *brave* choice . . . But I do think we should talk it over. I don't want you to have any regrets."

"About not having kids or about losing Ben?"

"Both," she says. "Because right now they seem to be one and the same."

I blow my nose and nod. "Okay."

Jess leans back in the couch and says, "So go ahead there. Leave no stone unturned."

I sip my coffee, think for a second, and instead of rehashing my usual reasons, I say, "Did I ever tell you about the study of mice missing the Mest gene?"

She shakes her head. "Nah. Doesn't ring a bell."

"Well, there was this study where scientists determined that mice missing this one particular gene—the Mest gene— have an abnormal response to their newborns. Basically, without this gene, they have no mothering instinct, and so they didn't feed or care for their young the way the other mice did."

"So? Are you saying that you're missing the Mest gene?"

"I'm just saying that some women probably don't have that . . . mothering instinct . . . I don't think I have it."

"Not at *all*? Not even a trace of it?" she asks. "Because I've heard a lot of women say that they thought they didn't have it until they had a baby of their own. And then, voilà! Nurture city."

"Is that a safe gamble?" I ask. "What if it doesn't kick in?"

"Well. I think there are a lot of effective mothering styles. You don't have to be Betty Crocker or June Cleaver to be a good mother."

"Okay. But what if I'm sorry I had a baby at all? What then?"

47

Jess frowns, looking deep in thought. "You're really good with kids," she says. "You seem to really like them."

"I *do* like kids," I say, thinking of my sister's kids and Raymond Jr. How good it felt to tuck his warm little body against mine and inhale his sweet baby smell. "But I have absolutely no desire to have one of my own on a full-time basis. And I firmly believe that if I had one, I'd wind up resenting Ben. Even worse, I think I'd resent our child. It's not fair to anyone."

Jess nods again, adopting that earnest "keep going, we're really making progress" shrink expression.

"I like my life the way it is. I like our lifestyle. Our freedom. I can't imagine the constant state of worry that parents have . . . From worrying about SIDS, to falling down stairs, to drunk driving accidents . . . that worry doesn't go away for eighteen years. In some ways, it *never* goes away. You worry about your children *forever*. Everyone says it."

Jess nods.

"And, truthfully, Jess, how many married people with kids seem genuinely happy to you?" I ask, thinking of my sister Maura and how her marriage started to become strained right after her firstborn, Zoe, arrived. And their relationship got progressively worse with her two sons that followed. I am not my sister, and Ben is not Scott. But it does not seem at all unusual for a relationship to change once children arrive on the scene. They are a drain on your time, your money, your energy, your patience. You can't put your relationship first anymore. So for better or worse, the dynamic of two people shifts and takes a new form. A form that sometimes seems to have more to do with surviving than truly enjoying life.

"I know what you mean." Jess looks sheepish and then

says, "Trey often refers to his family as the 'noose around his neck.' "

"Charming," I say. "My point exactly."

"I don't think he means his son," Jess says defensively. "Just *her*."

Jess goes out of her way not to say Trey's wife's name, Brenda. I think it makes her feel less guilty. She continues, "But I don't think he'd feel that way if he were married to the right person . . . And I don't think you and Ben would end up feeling like that. I think kids bring problems to the surface. Y'all don't have real problems. You would maintain a good marriage *with* kids."

I know it might ruffle Jess's feathers, but I risk it and tell her that Trey's wife probably thought she would maintain a good marriage *with* a child back in their early days. Trey probably thought so, too. Jess juts her jaw in protest, but I continue, "And I know for a fact that when Maura and Scott were hooking up strong in Scott's Jacuzzi and all over the rest of his bachelor pad, Maura would never have believed he'd someday cheat on her. That things would get so . . . *depressing*."

Jess continues, "Those are the exceptions. Most couples are even *happier* with children."

"I don't think so. The unhappy ones seem to be more the rule . . . Then you have Daphne's situation," I say.

"Daphne seems to have a solid marriage," Jess says.

"They do," I say. "But right now I think she and Tony seem so obsessed with having a baby that that one issue has completely swallowed them up. They don't talk about anything else. They don't *think* about anything else. They're . . . becoming *boring*."

Jess laughs and says, "Weren't they always sort of boring?"

Jess is the only person I let criticize my family. Still, I can't resist defending Daphne. "Boring in a very *sweet* way," I say, thinking of how excited she gets about things like scrapbooking. "I'd actually call her simple, not boring. *Refreshingly* simple . . . but lately she and Tony are just plain grim. Not that I blame them . . ."

Jess sighs loudly and says, "Well, anyway. The point is . . . there are plenty of happy couples who have kids."

"Maybe," I say. "But I have no confidence that we'd be joining their ranks. And I'm not trying to turn my life into some kind of science experiment."

"Like the Mest mice?" Jess asks.

"Like the Mest mice," I say.

I stay at Jess's place, only returning to my apartment once in four days, when I know Ben is at work, so that I can pick up my cell phone and some more clothes. I keep waiting for him to call me, but he doesn't. Not once. I guess I really don't expect him to, but every time I check my voice mail and hear "no new messages," I feel a fresh wave of devastation. Of course, I don't call him, either, so I hope that he is feeling the same way as he checks his messages in vain. Something tells me he's not, though, and there's something about this hunch that makes my pain feel exponentially worse. The whole "misery loves company" thing never applies more than when you're breaking up. The thought that the other person is doing fine is simply too much to bear.

Jess insists that I'm being paranoid—that *of course* Ben's just as sad as I am—but I have two good reasons for believing I'm in a worse state than he is. I share the first reason with Jess one night over Chinese delivery, reminding her that Ben is blessed with the ability to wall himself off from pain and settle into a comfortable numbness. You always hear that it's not healthy to repress emotions like this, but whenever I watch Ben skate on the surface of sadness, coping like a champ, I can't help feeling envious. I have never been able to shut down that part of my brain. I think of last year when Ben's cousin and best friend, Mark, was diagnosed with stage four testicular cancer. Ben remained stoic, almost defiant, throughout the whole ordeal, even when that phone call came in the middle of the night with the news that Mark was gone.

As Ben climbed back into bed after that brief conversation with Mark's mom, I asked if he wanted to talk. Ben shook his head before turning off the light and whispering, "Not really. There's not a lot to say."

I wanted to tell him that there was *a lot* to say. We could talk about Mark's way too short but still full life. We could talk about Ben's boyhood memories of the cousin who always felt more like a brother. We could talk about their days at Brown, each of them passing up their first-choice college so they could go to school together. We could talk about the end, how painful it was watching Mark slip away. We could talk about what would come next, the eulogy I knew Ben had been writing in his head for weeks.

But Ben said nothing. I remember sensing in the dark that he was wide awake, so I stayed up, too, in case he changed his mind and wanted to talk, or at the very least cry. But he didn't cry. Not that night or the next day. Not even at the funeral when his beautiful eulogy brought everyone else to tears.

It took six long months for Ben to break down. We were standing in the cereal aisle in Fairway when he picked up a box of Frosted Mini-Wheats, a look of sheer devastation on his face. I didn't have to ask what he was thinking about. He made it home and into our bedroom before I heard that strange, scary sound of a grown man stifling sobs. When he emerged, a long while later, his eyes were red and puffy. I had never seen him like that. He hugged me hard and his voice cracked as he said, "I miss him so *fucking* much."

"Not that I'm comparing our breakup to Mark's death," I say after I tell her the story.

Jess nods and says, "I know. But if you guys really do break-up, it sort of will be like a death."

"Yeah. Especially because Ben and I don't do that 'stay in touch with exes' shtick," I say. "If this is over, it's *over*. I don't want to be Ben's friend."

Jess sighs and then says, "Well. Maybe it's not over."

"I really think it is, though," I say. "Just think. It took Ben six months to really face the fact that Mark was gone. By the time he lets himself miss me, it'll be way too late."

Jess looks worried, which makes me think about the second reason Ben is suffering less than I am. This one I don't share with Jess. I have never said it aloud—or even written it in my journal. It is something I have always been aware of on some level, but have not allowed myself to dwell on. Until now, there wasn't any point in addressing it.

The reason is this: I am pretty sure that I love Ben more than he loves me. I know he loves me a lot. I know he loves me more than he loved Nicole or anyone else. But I still think I love him *more*. It's one of those things you never know for certain because there's no way to enter all the relationship data in a computer and have it spit out a definitive answer. You can't quantify love, and if you try, you can wind up focusing on misleading factors. Stuff that really has more to do with personality—the fact that some people are simply more expressive or emotional or needy in a relationship. But beyond such smokescreens, the answer is there. Love is seldom—almost never—an even proposition. Someone always loves more.

In our relationship, that person is me. With some couples, it can switch back and forth. But in the beginning, middle, and end of ours, I think I've consistently loved him more. Ben would tell me I'm being ridiculous—but if somehow he were forced to answer honestly, I think he'd acknowledge the truth of my claim. I think he'd also agree that it has nothing to do with our merits as people. I think we're roughly equally smart, successful, funny, and attractive, which seems to comprise the Big Four in the crass business of mate comparison. I am Ben's approximate equal and have always felt secure, confident, and worthy. But still. I happen to love Ben slightly more, which has the effect of making you fear losing someone more than if it were the other way around.

Which brings me to another point. I think I have always had the misguided sense that worry and fear serve as an insurance policy of sorts. On a subconscious level, I subscribe to the notion that if you worry about something, it is somehow less likely to happen. Well, I am here to say that it doesn't work like that. The very thing you fear the most can still happen anyway. And when it does, you feel that much more cheated for having feared it in the first place.

five

Sorrow comes with so many defense mechanisms. You have your shock, your denial, your getting wasted, your cracking jokes, and your religion. You also have the old standby catchall—the blind belief in fate, the whole "things happening for a reason" drill.

But my personal favorite defense has always been anger, with its trusty offshoots of self-righteous indignation, bitterness, and resentment.

I remember the first time I realized that people turn to anger in sad times. I was in kindergarten, and Jimmy Moore's dad had just died of a heart attack while lugging their Christmas tree in from the garage. A few weeks later, my mother and I ran into Jimmy and his mother in the grocery store. I peered at Jimmy from behind our cart with morbid curiosity while my mother asked Mrs. Moore how she was doing. Mrs. Moore shook her head and clenched her fist. "I'm so furious at God right now," she said.

Jimmy and I exchanged a glance and then cast our eyes down. I think we were both startled. And I know I was a little scared. I hadn't heard of anyone having a bone to pick with God. It seemed like a dangerous thing to be doing. I also remember thinking there must be something *very* wrong with Jimmy's mom for feeling anything other than pure, unadulterated grief upon her husband's death. Anger didn't seem like it should have been part of the equation.

But about six years later, when I was eleven, I learned how closely the two emotions are aligned. That was the year that my mother had an "alleged" affair (she still denies it) with my elementary school principal, Mr. Higgins. I steadfastly maintain that short of being orphaned or severely disfigured, it is about the worst thing that can happen to a fifth-grader, particularly when you're the very last person in the school to hear about it. I never had any illusions that either of my parents was perfect, as I frequently compared them to the ideal parents in books. I wished that my father were a little more like Atticus Finch, and that my mother would occasionally behave like Ramona Quimby's nurturing, understanding mother in my favorite Beverly Cleary books. But overall, I was happy with my parental lot. I appreciated the way my father always took us to do fun things on the weekends, rather than doing yard work or watching football like the other dads in my neighborhood. And I was proud of how beautiful and funny my mother was—and how much my friends admired her fashion sense.

And for the most part, I didn't think too much about my parents one way or the other. Most kids don't. If things are going well in life, parents are more of a backdrop and safety net than central characters who, say, take center stage during recess. Which is actually what happened on the playground one day when Chet Womble, a boy I hated for his nose-picking and name-calling, decided to break the big news of my mother's affair via chalk graffiti. He drew two large stick figures, complete with some vivid male-female anatomy, and the words CLAUDIA'S MOM DOES MR. HIGGINS. (The video cover for *Debbie Does Dallas* had just been passed around the cafeteria the week before, so even without Chet's clever graphic, there was no confusion about the word *does*.)

I remember staring at my mother's loopy, lopsided boobs, then desperately trying to rub out my name with my heel, all the while thinking that no matter what, I would never get over it. I had become a pathetic victim in a Judy Blume novel (although, at that moment, I would rather have been "Blubber" than my mother's daughter).

It didn't help that Chet was suspended for a week or that very few people saw the drawing before it was hosed off by a janitor. All that mattered was that upon one glimpse I knew in my gut that it was true: my mom *was*, indeed, doing Mr. Higgins. The pieces came together for me in a rush of shamefaced horror: my mother's sudden and uncharacteristic flurry of volunteering at our school; the care she took applying lipstick during carpool, followed by her excuses to come in the building with me; the fact that Mr. Higgins knew my name and seemed to go out of his way to smile and greet me in the halls.

The night of Chet's stunt, I went home and somehow made my way through my homework and a particularly horrible chipped beef dinner. I debated on when exactly I should confront my mother, and saw some merit in doing so with the five of us seated together around the table. She deserved as much. But for my dad's sake, I waited until dinner was over and he retired to the family room to watch his beloved Mets. My sisters stood to clear the table and load the dishwasher when I came out with it. "Mom," I said, "why are you cheating on Dad with Mr. Higgins?"

Maura dropped a plate and Daphne burst into tears while our usually brazen mother shushed me, looking frantic as she glanced toward our family room. I kept talking, saying that it certainly wasn't a secret, thanks to Chet Womble's vivid portraiture. Of course my mother denied everything, but she did not do so convincingly or strenuously enough to change my mind. Instead she sent me to my room. I obeyed not because I felt that I had to, but because the sight of her made me sick.

Over the next few weeks, I found myself remembering Jimmy's mother in the grocery store as I vacillated between anger and grief. I'd be sobbing one minute and then scribbling furious cursive in my journal the next, calling my mother names I had only heard uttered from boys like Chet. *Slut. Whore. Bitch.* Real healthy stuff for a fifth-grader.

Throughout that ordeal, I learned that getting mad was easier than being sad. Anger was something I could control. I could settle into an easy rhythm of blame and hate. Focus my energy on something other than the ache in my heart.

I think my mother and Mr. Higgins stopped seeing each other a short time later. But other affairs followed until she met Dwight, a tanned plastic surgeon who wore a pinky signet ring and ascots on special occasions and always conjured a rich, tacky character on *The Love Boat*. My mother was so smitten with Dwight and the lavish lifestyle he promised that she left us for real, giving up custody to my father when I was thirteen. Of course, that is a whole *nother* story (Ha! Screw you, Ben!), a chapter far more serious in our family lore. But somehow nothing that followed was as hurtful as that day on the playground, gazing down at my mother's white chalk breasts.

That brings me, of course, to the elephant in the room. The thing that Jess and Ben and my sisters all are thinking, but won't come out and say altogether: the fact that I don't want children because I have such issues with my own mother.

My first instinct is to deny these charges as I have always thought it a tiresome cop-out to blame your current predicament on your bad childhood. Everyone has a messed-up family—to one extent or another—but we all have an obligation to rise above it. Live in the present and stop sniveling about the past. I mean, who believes, for example, that an excuse for a child abuser is that, he, too, got cigarettes put out on his arm as a kid?

Still, I guess I can't deny that there is a life-shaping stigma in having a mother who cheats on her family and then finally leaves them altogether. A stigma that gets buried in your psyche forever. And those feelings must be playing at least a small role in all of this, just as I think my sister Daphne's obsession with *having* children has a lot to do with wanting to erase the pain my mother caused. On one level, Daphne's approach makes more sense. Yet the thought of a redo is not only unappealing, but terrifying. I don't want that kind of power over anyone. I don't want to be something that someone has to overcome. After all, I think everyone would agree that it's far worse to be a fucked-up mother than it is to have one.

So in the following days and weeks, I find myself spinning my hurt into anger. Anger about the whole situation. Anger toward Ben for turning his back on me. Anger that propels me along quite nicely, all the way to a fancy divorce lawyer on Fifth Avenue.

six

I can't decide whether the next few weeks pass too quickly or impossibly slowly. In some ways, it feels like Ben and I are breaking up overnight, way too easily. I keep thinking that only shallow celebrities end their marriages as easily as we are. Or young, stupid kids who get hitched on a whim and change their minds as soon as the hot-and-heavy period ends, thinking nothing of the sacredness of their vows and believing that do-overs in life are simply a given.

In other ways, though, the days leading up to our divorce seem to take a lifetime. I wake up every morning with the sick realization that my life is unraveling. That I will never really be happy again. Despite my best efforts to stay busy and distracted, I feel like I'm being punched in the stomach a dozen times a day. I find myself praying that Ben will change his mind.

In the meantime, I decide to move in with Jess. Living with her is a bit of a comfort, but it also feels like a setback. It's almost like moving back in with your parents once you've left home. I'm reverting to an earlier point in my life, and that never feels like a good thing. I recognize that it's a temporary measure—that eventually I will get my own place—but I still feel like somewhat of a loser. I also feel guilty for invading Jess, although she insists that she's thrilled to have me back. I offer to pay her—which is an awkward arrangement considering that she owns her apartment. She tells me not to be ridiculous and that she's never home anyway. "Besides, what are friends for, Claudia—if they can't pick up the pieces a man has left behind?" she says.

Still, I make a point to pay for our groceries and food deliveries. I also try to do more of my late-night reading at the office so that Jess still has some time in her apartment alone. I have always worked a lot of hours, but I've never been this inspired, this on top of things. I catch up on all of my reading and scratch through to-dos that have been languishing for months. Even my desk is neat for the first time in years, which my longtime assistant, Rosemary, marvels over.

"What's the special occasion?" she asks me.

"I'm getting a divorce," I tell her.

"I'm sorry," she says, which will be the extent of her commentary. Rosemary is as discreet as she is neat.

"Don't be," I say. "My office needed this."

Of course I am kidding, but I do find that throwing myself into my job and working crazy hours is therapeutic. I tell myself that there are benefits that come with being single again. I will be like a person who loses a loved one and, in turn, sets up a foundation. I will find the good in this loss. I will make something happen that wouldn't have happened otherwise. I tell myself to dream big, aim high. Maybe someday I will have my own imprint—*Claudia Parr Books*. Something that wouldn't have happened if I had had a baby with Ben. Something that might not have happened if I had stayed with Ben, even *without* a baby. I rather like the thought of Ben perusing the shelves of bookstores and seeing the spine of a book emblazoned with my name. Maybe I'll even acquire a coffee table book on architecture. Then he'd be sure to see it.

Meanwhile, during those early weeks apart, Ben and I talk very little, and when we do, neither of us says too much. There are a lot of awkward silences, fumbling questions about mail and bills and our respective schedules. It's clear that we don't want to be back at the apartment at the same time. We toss around a few "How are yous?," both of us answering curtly and quickly that we are fine, just fine. We are both prideful, stubborn, and eerily distant. It occurs to me that maybe we are both stonewalling, stalling, calling the other's bluff. At least I *hope* that's what is happening, but deep inside, I know we are becoming irreversibly estranged, and I can tell Ben knows it, too.

At the end of one conversation, Ben sighs and says, "I just want you to be happy, Claudia. That's all."

It is a *total* non sequitur as I've just told him that I checked the messages at the apartment, and his aunt called twice.

"Right," I say under my breath.

"Come again?" he says, an expression that has always annoyed me. Ben only uses it when he knows *exactly* what I said, but doesn't like it.

"Clearly that's not the *only* thing you want," I say, picturing him with a squalling newborn.

He says nothing back, and as we both register that there is nothing he *can* say to this, I feel a strange little rush of victory and satisfaction. It's always a good feeling when you can produce just the right one-liner to prove your point so tidily.

"Well, see ya," I say, to drive it home.

"Yep," Ben says flippantly. "See ya."

I hang up and promptly schedule another visit with my lawyer, Nina Raden. Nina is striking, hard-edged, and abrasive, the kind of creature you envision when you hear Billy

Emily Giffin

Joel's "She's Always a Woman." Her lips are pumped up with collagen, and she smiles a lot, which is in stark contrast to her obvious desire to make my divorce as contentious as possible. I can tell her bread and butter comes from playing cheerleader to wronged women all over Manhattan. I'd wager that she's said, "Let's get the bastard" more times than she's said, "Good morning."

During our second session, I have to tell her three times that I do not want to hire a private investigator, and that I'm sure there isn't another woman in Ben's life. She clearly is unaccustomed to breakups in our peculiar genre.

"You can never be sure of that," she tells me.

"I'm pretty *darn* sure," I say. "Unless, per chance, he has already selected a vessel to carry his baby."

She gives me a long look that says, *That's exactly what he has queued up*. Then she licks her thumb and flips to a fresh page in her notebook. She tells me that, based on what I told her in our first meeting, our grounds for divorce will be "constructive abandonment." It is a term that makes me sad as much for its formal sound as for the actual meaning.

I nod as Nina becomes all hyped up about our assets, telling me I should go for the gold, ask for the moon. She gestures a lot, her thick, enamel bracelets sliding up and down her long, slender arm. I give her a blank stare, insisting that Ben and I don't have all that much to divide. "We've only been married three years. And we rent, remember?" I say, grateful that Ben and I never took the plunge into New York real estate.

"Okay. Okay. But what about cars? Furnishings? Rugs? Art? Crystal? Stock? Time-shares?" she says, her palms facing up. Her Botoxed face strains to frown but can't quite get there.

I shrug. "We have a '99 Honda Civic. It's a piece of junk."

She gives me an exasperated look that says I can do better.

"I'll work on it," I say.

"Good. Good," she says, glancing at her watch. "In my experience, you only regret asking for too little."

"Uh-huh," I say.

"So shoot me an e-mail with anything—anything at all that you can come up with. I'll attach a list of all assets in Schedule A to the Separation Agreement."

I have never thought of our "stuff" as assets. I never thought Ben and I would be dividing anything; I thought we'd always be about sharing everything. Still, I decide to take my homework assignment seriously. I call my soon-to-be ex-husband and tell him I need to be at the apartment for a few hours that evening. Ben says fine, he has to work late anyway.

That evening, I walk through our apartment, poking through cabinets and drawers as I drink a bottle of wine and take notes on a sheet of paper. The whole exercise feels surreal, almost as if I'm seeing certain items for the first time. As I inspect all of our joint belongings, I realize with a mix of relief and pride that I want almost nothing. I try, but I just can't get myself too worked up about furniture, linens, and silver. I do linger briefly on our only expensive piece of art—a gorgeous Geoffrey Johnson cityscape in warm sepia tones. I love it and can't imagine not being able to look at it again, but Ben and I bought it together for our second anniversary, so I don't want that daily reminder.

For some reason, I focus on our CDs, music we acquired together, stuff we listened to during every range of mood and occasion. "Getting ready to go out" music. "Throwing a party" music. "Doing chores around the house" music. "Having sex" music. "Setting the mood for sex" music. "After sex" music.

I know CDs aren't the sort of big-ticket items Nina has in mind—as we're only talking a few hundred bucks for our entire collection—but the thought of going out to replace the music we enjoyed together feels too painful to bear. Besides, I know how much our CDs mean to Ben, and part of me wants to spite him. I have no desire to punish him financially, but I want him to suffer emotionally. I want him to feel a ravenous void, and taking a crystal carafe isn't going to get the job done.

So I pour another glass of wine as I jot down some of our favorite artists—James McMurtry, Bruce Springsteen, Bob Dylan, Tom Waits, Velvet Underground, Laura Cantrell, Van Morrison, Cowboy Junkies, Wilco, Tracy Chapman, and Dire Straits. Then, to reinforce my point, I take a black Sharpie and pen my initials on the CD covers. About halfway through the exercise, I catch myself using my married name— Davenport—and switch to my maiden initials, C.P. I tell myself that Parr—the name I've kept at work—sounds much better with Claudia. I've never been a fan of triple-syllable first names combined with triple-syllable last names. The wine starts to hit me around midnight, when I just give up, scribble through my list, and write "All CDs" at the top of the page.

The next day I call Nina and tell her I only want my personal property, all of our CDs, and my maiden name back. She groans into the phone, and says, "As your attorney, I feel it's my duty to tell you that I think you're making a mistake."

"This isn't about money . . . It's about principle," I say.

"That's precisely why I want you to include more," Nina says. "For the principle of things. *He's* the one checking out of this marriage." Then she sighs and tells me to give it a little more thought, and in the meantime, she'll draft the Separation Agreement.

A few days later the papers arrive at my office. I read the pages carefully. They mostly consist of boilerplate language about such things as waivers of maintenance, tax returns, and debts and obligations of the parties. The only lines that really get me are in the beginning:

> Whereas, as a result of certain disputes and irreconcilable differences between the parties, the parties have separated and are now living separate and apart, and they intend to live separate and apart from each other for the rest of their lives. . . . Whereas, there are no children in the marriage and none are expected.

I think, *You can say that again.* Then I call Ben and ask him to meet me for one last dinner so that we can review the agreement together. I think it's what we both need for closure. *Closure* is one of those words I've always hated, overused by melodramatic women. But I don't think it's melodramatic to use the term when your marriage is dissolving. When you need to see your husband one more time to come to terms with the fact that he's no longer going to be your husband. Although maybe, *maybe,* I'm just giving him one last chance to change his mind.

"Where should we meet?" I ask him.

I know that he will tell me that he doesn't care where we meet, that it's up to me.

Sure enough, he sighs into the phone. "You pick a spot, Claudia. It doesn't matter to me," he says. As if *he* has earned the right to be weary.

I want to be passive-aggressive back, insist that he choose our final meeting place, but I decide that taking control is a pretty foolproof way to keep from losing control. I tell him I will think about it and get back to him. My voice is cold and detached.

"Okay. Just let me know," he says, and I must face the fact that if we were having a "try to sound as detached as possible" contest, he would have just beaten me by more than a hair.

For the next few hours, I look through virtually every entry in my *Zagat*, paging through the guide that once held the key to fun evenings out with Ben. There are one thousand nine hundred and thirty-one restaurant entries, and yet not a single venue seems to be an appropriate one to meet with your soon-to-be-ex-husband to discuss the division of your assets. I peruse the categories—*late dining, people-watching, power scenes, romantic places, special occasions, singles scenes*. None seems right. In a city like New York, how could the good people at *Zagat* include categories like *bathrooms to visit* and overlook the ever-important *places to break up*?

While I'm reviewing restaurants, Michael Brighton, a publicity manager, stops by to say hello. Michael and I graduated from college the same year, thirteen years ago, and both started working here the same day. He is one of my closest friends at work, and his matter-of-fact manner and wry wit make it easy to discuss my divorce. I can count on him not to give me too much sympathy.

"What's shakin', Claudia?" he asks, as he picks up my Magic 8 Ball from my bookshelf and shakes it. It is a gadget I've been avoiding lately, for obvious reasons.

"Not too much," I say.

He peers down at the ball and says, "Damn. My dry

cleaner isn't going to get that stain off my suede jacket."

I laugh. "Why are your questions posed to the Eight Ball always so inane?"

"Because my life is inane. You know that," he says, running his hand over his clean-shaven head. Michael has the smoothest brown skin I've ever seen. He almost looks airbrushed. Ben has always said that Michael looks like Charles Barkley—and I guess I can see the resemblance around the eyes and eyebrows—but Michael isn't nearly as bulky as Barkley, and his features are sharper.

"Right," I say sarcastically. Michael's life is anything but inane. Just last week, he accidentally sent an e-mail to the entire company about his assistant being incompetent.

"So anyway. Where are you with Amy Dickerson's novel? Is *Time* going to review it or what?" I ask.

"I'm getting there," he says, yawning. Michael is a total procrastinator, but can usually charm his way into getting any review for me. Everybody in the business loves him, and I'm always thrilled when he's covering one of my books. "No worries." He points to my *Zagat*. "What? Do you have a hot date already?"

"No," I say. "I'm trying to pick a place to meet Ben tonight."

"To discuss reconciliation?"

"No. To discuss the division of our assets."

"Hmm," he says. "How about Kittichai? I have a reservation I'd rather not use."

I raise my eyebrows.

"Long story."

"I have time."

"She's too needy."

"Ahh," I say, flipping to the *K*s. "So, Kittichai. That's in the Thompson Hotel, right?"

"Yeah," he says. "I have a table for two at eight. It's yours if you want it."

"I've actually never been," I say. "And I don't think this is the night to be trying something new."

"So go to an old standby . . . Gramercy Tavern? Aquavit? Balthazar?"

I shake my head. "Can't do those, either. Old standbys are imbued with too many memories. Good memories. Celebrations. It would be . . . conflicting," I say. "I can't very well be sitting there telling Ben that I want our Calphalon pots, all the while thinking about our first anniversary or the night we got a little crazy in the back of a cab . . ."

"You don't even cook. You really want the pots?" he asks.

"No. I don't really want anything."

Michael nods and then squints up at the ceiling as if he has something in his contacts. "Just curious on that back-of-a-cab thing—I'm testing a theory—did that happen before or after you guys got hitched?"

"Before," I say, pushing away the memory as I continue. "I think I have to aim for something in between trendy, new hotspot, and tried-and-true favorite. A place we've both been before, but a place with no particular connotation. A place with a decent vibe, but not too much gaiety," I say. "And I'm thinking low marks in service. I don't want a lot of interruptions or too much food and wine description."

Michael laughs.

I shoot him a look. "This isn't funny."

His smile fades and he says, "My bad. You're right, this isn't funny."

"Okay. It's a little bit funny," I say, thinking that maybe those people who crack jokes in the face of hardship are on to something.

He shakes the 8 Ball again and says, "Uh-oh."

"What?" I say.

"Never mind," he says. "I don't believe in this thing anyway."

The night of our final "date," I arrive at a random bistro in Hell's Kitchen (a neighborhood with which Ben and I have the fewest ties) ten minutes late but still before Ben. This annoys me because I have to have a drink at the bar, which makes the evening feel too much like a date, rather than the business transaction it is. I wonder if perhaps we should have met for lunch instead.

Ben saunters in after I've ordered my wine and taken my first few sips. He is wearing loose-fitting jeans and a new white shirt that makes his chest and arms look especially cut. Ben has one of those not-too-big, not-too-small, hard bodies that always looks perfect in clothes. And unfortunately for me now, even better without.

"Nice shirt," I say with a trace of sarcasm. I want him to know that I know that he's been shopping during our turmoil.

He gives me a defensive look and then mumbles something about picking a few things up at the Gap. Picturing Ben trying on casual clothes that he will surely be wearing on dates with blushing, fertile girls in their early twenties makes me almost hate him. This is actually a good, healthy thing, though, because hating him takes the sad edge off the night. I settle up at the bar, and we walk over to the maître d's podium.

"He's here," I say, pointing at Ben.

She smiles and leads us to a small table in the very center of the dining area. I immediately target the table as the worst one in the restaurant. We will be surrounded on all sides. I don't anticipate a scene. Nor do I expect tears. Ben and I are very controlled and feel the same way about drawing attention to ourselves. But still. A corner table would work so much better for our purposes. I glance at Ben, hoping he'll ask to switch. He almost always does. Even when we were at McDonald's and I'd pick our table, he'd ask if I wouldn't mind moving. It became almost a game. I'd anticipate where he wanted to sit, and he'd find something problematic with it. A draft from air-conditioning, sunlight too direct in his eyes, a nasty spot of ketchup on his chair. Of course, Ben picks *this* night to debut his new shirt *and* become complacent with our seating.

"So. How is everything?" Ben asks me after the waitress hands us our menus and a wine list.

"Fine," I say.

"How's work?"

I tell him work is great and then, at his prodding, give him a few-sentence update on recent books I've been working on and some I'm trying to acquire. I know Ben is proud of all that I've accomplished at work, and I can't help sharing a few details with him. I wonder how long it will take to lose the urge to share my stories with him. "How's work going for you?" I say.

"It's okay," he says. "Same old."

"Your family?" I ask.

"They're fine. Good."

"Did you tell them yet?" I ask.

"Tell them what?"

"Gee, Ben, I don't know. Tell them about your new shirt."

"I didn't know which *specific* part of this you were referring to," he says.

"The whole thing? The general breaking up that's happening here?" I say, pointing back and forth in the space between us.

"I told them we were having problems," he says.

"Did you tell them the nature of our problems?" I ask.

He nods.

"So now they all think I'm a cold bitch?" I ask.

"Nobody thinks anything bad about you, Claudia."

I look down at my menu, raise my eyebrows, and mutter that I doubt this very much.

He ignores my comment and says, "Did you tell your folks?"

"No," I say. "Not yet."

He doesn't look surprised. He knows I avoid my mother and that I don't want to upset my father. "What about your sisters?"

"Not yet. Just Jess," I say. "And Michael."

"Annie?" he asks.

I shake my head. "No . . . Why? Have you talked to Ray?"

"A little bit," Ben says.

I want to ask him what he's said, but decide against it. I pretty much know anyway. I also know what a new father is going to be saying back to him. It confirms what I have always said—people seek out selective advice. They ask it from people who will echo their own instincts. Tell them what they plan on doing anyway.

Our waitress comes by and takes our order. We have not discussed our orders in advance, yet we both opt for the salmon. We never used to duplicate, preferring to order two entrées and share. Clearly our sharing days are over.

"So," I say.

"So," Ben says. "What next?"

I can tell he is talking about logistics, not our relationship. We are over, and we both know it. I hand him Nina's draft papers and say, "It's all pretty standard when it comes to uncontested divorces in New York."

He takes the papers and glances down at them. He flips through them, page by page, until he gets to the part that discusses the division of assets.

"I just want the CDs," I summarize for him.

He looks up at me, surprised. "That's all you want? The CDs?"

"Yeah. I just want our music," I say, vowing that it will be my very last *our*. "Is that okay?"

"Sure, Claudia. The music is yours."

"Even all the James McMurtrys?" I say, hoping that he'll balk—or at least look upset. Ben has his favorite bands, and I have mine, but as a couple, James McMurtry is our number one. Maybe it's because we discovered and fell in love with his music together. I see Ben's chest rise slightly as he inhales. He exhales and looks at me. I hope he's thinking of last summer when we flew to Austin to see James perform at the Continental Club. I hope he's thinking of how we drank too many beers, our arms around each other, as we soaked up James's wrenching lyrics.

"Sure. Even James," he says sadly, as I make a mental note to leave just one CD behind, as if it were only an oversight. I pulled a similar stunt when I broke up with my college boyfriend, Paul. There were a lot of reasons for our demise, but among them was that we weren't geographically compatible. I wanted to live in New York—and he wanted to live anywhere *but.* I held out hope that he'd change his mind and strategized ways to increase those odds. So when I gathered up all of his stuff that had accrued in my apartment over the prior year, I stuck one random Uno card in the crate because Paul and I played Uno together all the time, and had kept a running score into the triple digits. The card was a red "reverse" which I thought was somehow symbolic. I hoped that he'd find it and have a moment of intense regret for letting me go, a desire to "reverse" his life, leave Denver and move with me to New York. Maybe he would even tape that card to his mirror, look at it every morning when he shaved, thinking of me and what could have been.

I try to imagine what Ben's expression will be when he comes across one of our McMurtry CDs. I picture him sliding the disc in the stereo, listening to one of our songs, and cursing himself for picking a baby over me.

"Claudia?" Ben says, interrupting my thoughts. "What are you thinking?" His voice is soft.

"You know," I say, shaking my head. I feel another enormous stab of sadness. I have to work hard to fight back tears.

"Yeah. I know," Ben says. "This *sucks.*"

I nod and look away, over to a couple sitting near us, seemingly on a first date. They were seated just after we were and I noticed that he pulled her chair out for her. They are young and eager, all smiles and perfect table manners. They are off to a good start, happy and hopeful.

I nod toward their table and say, "Check out those two. First date?"

Ben turns slightly in his chair, studies them for a second, and says, "Yeah. Second tops. I bet they haven't even kissed yet."

"Maybe tonight," I say.

"Yeah. Maybe."

"I wish I could skip ahead and see *their* ending," I say sarcastically.

Ben gives me a look and says, "You always were a cynic."

I say, "Go figure."

"Maybe they'll live happily ever after," Ben says.

"Yeah. With two point two children."

"Or at least one," Ben says.

I let him have the last word—and the check when it mercifully comes.

seven

There is more than a sliver of me that wonders if I'm making a mistake as I let Ben slip away from me for good. I tell myself that second-guessing just comes with the territory. Whenever you make a big decision in life, at least any decision where you have a viable alternative, there is an inevitable uneasy aftermath. Anxiety is merely a sign that you're taking something seriously.

In this sense, divorcing Ben conjures up a similar set of emotions that I had when I *married* Ben. I knew I was doing the right thing then, too, but couldn't escape the occasional worry that kept me up in the middle of the night even after I took a few swigs of NyQuil. In the days before our wedding, I knew that my love for Ben was the most real thing I had ever known, but I still fretted that I was setting myself up for disappointment. I remember looking at Ben while he slept one night and fearing that I would someday let him down. Or that he would let me down. That things, somehow, wouldn't turn out well for us, and that I would look back and say, "How could I have been so stupid? How could I have not seen this coming?" Which of course is *exactly* what is happening.

And now, as I watch Ben slip away from me, I have the nagging feeling that I will someday look back at this fork in the road and point to it as the biggest mistake of my life.

So given my fragile state, I am very nervous about being around my outspoken family. I tell them nothing and put off seeing them for several weeks, until the day of my niece Zoe's sixth-birthday party when I can put it off no longer.

That morning, I take the train to Maura's house in Bronxville, staring out the window at scenery I have come to know by heart. I only let myself listen to the upbeat songs on my iPod, skipping over any faintly melancholy ones on my playlist as a precautionary measure. The worst thing I could do is show up at Maura's with any trace of sadness on my face. I have to be tough, I think, as I ponder my strategy for breaking the bad news.

By the time I pull into the station, I have decided that I will tell my family of my pending divorce after the guests have departed, and Zoe has gone to play with her new toys. It would probably be less dramatic to give everyone the news individually over the phone, but this way, I'll only have to say it one time. I'll hold one press conference and field one set of questions. When I can stand it no more, I'll thank my family and make my exit. Just like an athlete after a painful loss. *Yes, I'm disappointed. I feel bad for letting my team down and missing that easy layup in the second OT. But I did the best I could. And I gotta move on . . .*

My dad, who still lives in Huntington in the house we grew up in, drove to my sister's earlier this morning and picks me up at the train station now. Before I close the car door, he starts in on my mother. "That woman is so impossible," he announces. My father is usually very positive, but my mother brings out the worst in him. And apparently, he never got the divorced-parent memo that explains that it's not healthy for a child (even an adult child) to hear one parent tear the other down.

"So what did Vera do this time?" I ask.

"She made one of her trademark snide remarks about my trousers," he says.

I smile at my dad's old-fashioned term. "What's wrong with your pants?"

"Ex-*actly*! There's nothing wrong with them, is there?"

"Not at all," I say, but upon closer inspection I can see that he has paired cuffed suit pants with a collared golf shirt. It is the sort of offense my mother can't tolerate. Still, I have to wonder why she still takes his fashion faux pas so personally. *What's it to her?* I always think.

"Is Dwight with her?" I ask.

"No. He had an early golf game," my dad says, flicking on his turn signal. "I'm sure he'll make a grand entrance later, though."

"They have that in common," I say.

"Yeah. She's been prancing around all morning," he says. I picture my mother, head thrown back, perky nose in the air, just like a proud circus pony.

"Yeah. Everything is about *her*," I say.

My mother aims to be conspicuous at all times. She is sure to be overdressed, will likely give Zoe the largest and most expensive present, and will have a crowd of admirers around her at all times. That is one thing that has not changed since my sisters and I were young—our friends adore our mother. They call her things like "zany" and "a hoot" and "one of the girls." But deep down, I think they are all glad that she's somebody else's mother.

"Don't let her get to you, Dad," I say.

My dad smiles as if mentally shifting gears. Then he says, "So where's Ben?"

I knew the question was coming, but I still feel a sharp pain in my side hearing his name. I take a deep breath and muster a breezy tone. "He had to work."

"Not like Ben to miss a family party."

"Yeah. He's quite the family man," I say. I am being sarcastic, but it occurs to me that this much is actually true—he *is* quite the family man.

A minute later we pull into my sister's horseshoe-shaped driveway as I survey her four-million-dollar mansion (Maura insists that her house is not a mansion, but I consider any home with more than six bedrooms a mansion, and her house has seven) with my usual mix of admiration and disdain. I'm disapproving not because of the sheer magnitude of their riches—because that is all relative. Rather, I dislike how Scott earned his money—not from hard work or brains, but by being at the right place at the right time. He was working as the CFO of a small software start-up that was purchased for a ridiculous amount of money during the technology bubble. He has so much money, in fact, that I've heard him refer to guys with smaller fortunes as "nickel millionaires."

If he were good to my sister, all of this would be great, and I would applaud his good luck. But Scott is a cad (to use one of my father's expressions) and their home is a constant reminder to me of the daily trade-off Maura makes: nice things, philandering husband. I often wonder whether my sister would leave if she didn't have children with Scott. She says she would. I'm not so sure she shouldn't anyway.

My dad parks behind a large white van marked ENDIVE CATERING. Maura spares no expense for her parties; even the ones for her children are extravagant affairs, so I'm not surprised as I walk through the front door and witness the sort of bustling last-minute preparations that would suggest a wedding reception, rather than a child's birthday party.

"Hello! Hello!" Maura says, giving me a quick, distracted hug before returning her attention to a gigantic vase of exotic flowers surrounded by elaborate party-favor bags. I can tell she is nervous, the way she always gets before any social function. A typical firstborn, Maura is a perfectionist in all that she does, and I always find myself thinking how exhausting it must be to be her. I can be anal, too—when it comes to my work—but Maura is that way about *everything*. Her house, her yard, her kids, her appearance. It is actually a good thing she quit her high-powered HR job when she had kids, because I can't imagine how burdened she'd be if she had to include a career in her quest for perfection.

She frowns, tilts her head to the side, and says, "Do these flowers look okay here? Is the scale . . . off?"

I tell her they are beautiful. Maura's home *is* beautiful, although there is nothing relaxed or comfortable about it. Instead it is a bit contrived in its eclectic perfection, bearing the heavy mark of an upscale designer who has painstakingly achieved a predictably sophisticated blend of old and new, modern and traditional. Maura's predominant color scheme is warm—yellow walls, cherry upholstery, tangerine abstract art—and yet something about her house still reminds me of a showroom. You would never guess that three children, six and under, reside there, despite the oil paintings in their likeness and photographs covering her baby grand piano. My sister is proud of her home's sophisticated, sleek feel. In fact, she points it out often, as if to say to me, *You don't have to be swallowed up by clutter and crumbs just because you have children.*

She has a valid point, but as Ben used to say, one can accomplish pretty much anything with her fleet of employees, including a nanny, a gardener, a pool guy, a personal assistant, and a live-in housekeeper. I've watched her delegating tasks to her staff, in her designer sarongs and Juicy Couture sweats, Venti Starbucks in hand, and thought to myself that although she quit her job, she is still running a small corporation of sorts—and she does a seamless job of it.

But despite the fact that Maura's life might seem shallow and indulgent upon first blush, she has a lot of underlying substance. She is an excellent mother. She subscribes to the Jackie O school of mothering, often quoting her idol: "If you bungle raising your children, I don't think whatever else you do matters very much." As a result, Maura's children are sweet, well mannered, and against all odds, relatively unspoiled.

"Where are the kids?" I ask Maura now, just as Zoe, William, and Patrick come tearing around the corner, hyper and wide-eyed, as if they've already consumed too much sugar. With light hair and fair skin, Zoe looks more like me than her own olive-skinned, brown-eyed parents, which I find to be a fascinating case study in genetics. Maura phoned one day recently to tell me that Zoe took a snapshot of me to the hair salon and told the stylist that she wanted her hair in a wavy bob so that she'd look like her aunt Claudia. I can't help feeling gratified by the fact that my niece resembles me, and recognize it as the narcissistic urge that compels many to have children in the first place.

"Happy birthday, Zoe!" I say, bending down to give her a big hug. She is dressed in full ballet regalia as "blushing ballerinas" is the theme of her party. Her pale pink leotard and lime-green tutu and ballet slippers coordinate, hue for hue, with the pink and green balloons tied to the banister and the three-tiered cake surrounded by yards of tulle. "I can't believe you're six!"

I think about the fact that Ben and I went on our first date the week after Zoe turned two. I wonder how long I will measure time in terms of Ben.

"Thank you, Aunt Claudia!" Zoe says in her low, throaty voice that seems so funny on a little girl. She slides her feet from second position into third. "The gift table is in the family room! In case you remembered to bring one?"

"I just might have," I say, opening my tote bag and giving her a glimpse of her wrapped present.

William and Patrick, ages three and two, both thrust matching gadgets into the air. "Look what we got!"

"Cool!" I say, although I haven't a clue what they've just shown me.

Zoe informs me that her dad bought them the new robots so they wouldn't be jealous of all her presents. Scott is a good father, although he's a little too much about bribery and threats. My favorite of his threats was "No Christmas if you don't stop the whining." When Ben heard that one, he laughed and asked how exactly Scott planned on going from December twenty-fourth to the twenty-sixth.

Zoe grins and leads me by the hand into the family room where Daphne and my mother sit knee to knee on the couch, sipping Kir Royales.

"Where's Benny?" my mother demands before even saying hello to me. It has always set my teeth on edge when she calls him Benny. I hate it even more now that we're not together.

I can feel myself stiffen as I sit on an armchair across from them and say, "He can't make it today."

"Why not?" my mother asks.

"He had to work." I smile brightly. "Business is booming."

This statement should be a dead giveaway. I don't use expressions like *business is booming*.

"But Benny never works on Saturdays," my mother says, as if she knows him better than I do. "Is there trouble in paradise?"

I marvel at my mother's ability to sniff out any controversy. Her favorite expression is "Where there's smoke there's fire" (which, incidentally, is her stated rationale for believing the tabloid press, no matter how outrageous the story).

"We're fine," I say, feeling relieved that I made the decision to wear my wedding ring one final time.

She looks around fervently, then leans in and whispers, "Don't even tell me he's pulled a Scott on you."

I shake my head, wondering how she, of all people, would dare cast stones at Scott. Then again, my mother is one the finest revisionist historians in the world, giving O.J. Simpson a run for his money. O.J. seems to have convinced himself that he didn't kill anyone, and in my mother's mind, she never did a *thing* wrong. At the very least, she has rationalized that my father drove her to cheat—which is absolute nonsense. My father was a better husband than she ever deserved.

"No, Mother," I say, thinking how much easier and clearcut an affair would be. I could never stay with a man who cheated on me. No matter what the circumstances. I am more like most men in this regard. No second chances. It's not so much about morality, but about my inability to forgive. I'm a champion grudge holder, and I don't think I could change this about myself even if I wanted to.

"Don't you lie to me, Claudia," she says, enunciating each word for maximum impact. Then she nudges Daphne and asks in a loud voice if she knows something. Daphne shakes her head and takes a sip from her champagne glass.

"Mother. It's Zoe's day," I say. "Please stop."

"Oh, dear *God*! There *is* trouble!" she practically shouts. "I *know* when there's trouble."

My dad mutters something about how fitting that is, on account of her being the cause of most of it.

My mother narrows her eyes, spins in her chair to face him. "What did you just say, Larry?"

"Mother," Maura calls from the powder room where she is doing her last-minute preening. "Please stop whatever it is you're doing in there!"

"Unreal. How is it that I'm being blamed for concern for a child?" she says to Daphne, her only potential ally in such situations. Daphne feels the same way about our mother as Maura and I do, but she can't help sucking up to her. She is vulnerable and sensitive and needs my mother's love in a way that both angers me and fills me with profound pity. Maura and I long ago walled ourselves off from caring about what my mother does or does not do. For some reason, Daphne can't do the same.

"Unreal," my mother says again, looking wounded.

"*You're* the one who is unreal, Vera," my dad says from across the room.

The unfolding scene is so predictable that I have another sharp pang of missing Ben. We often scripted the day ahead of time, placing wagers on who would say what and how long it would take for the words to be uttered.

My brothers-in-law, Scott and Tony, look up from their task of submerging beers in a large bucket of ice on the back porch and make their way into the living room where they exchange a "we're in the same boat, pal" glance. They have little in common—Tony is a plaid-shirt-wearing, sports-page-reading guy's guy and Scott is a cologne-wearing, *Wall Street Journal*-subscribing slickster—but they have bonded over the years in that in-law way that is common in many families. Always the perfect host, Scott pours an Amstel Light into a chilled glass and hands it to me with a cocktail napkin.

"Here you go, Claudia," he says.

I thank him and take a long swallow.

"What's all the commotion about?" Tony asks. He and Daphne have been together since high school. Their long history coupled with his unwavering fidelity has earned him the right to chime in—a right that Scott lacks even in his own house.

"Ben's not coming," my mother informs them. "What do you make of that? Am I the only one who thinks this is suspicious?" She looks around, hand pressed to her cleavage.

"Mother. I mean it. Not another word," I say. It is hardly a denial, but any normal person would take the cue and shut up. My mother proves she is anything but normal by glancing up at the ceiling, moving her lips in silent prayer, and rising slowly. "I need a cigarette," she announces. "Daphne, dear, won't you join me in the backyard?"

My sister gives my mother an obsequious nod. Only after she stands and follows my mother does she turn back and give me a slight eye roll. Daphne wants to please everyone. It is her best—and worst—trait.

The doorbell rings a few seconds later. I glance at my watch and realize that the party is officially under way. I am safe for a few hours. I hear Maura squealing at the door, and the sound of her best friend, Jane, squealing back. Maura and Jane were roommates and sorority sisters at Cornell, and like Jess and I, the two have been inseparable ever since. In fact, Bronxville was their joint decision. After living in Manhattan for years, they researched the New York and Connecticut suburbs exhaustively until they came up with two houses in the same neighborhood. Maura is wealthier than Jane, but Jane is prettier—which makes the friendship fair and balanced. Evidence of this is the conversation I overhear now:

"Your house looks amazing!" Jane says. "That floral arrangement is to *die* for!"

"Your *highlights* are to die for! Did Kazu do them?"

"Of course! Who else would I let touch my hair?"

As the rest of Maura's friends file in, I think what I always think when I'm in Bronxville. Everyone is *exactly* the same: smug, polished, and if not downright beautiful, they have, at the very least, maximized their genetic lot. And most of them have had at least two forays into the magical and seemingly addictive world of plastic surgery. *Having a little work done*, they whisper. My sister had her nose tweaked and her boobs lifted after William was born. She is not outright beautiful, but with loads of money and sheer force of will, she comes much closer to the mark than Daphne or I do. Her whole crowd, in fact, is tweezed, tanned, and toned to perfection. Their clothing is magazine-layout perfect, and their style so similar that their collective garments and accessories could easily belong in the same closet or photo shoot. I need not consult a fashion magazine this month—because one look around the room, and I know the latest trends include billowy skirts, bejeweled ballet flats, and chunky turquoise necklaces.

Their husbands are all dashingly handsome, at least upon first glance. Some have receding hairlines, others have weak jaws or overbites, but such shortcomings are overshadowed by a patina that comes with having money. A *lot* of money. They are confident, smooth talkers with full-bodied laughs. They wear Gucci loafers with no socks, pressed khakis, calf-skin belts. Their hair is gelled in place, their skin smells of spicy aftershave, and their custom linen shirts are rolled in neat cuffs just high enough to reveal their fancy yet still sporty watches.

Their conversation is self-congratulatory and ever-predictable. The women talk about their children's private schools and their upcoming vacations to the Caribbean and Europe. The men discuss their careers, golf games, and investments. There is occasional gossip about neighbors not in attendance—the women are biting; the men disguise it as banter.

What strikes me the most on this day is that Zoe and her friends seem to be on display as the ultimate accessories, coordinated with their siblings and, in one painful case, their same-gender parent. The girls wear oversized grosgrain bows in their hair and expensive, smocked dresses and have already learned how to flirt outrageously. Their brothers wear monogrammed john-johns and knee socks, and they have already learned to swagger and brag.

Following our lunch of tea sandwiches and elaborate pasta salads (and goat-cheese pizza for the kids), a professional ballerina from Ballet Academy East arrives to dance en pointe for Zoe and her fifteen closest friends, who scurry to change into their own leotards and tutus. They are treated to a group lesson in the pool house along one mirrored wall. The mothers line up like paparazzi and snap photos of their own. I switch to wine, keeping my glass filled while I sneak glances at my watch. The sooner the party ends, the sooner I can break my news and move on with the rest of my life.

When the ballet lesson concludes, it is time for cake, the highlight of any party. There are few things as satisfying as very expensive cake. We sing to Zoe, watch her blow out her candles in two tries, and wait for a piece of cake. A few women accept a slice from the caterer, but most decline and sneak dainty bites from their husbands. I find myself with the B for *birthday* and think B for *Ben*. I miss him in so many ways, but right now I miss him in the way you always miss someone when you're single among a room full of couples.

I pour another glass of wine and follow the crowd into the living room where Zoe begins to open presents despite Maura's prodding to wait until the guests have departed. Luckily Zoe is at the age where it is not possible to rip through the wrapping fast enough, so in no time at all she is surrounded by a pile of pink and lavender plastic and stuffed toys. American Girl dolls, bead-making kits, board games, Polly Pockets and Barbies galore. She saves my present for last. It is a monogrammed, wooden jewelry box with a twirling ballerina inside. I am pretty proud of the fact that I made the selection with no help from Maura, whom I usually consult at the last minute.

Zoe opens my card first, after being prompted by Maura to do so. We all listen to her read it aloud, sounding out the harder words. She gets to the bottom and reads, "Love, Aunt Claudia." Then she looks up at me and says, "Why isn't Uncle Ben's name on the card?"

Shit, I think.

"Yes, Claudia? Why?" my mother says.

I say something about it being an oversight.

Zoe gives me a puzzled look. Clearly she does not know the word *oversight*.

"I forgot to write his name," I say weakly.

"Are you getting a dee-vorce?" Zoe asks in an anxious tone that suggests her own parents' marriage is on the rocks. "Nanny V told Aunt Daphne that you're getting a dee-vorce."

My mother, aka Nanny V, finally has the opportunity she has been craving. She glances around the room, making maximum eye contact with her best "who me?" expression. Then she turns to me and trills in her eloquent soap opera voice, "Well? Is it true?"

All eyes are on me. Even Maura's friends who have never met me are staring at me waiting for my answer. It occurs to me to lie one final time, but I just don't have it in me. So I say to Zoe, "Sometimes things don't work out."

Maura looks as if she might faint, as much from the news as the black mark my announcement is making on her party. My dad practically runs toward me and gives me a big hug, whispering that everything will be okay. My mother starts bawling.

"I knew it. I knew it," she sobs as Dwight, who arrived only minutes before, fans her face with a pink ZOE IS SIX! cocktail napkin.

I break away from my dad, and say, "I'm fine."

One of Maura's friends, a woman with jet-black hair and the largest diamond earrings I've ever seen off a red carpet, gives my mother a Kleenex. She then doles one out to Daphne, who is tearing up in a Pavlovian response to my mother's sobs.

A hush falls over the room and Zoe, who looks stricken but stoic, poses another careful question, "Is it because you don't want children, or because you don't love him?"

This question is similar to "Are you still beating your wife?" and I can't help marveling at a six-year-old's astute ability to slice through the issues, boil my divorce down to its naked essence.

Of course the answer is simple: I don't want children so therefore Ben doesn't want me. I almost say it, exactly like that, but instead I smile and give one of those awful adult explanations, the sort of response that puts me squarely in the evasive, bad-mother camp. Or at least the bad-aunt camp.

"It just wasn't meant to be, Zoe," I tell my niece.

Zoe gives me a look that makes it clear that she has no idea what this means. Hell, *I* don't even know what it means. But before she can formulate her next question, I smile, stand, and stride to the dining room where I help myself to another piece of cake. This time I get a *D*—for *divorce*—all piled high with pink and green icing.

eight

The follow-up phone calls come fast and furious, and it is clear, by the pattern and intervals between messages, that the callers are in cahoots: Maura, Daphne, Dad, Maura, Daphne, Dad. My mother's messages are more random—just as she always is.

I take my time before I phone anyone back, which is a good decision because I can tell they've moved beyond their hysteria when we finally talk. I can also tell that they've come up with a unified party line—*we just want what's best for you, and although we dearly love Ben, we are on your side*. I credit Maura's fancy Upper East Side therapist, Cheryl Fishstein, for this reaction. Being rational and calm is never the first instinct in my family.

The only comment that throws me for a loop is Daphne's request to contact Ben.

"And say what?" I say.

"And say that I'm sorry you guys couldn't work things out . . . That I'll miss him . . . Maybe ask him how he's doing . . . But I'll only call if it's okay with you."

I tell her that she can do whatever she wants, but I don't want to hear the details of their conversation—which will likely revolve around how much both of them want babies. (In point of fact, Daphne actually started this conversation with the report that she got her period; I think I know Daphne's menstrual cycle better than I know my own.)

"Has his family contacted you?" she asks.

I tell her no. It occurs to me that this should hurt my feelings, but for some reason it doesn't. I think Ben's family respected me and liked me, but I never sensed real warmth between us. So their silence now is not a big surprise. And I think to truly get your feelings hurt, something has to come as a surprise. (Maybe this is why I'm immune to my own mother's actions.) I'm sure Ben's mother will send me a note at some point on her formal, monogrammed stationery. She's probably just reviewing her Anne Landers clippings for what exactly one should say to one's ex-daughter-in-law. Unless she's too busy getting started on her quilt for Ben's firstborn, that is.

The following Saturday afternoon I am traipsing across the Brooklyn Bridge with Michael in a throng of walkers, runners, and bikers, as he swears to me how therapeutic the view will be at the halfway point. We are here because yesterday at work I confessed that I was a little bit depressed. He stood across from my desk and said, "Of course you are. It would be weird if you *weren't* depressed."

Then he said he had an idea of something that might cheer me up, did I have plans for the next afternoon? I told him no, when you shift from married to divorced as abruptly as I have, it tends to do a number on your weekends. I told him that Jess and I had planned on making it out to the Hamptons, but she had a last-minute "business trip" (which is really a boondoggle to see Trey). Michael told me to be at his place in Alphabet City at ten. I sensed that it was a pity-invite but decided not to let pride get in the way of a good time. And Michael is always a good time.

So this morning, we met near his apartment, and now here we are on the Brooklyn Bridge pedestrian walkway. It is a hot June day—hotter than June usually gets in New York—and it's made even warmer by the sunlight reflecting off all the steel. Our pace is sluggish, and people pass us on both sides.

I keep thinking of how this is my first summer without Ben in a very long time. My first change of season without him. I haven't spoken to him at all in almost two months. Our divorce is final—the papers came in the mail a few days earlier, arriving without ceremony or fanfare. I filed them along with my birth certificate and social security card in a green hanging file marked IMPORTANT DOCUMENTS. And that was that.

I am thinking of the word *ex-husband* now—how both sad and oddly sophisticated it sounds—while Michael is saying something about the bridge's foundation being made of wood.

"You'd think the wood would rot and decay, wouldn't you?" Michael says.

"Yeah," I say. "But Venice is built on wood and it's a hell of a lot older than this."

"Good point," he says. "Maybe the bacteria that rots wood needs air to live?"

"I dunno," I say.

Ex-husband. Ex-husband. Ex-husband.

"So you've crossed this bridge before?" I ask Michael.

"Yeah. A few times . . . including a few days after September eleventh. It really gives you a sense of perspective. You'll see what I mean," he says. "It's the urban equivalent of going on a hike. Very peaceful."

I look ahead at the stone Gothic towers and backdrop of cobalt-blue sky, crisscrossed by a lacework of suspension cables. It creates an awesome visual effect, but I still tell Michael that I've always put the Brooklyn Bridge on par with the Statue of Liberty or the Empire State Building.

"New York landmarks are typically better on a postcard. Or from above on an airplane," I say, swerving to avoid full-body contact with an obese, wheezing man in a Derek Jeter jersey. "Away from the grime and crowds."

Michael smiles knowingly. "You can be a bit of an elitist, you know."

"I'm *hardly* an elitist," I say.

"Well, with comments like that one, I'd say you're certainly not down with the people," he says. I can tell he's mentally preparing his checklist of examples. Most people can't think of examples in the clutch, but Michael can always conjure up a good set of facts to use against you.

"I'm down with the people," I say.

Sure enough, he says, "Nuh-uh. You don't like amusement parks. You don't like fans who wave those big Styrofoam fingers at Knicks games. You wouldn't be caught dead in Times Square on New Year's Eve."

"Neither would you," I say. "Name someone we know who would?"

He holds his hand up and walks at a faster clip. "And," he says, signaling his grand finale, "you hated *Titanic*. For God's sake, I don't know another chick who hated *Titanic*. It's practically *un-American* to hate *Titanic*."

"I didn't *hate* it," I say, thinking of the Oscars from years ago. "I just didn't think it was best-picture material."

"You're not down with the people," he says again.

I think for a second and then say, "I take the subway. You can't get much more down with the people than that."

"Mere convenience."

"No. I actually *like* the subway."

"Bullshit. I've watched the way you gingerly hold on to the pole," he says, imitating my grip. "And make sure your legs don't touch the person next to you. And you use that antibacterial gel afterward."

I shake my head. "So I have a mild case of OCD . . . What's your point, anyway?"

"My point is . . . your standards are too high."

"In movies? Public transportation?"

"In general."

I have the distinct feeling we are about to cover my personal life. Michael's been telling me for weeks that I need to get back on my horse. Check out Match.com. Pick up a random, pretty stranger at a bar. I told him that I wasn't interested in random guys, pretty or otherwise.

"I know Ben was the man and all . . ." Michael says. The way he says it makes me think that he doesn't think Ben was the man at all. "But—"

I interrupt him and say, "I *knew* this was about my love life. Jeez, Michael, I've only been divorced for a few days."

He looks over his shoulder as if we're being followed and says, "I know. But you've been separated for longer . . . And in my experience, after a bad breakup—and I think a divorce qualifies—it helps to just go ahead and get the first hookup over with. Take the plunge."

"Are you volunteering?"

He looks at me and grins. "Are you taking volunteers?"

"No," I say. "I'm not."

"I didn't think so . . . But if you change your mind, I'd be up for it."

"Are you trying to tell me something, Michael? Have you been secretly in love with me all these many years?" I joke back, giving him a sideways once-over. He is wearing a canary-yellow T-shirt, Adidas flip-flops, and khaki cargo shorts that show off his long, sinewy calves. There's something about the confident way he walks, slightly bow-legged, that hints at high marks in bed.

He smirks. "Nah. Don't worry. I'm not trying to get all *Harry Met Sally* on you or anything . . . I just think you should know that I'm always willing to help out a friend."

"Help *me* out?" I say. "Aren't you in a bit of a drought yourself?"

"Six weeks does not a drought make," he says. Then he clears his throat and says, "Look. I'm just saying that I think you're very attractive. A solid eight. So if you need a volunteer or anything, I'm here for you."

"Gee," I say. "Who needs the view from the Brooklyn Bridge with that kind of pep talk?"

Michael smiles as he leads me over to the side of the bridge. "This is a good spot," he says.

I follow him and look across the sparkling water toward Manhattan. The skyline is stunning, even without the World Trade Center. Around us, people are snapping photos and pointing out landmarks. I look down the bridge toward Brooklyn and see a teenaged girl flash a peace sign and then blow a kiss at a boy approaching her. I imagine their earlier conversation: *Meet me on the Brooklyn Bridge, baby.* I close my eyes, listen to a helicopter overhead, and feel a breeze against my face.

After a long moment, I reach into my pocket for my wedding ring, which I brought with me at the last minute. I give it one last look, running my hand along the inside engraving— FOREVER, BEN. Then I roll my shoulder back and forth to loosen my muscles before chucking it overhand into the East River. I am proud of my nongirly, hard throw, a benefit of having no brothers and a father who adores baseball; he poured all his effort into me. I try to keep my eye on it to see the precise spot it drops, but lose sight of it about halfway down, the platinum band getting lost in the background of the pewter-colored river.

"Was that what I think it was?" Michael says. He looks impressed.

"Yup," I say, squinting down at the water.

His black eyebrows arch high over his Oakleys. "Rather *Titanic*-esque, huh?"

I laugh. "See that? Rose and I have a lot in common."

"Seriously. That was a strong move," Michael says.

"Thanks."

"Almost makes me want to kiss you," he says. "The cherry on top of your little ceremony, ya know?"

I consider his proposition for a moment and the fact that it might add a little texture to our friendship. Whenever I get that inevitable question, the one always posed to male-female friends: "Have you two ever kissed or anything?" I can say, "Indeed we *have*. Once upon a time, right after I hurled my wedding ring off the Brooklyn Bridge." It would make a good story in my romantic repertoire, one that Jess would surely enjoy—particularly because she thinks Michael is hot. Besides, maybe a simple kiss, like my symbolic ring toss, could serve as a catalyst of sorts.

Even though I think Michael's mostly kidding, I fleetingly study his full lips and think I'm going to do it. But I hesitate one second too long, leaving the realm of spontaneity and entering into awkward territory. I decide it's for the best. Why complicate my life by kissing a friend, especially a friend from work?

I look back toward the skyline and shrug noncommittally. "Would you settle for getting loaded in Brooklyn?"

"Sure," Michael says. "Twist my arm."

We cross the bridge into Brooklyn, not breaking stride once until we arrive at Superfine, a restaurant on Front Street that Michael says has great food and a good, casual atmosphere. The tables are all full so we sit in the bar in a blast of blissful air-conditioning. I curl my legs around my stool as Michael asks the bartender, an older woman wearing pigtails (which I think is a frightful combination), what they have on tap. She rattles off our choices. Nothing grabs our fancy so we order two Heinekens in bottles. Michael says we'll be starting a tab. I gulp my first beer quickly, more for thirst than taste. Then, while Michael sticks with beer, I ramp it up with a dirty martini. Michael raises his eyebrows and smiles.

We order one burrito, and split it because it's huge. We also share an order of fries. Despite the food, I still catch a strong buzz quickly. Time begins to fall away, along with any thoughts of Ben. Michael and I talk about the books we're working on and people at work. Then I tell him the latest scoop on Jess's relationship with Trey, knowing that she wouldn't mind. Jess is very open with details of her life.

I remove a vodka-soaked olive from my toothpick and pop it into my mouth, telling myself to slow my pace. I need to stay in the buzzed, lighthearted zone and out of the morose, drunk one. Of course, that's a tall order when you're dealing with martinis. And the more I drink, the more my thoughts drift back to Ben.

At one point, I can't help blurting out, "I didn't think I'd miss him this much."

Michael runs his hand along the sides of his glass and then wipes the condensation on his shorts as he says, "So what exactly went down there anyway?"

I answer quickly, "We wanted different things."

He rolls his eyes. "Jesus, Claudia. That's worse than the 'we grew apart' song and dance."

"Fine," I say. "Ben wanted a baby."

"And you?"

I pause and then say, "I didn't—*don't*—want a baby."

"What *do* you want?"

Nobody has ever posed the question quite like this before, and I have to think for a minute before I can answer. "I want a really good, committed relationship. I want close friends and good times. Like right now . . . I want freedom to do my job well without feeling guilty or beholden to anyone. I want freedom generally."

"Oh," Michael says, and then takes a long swallow of beer. "I see."

"Tell me what you're thinking," I say, recognizing that you're more likely to invite or tolerate criticism when someone isn't so free with it.

"I don't know," he says. "It's just that . . . being married cuts down on your freedom. Having a husband—or a relationship at all—puts constraints on you. You handled that fine. I don't think I could deal with those sorts of constraints. It's why I had to call it quits with Maya," he says, referring to his ex-girlfriend. It was Michael's most serious relationship to date, one that he ended when she demanded a ring—or at the very least, a key to his apartment. He continues, "I was so afraid that I wouldn't be good at it that I didn't even want to try . . . It seems to me that you left Ben more because of fear than anything else."

"Fear of what?" I say.

He shrugs and then says, "Fear of failure. Fear of change. Fear of the unknown."

I look at him, feeling dizzy.

"And yet, here you are anyway . . ." he says, his voice trailing off.

He doesn't have to say the rest. I know the rest. Here I am anyway, facing all of the above. Fear of failure, fear of change, fear of the unknown. And right here, in a bar under a bridge in Brooklyn, I feel a very small pang of regret.

Michael says he has to get back home, that he has a hot date tonight. Actually, he doesn't say it's hot, but I assume that part. Michael only dates hot women. So we take the subway back to Manhattan and part ways on the Lower East Side.

"Are you going to be all right?" Michael asks.

"Yeah," I say, kissing his cheek. "Thanks for today."

"It was my pleasure," he says, tipping an imaginary hat.

As we say good-bye, I wonder if, come Monday morning, I will confess to Michael the very stupid thing I'm about to do.

nine

I really can't say *exactly* what makes me take the subway up to my old apartment when, prior to this afternoon, I was convinced that short of mere happenstance I would never see Ben again. Of course the martinis are a factor, but I've never been one to radically change my behavior when I'm drunk. I've never, for example, hooked up with someone while drunk whom I wouldn't have hooked up with otherwise. Besides, by the time I get off the subway at Seventy-second and Broadway, I'm not nearly as intoxicated as I was in Brooklyn. I could easily regroup and head back to Jess's place.

So I think my little detour has less to do with alcohol and more to do with what Michael said to me in the bar. The stuff about fear motivating my decision to divorce Ben. As I walk the several blocks to Ben's apartment, I consider my faults, ticking off the list of adjectives that other people have thrown at me during arguments—and that I've thrown at myself during quiet, introspective moments: *stubborn, judgmental, moody, impatient*. I have my share of character flaws, but I've never counted cowardice among them. To the contrary, I have always thought of myself as one to accept challenges and take risks. It is part of the reason I've been so successful at work.

Still, something rings true in Michael's words. Maybe I *am* just afraid. Maybe I let Ben go because the *fear* of having a baby actually outweighed the fact that I didn't *want* one. Maybe I feared the person I would become. Maybe I feared something I couldn't quite name, even to Ben, even to myself.

Somehow I think I believe that seeing Ben will give me these answers. Or maybe it's just an excuse to see him again. In any event, it doesn't really matter. Nothing has changed. I still don't want a baby, and Ben still does.

But here I am anyway, standing on the sidewalk, looking pensively up at the third-floor kitchen window I used to look out of every morning and every night. I picture Ben, unshaven and barefoot, making a late-afternoon snack. I can see him pouring a glass of milk and arranging Ritz crackers on a plate before smearing just the right amount of peanut butter across the face of each one. I can see him licking both sides of the knife and dropping it with a clang into the sink. I can see him eating his crackers peanut butter side down, while he sits on the couch and watches golf. I can see all the little ordinary things he used to do, things that now seem like faraway memories.

I take a deep breath and climb the outside stairs to the front door. My heart is racing as I close my eyes and press the buzzer over my old last name. "Davenport, Apt 8C." I wait to hear static and Ben's voice saying, "Hello?" but there is only silence. I look at my watch. It is 5:15. Maybe he went for a run. Ben loves to run in the park at this hour of the day. Sometimes I'd go with him.

I decide I will kill a few minutes and go get some soft-serve ice cream at the little candy store around the corner. I walk there slowly, looking around at my old neighborhood, noticing things I never noticed before. A green wire waste can. A jagged break in the sidewalk. A row of red geraniums planted in a second-story window box. When I enter the candy store, the Middle Eastern clerk working behind the counter smiles and says hello as if he recognizes me. Maybe he does. Maybe he has noticed that Ben now comes in alone.

I smile and order a chocolate-vanilla swirl in a sugar cone with rainbow sprinkles. I also buy a bottle of Evian and a pack of spearmint Trident. I am four cents short, so I get out my credit card, but the clerk says don't worry about it, you'll be back. I almost tell him that I won't actually be back, but instead I just thank him. I take my cone, retrace my steps, and try the buzzer again, just in case Ben returned while I was gone. Still no answer.

I sit on the top stair and take a few bites of the vanilla side of the cone. I don't know why I consistently order the swirl when I like vanilla so much better. It just seems like I *should* prefer chocolate. I also decide that the rainbow sprinkles were a bad idea. They are good in a dish, but too messy on a cone. I eat a little faster as the ice cream begins to melt. I tell myself that I will only wait for Ben as long as it takes to finish my cone. Anything longer than that might make me feel like a stalker. The last thing I need right now is to feel like a stalker. Besides, my buzz is *completely* gone now, replaced with a faint headache, the kind that is sure to get worse. I hold my cone in one hand, unscrew the bottle of Evian with the other, and down about half of it without stopping. I am starting to panic a little, wondering what I will say to Ben. Wondering if there is any point to my being here at all.

A lone pigeon bobs his way toward me. "Rats with wings" Ben calls them. I lick the chocolate side of the cone and contemplate walking back to the subway when I suddenly spot Ben jogging in place, about a block away, waiting for the light to turn green so he can cross West End Avenue. He is wearing burnt-orange running shorts, a gray Wake Forest basketball T-shirt, and his favorite White Sox baseball cap. I feel a nervous flutter in my stomach and then a sense of comfort for having correctly guessed that he was on a run. *I still know you,* I whisper, and then I wave just in case he can see me. It's not an eager wave, just a casual, hand-in-the-air acknowledgment. I wait for him to wave back, but he doesn't, just adjusts his cap, bending the bill with one hand. I wipe my mouth with my napkin, and stand, thinking he'll see me any second.

Instead, he turns in the other direction to face a girl jogging toward him. My mind freezes and then clicks into place. *Ben is running with a girl. He is on a date. A late afternoon, summer date. A run-in-the-park-together date.*

I think back to our first run together. It was *after* we had slept together. About a week later. Two tops. I know this for a fact. I have an excellent memory, especially when it comes to dates. And Ben.

I study this woman—this girl—he is with. She has long, thick, white-blond hair pulled back in a perfect, silken ponytail that swishes back and forth just right. It is the kind of hair that I coveted when I was much younger, believing that I could somehow train mine to look and behave the same way. The girl strides forward, once, twice, three times and is now beside him. Ben says something to her and then leans down and grabs the bottom of his shorts as if to catch his breath. I can see his profile. He stands, and I watch his chest rising and falling with the effort that comes from a hard finish. His shirt is damp across the chest. The girl stretches her left hamstring. She has long, thick legs, reminding me of a beach volleyball player, only without the tan. Her skin is as pale as her hair.

103

Her face is long and angular. I wouldn't call her pretty, but she is attractive, and unfortunately for me, very memorable. I can't tell how old she is, but something about her expression and stance makes me think she's still in her twenties.

All of these observations transpire in a few seconds, but that is long enough for a stream of ice cream to melt down the side of the cone and trickle onto my hand and forearm. It is also long enough for the light to change and Ben and his date to come bounding toward me. And it is plenty long enough for me to realize that I am completely trapped. If I still had my key to the front door, I would duck into the building and hide behind the stairwell near the mailboxes. Gamble that Ben already picked up the mail. I cannot turn and walk in the other direction because Ben knows my back as well as he does my front. I will be tortured wondering whether he saw me and just chose to let me walk away. And my third option—aggressively approach them—is something I just can't make myself do. So I just stand there, my feet rooted to the concrete. I frantically try to clean myself up. By now another half-dozen drips of ice cream are trickling down the side of the cone, carrying sprinkles downstream with them. I am a total mess.

You dumbass, I think to myself, for coming here at all and, even more, for ordering a cone on a hot day. A cone with rainbow sprinkles. What am I, *twelve*? This is my last thought before Ben sees me. His expression is confused at first, as if I'm completely out of context standing in front of a place where I lived for years. Then he smiles tightly, obviously flustered over the impending introduction. His eyes are casting wildly from me to the girl. Me to the girl. She is still oblivious. She doesn't seem to notice me at all, looking right through me in the way you look right through so many people every day.

Especially in a big city. She is in the middle of telling a story. Something about a stress fracture she got from running around the reservoir in the same direction, day after day. It was diagnosed right before last year's New York marathon. She had to pull out of the race. One of the saddest days of her life.

I can tell Ben wants to interrupt her, save everyone the extra layer of embarrassment that comes when a third party has a delayed understanding of the awkward thing transpiring. But short of telling her to shut up, he can't stop the story. She finishes by saying this: "But that's one of my goals in life. To run a sub-three-and-a-half-hour marathon."

I am angry that we have one of the same goals—but I was only aiming to *finish* a marathon. I wonder what her other goals in life are. And if they include Ben. Motherhood. I feel as though I'm going to throw up. Ben has a pained look on his face, too, and this helps a little, but not much.

"Hi, Claudia," he says, looking up at me.

"Hi, Ben."

"It's good to see you," he says.

"Good to see you, too," I say. "How are you?"

"I'm fine," he says. "Just . . . went for a little run."

I make direct eye contact with the girl, and wonder if Ben told her about me. Told her that, technically, I was his wife until last week.

"Oh, sorry, um, this is my friend Tucker Jansen," Ben stammers. "Tucker, this is Claudia Parr," he says, pausing for one beat before using my maiden name.

I memorize her name as she flashes me a polite, friendly smile. Unfortunately, it reveals absolutely nothing. I still don't know if she knows who I am. I do notice, however, that she has very few lines around her eyes. She is definitely in her twenties. I'd put her no older than twenty-six. The name Tucker seems to corroborate my guess. Nobody born in the sixties and seventies has a name like Tucker. The surname craze didn't start until later. She is an eighties child. She was probably five when *St. Elmo's Fire* came out. Three when *Flashdance* hit theaters. It is entirely possible that she hasn't even *seen* those movies.

I swallow, descend the stairs, and shake her hand. "Hi, Tucker. It's nice to meet you." Luckily I am left-handed so my right hand is not the sticky one.

Tucker's grip is firm, but her skin is soft. *Alarmingly* soft. "Nice to meet you, too," she says.

We are all stuck at this point. What else can we say? If Tucker knows who I am, she can't say anything. And if she doesn't know who I am, she can't say anything. Ben really can't offer up, "This is my ex-wife." Or, "This is my new girl-friend." Or, "You two actually have a lot in common. You've both had stress fractures! Only Claudia got hers from tripping on an escalator rather than training too hard. And she only ever aspired to *finish* a marathon."

And I certainly can't say, "So, Ben, do you think that I'm allowing fear to govern my life?"

So we all just stand there for a second, smiling unnaturally, until I say, "Well, I was just in the neighborhood. Thought I'd say hello."

"I'm glad you did," Ben says.

"Yeah. But I have to get going now," I say, glancing at my watch. I am still holding the half-eaten cone, which is begin-ning to drip from the tiny opening in the bottom. Note to self: *the next time you stalk your ex-husband, go with a waffle cone.*

Tucker says, "Well, I better get going, too . . ."

This statement is a strong indication that she knows exactly who I am. She feels rude and awkward standing there with my ex-husband while I am forced to slink away. It is arguably a compassionate move on her part, but it makes me feel even more pathetic. Then again, maybe she really *does* have to get home. Maybe she has to shower and get ready for the dressed-up, nighttime portion of their date. Or maybe they are already showering together. She appears to be completely unself-conscious, the sort of girl who might hop in the shower with a new boyfriend, under bright lights.

I feel tempted to let Tucker go so I can stay and talk to Ben. But I feel too humiliated and decide it's better to walk away first. Show both of them that I am fine with whatever they have going on. I give Ben a small, formal smile and say goodbye. Then I shuffle away quickly. I hear Ben and Tucker exchange a few words and then she is behind me, saying my name. She *so* knows the deal.

She asks if I'm going to the subway. I detect a Chicago accent and think, *Midwestern, wholesome.*

I say yes, I am.

"Me, too," she says.

Great. I am now stuck walking several blocks to the subway with her, maybe longer if we're going the same direction. Now I *really* think I might puke. I can actually feel the martinis and rainbow sprinkles in my throat as I ask, "So how do you know Ben?"

"We met at a party."

"Oh. That's nice," I say, and then can't resist asking, "When?"

"Memorial Day."

"That's nice," I say again, feeling somewhat relieved that we didn't overlap.

"Ben and I are just friends," she offers clumsily.

"Oh."

"Yeah."

After a long silence, I say, "Us, too. Although we used to be married."

"Yeah. I know."

"Well," I say with a nervous laugh.

"Yeah," she says with her own anxious chuckle.

And that's about when I think to myself that I'd rather be a contestant on *Fear Factor* than continue a conversation with Ben's new "friend." So I manufacture an Upper West Side errand.

"I have to run in here and check out some things," I say, pointing up to a random store we are walking past.

"Oh," she says. "Do you have a dog or a cat?"

Leave it to me to pick a pet store when I don't have a pet.

"Neither . . . I, um, just need to get a few gifts . . . I have some friends with dogs," I mumble. "So . . . it was nice to meet you, Tucker."

"It was really nice to meet you, too, Claudia. Hope to see you again."

Not if I see you first and actually have a chance to escape.

"So. Bye," I say.

"Buh-*bye*," she says.

Buh-bye?

I duck into the store and pretend to be enthralled with a tank full of goldfish, comforting myself with the knowledge that Ben *hates* when girls say *buh-bye*. It will never last between them. She is young, athletic, and sweet. And I'm sure she's *dying* to have children. She even *looks* fertile. But she says *buh-bye*. At least I have that much to hold on to as I face another Saturday night alone.

ten

Ben calls me twice that night. The first is when I am still at the pet store, gazing at those goldfish and wondering who the hell thinks that fish make good pets. Then he calls again just after I've returned to Jess's apartment, showered, and dumped two manuscripts and a sharpened red pencil onto the kitchen table. Both times, I feel too sad and queasy to answer. I never fancied myself irreplaceable. I mean, our divorce is proof that I *am* totally replaceable. But I really didn't think Ben would be out there so soon, meeting women already, as if he is up against some male biological clock. And whether Tucker *is* just a friend or his actual girlfriend or someone he's sleeping with or someone he aspires to sleep with or his second wife or the mother of his future children isn't the point. Tucker actually is *entirely* beside the point.

The point is—Ben is moving on and I am not. Instead, I'm trekking up to his apartment with some half-baked inquiry about a purported fear. A total, transparent, pathetic excuse. The kind of thing I would rip Jess apart for. All of this not only confirms that I'm taking the divorce harder than he is, but now I also know that *Ben knows* that I am taking the divorce harder than he is. And this part probably sucks the most.

I try to concentrate on my work, but my mind keeps returning to Tucker. I remember Ben's introduction and say

110

her name aloud: "Tucker Jansen." Then, against my better judgment, I slowly get up from the table and make my way to Jess's computer, set up in a corner of her bedroom. My heart is pounding as I log on to Google and prepare to do a search of my ex-husband's new friend. I put *Tucker Jansen* in quotes, just as Jess taught me to do. Jess is a masterful cyberspace stalker. She has found numerous ex-boyfriends online. Wedding gift registries on theknot.com are her bread and butter. She pores over the selections, recruiting me to help rip on her ex's fiancée's taste. ("Have you ever seen such a hideous china pattern?") She has also found houses on domania.com ("Jack's doing well—he just bought a five-bedroom chateau in Greenwich.") and baby registries on Amazon.com ("Brad's wife is due on April fifth—they don't know the gender because they only registered for yellow things.").

But my favorite of her hits was when she found one ex on an obscure cooking Web site. She read details about his upcoming dinner party for twelve, which happened to be planned on her birthday, shortly after their breakup. It just added insult to injury to read his chipper online chat about how to make venison taste less gamey with a milk marinade. Of course she couldn't resist posting an anonymous response: "Who the hell serves venison at a dinner party? And if you want it to be less gamey, skip the milk marinade and just go with steak."

I hesitate for a moment, worried about what I will find on Tucker. Then I close my eyes and hit return. I am beyond relieved when I open my eyes and discover that Ben's new friend does not exist on the Internet. Clearly she is too young to have accomplished much of anything. To reinforce the point, I do a search of myself. I feel an enormous sense of satisfaction when my name retrieves four hundred and thirty hits, including articles in *Publishers Weekly*, mentions on author Web sites, and quotes from various conferences and speaking engagements. I scan some of the articles and start to feel the tiniest bit better. Tucker *needs* a baby to give her life some meaning. I do not.

I log off and return to the kitchen table, determined to get some work done. I tell myself not to listen to Ben's messages. It was bad enough that I Googled his (girl)friend. But after twenty minutes of rereading the same paragraph, I cave and dial my voice mail. In his first message Ben is all business. He simply says, "Claudia. It's Ben. Please call me when you get this."

In his second message, he says virtually the same thing, word for word, but then he pauses for several seconds and says, "It was great to see you . . . It *really* was."

His *really* is so sincere and has something of a desperate edge—an edge you could only detect if you know someone well. I listen to the message again and can't stop myself from dialing his cell even though I know he could be reunited with Tucker by now. I figure I've already blown my pride for the day. Besides, he *asked* me to call him. Blowing him off might appear more pathetic. Like I'm too wounded or angry to talk.

Ben answers on the fourth ring, and before I can say hello, he says my name, sweetly and softly: *Claudia*. I shiver, but quickly tell myself not to get sentimental. There is no point.

"Hi, Ben," I say, careful to keep my voice even. "Look. I'm really sorry to drop in on you like that. I didn't mean to interrupt . . ."

"You didn't interrupt anything," he says quickly.

I laugh, as if to say, *I sure did interrupt something*.

"Tucker's just a friend," he says.

"Uh-huh," I say.

"It's not like that," he says. "We just went for a run. It was nothing."

"Whatever. It's none of my business," I say a little too emphatically. I don't want to come across as bitter. The last thing I want to be is bitter.

"It's not like that," he says again. "Truly. It's not."

"Okay," I say.

After a long pause, he says, "So. Was something on your mind when you came by?"

"No. I was just in the neighborhood . . . and I thought I'd say hello."

"Claudia. C'mon."

"What?"

"Talk to me," he says, his voice a near whisper.

My heart is pounding in my ears, and I can't get any words out. Not that I know what to say anyway.

"Are you okay?" he says.

"Yeah. I'm fine," I lie. "I just . . . I don't know."

"Say it," he says. "Tell me."

"I don't know . . . I guess I was just wondering if we did the right thing?"

He says, "Sometimes I really don't know . . . I miss you so much."

I want to tell him that I miss him, too, but instead I deflect with a laugh and say, "Yeah. This whole divorce business ain't easy."

We're both quiet for something close to a full minute and then he says, "You want to come over? Watch a movie or something?"

I feel goose bumps rise on my arms and legs but shoot back,

113

"I don't think that would be a very good idea . . ."

I know I am right, but I still hate myself for saying it. I want nothing more than to go back to my old apartment, sit with Ben on the couch, and watch a movie. At this moment, I miss our friendship more than anything else.

Part of me hopes he'll talk me into it, but he just says, "You're probably right."

"Yeah," I say.

"Okay," he says.

"Well. I better go," I say, my eyes filling with tears.

"Okay. Good-bye, Claudia," he says softly. "Be well."

"You, too," I say, feeling unbelievably empty inside. I can't ever remember feeling this lonesome. As I hang up, I tell myself to memorize the ache in my chest just in case I ever get any more bright ideas to get in touch with Ben. I don't want to be reminded of what I no longer have.

Jess returns the following morning from her red-eye flight, bursting into my bedroom. The best way to describe her is giddy.

"I'm so glad you're awake!" she says, running and jumping on the foot of my bed.

"What's up?" I say, just as Tucker's vivid features come into sharp focus. "How was your trip?"

Jess sings, "Trey's leaving his wife!"

"That's great!" I say, my voice sounding stilted. It's hard for me to muster up a lot of enthusiasm around the subject of divorce.

"He's telling her this week," she says. "She's going on her annual girls' trip to the beach this Friday—and he's going to tell her right before she leaves."

How thoughtful, I think. *The girls will have something to talk about now.* But I say, "And then what?"

"What do you mean 'then what'?" she says. I know she is hungry for my approval in the way that all single women need the approval of their best friends. In the way that I now need her approval.

"I mean—what are the logistics? Is he moving to New York?"

"We haven't talked about that yet," she says.

"Oh," I say, and then worry that I'm probably not sounding jubilant enough. The last thing I want to do is rain on Jess's parade when every single one of her parades over the past decade-plus has been rained out. Besides, nothing I say is going to change what she does so I might as well be supportive. Sometimes you just need someone to be happy—or sad—along with you. Still, I can't help having a very bad feeling about Trey. Except in a few, very rare circumstances, I am a firm believer in the saying, *Once a cheater, always a cheater.*

I know Jess can sense my skepticism because she says, "You don't like him, do you?"

"I don't know him," I say quickly. "I just . . . I don't know . . ."

"Say it," she says.

I hesitate and then say, "Do you think you could ever really trust him?"

"We're totally in love," Jess says, which doesn't really address my question. You can love someone you mistrust. "He's my soul mate."

My legs feel weak just hearing the words *soul mate,* words I once used to describe my relationship with Ben. There is no better feeling in the world than believing you have found your

115

soul mate. It's utter euphoria. Which is sort of the exact opposite of how I feel right now.

"I'm happy for you, Jess," I say. "I really hope things work out."

She grins and then disappears, returning with her digital camera. "I took photos of him. Just so you could see him," she says, clicking through highlights of their tryst at the Four Seasons. There is one picture of Trey holding a towel loosely at his waist. He has a six-pack, maybe even an eight-pack, complete with those ledgelike indentations where ripped stomach dips into pelvis territory.

"Wow. He's gorgeous," I say, wondering how an investment-banker-father-husband has time to carry on an affair *and* hit the gym that hard. It confirms something else I've always said—I don't trust men who have bodies that fabulous.

Jess blushes and says, "I know! He *really* is . . . I think this is *it,* Claudia. This is really *it* this time."

"We'll see," I say, crossing my fingers with feigned optimism.

I don't tell Jess about Tucker until the following Saturday morning, after Trey—*surprise, surprise*—does *not* tell his wife that he wants a divorce. He had his reasons, of course. They always do. Something about his son having a high fever and his wife's beach trip getting canceled. I think to myself that it's so unfair that shit marriages seem to have a way of limping along for decades—while perfectly good ones like mine can just end overnight.

Meanwhile Jess is telling me how she doesn't hold the delay against him. That this just proves what a good father he is.

I guess it's the "good father" reference that makes me think of Ben because I tell her the whole Tucker story.

Jess looks surprised that I didn't confide in her sooner, so I shoot her a look of apology and say, "I had to digest it before I could talk about it."

She nods as if she understands. Unlike my sisters, she's not one to get her feelings damaged around these sorts of things. In fact, she's not one to get her feelings hurt around much of anything. She has developed an extremely thick skin over the years—which probably stems as much from her bad luck in love as her hardass profession.

"Did you Google her?" Jess asks.

I laugh and admit that I did. "You taught me well."

"And?"

"Nothing. She's nowhere to be found."

"You put her name in quotes?"

"Yup," I say. "Nothing came up."

"Good," Jess says, flashing me one of her devilish smiles. "Just proves what we already knew."

"What's that?" I say.

"That he doesn't have a prayer of upgrading from you."

"Say it again," I say.

So she does, with a little extra flair the second time.

Later that afternoon, Jess and I meet my sisters at Union Square Cafe for lunch. Jess and I were working all morning while Maura and Daphne shopped. They are loaded up with bags from Barneys (Maura's favorite store) and Blooming-dale's (Daphne's favorite). I'm in the best mood I've been in for a long time, likely because I'm spending time with my three favorite women. I can literally feel my heart healing just being in their company.

The waitress is grinding fresh pepper on Daphne's ravioli

when Maura comes right out and asks if I've heard from Ben. I glance at Jess and fleetingly consider saying no. It's not that I don't want to tell my sisters. I'm just not in the mood to relive the whole tale. But I have a very difficult time keeping track of those sorts of deceptions. I know I will forget in several months that I *didn't* tell them and will make a Tucker reference—and then it will become an issue: why did I tell Jess and not them? So I just go ahead and divulge everything, down to the rainbow sprinkles and the pet store and my Google search and short conversation with Ben later that night. Daphne's brown eyes look pained and downright teary. Daphne cries a lot. It is her natural reaction to any extreme emotion—anger, happiness, worry, fear. Meanwhile, Maura puts on her determined, competitive face. I can tell she wants more information. Sure enough, she starts firing questions. "How pretty was she?" she asks, even though I just completed a rather detailed physical description for the express purpose of preempting this line of questioning.

"I told you," I say with a shrug. "She was attractive. She had good hair and skin. And a decent body."

"Decent?" Maura asks. "Define *decent,* please."

"It was pretty good," I say, and then amend my statement as I consider my audience. "Actually, you probably wouldn't think so."

Maura's standards are ridiculous—for herself and everyone else. She is extremely thin—and with frequent workouts with a trainer, she is also toned and fit. You would never guess that she had three children. Some might even call her *too* thin. Daphne thinks so, but that might be because Daphne and she look so much alike except that Daphne is perpetually trying to *lose* fifteen to twenty pounds. In fact, one of my sisters' biggest arguments of the last five years came when Daphne was complaining about some bizarre diet not working and Maura said to her, "I don't get it. Just don't eat, Daph. Just don't put the food in your mouth. What's so hard about that?" To Maura, it's *not* hard. I've never seen someone with so much self-discipline. To Daphne—and millions of other Americans—it's just not that easy. If it were, nobody would be fat.

So Maura continues now, "So she was chunky? I can't see Ben with a chunky girl."

"No. She *wasn't* chunky. Big-boned maybe," I say. "Lush." Jess laughs. *"Lush?"*

"Young . . . curvy . . . strong," I say matter-of-factly.

"Yikes," Daphne says. "I don't care for that description."

"Well," I say, scraping my container of dressing onto my salad. I don't know why I ever bother getting dressing on the side when I always eat all of it. "What're you gonna do? We knew that Ben was going to date. That was the point of our breakup, right? Find a good woman with an available womb."

Daphne makes a face. I usually try to avoid words like *womb* around Daphne. Unlike my insensitive mother who tosses around expressions like *shooting blanks* and *barren*.

I field another few questions about Tucker's looks.

Probably a size ten.

About Ben's height.

Green eyes, I think. Maybe blue.

"So it sounds like her hair is her only decent feature?" Maura concludes.

"It's probably her best feature, yes," I say.

"So she wouldn't pass the Rosannadanna-do test?" Daphne says, smiling.

I laugh and say probably not. The Rosannadanna-do test is pretty self-explanatory, but this is how it works: give an otherwise pretty girl frizzy, brown Rosannadanna hair and ask if she's still pretty. Maura devised the litmus test when we were in high school and she insisted that the only reason Tiffany Hartong beat her out for homecoming queen was that Tiffany had this gorgeous blond hair that *fooled* everyone into thinking she was pretty. Of course, I would argue that that's sort of like a test that says, "Give the girl a buttass ugly face and ask if she's still pretty." Hair is a pretty integral part of the package.

Still, I resist the urge to announce that I'm not as all-consumed with looks as some other women seem to be, and that I'd rather Tucker be a Victoria's Secret model than a concert pianist or fighter pilot or something else that Ben would really respect. Of course if I were in Maura's shoes, and my husband had cheated on me with his secretary, a Norwegian bombshell who refused to lick envelopes because she once heard that the gumming on the flap equals three calories, I'd probably be obsessed with body fat, too.

"Well, who gives a *flying fuck* about Tucker," Jess says, raising her glass of wine. "She's clearly just his rebound. In fact, I bet he'll stay in the rebound stage for years. Nobody's going to measure up to you, Claudia."

This is more like it. I flash Jess a grateful smile and raise my glass. "I'll drink to that!"

Maura takes Jess's lead and says, "Yeah. He'll never find someone like you."

"Not in a million years," Daphne says. "Hear, hear!"

I clink my glass against theirs and say, "Thanks, guys."

This is the moment Jess chooses to begin her smitten chatter about how wonderful Trey is.

"Wait. Which one is Trey?" Maura asks.

"The married guy with the hot bod. Right?" Daphne says. Daphne lived with Jess and me for a year before she married Tony, so she and Jess occasionally e-mail and talk on the phone. In fact, Jess has told me before that Daphne will likely be one of her bridesmaids, an exercise I find just as silly as picking baby names before you're pregnant.

" 'Married guy' hardly narrows things down," Maura says.

Jess laughs and flips her off.

"Don't tell me you're dating *another* married man, Jess," Maura says. She pushes away her salad with disgust and crosses her arms.

I was worried about the Trey topic for this reason, and suddenly wish that I had warned Jess to tread carefully.

"This time it's different," Jess says, dabbing at her mouth with her cloth napkin. "Trey and his wife are totally wrong for each other. They married really young."

The "married too young" theme, of course, rubs Daphne the wrong way so she says, "Hey! Nothing wrong with that. If you find the right guy, you can't help it if you're young."

"That's the point," Jess says. "He's *not* the right guy for her. Clearly. And he's going to leave her soon. Tell them, Claudia."

"He's leaving her soon," I echo, keeping my eyes focused on an orb of hardboiled egg.

Maura sniffs. "Jesus, Jess. Is *nobody* off-limits to you?"

"Hey. It's not my fault that there are bad marriages out there," Jess says. "I didn't create that dynamic. It was preexisting."

"There are bad marriages out there in part because of women like you!" Maura says. "You don't have to be so *predatory*."

121

"And you don't have to be so *naïve*," Jess says. "Affairs happen when people aren't happy. A third party can't penetrate a happy, mutually satisfying marriage."

"I beg to differ," Maura says, looking pissed.

I don't really blame her for being upset. The topic hits a little too close to home.

But instead of backing off, Jess goes for shock value and says, "So I guess you'd disapprove of me getting pregnant on purpose?"

"What do you mean?" Maura says, aghast.

"You know . . . *forgetting* to take my pill. To sort of move the process along." She makes an investment-banker hand gesture.

Maura's eyes widen. "You have *got* to be shitting me."

Jess looks pleased with herself. I can tell she is mostly kidding, but not entirely. Of course, beyond the obvious unethical nature of such a dirty trick, this whole topic strikes a chord with me as I think of how I would have felt if Ben had, say, replaced my birth control pills with placebos. The word *unconscionable* comes to mind. So I say, "What if Ben had pulled something like that with me? Punched tiny holes in our condoms, so to speak?"

Jess says, "That's *totally* different."

"Not really," I say.

"Sure it is. It's *your* body. You should have ultimate say."

"Well, it's *his* sperm," Maura says. I can tell she's imagining what she would do if Scott had an illegitimate child on the side. It's not beyond the realm of possibility, that's for sure.

Daphne, on the other hand, looks suspiciously conspiratorial. *Anything* for a baby. I am pretty sure that she would steal a bit of seed if she had to.

I call her on it. "You think it's okay, Daph. Don't you?"

"No," she says unconvincingly. "Well . . . it depends . . . I guess."

"Depends on *what*?" Maura says.

"On why she's doing it," Daphne says, turning to Jess. "Would you be doing it to get Trey to leave his wife? Or would you be doing it to have a baby?"

"Look, Daph, motherhood ain't so noble that it overrides basic morality," Maura says.

Daphne kicks me under the table, as if the argument brewing at the table is subtle, something that I could somehow miss. She gives me a "do something" look.

"C'mon, guys," I say. "Enough. We gotta stick together."

"That's *my* point, Claudia," Maura says. "*Women* should stick together."

"*Friends* should stick together," Jess says. "I don't know Trey's wife from Adam. Eve. Whatever. I owe her nothing."

"I'll remind you of that someday," Maura says, her voice shaking a little. "When you're married to a man who once looked into your eyes and promised to forsake all others. I'll remind you of that after you've just had his baby and you have postpartum depression and feel as fat as a cow and you are pumping milk into little plastic containers in the middle of the night while he's running around with some twenty-two-year-old named Lisette. I'll remind you of that."

"Wait a second," Daphne says. "You didn't breast-feed."

I give her a look that says it's probably not the right moment to play the role of superior-earth-mother-to-be.

"I nursed Zoe for three weeks!" Maura says. "And then I had to quit because of mastitis. Remember?"

Daphne shakes her head.

"Well, I did . . . And *besides,* Daph, talk about missing the point."

"God. Well. Excuse me for living," Daphne says.

I give Daphne a sympathetic look, knowing that she would *kill* for a raging case of mastitis right about now. Remarkably, I also think she'd settle for a philandering husband if it meant she could be a mother.

A few minutes later, with a lot of cajoling on my part and the ordering of another bottle of wine, the storm has passed and we are on to safer topics. But as I listen to the three women I love most, I can't help but think how crazy it is that we all want something that we can't seem to have. Something that someone else at the table has in spades. I want my husband back, hold the baby. Daphne wants the baby, these days never mind her husband. Maura wants her husband to stop straying. Jess wants someone else's husband to stray a little more.

I consider what we did to get to this place. Whether any of us is entirely blameless for our predicament. Should Daphne have tried sooner to have a baby? If she knew that she wanted a child more than anything else, should she and Tony have tried to conceive in their twenties, rather than saving their money to buy a house? Should Jess use her head and follow her heart a little less? Should she only date available, unmarried men—for reasons of morality and practicality? Should Maura have seen the signs in Scott earlier? Should she have married a nicer guy, someone more like Niles? And what about me? Should I have just sucked it up and had a baby to keep the only man I've ever truly loved?

Things certainly aren't the way you imagine them when you're a kid and dreaming big dreams about what your life as a grown-up will look like. Even with a mother like mine, even with my untraditional wishes, even with all the books I've read about all the people with lives screwed up in one way or another, I still could have sworn things would be so much neater and easier than they're turning out to be.

eleven

Word of Tucker clearly works its way to my mother because she decides to make a surprise appearance two days later. As I return home from work, I can hear her voice, high and animated, chatting with Jess about her "marvelous day" on Fifth Avenue. My mother still lives in Huntington, but since she married Dwight and can afford her expensive Manhattan haircuts and spa treatments, she comes into the city a lot more often.

I curse softly to myself and seriously consider creeping off to a nearby bar for a beer. But I decide that this wouldn't be fair to Jess. Besides, my mother is a night owl, keeping hours more consistent with a college girl than a sixty-three-year-old. She will only outwait me and likely even spend the night with us, lapsing into her giggling, bunny-slipper-wearing mode, as if she just watched the Sandra Dee sleepover scene in *Grease*.

I take a deep breath and walk through the door with a forced smile.

"Hi, Mother!" I say, noting her salon-perfect hair and long nails freshly painted in a bright plum color. She is always well groomed, but today is one of her more impressive days. She does not look her age and is one of those rare women who really *does* look more like our sister than our mother (as opposed to all the women who get this false compliment from cheesy men).

"Hello, Claudia darling!" she says, standing to give me a prim hug, the kind where there is virtually no body contact other than our cheeks and shoulders.

"I didn't know you were coming into the city today?" I say, which clearly means, *Good Lord, woman. How many times have I told you that I hate drop-ins?*

"I've come to photograph you, Claudia," she says, throwing the thick black camera strap over her head.

My mother fancies herself an artist. I've even heard her end the word with an *e*, for an affected *artiste*. It's pretty amusing, especially when you know the truth—that she dabbles in watercolors and ceramics. But to be fair, I will say this for her: at least she has interests and hobbies and passions, even if those passions often include inappropriate romances. She was never one of those idle, soap-opera-watching moms. She actually *did* watch soaps, but she also made sure her life was as scandalous as the most outrageous character on all her favorite shows. For a while, she had this weird obsession with Erica Kane and once phoned the *All My Children* set to inquire about a black clutch Erica was carrying in a funeral scene. She got the information, phoned her personal shopper at Nordstrom, and shamelessly ordered the same one for her own Mother's Day present. (My mother always picked out her own presents. Whenever my father tried, his effort would go unrewarded. "Did you get a gift receipt?" would be the first thing out of her mouth.)

In any event, her latest hobby is black-and-white photography. I haven't seen her in action, but Maura assures me that she tries way too hard, comparing my mother's photos to her painful haikus. Maura also said that photography is one of her more annoying hobbies to date; in mid-conversation, my mom will whip out her Nikon, zoom in on your face and start snapping away, making comments like, "Chin down. Yeah. Just like that. *Oh!* Fantastic! Work with me." Apparently she also takes roll after roll of random inanimate objects, like coffee mugs and stools and titles them "Mug Series" and "Stool Series." It's all too pretentious to bear.

"I would have phoned first, but I wanted you *au naturel*."

"Well, that's what you got," I say, looking down at my work outfit—black pants, black heels, gray blouse, no accessories. Unless I'm meeting with an author or agent, I put almost no effort into my work wardrobe.

"I wanted to capture you as part of your normal workday routine. No frills. Just you."

As if I would have primped for you, I think, but instead I say, "Get outta here." I mean it literally, of course, but try to sound playful. I can't deal with her wounded routine.

"I'm serious. I need to take a roll or two. It won't take long."

I grab a bottle of water from the refrigerator, make my way over to the armchair across from her, and plop down with an exaggerated sigh. "I'm too tired for this, Mother."

Jess is standing behind my mother, sorting through a stack of mail. She stops and makes the cuckoo sign that was popular in elementary school—little swirls in the air, pointing at your own head then gesturing toward the other person. Then she crosses her eyes, which adds a nice psychotic touch.

I start to laugh, and my mother turns to see what's so amusing.

Jess sombers up quickly, taking great interest in a catalogue.

My mother faces me again and continues, "I already shot a roll of Jess while we waited for you. But that wasn't for my assignment. It was just for fun. Jess is so damned photogenic, isn't she?"

"Uh-huh," I say. Jess does look great in just about every photo I've ever seen of her. I think it's because her face is so symmetrical, which I once read is the very thing that makes someone beautiful. The article said that even babies are drawn to faces with symmetry.

"*Your* portrait is for my assignment," she says to me.

She couldn't be any more desperate for me to ask about her assignment. So I fold and say, "What assignment might that be, Mother?"

"I did tell you about my photography class, didn't I?"

I nod, thinking, *Only a dozen times.*

"Well. We're working on portraits now."

"Sounds neat," I say.

She misses my sarcasm and says, "Yes. It is *so* much fun. But quite challenging to capture a fleeting expression on your subject's face."

"Right. I'm sure."

"Which brings me back to you. I've chosen you as my subject."

I can tell she expects me to be excited by being the chosen one, but I say, "Why not photograph Maura's kids? Or Dwight?"

"Because," she says hesitantly, as if about to unmask a dark truth.

Jess nods vigorously and makes another gesture, like, *Getta load of this one.*

"Our assignment is to photograph pain." She frowns as she says it as if she, herself, is carrying quite the emotional load.

I can feel my eyes narrowing. "And you think I can help you out with that?"

"Claudia, dear. Please don't get defensive."

"I'm not," I say, well aware of how very defensive I sound.

"I want to capture your pain."

"I'm not in pain."

"Yes you are, Claudia. You're hurting over Ben. I heard about Tucker," she says.

"I'm fine," I say.

"No, young lady, you are not fine. You are not fine at all."

Jess makes a face as if she's bracing for a traffic accident and then exits, likely to call Trey.

"You are hurting right *here*, Claudia," she says, crossing her hands and placing them tenderly over her heart. "I'm your mother. I know these things."

"Mother. I *really* can't deal with this right now."

She purses her lips, stares at me and shakes her head. Then she loads a fresh roll of film, fiddles with her monstrous lens, and raises her camera to shoot me.

I put my hand in front of my face, palm out. "Stop it, Mother."

Snap. Snap.

"Mother!" I say. Then I gather myself, recognizing that my mother probably loves having a pained *and* angry Claudia, and say more calmly, "Why not photograph Daphne?"

I feel a bit guilty for the suggestion, but then consider that it was likely Daphne who spilled the beans. Besides, Daphne has a much higher tolerance for my mother. They talk nearly every day.

"Because of her infertility, you mean?" my mother asks, as if it is only a minor travail rather than a heartbreaking ordeal.

"It's not the same. There is no grief like heartbreak."

I want to refute what my mother has just said, but I can't,

130

so I just say, "I'm not heartbroken."

"Yes. You are."

"What about Maura? She and Scott are in a constant state of turmoil," I say, figuring that I might as well throw my other sister under the bus, on the off chance that it was she who spilled the beans about Tucker.

"Maura's not in love with Scott," my mother says. "They never had what you and Ben had. You and Ben were so in love. And I suspect you still are," she says, raising her camera again. She squints, zooms in with a flick of her wrist.

Snap. Snap.

"Mother. Enough."

Snap. Snap. Snap.

"I mean it, Mother!" I shout, and as she stands to capture another angle of my angst-ridden profile, I feel incredible sadness commingling with my anger. I put my face in my hands, telling myself not to cry, telling myself not to prove my mother right. When I look up, I see Jess in the doorway with a questioning look: *Do you need me?* I shake my head, thinking that I don't need anyone. Jess retreats, looking worried. I watch my mother load another roll of film and sling her camera strap back over her head.

I am back to being only enraged as I say, "Don't you dare take my picture again. I'm your daughter. Not your project."

My voice is eerily calm, but I also hear something in my voice that almost scares me. I wonder if my mother can hear it, if she's listening at all.

I suddenly know that if this woman, who happened to give birth to me almost thirty-five years ago, takes my picture in this moment and seeks to benefit from my grief, I will be done with her forever. I will not speak to her again. I will refuse to see her under any circumstance, deathbed scenarios included.

Of course I've had this thought many times before, but I have never followed through. I always cave—not for her sake, nor because I need or want a mother—but because I don't want my mother to define who I am, and *not* talking to her would do that in some bizarre sense. Whenever I read of a celebrity estranged from her mother (Meg Ryan, Jennifer Aniston, Demi Moore; I know these women by heart), I think it says something about the mother *and* the daughter. No matter how atrocious the mother's offense, it still marks the daughter as unforgiving, self-righteous, cold.

My mother is a nuisance and a trial, but she is not important enough to write off in any bold terms. Still, despite my general feelings about avoiding total estrangement, I have the sense that I am at a crossroads. This time I mean business. If I can get a divorce from a man I love, I can cut off this woman.

I watch my mother furrow her brow and give me her standard look of sympathy. Her best funeral expression. *I know what you're going through. I'm here for you.* All of that bullshit. She has a deficiency of empathy, even for her own daughters, but has mastered the art of appearing to care. She is a fraud. People outside her family might find her engaging, intriguing, compassionate. Sometimes she even fools Daphne. But I know the truth about her.

My rage gives way, in small part, to curiosity. How bad is my mother? Will she take my picture again, even after I've come to the brink of tears? Even after I warned her in no uncertain terms? I almost want her to take one final photo. I almost want this to be our defining mother-daughter moment. I watch her as she freezes, then lowers her camera to her lap. Nobody ever stops my mother from doing what she wants, and I can't help feeling triumphant. And very surprised.

She presses her lips together and says, "I'm sorry."

I am both relieved and disappointed by her apology. I can't think of a single time she's ever apologized to me for anything, despite scores of occasions she owed me one. At least she's never apologized without blaming someone else or adding a *but*. I don't want to let her off the hook so easily, but I am completely drained. So I say, "Okay, Mother."

"But *is* it okay?" she asks.

I roll my eyes and say yes.

We are both silent as she awkwardly packs up her camera equipment. When it is all stowed at her feet, she looks at me and says another quiet but sincere, "I'm sorry."

I look away, but can still feel her eyes on me. I can feel how much she wants me to say something. Absolve her. Embrace her.

I do none of these things. I just sit there in silence.

A long while later, my mother says, "I need to tell you something, Claudia."

"What's that?" I ask her, expecting something frivolous. *The sun will come out tomorrow. The sky is darkest before dawn. Look for the silver lining.* Why are there so many trite expressions involving the sky?

But my mother clears her throat and says, "I want to tell you something I've never told you before."

"Go ahead," I say to my mother as I see Jess's shadow in the doorway. She isn't really eavesdropping; she's just saving me the trouble of repeating everything later.

"You were an accident," my mother says. "An unplanned pregnancy."

"I *know* that, Mother," I say.

She never tried to hide the fact—it was something I knew at a very young age. She'd tell people right in front of me, "I thought I was done. But Claudia here was an 'accident.'" She'd whisper the word *accident*, but of course I heard it every time. And even if I hadn't heard all the whispers, I certainly heard her when she shouted the word at me after I told her I was boycotting her lavish wedding to Dwight and that she could shove my lavender bridesmaid dress where the sun don't shine. (My favorite expression involving the sky.)

"Please," she says now. "Let me finish."

I shrug, thinking that she sure has a hell of a way of apologizing.

"So you weren't planned," she continues. Then she raises one finger in the air as if poised to make a grand proclamation. "But just the other day, I was reading the acknowledgments in one of your novels. The one about the guy with the harelip?"

"Cleft palate," I say. She is referring to John Skvarla's memoir. John's birth defect was such a miniscule part of his life story that I wonder if she ever made it past the first page. My mother postures herself as well read and buys hardcover books all the time, but they typically go straight to her living room shelves, unopened. All for show.

"Whatever," she says. "The book isn't the point. The point is—I was reading his acknowledgments, the part where he thanked you for being his editor and friend. And I was filled with this profound sense of pride that you are my daughter."

I know that my mother basks in any form of public attention. She loves telling her friends that she raised a successful editor at a prestigious New York publishing house, and pointing out her daughter's name in the front of a book is just icing on the cake. Still, I am surprised by her words. This is not the language my mother normally speaks in.

"I am so proud of you, Claudia," she continues. "Not just for how smart you are and for all you've accomplished. But because you're the kind of person that people *want* to thank in the front of a book. People love you and respect you. You are special that way," she says quietly. She looks down at her feet and slides her orange driving moccasins together. Her hands are folded in her lap. She looks contrite and shy and sincere.

"You are the very best thing I've ever done in my life," she finishes.

I don't want to feel moved or grateful, but I am. So much so that I am on the verge of tears *again*. I wonder how one woman can create such a tsunami of emotion in me—and in such a short span of time? I tell myself to get a grip. I remind myself that my mother is, in a sense, taking credit for the way I've turned out, when she deserves relatively little credit. She used to tell me to get my nose out of my book and go get some fresh air. She was devastated when I was sixteen and applied to work at the library instead of lifeguarding at the country club. I am who I am in spite of my mother. But I can't help it—I know I will not forget what she has just told me. I know I will replay her words a hundred times or more. I know that, as much as I don't want to admit it, my mother is important to me.

"Why are you telling me this?" I say.

"Because of the recent choices you've made in your life."

"What about them?" I ask. I know she is talking about Ben and babies, but I am not sure how it all ties in with her out-of-the-blue compliment.

She looks contemplative, as if carefully considering her wording. "I'm not the best mother in the world . . . I never have been," she says slowly. "But always remember, Claudia, you are not me. You are a lot of things to a lot of people. But you are absolutely *nothing* like me."

twelve

I never did think I was anything like my mother, nor did I peg her as the main reason I didn't want children. So, despite her intent, my mother's speech did nothing to reverse my position on motherhood.

But there was *still* something about my mother's words that felt like a revelation to me. Perhaps because it was the first time my mother had ever apologized to me for anything. Perhaps because everyone wants her mother to be proud—and, to some extent, we can't help seeing ourselves as our mother sees us. Perhaps because it was a reminder of all that I still have in my life. I have my career, of course. But more important, I have rich relationships that I cherish. I am a good sister, daughter, and friend. My life has meaning—and will continue to have meaning—without Ben.

So it was my mother, albeit unwittingly, who helped me get to the next level of emotional recovery. Achieve that postdisaster glimmer that life goes on. I even began to think about dating again. Not so much because I *wanted* to but because dating is always the best inward and outward sign that you've moved on after a big breakup. In some ways, I think it might be the *only* way to move on.

So when Michael strolls into my office one day and says, "Guess who has you in his number two spot?" I feel a bit excited. I know exactly what he means by "two spot." Whether you're an insurance adjuster in Iowa, a schoolteacher in Florida, or an editor in Manhattan, you are familiar with the practice of gathering around the water cooler (or in our case, the automated Euro-coffee machine) and discussing who among your esteemed colleagues is most attractive. It's an exercise largely born out of boredom or long hours at the office, but it is nonetheless approached with tremendous gravity. (And is only rivaled by the list compiled by couples: "Celebrities I Am Allowed to Cheat on My Significant Other With." Obviously my cheating list is null and void—I can do what I want now without an exemption—which, unfortunately, brings me no closer to sharing a bed with (1) Sting, (2) Colin Firth, (3) Johnny Depp, (4) Tom Brady, or (5) Ed Harris.)

Of course, the problem with playing this ranking game at most publishing houses is that there are slim pickings for a woman. First, the general breakdown of women to men in publishing is about 3 to 1. And of the men, about 70 percent are gay. So you're talking a 10 to 1 female-to-heterosexual-male ratio. On top of that, aside from a few more high-profile departments like publicity, publishing is filled with a high percentage of former nerds (myself included) who spent the majority of their childhood indoors, reading books. My friend Jacqueline, for example, was featured in her local newspaper in North Carolina for reading over five hundred books in one year; she was five at the time. Not that I should talk—my greatest accomplishment as a kid was making it to the state tournament spelling bee, losing in the final round on the word *precipice*. This is not to say that all former nerds are unattractive. To the contrary, I think we're a great breed—quirky, smart, and far more interesting than your average former cheerleader or ex-jock. Still, the list is not about being quirky and smart or appealing in an offbeat way; the list is about being sexy.

Anyway, one of the perks of being close to Michael is that I'm always privy to the male lists floating around, which is particularly interesting on the few occasions when I've been mentioned. It works like this: Michael tells me I'm on someone's list whereupon I pretend to be some combination of embarrassed, nonplussed, or annoyed, all the while feeling secretly flattered. Who wouldn't be? Even when chosen by a downright geek, it's nice to know you rank.

But I still say, "Two spot?" because the last thing I want to appear is desperate or eager.

"You know. He thinks you're the second-hottest girl at work," Michael says.

"Who?" I say, rolling my eyes. "Gerald from the IT department?"

"Nope."

"I give."

"Richard Margo," Michael says smugly.

He now has my full attention. Richard Margo is our executive vice president and director of publicity and is very well-known at our house, as much for his prestigious position as his reputation for pitching in the minors for one season and for being a bit of a womanizer—not the sleazy kind, but the "never been married smooth intellect who wines and dines beautiful women" kind. He's in his late forties but, unlike many men his age who are lucky to fetch descriptions like "handsome" or "attractive," Richard can fairly be called hot. He has a very square jaw, deep-set blue eyes, and a slightly receding hairline, a combination of traits that conjures a certain rugged confidence. Even his nose—which looks as if it has been broken at least once—is sexy.

Richard has not only been on my list since I arrived at Elgin Press, but he has consistently occupied my top slot, a fact that I've only admitted to Michael and a few other close friends (with others, I hem and haw, pretend to never have considered the subject, and then issue the preamble, "Please know that they are in no particular order," which somehow makes the exercise seem less serious). In fact, Richard not only consistently tops my workplace list, but when Jude Law was caught in bed with his nanny, all his appeal went out the window, and a spot became available on my celebrity list. A spot I gave to Richard. At the time, Ben insisted that I couldn't commingle my lists, whereupon I argued that he was "famous" at work. The point did not go over so well (Ben insisted that the whole theory behind the celeb list was their unattainable nature). So I bumped Richard, replacing him with Ed Harris—who, incidentally, could pass for Richard's brother.

"Where'd you hear that?" I ask Michael, feeling somewhat shamed by my racing pulse. But in my defense, I haven't had sex in months.

"From the horse's mouth," Michael says, proudly cracking his knuckles.

"You asked your *boss* that question?" I say, marveling over Michael's ability to elicit illicit information from people, including higher-ups.

He shrugs. "Yeah, so what. Guys over lunch, you know. Phil Loomis and Jack Hannigan were with us, and incidentally, Hannigan had you on his list, too."

"Damn Phil screwed me out of the hat trick?" I say.

Michael laughs as I casually return to the subject of

Baby Proof

Richard. "So who is Margo's number one? Stacy Eubanks?"

Stacy Eubanks, a secretary in sales, is Beyoncé's blonde, blue-eyed twin and word has it that she moonlights as a porn star. (Michael claims to have spotted her in a video called *Lezzie Maguire*.)

"Nope. Stacy didn't make his cut."

"Imagine that," I say, giving Richard's list even more credence.

"I know. Shocked the hell out of me, too."

"So who *is* his number one?" I say nonchalantly.

"That new French chick in sub rights."

"Oh, yeah. Marina LeCroy. She's very . . . French."

"Uh-huh. But apparently Richard's got a thing for red-heads because Naomi Rubenstein is in his mix, too."

"I'd hardly call that a *thing* for redheads."

"Two redheads out of five *definitely* qualifies as 'a thing.' I mean, you all don't exactly make up forty percent of the general population."

"Fair enough," I say, wondering who the other two non-French, nonredheads on his list are.

"So what are you going to do about this?" Michael asks.

"Nothing," I say, laughing.

"Nothing? Why not?"

"Because . . . I'm a professional," I say in a jokingly prim tone.

"There's no antifraternizing policy here. And you don't work for the guy," Michael says. "You're not even in publicity. What's the conflict?"

"I don't know. It might show an air of favoritism. Somehow discredit my books."

"C'mon. That's a reach," Michael says.

Technically he is right. Richard runs the publicity department, and as such, has responsibility for all titles in the house.
But many different publicists cover my books, and there are
other checks and balances in sales and marketing, so it would
be virtually impossible for Richard to make much of a single-
handed impact on my career or the success of my books. Still,
publicity has a huge say in book proposals and they can easily
quash a book, so there could be an inference of favoritism col-
oring my success. Bottom line, I've never dated anyone at
work, and I have no intention of doing so now. I tell Michael
this and then say, "The whole discussion is moot anyway
because Richard Margo is not interested in me. He was only
humoring you by playing your little game."

"I wouldn't be so sure about that," Michael says. "Besides,
I totally teed you up."

"How so?" I ask nervously.

"I told him about your divorce," Michael says. "He had no
idea."

"Michael!" I say. I know it's ridiculous to keep hiding the
fact from everyone, but I can't help it—I don't like my personal affairs being discussed at work. And there's something
about divorce that is equated with failure, which is never a
perception you want to parade around in the workplace.

"It's no big deal," Michael says.

"What did he say?" I ask.

"That he was sorry to hear it . . . But I think you should
know that he didn't look one bit sorry to hear it. If you catch
my drift."

Michael leaves my office after giving me a final, dramatic
brow raise and a skilled drumroll on my desk.

As much as I try to downplay my interest in Richard's list,

I report the news back to Jess that evening. She has never met Richard, but has heard me speak of him over the years and relishes the mere scent of an intraoffice romance. So instead of taking the story for what it is—a juicy, self-esteem-boosting bit of trivia—she becomes wildly animated, saying that he is perfect for me.

"He's way too old to want kids," she says.

I shake my head and tell her not to be ridiculous.

But a week later when Richard calls me out of the blue, saying he wants to discuss some matters over lunch, I can't help wondering about his intentions. I've sat with him in numerous meetings, but have never had a one-on-one meeting with him. And certainly not over lunch.

"Sure," I say, reminding myself that, our work lists notwithstanding, I have no interest in Richard (or vice versa). I'm sure that he only wants to discuss business. After all, I am becoming more senior all the time, and maybe an occasional lunch with Richard just reflects my status in the house. Perhaps he wants to go over publicity plans for my upcoming Amy Dickerson novel. Or maybe he wants to formulate a strategy to handle my most difficult author, Jenna Coblentz. Jenna's been a huge commercial success for over a decade, but she is so demanding with publicity that her behavior borders on abusive, and it's an editor's responsibility to act as a buffer for the publicists.

"How does Thursday look?" Richard asks me in his rich, radio-DJ voice.

"Thursday's perfect," I say, without consulting my calendar.

"Bolo at one?" he says. Bolo is a popular spot with people from work and the publishing scene generally. He'd never choose Bolo if his intentions were at all impure.

"That works for me," I say, all business.

On Thursday, I wear my most flattering pair of jeans and green seersucker jacket to work. I look casual, but stylish. Then I spend about ten minutes touching up my makeup at my desk before leaving for lunch. I stand by my claim that I have no interest in Richard, but figure that it never hurts in life to look nice, particularly when you're going to be in the company of a hot man.

Richard e-mailed me earlier to tell me he was coming from a dentist appointment and would meet me at the restaurant. I walk briskly the few blocks to Bolo, but still arrive five minutes late. I spot Richard right away at a corner table wearing a sport coat and tie. A glass of red wine and a bowl of olives sit on the table before him. He is talking on his cell phone, looking somewhat agitated as he glances down at a small notepad, the old-school kind reporters carry. He has an air of importance. Then again, maybe I just *know* that he is important.

When he looks up and sees me, his face brightens and he waves me over. I give him a signal, as if to say, "Finish your call. I'll wait here." He shakes his head, says good-bye quickly, and snaps his phone shut, sliding it into his jacket pocket along with the pad. As I approach him, he gives me the half-stand and says, "Hello, Claudia."

"Hi, Richard," I say as I inhale his aftershave, something I first noticed on him during a shared elevator ride years ago. I love aftershave or cologne on a man. Ben never wore it. Even his deodorant was scent-free. It feels good when I stumble upon something *not* to miss about Ben. Unfortunately, I haven't racked up many of those so far. "Any cavities?"

"Not a one," he says.

"You're a flosser?" I say.

"Nope," he says, looking sheepish. "Just good genes, I guess."

Our waiter, a young, blond kid with so much exuberance that I peg him as a Broadway performer, stops by, introduces himself as Tad, and asks what I'd like to drink. I don't usually have wine at lunch during the week, but because Richard is drinking, I order a glass of chardonnay.

"Good. I don't like to drink alone," Richard says after Tad departs. "Unless I'm alone, that is."

I laugh.

He laughs.

Then, as if to offset our beverage selection, Richard skips further small talk and immediately launches into business. Our summer list generally. A new author I just signed on board. A recent, mixed review of the Skvarla memoir in the *Times*. (Not that publicity ever cares too much about the content. Even bad publicity is good publicity.)

"And the big news is," Richard says, as if signaling the reason for our lunch, "I'm *this close* to getting Amy Dickerson on *The Today Show*." His index finger and thumb are a millimeter apart.

"You're kidding me?" I say, even though I had already heard this news from Michael. It is huge deal for any book, but particularly a novel. Still, it's usually not the sort of thing that necessitates a one-on-one lunch with the head of publicity.

Richard nods. "Apparently Katie really digs the book," he says.

I smile at his use of the word *digs*. Richard frequently uses jargon from the seventies. Most people sound washed-up or silly when they drop slang from a prior generation, but with Richard, it's endearing. I guess if you're handsome and successful enough, you can pull off just about anything.

I resist the urge to say, "Groovy," and instead cross my fingers in the air.

Tad returns with my glass of chardonnay and two menus. He asks if we'd like to hear the specials.

"Sure," we say in unison, and then listen as Tad rattles off the longest and most detailed shrimp bisque description in the history of the world. Ben always hated food adjectives— particularly the words *moist* and *chewy*. Cookie commercials presented a problem for him. I tell myself, *No more thinking about Ben!* I peruse the menu, trying to find something that's not too messy to eat. I decide on the seared-tuna salad. Richard goes with the pressed burger. I like the burger-wine combo.

"So read anything good lately?" Richard asks.

"You mean generally—or are you talking manuscripts?" I ask.

"Either," he says.

I reel off a few titles in the first category—and a couple of projects in the second.

"What else can you tell me?" Richard says after Tad takes our order and trots off. He looks at me expectantly, as if I'm the one who scheduled our little "business" lunch.

I take a sip of wine and say, "As far as work goes?" My mind races to various bits of gossip in the business generally. Just as I'm about to ask him if he's heard the rumors that the mystery writer Jennifer Coats is unhappy with her editor at Putnam, and is shopping her new manuscript around, Richard shrugs and leans back in his chair. "Or whatever." His *whatever* signals that this is most definitely not a business lunch.

I consider my response carefully, feeling as if I have just arrived at a fork in the road. Like the kind in one of those choose-your-own-adventure books I loved so much in elementary school. I could easily discuss the Jennifer Coats rumor or turn the conversation back to Amy Dickerson's *Today Show* booking.

Instead, I hold up my left hand, wiggle my ring finger, and blurt out, "I got a divorce."

Richard looks surprised, and I hope that he's not going to play dumb and pretend that he knew nothing of my recent news. Then again, maybe he's just surprised that I'm sharing it with him so readily. I'm a little surprised myself.

Richard tugs on his earlobe and says, "I heard. I'm sorry."

I consider saying, "That's okay," but I've always hated when people respond that way after a death or any sad event in life. After all, it's *not* really *okay*. So I say, "Thanks. It happens."

Richard nods as he swirls the wine in his glass. He takes a long swallow, then says, "Half the time from what I hear."

"Yup," I say. "Odds you've never played, right?"

The first personal-question card has officially been played.

Richard laughs. "You got that right."

"Ever come close?" I ask.

Second.

"Sure."

"How close?"

Third.

"Not that close, actually."

Richard gives someone across the room a quick salute. I

consider turning around to see who it is, but don't want to appear as caught red-handed as I feel.

As if Richard knows what I'm thinking, he says, "Jason Saul."

I give him a puzzled look and he says, "Little fellow in marketing? With the soul patch?"

"Oh, yeah," I say. "It's actually a goatee. Not a soul patch."

"What's the difference?"

I describe the difference, pointing to my chin. Richard nods, looking enlightened. I am reminded of my favorite facial hair story. Years ago, Michael was in a moustache-growing contest with another guy at work. Michael was badly losing, and to demonstrate his point over lunch, he nodded toward a girl named Sally whom he actually had a minor crush on and said, "Even Sally would kick my ass." He was trying to be funny, but unfortunately, Sally was a dark-haired Italian and one of those girls who waxes her upper lip. Sally was horrified and humiliated, as was Michael when he realized his slip. I tell Richard the story now, and he laughs.

"Is Sally still around?" Richard asks.

"No. She left a short time later. Guess she was traumatized."

Richard nods, and then says, "So where were we?"

"Why you never married?" I say.

Fourth.

"When I meet someone I like being with more than I like being alone," he says, "I'll marry her."

I laugh and tell him that had been, more or less, my philosophy when I met Ben.

"So, what? You figured out late in the game that you still preferred your own company to his?"

Fifth.

"Not exactly . . . Just . . . irreconcilable differences."

Richard pauses, as if considering a follow-up. Then he stops himself and gives Tad a signal that he'd like another glass of wine.

I decide to just tell him. "I didn't want kids. He did."

Maybe I should get a T-shirt made. Most divorces aren't so neatly summarized.

"Shouldn't you have covered that one while you were in the courting stage?" Richard asks gently.

"We did. He reneged on our deal. Now he wants them. Or at least *one.* One more than I want."

"Bastard."

I laugh. I like the sound of Richard calling Ben a bastard.

Tad returns with Richard's wine. So here we are, I think, having multiple glasses of wine at lunch as we discuss my divorce and his perpetual bachelorhood. And maybe he's thinking the same thing, because the floodgates open and we are firing off the personal questions too quickly to keep track of them.

At one point I say, "So, I hear that you and Hannigan had me on your lists?"

"And I hear that I've topped yours for thirteen years."

I say, "That Michael is a gossipy little girl."

"So it's true, then?"

My heart races as I tell him yeah, it's true.

"I'm honored," he says.

"You should be," I say.

He leans across the table and taps the base of my wineglass. "And believe me, I am."

I work hard at not averting my eyes before I lean back

149

across the table and tap the base of his wineglass. "So am I."

We finish our lunch, talking and laughing. Then, at Tad's chipper suggestion, we agree that a cup of coffee sounds like a fine idea. When the check arrives, Richard gets it, saying he'll expense it.

"Since we talked so much shop?" I say.

"Righto," Richard says.

I smile, feeling both relaxed and excited, the mark of a good date. Which this is shaping up to be. And although I don't recognize it until later that day, after Richard and I have strolled back to the office together and I've hunkered down to read a revised manuscript, it is the first time in a very long time that I am thinking about a man other than Ben.

thirteen

Over the next four workdays, Richard and I exchange about thirty e-mails a day. It's all disguised as friendly banter, but the sheer volume of traffic suggests otherwise.

At one point, when Michael comes into my office, he catches me laughing at the computer. He darts around my desk, and takes instant note of my in-box filled with Richard Margo's name. There are at least ten in a row.

"Busted," he says.

"Whatever," I say, but my goofy grin suggests that I am, indeed, busted.

"What the fuck's going on here?"

I minimize my in-box and work hard at ridding my face of the guilty smile I can still feel straining at the corners of my mouth.

"Are you schtupping my boss?"

"No," I say with pretend indignation.

Ding! My e-mail notifier rings loudly.

"Is it from him?" Michael demands.

I can't resist checking. It is. Which Michael sees over my shoulder.

"Holy shit. You're *so* schtupping my boss!"

"There's no schtupping going on," I say.

Yet.

"Now. Can I have some privacy, please?" I say.

When Michael leaves, shaking his head, I read the latest from Richard.

I type back, "Yes." Then backspace and type, "Would love to" before clicking send.

I reread the entire exchange, beginning with another one of his weak attempts at a legitimate business purpose.

From: Richard Margo
Sent: July 27, 9:30 A.M.
To: Claudia Parr
Subject: Timothy Lynde

Timothy Lynde just rang. He's interested in paying to take himself on the road for a book tour. I think it's worth it. Any ideas on what markets might work best for him? Let me know what you think . . . By the way, did I tell you I had a nice time at lunch the other day? Thanks for joining me.

From: Claudia Parr
Sent: July 27, 9:33 A.M.
To: Richard Margo
Subject: Re: Timothy Lynde

I'll think about cities and touch base with Tim. He's a Mormon so Salt Lake's probably a safe bet . . . As for lunch, yes, you mentioned that . . . I had a lovely time, too.

From: Richard Margo
Sent: July 27, 9:38 A.M.
To: Claudia Parr
Subject: Mormons

A Mormon, huh? I went out with a Mormon once . . . It didn't go so well.

From: Claudia Parr
Sent: July 27, 9:44 A.M.
To: Richard Margo
Subject: Re: Mormons

Did she try to convert you?

From: Richard Margo
Sent: July 27, 9:50 A.M.
To: Claudia Parr
Subject: Re: Mormons

No, I slept with her and she was excommunicated . . . It wasn't good.

From: Claudia Parr
Sent: July 27, 9:55 A.M.
To: Richard Margo
Subject: Re: Mormons

Shame on you. When did this happen?

From: Richard Margo
Sent: July 27, 9:58 A.M.
To: Claudia Parr
Subject: I'm old

High school. The '70s . . . What are you, Class of 2000?

From: Claudia Parr
Sent: July 27, 10:00 A.M.
To: Richard Margo
Subject: And you're funny, too

Ha ha.

From: Richard Margo
Sent: July 27, 10:03 A.M.
To: Claudia Parr
Subject: You

I bet you were cute in high school.

From: Claudia Parr
Sent: July 27, 10:08 A.M.
To Richard Margo
Subject: Nope

I so wasn't. I was spectacularly lame.

From: Richard Margo
Sent: July 27, 10:08 A.M.
To: Claudia Parr
Subject: Re: Nope

I bet I was lamer.

From: Claudia Parr
Sent: July 27, 10:10 A.M.
To: Richard Margo
Subject: Re: Nope
You were corrupting hot Mormon chicks. I was student body treasurer. Top that.

From: Richard Margo
Sent: July 27, 10:19 A.M.
To: Claudia Parr
Subject: Re: Nope

Well, I was the school mascot . . . and who said she was hot?

From: Claudia Parr
Sent: July 27, 10:25 A.M.
To: Richard Margo
Subject: Yeah, right

Something tells me that she was hot.

From: Richard Margo
Sent: July 27, 10:26 A.M.
To: Claudia Parr
Subject: I was a stud

Okay. I wasn't really the school mascot. And she actually was pretty hot. A dead ringer for Marcia Brady. Which, at the time, was a big deal. Have I impressed you yet?

From: Claudia Parr
Sent: July 27, 10:44 A.M.
To: Richard Margo
Subject: Re: I was a stud

Man, you are ancient. Yes, I'm impressed . . . My boyfriend was more like Screech on Saved by the Bell . . .

From: Richard Margo
Sent: July 27, 10:49 A.M.
To: Claudia Parr
Subject: Still a stud

I know the show, but you lost me on Screech? . . . I was a big X-Files fan, though. Wasn't that during your high school days?

Baby Proof

From: Claudia Parr
Sent: July 27, 11:01 A.M.
To: Richard Margo
Subject: Re: Still a stud

Don't tell me—you had a crush on Scully, right?

From: Richard Margo
Sent: July 27, 11:09 A.M.
To: Claudia Parr
Subject: Re: Still a stud

Ah, Scully. Yes, I did have a crush on her . . . You actually sort of look like her. All you need is a navy suit and one of those FBI badges pinned on you and you'd be set to go. Can you spout off medical jargon on cue? If so, I might fall in love with you.

From: Claudia Parr
Sent: July 27, 11:22 A.M.
To: Richard Margo
Subject: This do the trick?

White male, 38. Stress lesions along the superior vena cava, anterior left lung and bronchi . . . Code Blue! He's bradying down! We need a pericardiocentesis stat!
Are you in love with me yet?

From: Richard Margo
Sent: July 27, 11:23 A.M.
To: Claudia Parr
Subject: Sure did

Totally am. Want to have dinner Saturday night?

On Saturday Daphne comes into the city to go shopping with Jess and me. Our mission: date wear to impress Richard. Jess guarantees that a new outfit will give me all the confidence I need to make the evening a success. I hope she's right, because ever since I agreed to the date, I've been feeling more nervous than excited. I'm nervous about dating again generally, and I'm nervous about dating someone from work. Compounding my anxiety is the fact that Richard and I have not talked face-to-face since our lunch at Bolo. We haven't even spoken on the phone. I recognize that e-mail allows you to be much bolder than you truly feel inside. Part of me worries that it's the cyberspace equivalent of having sex too quickly and then having to face your guy the next morning, sober and without makeup. Richard and I have said an awful lot of flirtatious things over the computer, but sitting across the table from him is a different matter altogether, and anticipating the first moment in the restaurant makes me nothing short of queasy.

So Jess, Daphne, and I start out bright and early on our shopping spree. We hit Intermix on lower Fifth first as it is only a few blocks from Jess's apartment. The dance music blaring through the store is a pretty good indication that the clothes are too trendy for me. I don't do clubs anymore, and I'm over having to yell to be heard at a bar—so certainly the same applies when I'm shopping.

I shout this sentiment to Jess, but she holds up her hand to signal that she's not ready to leave. I watch her whip expertly through a rack of clothing, finding a funky pair of white pants, a paisley silk halter, and a fuchsia shrug. They are items that I would never pick up on my own—as an ensemble or even individually—but Jess has an amazing sense of style. She also has a knack for pairing garments you would never imagine going together to create a completely original look. Of course, having gobs of money helps in that department. She can afford a lot, but she can also afford the inevitable mistakes all women make when shopping. Who doesn't know the phenomenon of loving something in a dressing room and hating it at home? If I buy something I don't end up wearing, I berate myself for months, but at any given moment, Jess has a dozen designer rejects still hanging in her closet, worn once, if at all. The great tragedy of our friendship, at least from my perspective, is the fact that we don't wear the same size. I would especially kill to make my feet grow one inch and fit into Jess's rainbow of Jimmy Choos.

Still, despite trusting Jess in matters of fashion, I am skeptical of her selections now. "That's *so* not me," I say, pointing to the halter she is holding up against my torso. I glance at the white pants in her other hand. "And there's no time to get those hemmed." Pants off the rack never work when you're only five four.

"Daphne can do a makeshift job. Right, Daph?" Jess asks.

Daphne nods eagerly. She is a whiz on the domestic front. She knows how to do little things, like fold egg whites, get red wine stains out of garments, or arrange flowers. I don't know where she picked most of the stuff up. It certainly wasn't from our mother, who has trouble lining up the seams of pants on a hanger. Not that I can talk. Hanging pants was one of the things Ben always did for me. Before I lived with him, most of my wardrobe could be found draped over the backs of various chairs. Which is exactly where they've returned.

"Just try them." Jess points to the dressing room again, with authority. I obey her instruction, thinking to myself that when she does have kids, she'll be the rare mother who gives teeth to the concept of time-out.

"A total waste of time," I mumble, but it's doubtful that she can hear me over the pulsing remix of George Michael's "I Want Your Sex." I am reminded of the time Jess went out with colleagues for a little karaoke and picked this tune. Talk about bold—taking the stage to a song that, as a grand finale, has you screaming the words *Have sex with me!* over and over again to a room full of drunken bankers. Par for the course for Jess.

A moment later, I emerge from the dressing room, thinking for sure that I've proven my point. The pants look and feel baggy, which is shocking because they're a size six, and I'm usually an eight. Then again, I know I've lost some weight since my divorce—at least ten pounds, maybe more. I was just telling Jess last night that there are two kinds of women—those who eat in a crisis and those who lose their appetite in a crisis. Most fall into the chowhound crowd, so I consider myself blessed to be in the second camp.

"Those are incredible," Jess says. "Whether you wear them tonight or not, they're a definite yes."

"Aren't they too big?" I ask, tugging at the waist and checking my reflection in the mirror.

Jess slaps away my hand and explains that they're supposed to hang low, on my hips. "Besides, you can't go tight with white pants. You'll look ghetto. Tight black pants are one thing, but tight white pants are so . . . Britney Spears," Jess says to push Daphne's buttons.

It's sort of a contradiction to her traditional, homemaker side, but Daphne is one of those full-grown women who loves all things cheesy and adolescent. She has the complete DVD box set of *Dawson's Creek*. She still keeps stuffed animals on the window seat in her bedroom. She also orders those glittery tank tops from the back of *US Weekly* that say things like DIVA IN TRAINING. So obviously, Daphne's a Britney fan. At one point, Daphne went so far as to see her teen idol perform out on Rockefeller Plaza on *The Today Show*. She was one of the only women in her late twenties, rocking out without a preteen in her company. The funny thing was, a couple of kids in her fifth-grade class spotted her on television the morning before school and seemed to be profoundly impacted by the sight of their teacher singing along to "Hit Me Baby One More Time." I told Daphne it would be like watching your teacher dance on *Soul Train* or *Solid Gold*. Impressive, but a little bit unsettling. Teachers, after all, were supposed to freeze in their classrooms at night while we went home and had a life.

Anyway, Daphne and Jess agree that my white pants are fabulous, and Daphne insists that she can hem them, no problem. They agree that the silk halter is flattering, too. It displays what little cleavage I have and is tight in just the right places (which adheres to another of Jess's fashion rules—if the pants are loose, the top should be tight—or vice versa). And the fuchsia shrug is the perfect finishing touch.

"In case the restaurant is chilly," Jess says.

"Or *in case* Richard keeps the air low in his apartment . . ." Daphne says, giggling as I spin in front of the mirror on my tiptoes. I have to admit that I do look pretty good. Above all, the thought of being finished with our spree holds tremendous appeal. I *really* hate shopping. If I won the lottery, one of the first things I'd do is hire a personal shopper—for groceries, clothing, Christmas presents, everything. So I change quickly, hurry over to the cash register and toss down my Amex, purchasing the ensemble guaranteed to give me confidence and make Richard swoon.

That night, I can tell straightaway that Jess and Daphne were right about the outfit. For starters, I fit right in with the crowd at Spice Market, the lavish duplex restaurant in the Meatpacking District. More important, Richard comes right out and tells me that I look fantastic.

"I've never seen you in anything like that," Richard says as we follow the maître d' to our table. His hand rests for a beat on the small of my back. "But I guess I've never seen you outside of a work function . . ."

"You, either," I say, admiring Richard's corduroy jacket.

I'm suddenly reminded of Richard's flamboyantly gay ex-assistant Jared Lewison. Jared used to keep cards marked 1 through 10 at his desk and would rate people's outfits as they walked by (behind their backs, of course) as if he were a gymnastics judge at the Olympics. Michael, who was pretty good friends with Jared, derived much amusement from the exercise, passing on the results to the rest of us. In fact, I owe Jared gratitude for teaching me one of life's crucial lessons: do not wear patent leather after Labor Day. Michael informed me that I earned myself a 3 for that fashion lapse.

I ask Richard now if he knew about Jared Lewison's cards.

"Sure did," Richard says. "Apparently I was regularly rated

between a two and a four . . . With a high score of six."

"What were you wearing when you got the six?" I ask as our waitress, wearing an orange kimono, delivers us our menu.

"I think it was some kind of turtleneck sweater," he says, laughing.

I smile, recognizing that I'm no longer nervous.

Richard looks as if he's still considering Jared's cards as he says, "I heard that if you had on any sort of Louis Vuitton or Prada, Jared automatically gave you an extra point, while if you wore anything from the Gap, or God forbid, Old Navy, you were docked three points."

I laugh and then say, "Where is ol' Jared now?"

"I'm not sure. But something tells me he's sitting at a bar somewhere with his fashionista friends, all of them telling each other how fabulous they look."

I smirk as I recall another Jared story.

"What?" Richard says.

"Nothing," I say, as I spot a man who I am pretty sure is Chris Noth sidle up to the bar with a gorgeous blonde. He is way shorter than I thought he'd be, and I think to myself, *Mr. Medium*. "I'm just smiling."

"C'mon. What's so funny?" Richard says again, because it's clear that I'm smirking rather than merely smiling. There is a difference between a smirk and smile—which is especially apparent to the recipient.

"I was just thinking of something Jared did to you once," I say.

"And what was that?" he says, looking worried. Or at least pretending to look worried.

"Well, I heard that he went through your garbage and found a postcard with rather colorful sexual references."

He looks sheepish and says, "Now, *when* was all this?"

It's hardly a denial, which I point out by saying, "So it happened more than once?"

He makes a hand motion as if to say, *Continue with your evidence.*

"I dunno. It was about three years ago. I heard that Jared suspected you of sleeping with some woman in the art department," I say, trying to remember her name.

"Lydia," he says.

I snap and point at him. "That's the one. So it was true?"

He nods. "I was, in fact, sleeping with her . . . But I didn't think she signed her name to that postcard."

"She didn't," I say. "Jared recognized her handwriting. He trotted the postcard and a handwriting sample from her notepad all over the office. That was one of his proudest moments."

"Wow. He was *good*," Richard says.

"And so were you, apparently. At least according to Lydia."

I surprise myself with this last comment as I've never been one for sexual innuendo. As we study our menus, both of us still smiling, I try to analyze why I feel so open with Richard. I decide that it has less to do with him (although he does put me at ease) and more to do with my divorce and new mindset. I hate to be jaded, but I can't help feeling that all my fears about marriage were confirmed when Ben and I broke up. I'm not sure I believe in permanent monogamy anymore, and in any case, I don't plan on attempting it again.

Therefore, I don't need to follow any rules. If I thought I was free when I didn't want children, I'm especially free now that I don't even want a *husband*. Instead of playing hard to get or worrying about perception, I can do exactly what strikes my fancy. Which at the moment is to flirt outrageously with a very hot colleague.

As the night progresses, Richard and I fall into an easy rhythm of talking, laughing, and mocking each other in a way you only can when you feel comfortable with someone and like them a lot. No topics are off-limits. We cover the basics, but spice them up with shock value and humor. We talk about work—and about publishing in general. We talk about travel, books, music, and families. We talk about past relationships.

When we touch on Ben, I expect to feel a bit sad or defensive, but I am neither of these things. I find myself embracing the past tense with a strange sense of relief: *I felt, he was, we were*. Then I look into Richard's eyes and say, "Enough of all of that."

He nods in agreement as I mentally shift back to the present, feeling happy to be in Richard's company, happy to be moving on.

fourteen

Despite the success of that first date with Richard, and our nightcap at his apartment afterward (I teased him that only old men use the term *nightcap*), we don't even kiss on that first date. Or the one after that. I'm not sure what the delay is—because it's safe to say that neither of us is playing things close to vest, nor are we striving to be prim and proper. I also know that I am very attracted to Richard, and I can tell that he is attracted to me. And I'm positive that the wait has nothing to do with Ben; I refuse to dwell on him.

So the only explanation is that we are relishing the growing sexual tension and intrigue. I've always enjoyed going to work, but never has the office been such an enticing, tantalizing playground. I come in early every day, hungry for Richard's first phone call. I end up working late every night, to make up for my three-hour chunks of time spent e-mailing a man sitting two floors away. When we pass each other in the halls, we exchange formal pleasantries before returning to our offices and e-mailing things like, *"You look hot."* . . . *"No, you look hot."*

So I suppose it's fitting that our first kiss happens at work.

It is a late Monday night—close to ten o'clock—and I've just e-mailed Richard a question about one of my authors. As I wait for his reply, he suddenly appears in my doorway with the answer.

I jump and say, "Shit, Richard! You scared me."

He gives me his standard-issue grin and then makes a sarcastic comment, something about my guilty conscience.

I shake my head, smiling. Then I stand and head for the door.

"Where do you think you're going?" he asks, blocking me.

Our bodies touch—and the contact gives me a little rush.

"To the copier," I say, attempting to exit again.

He blocks me again and then pulls me back into my office, closing the door behind us.

"What's the big idea?" I say, knowing *exactly* what his big idea is.

His face comes closer to mine. I tilt my head to the right, my preferred angle to kiss. At the same second, he tilts his head to the right. Our lips meet effortlessly, softly. Then more urgently. We swiftly become two movie stars, making out in a forbidden place. I am watching myself kiss Richard, aware of how good we must look. Richard is the sort of man who can make any woman look good.

He backs me up, over to my desk, where he lifts me up and puts me down with the exact right mix of passion and care. His hands slide under my bare thighs. I am glad I wore a skirt today. And—hallelujah!—lacy, matching underwear. Sometimes things really *do* work out; I make a mental note to remember this small blessing the next time I'm complaining about bad luck, when, say, I am stuck in a middle seat on a flight between two oversized passengers.

Richard keeps kissing me, mostly on the lips, but also on my neck and collarbone. The man is an expert, and there's really no doubt about where he got his experience. I think of Lydia in the art department—and so many other women before me. Some he met at work, others from bars or restaurants or blind dates or the subway. But I don't care about any of them. I don't care if he's seeing other women right now. I just want him to keep touching me, everywhere, right under these fluorescent lights.

"Will you come back to my place?" Richard breathes in my ear.

I nod and whisper, "Yeah," as he continues to kiss my neck. My hands are on his back—which feels stronger than I imagined. I decide that forty-eight is not very old. He presses harder against me. Not so old at all.

"Now?" he says.

"Uh-huh," I say. "But you'll need to stop kissing me first."

There are a few more false stops before we finally disentangle ourselves and breathlessly formulate a plan: I am to go get a cab and wait for him while he picks up his things in his office. We kiss one more time. Then he opens my door. I consider it a victory when we are only spotted by Jimmy, the janitor on my floor, who nods hello. In truth, though, I really don't care who knows about us. I am beginning to wear our relationship as a badge of honor. An outward emblem of my well-adjusted, "pick myself up by my bootstraps" mentality. I am no victim, no embittered divorcée. And Richard is proof of that.

I get a cab right away and wait for Richard. He hops in a moment later, swinging his briefcase in by his feet. We do not kiss in the cab, but we never stop touching. He tells me, more than once, that he can't wait to get me home.

When we do get to his apartment, we head straight for his bedroom. I am glad he doesn't ask me if I want something to drink. Because I don't. I'm glad we don't sit on the couch and talk. Because I just want to be in his bed, touching him. And within two minutes of the dead bolt being locked behind us, that's exactly where we are, exactly what I am doing.

Everything about Richard is cool and smooth—his sheets, his music (Sam Cooke), even his choice of pets—an uppity Siamese cat named Rex who is disdainfully surveying us from his windowsill. There is only one awkward beat—the predictable one where Richard stops, looks at me, and says, "Do I need to get something?"

"Are you . . . fine?" I ask, thinking of Lydia again and the disease that rhymes with her name.

"Oh, yeah. I'm completely fine," Richard says, kissing the inside of my left thigh. "But . . . are you on the pill?"

I breathe a yes.

"Of course you are," he says. His comment jolts my mind back to Ben and babies, and I can't help but feel a quick jab of longing. I tell myself that my ex-husband is likely doing the same thing with Tucker. Or someone like her. I tell myself to stay in the moment. I tell myself that I would so much rather be here with Richard than having a baby. It's no contest. No contest at all.

Moments later, Richard and I are having sex.

"You're so good," he whispers to me at one point.

"You say that to all the girls," I whisper back.

"No. I don't," he says. "I say only what I mean."

I smile because I believe him. There is nothing gratuitous about Richard.

We both come, seconds apart, but do not cuddle in the aftermath. I already sensed that Richard is not the cuddling kind, and that is fine with me. I can skip the cuddling as long as there is some sense of lingering connection, physical or otherwise. Richard and I have both. We sit side by side, leaning against his pillows and leather headboard. We are still undressed, but covered up to our waists with his taupe sheets. His arm is draped over mine, his fingers resting on my wrist, occasionally tapping my skin.

We talk about work, but not in a "we have nothing else to talk about" sort of a way. More in the "tell me what I don't already know" kind of way. He asks me if I love what I do, and I tell him yes.

"What do you like the best about your job?" he says.

I consider all the standard answers that editors give—stuff about loving books and the written word and escaping to a different world. Of course that's all true, but that's not what I love *most* about editing. There's something else—something that has more to do with discovering a fresh talent.

"It's hard to explain," I say. "But I guess it's that rush I get when I read something and feel hooked. When I think, 'This person can really, *really* write,' and I just *have* to work with her."

Richard smiles and takes my hand as if to say, *Go on.*

So I do. I say, "You know that almost smug feeling you have in high school when you listen to a band before they get really big—and then you can say, 'Oh, Depeche Mode? I've been listening to them *forever*. I just *love* their old stuff'?"

Richard laughs and nods.

"Well, that's what it's like to uncover a new author," I say. "Like you were in on the secret *first*." I suddenly feel self-conscious, like I've exposed too much of myself.

"So what about you?" I say. "What do you like best about your job?"

"Oh, I don't know," Richard says. "I guess I like that it's

personality-driven . . . And I like contributing to a book's success . . . that feeling when everything is clicking for a book and an author and you're getting a whole bunch of reviews . . . But sometimes it feels so all-or-nothing. Like, 'what have you done for me lately?' You know how that goes."

I nod. I know *exactly* how that goes.

He continues, "And there are many more times when you can't get shit for a book. Which really sucks when you like the book and like the author . . ."

I nod again. It's heartbreaking when you love a book that fails. And it always seems to happen to the nicest authors.

Richard says, "And I don't know . . . publicity tends to breed a certain kind of person who feels the need to try to take credit for everything and who can't seem to ever quite turn off that publicist persona. It's like they're perpetually in schmooze mode and in a rush to get into the spotlight all the time."

"You're not that way," I say, thinking that Richard is just *naturally* in the spotlight. He's not rushing to get there.

"God. I sure hope not. Because I'll tell you, Parr, there is nothing that makes me loathe my job more than heading to some sort of industry cocktail party and watching all the hyperpublicists chase around media folks to introduce themselves while not-that-subtly trying to pitch their projects and doing the whole nametag surfing thing. It's brutal."

"Nametag surfing?"

"You know—when someone starts talking to you like they're your new best friend. Then, when they think you're not looking, they glance down at your nametag really quickly to see who you are. And if they deem you worthy—and important enough—they'll keep talking to you. It's sort of like peeking at someone's cleavage. And man, if there is someone from the *Times* or something at one of those things, it's like a feeding frenzy. I can't imagine why those guys even *show up* to those things, unless they just need some sort of cheap ego boost."

I laugh and say, "Yeah, but nobody has to read your nametag, Richard."

"That's true," he says with feigned bravado.

His phone rings, but he doesn't even glance in its direction. I return the gesture when my cell spits out Jess's personal ring tone, The Verve's "Bittersweet Symphony." But then she rings again. And again.

"I better get that," I say. "It's Jess. Sounds important."

Richard knows that Jess is my best friend and roommate. He leans over, kisses my cheek, and says, "Go ahead. Call her back."

I retrieve my underwear on the floor next to the bed, put it on as quickly as possible, and walk the five or six steps over to Richard's ottoman where I dropped my purse. I find my phone and call Jess at home.

"Where are you?" she asks.

"I'm with Richard," I say, liking the way those words sound. I hope that I'll be saying them for a while. "What's going on?"

"He dumped me," she says. Her voice cracks as if she's been crying or is about to. "He says he still loves his wife. He wants to make it work with her."

"I'll be right home," I say, snapping my phone shut.

I cast Richard an apologetic look as I finish dressing. "I'm really sorry, but I gotta go."

"Everything okay?" he asks, swinging his legs over the side of his bed and pulling on his boxers.

Baby Proof

"A crisis of the heart," I tell him.

"I'm not familiar," he says.

Must be nice, I think.

He walks me to the door and kisses me good-bye.

I pause for a second as I think of something appropriate to say. I settle on, "Thanks for tonight."

It sounds a little formal, so I smile and add, "I enjoyed it."

"Anytime," he says. "And I mean that."

Jess is a mess when I return to her place. She is sitting cross-legged in the corner of her room and there are at least a dozen cigarette butts in one of her white saucers on the floor beside her. She quit smoking a few years ago, but picks the habit back up whenever she's in the middle of a stressful deal or an emotional crisis. She looks fragile, vulnerable. To see her now, you'd never guess that she can buy and sell companies worth billions of dollars.

I hug her and say that I'm sorry. That I know how badly she wanted things to work out with Trey. I refrain from calling him a lying bastard. For now.

She says, "I really believed in him," and then starts to cry. It's heartbreaking to watch. Another reason not to have a child. The thought of watching your child suffer feels unbearable. Still, as I listen to Jess romanticize her relationship with Trey, I can't help feeling the way I do when friends lose pets and grieve as if a person died. Yes, it's sad, but it's not *that* sad, I always think. I know you loved Flash, but he was a basset hound, for God's sake, not your son. But maybe that's because I never had a dog growing up (my mother is allergic to them). I feel sort of the same way about Trey. I've never been with a married man, but I want to say to Jess, "Yes, you liked him, and you loved having sex with him. But how could you love *him*? He is *married* to another woman. With children. He is emotionally unavailable to you. He is a fraud. You were never, even at your peak romantic moment, really together. So you haven't really lost anything."

I might say all of this at some point, but now is not the time. I just let her cry. I remember that she did the same for me. Not that Ben and Trey should ever be compared.

"I know you couldn't *possibly* understand this," Jess says after a long silent stretch. "But I thought he was going to be the father of my children. I've invested two years in him. *Two* years. I feel too old to start looking again."

"You're not too old," I say. "That's ludicrous."

"I'm almost thirty-*five*," she says. "I'm running out of time. I'm running out of eggs."

"You have plenty of good eggs left," I say. I am trying hard to be a supportive friend, but I can't help fixating on the other part of her statement. The part about me not understanding. I don't want to make her angst about me, as my mother does whenever someone else is experiencing trauma, but I can't help asking, "Why do you think I can't understand this?"

Jess and I never argue, so she has no experience in detecting the edge in my voice now. She has no way of knowing how annoyed I am. How much I am regretting calling her back at all. I could still be at Richard's. I wish I were. Almost. Actually, I'm not sure about that—in some ways it was nice to get the natural out. Much easier than deciding for myself whether I should spend the night.

But what I *do* know is that a man like Trey should not have the power to infiltrate *my* romantic life. It's bad enough that he has impacted my best friend's.

I look at Jess, waiting for an answer. She lights another cigarette as she says, "Because you don't want kids."

Right, I think to myself. And I guess that means that I also have no imagination, no empathy, no feelings. I can't possibly fathom how another woman feels when I don't want to be a mother myself. After all, what kind of a woman doesn't want to be a mother?

fifteen

The next day Daphne calls me from the waiting room of her fertility clinic. I'm about to go into our weekly editorial meeting, and I want to take the time to either review my notes or say good morning to Richard or both. I called him back last night, after my conversation with Jess, but I still feel strange about leaving so quickly after we slept together for the first time. I tell Daphne that I can't talk and will call her back after my meeting.

"But it's nine-twelve," she says.

"Yeah. So?"

"So your meeting doesn't start at nine-fifteen, does it?"

I know precisely where she's going with her line of questioning, but I still fall into her trap and say, "No. It starts at nine-thirty."

"You have a few minutes then, right?"

I shake my head and sigh. Daphne seems to think that because I have my own office and phone, I should always be able to talk. But instead of delving into the details of my meeting or anything of my evening with Richard, I say, "Okay, Daph. I have about three minutes. What's up?"

I can feel her victory smile over the phone. "So," she says, "we're here at the doctor's office. Tony is getting his tests. You know, to see if something is wrong with him."

176

"Right," I say, checking my e-mail. I have one from Richard. Just the sight of his name makes my heart flutter. He was so good last night.

She says, "The first step is his semen analysis."

"Uh-huh," I say. "That makes sense."

"So they put him in this little room with all these porn videos and girly magazines and stuff."

I laugh and say, "Poor Tony."

"Poor *Tony*?" Daphne says. "He's looking at naked women right now. I don't think you need to feel sorry for *him*."

"I'm sure he's embarrassed, though," I say as I quietly click open Richard's e-mail and read, *When can I see you again?*

I smile and type back, *At 9:30. Aren't you coming to the editorial meeting?*

Daphne continues, "He's not embarrassed in the slightest. He thinks the whole thing's hilarious. He was cracking jokes, asking the nurse if they had any girl-on-girl videos."

"Tony cracks jokes when he's embarrassed. Remember when he forgot to put his car in park that one Thanksgiving?" I say, remembering how his new, black Acura rolled backward, causing a four-car pileup. "He made self-deprecating remarks about that maneuver for years. He still brings it up."

"That's different," she says. "That *was* sort of funny. After the fact, anyway."

"This will be funny someday, too," I say as I read Richard's virtually instantaneous response: *See you alone. As I saw you last night.*

"So is it totally unreasonable for me to be annoyed?" Daphne asks.

This is her trademark question; Daphne always wants me to gauge the unreasonableness of her emotional reaction to

177

something. I consistently want to tell her that, yes, she's being unreasonable, an instinct Maura gives in to, but I've learned to tread carefully.

"I can see why you would be annoyed," I say to Daphne as I compose an e-mail back to Richard: *As soon as possible.*

"I mean, it's just *gross,*" she says. "And it adds another layer of humiliation to this whole process."

"Try not to think of it that way," I say. "Just get through it."

"Well, don't you think Tony should have told them he didn't need . . . props? Don't you think he should be thinking about his wife? Instead of jerking off to porn?"

"I'm sure he *is* thinking about you. Give him the benefit of the doubt, Daph."

"Yeah, right," she says. "Our sex life sucks. Unless I'm ovulating, it's nonexistent. And when I am ovulating, it's a total chore."

"It will get better," I say, thinking of Richard again. How good last night felt. How I will never have to experience the drudgery of procreational sex. "You guys are just under a lot of pressure."

I glance at my watch. It is 9:19, and it takes approximately four minutes to take the elevator up three floors and walk to the conference room. Which leaves me only seven minutes to look over my notes.

Just as I'm about to say good-bye, she says, "Do you think this is his fault?"

"Fault? What do you mean?" I ask.

Clearly it's not Tony's fault that their clinic—the clinic Daphne researched and selected—keeps pornography on hand.

"You think it's his problem or mine? The reason we can't get pregnant?"

178

Surely Daphne must realize that I have no possible way of knowing an answer that requires extensive diagnostic testing, but this sort of thing never stops her from asking the question; she is a big believer in random speculation and blind guesswork.

I humor her and say, "I think it's probably his issue. But I also predict that it will be a *fixable* issue . . . Listen, Daph. I really gotta run. I'll call you after my meeting. Okay?"

"Okay. But cross your fingers that you're right . . . and that it *is* his fault," she says before we say good-bye.

Her last comment about fault disturbs me so much that I frown at the phone as I hang up, something that people usually only do on badly written television shows. I'm not sure what about it bothers me, but I tell myself I can analyze it later.

For now, I must get in my saleswoman frame of mind. The purpose of the weekly editorial meeting is for editors to pitch manuscripts to the editorial director and heads of other departments who have the opportunity to shoot the proposal down for any number of reasons: *this won't sell; this book is too much like another book released last year;* or just a plain old, *this manuscript blows*. Obviously a lot is at stake for editors so the meetings tend to have a Darwinian feel with plenty of office politics coming into play. Emotions run high, and it's not uncommon for junior editors, who are desperate to make a name for themselves, to leave the conference room in tears. I have had my share of traumatic meetings as I came through the ranks, but I'm actually six for six for novels pitched this year (which could be a house record), and I'd like nothing better than to keep my perfect track record alive. I also want to impress Richard. It would be a real shame for my streak to be broken on the heels of last night.

When I walk into the conference room, I can instantly

sense Richard's presence. I hear his robust laugh and, out of the corner of my eye, can see him pouring coffee into a Styrofoam cup. I don't have the gumption to approach him or even look his way. Instead, I avoid all small talk and sit at the long, oblong table where I diligently scan my notes as Jacqueline Dody, my good friend and closest editorial ally, takes a seat next to me and asks if I want a doughnut. I say no, thanks, which might be the first time in my life I've declined a Krispy Kreme doughnut. But I'm too nervous to eat today. I've never had to speak professionally in front of someone I've just slept with—or slept with at all, for that matter.

That's when I hear Richard say, "What the hell? Parr's turning down doughnuts?"

"No kidding!" Jacqueline says. "What's up with *that*, you skinny bitch? You can afford the calories."

"Yeah," Richard says, "don't you know that it is bad form to turn down sweets when you're model thin?"

I look at him, both surprised and impressed that he's managed to compliment my body inside five minutes.

"Hey. I'm trying to focus here," I say as Richard takes a seat on the other side of me. I feel unnerved and even more so when I feel his foot against mine. I shake my head and move my foot, wondering how many times he's played footsy under this very table. I wonder if Richard has ever slept with any other editors, and hope that the answer is no.

When his foot moves back against mine, I shoot him a pretend look of warning.

He smirks and says, "What?"

"Nothing," I say, shaking my head again.

Our editorial director, Sam Hewlett, calls our meeting to order with his usual dry, no-nonsense tone, and then turns things over to Molly Harrington, an editor who is pitching a young adult historical novel set in Bruges. I try to focus on Molly, but can only think of what happened last night. At one point, Richard starts doodling squiggly lines on his pad, and I find myself transfixed by them—and by his hand. When he catches me watching, he writes the words *I can still* on his pad. Then he scratches them out, looks around to make sure nobody is paying attention, and writes *taste*. Then he flips his notebook to a fresh page and writes *you*. My heart starts pounding in my chest as I think of his mouth on me last night. I vow not to look at his pad again.

Two hours and six books later (four of which are rejected), it is my turn to present. Richard turns his chair toward me and smiles. I try to ignore him, but I still start out a little bit rocky as I introduce my novel and rave about how witty and charming I found it to be. Then I say, "More specifically, the story is about a woman who is living in Chicago when, for various reasons, she decides to give up her wonderful, stable life to go live in the South of France. She faces a lot of obstacles and adversity, but in the end, she makes some surprising discoveries about herself . . . The book is *incredibly* heartwarming and engaging."

Sam interrupts me and says, "Who do you see as the audience?"

I say, "I think it will appeal to anyone who likes Peter Mayle. But the story has a very down-to-earth quality to it, so I actually think it will have an even broader appeal than Mayle's books. I think women of all ages will love it. And honestly, men will enjoy this story, too."

Another editor, Dawn Bolyn, leans forward with a smug expression. Dawn is one those sniping, ultracompetitive types who seems transparently jealous of anyone's success, particularly mine. So I'm not surprised when she says, "It sounds like an *Under the Tuscan Sun* knockoff."

"Well, Dawn," I say with exaggerated patience. "For starters, this is *France,* not Italy."

To Dawn's obvious dismay, my comment earns a few chuckles. Then I say, "And the books are actually *nothing* alike."

And please use a toner on that greasy face of yours.

Jacqueline chimes in on my behalf. "Well, I loved the writing. It was very vivid and descriptive without being overwritten . . . And the story was riveting. I had a vicious hangover all day on Sunday and I couldn't stop paging through it."

Everyone laughs because Jacqueline is known to overindulge when we go out for drinks after work.

Sam says, "Well, I agree with Jacqueline that the writing was descriptive and vivid . . . but there was something about the book that just felt . . . *small.*"

It feels pretty damning when Sam calls a book small so now I'm beginning to worry. As I'm grappling for a retort, Richard removes the pen cap from his mouth, and says, "Claudia, tell us, did the author actually move to France?"

I shake my head. I know he is driving at review angles.

"So, unfortunately, we wouldn't be able to get nonfiction, feature coverage for her, but it still sounds good to me. I can picture a great cover on it . . . Besides, I think Claudia's track record speaks for itself. Close calls should go to her."

All eyes are on Richard. He doesn't speak often in meetings, but his opinion carries great weight so I feel pretty sure he's tipped the balance in my favor. Sure enough, Sam calls a vote, and my proposal passes by a narrow margin.

I look at Richard who gives me a quick, surreptitious wink.

I think to myself, *Omigod, did I just get ahead at work because of sex?*

I'm not sure of the answer, but it suddenly strikes me that there is a mighty thin line between a wholesome life and a scandalous one.

I call Daphne as soon as I return to my office. She is in the car, alone, on her way to the grocery store.

"How did it go?" I say.

"It went. Apparently he delivered a few sperm," she says caustically. "With the help of coeds Shari and Shelli."

"And the verdict?"

"The tests take a few days . . . But what's another few days when you've been waiting a decade to have a baby, right?"

I want to point out that she hasn't *really* been waiting a decade. You can't count the years of not trying. Of wearing condoms, taking the pill, and "pulling and praying," Daphne and Tony's method of choice during their impoverished, ramen-noodle college days.

"You'll get to the bottom of this soon," I say as I glance down at my cuticles and make a mental note to get a manicure before I see Richard again.

I listen to Daphne start ranting about an elderly driver not using his turn signal. Ever since an old man plowed into several schoolchildren at a crosswalk in our hometown last year, Daphne routinely scribbles down license plates and reports careless drivers to the DMV. "I mean, God bless them, you know . . . I'm sure they don't realize that they shouldn't be driving. But it's just not safe, you know?"

I interrupt her tirade and say, "Listen, Daph, I was wondering something . . . You know how you said that you hoped that it was Tony's problem? Fault?"

183

"Yeah."

"What did you mean by that exactly?"

"I meant that I don't want to get blamed for this."

"Blamed by Tony?"

"Yeah."

"You really think he'd *blame* you?" I ask. "That's not like Tony."

"I know . . . But sometimes I get that feeling."

"I don't think anyone should be blaming anyone," I say.

"Yeah. Well. This whole thing is *really* stressful . . ." Her voice trails off.

"I'm really sorry, Daphne. I wish you didn't have to go through this."

"I know . . . Just tell me that it will happen for me. Tell me I'll be a mother someday."

"It will happen," I say, believing it. "And worst-case scenario, you could adopt. Right?"

"I guess so. But that is a *last* resort. I want my own baby."

"But it would be your baby," I say.

"You know what I mean," she says. "I want to carry a child. I want to fully experience every part of motherhood . . ."

"You will," I say.

"Maybe that's the real reason I want this to be Tony's fault," she says. "If it's his fault, I can still have a baby."

"You mean with someone else? You'd leave Tony?" I say, horrified.

"Oh, God, no," Daphne says. "I was more talking sperm banks . . . something like that," she says.

I almost ask her if Tony would be willing to go down that road. It would surprise me if he would. He would do most anything for Daphne, but he strikes me as the sort of macho guy who wouldn't be able to handle that. But I decide not to stir the pot. Daphne has enough on her mind.

That afternoon, after I return about a dozen phone calls from various agents and authors, I find myself thinking about Ben and our marriage and how it wasn't what I thought it was the day we said *I do*. After all, people who belong together *stay* together despite major setbacks and disagreements. They may deal in fault and blame temporarily, but ultimately they work things out. *Love conquers all. In sickness and in health.* That's what good marriages are all about. I think of an extreme example—how Dana Reeve stayed with Christopher even though she couldn't have possibly wanted to be married to a quadriplegic. Their love was strong and real and more important than all the collective things they could no longer do together. It was more important than fantastic sex, or horseback riding, or having more babies. Dana had to let a lot of dreams die, but she did so willingly. He was worth any sacrifice.

I sit at my desk for a long time, my back to the computer, ignoring the *ding* of new e-mails, likely from Richard, and wondering whether Ben would have left if I had been diagnosed with a serious illness. If I had only a few years left to live. Or, if I *couldn't* conceive—as opposed to being unwilling to do so. I can't imagine Ben leaving me under any of those circumstances. So how could he leave simply because I didn't want kids? I wasn't throwing hardship at him; I just wanted things to stay the same. Couldn't my husband just love me enough to stay? Was that really so much to ask?

sixteen

It takes me a good three days to really shake the Ben funk set-tling back into my psyche. During this time, I avoid Richard. Not completely—we still talk and e-mail with staggering fre-quency. But when he inquires whether I'm free for dinner, I make up an excuse and ask for a rain check. I do not want to have sex with him while dwelling on Ben even though Jess insists that sex with Richard could be the very thing to help me get over the unexpected hump. I know from experience that having sex with a man while you're thinking of another can have the catastrophic reverse effect, and I remind her of my breakup with my college boyfriend Paul. My only other truly significant split.

During those early days in New York, right after gradua-tion, Jess went out virtually every night, but I spent most of my evenings in, doing pathetic things like listening to The Cure's "Pictures of You" on repeat and calling into radio shows to dedicate songs to "Paul in Denver." I couldn't snap out of my misery—nor did I really want to—until I met Anders at a roof party on the Upper East Side. Anders was a twenty-year-old Swedish tennis pro with long blond hair and a lopsided grin. We hit it off right away, although I recognized that he was the sort of guy with whom everyone hits it off and girls easily fall in love.

So I was psyched when he found me at the end of the night and asked for my phone number. We went to dinner and a movie the following week and began to hang out pretty regularly, although we never really analyzed what we were or where we were headed.

About a month later, we had sex on his futon, under a scratchy rainbow-colored afghan his grandmother had knitted for him. It didn't top the best of my sex with Paul, but it was way better than my first time with him, which I thought was significant and promising. Afterward Anders made us a midnight snack of Fritos and boiled hot dogs. Then he fired up his lava lamp and we danced to Marky Mark's "Feel the Vibrations" until his neighbor pounded on the wall for us to shut up. I remember thinking that although I wasn't in love with Anders, I couldn't rule out the possibility of it happening. In fact, I was hopeful that it would.

A few days later, right before another date with Anders, I got out of the shower and noticed a blinking red light on my answering machine. Even though we hadn't talked in nearly three months, I knew right away it was Paul—which marks the closest thing I've ever had to a psychic moment. I hit the play button, and sure enough, it *was* Paul, drunk and rambling about how he really hoped that I was well. It was hardly an "I miss you like crazy and wish I had moved to New York with you" sort of message, but still, he was calling me on a Friday night while drinking—something I had, with Jess's resolve, managed not to do. I listened to the message twice and then made myself delete it, fighting the urge to save it for further analysis. (Jess is gifted at reading between the lines and interpreting things like drunken voice-mail messages, perhaps because she had left her fair share up to that point. Then again, who doesn't drink and dial in their early twenties?) I had serious pangs as I erased Paul's familiar husky voice, but mostly I just felt proud of myself. I was a well-adjusted young urbanite dating a European with longish hair and a ferocious serve. I was *so* over my college boyfriend.

So in keeping with my image, I saw to it that Anders and I had a blast that night. We ate at El Teddy's, my favorite Mexican restaurant (one that has since closed) in Tribeca and got wasted on margaritas on the rocks with salt, which made me feel sophisticated with every sip as I only drank frozen margaritas in college. Then we met up with Anders's friends, mostly fellow tennis players, and danced at a velvet-rope club in SoHo. Anders was a great dancer, but didn't take himself at all seriously. Every once in a while he'd break into his hilariously manic "running man" dance. He cracked me up and made me feel buoyant, in a way you can only feel in the aftermath of true misery.

Then something very strange happened. Back at Anders's apartment, as we were having sex for only the second time, I found myself thinking about Paul's message. Then, seemingly out of nowhere, I was crying. I told myself that it was just the margaritas. I reminded myself that I was happy. I prayed that the moment would pass quickly and that Anders's room was dark enough for my tears to go undetected. But no such luck. Seconds later, I felt Anders freeze over me. He gently touched my cheek. "Are you crying?" he asked, sounding more horrified than worried. He didn't wait for an answer, just sat up, snapped on the light, and gave me a fearful look. I told him I was sorry. He hugged me and said, "Don't be." Then he asked me questions, about what was wrong, about why was I sad, had he done something wrong? I told him I wasn't that sad, just drunk and tired. He pressed me on it, so I told him all about Paul, what had changed in our relationship, his unwillingness to move to New York, how I still sometimes missed him when I heard certain songs—all the typical postrelationship melodrama. I even told Anders about Paul's message earlier that night, how I had deleted it after only listening twice. I apologized along the way, and Anders was an excellent sport. He said it was fine, and at my insistence, shared some of his own stories of past loves.

Of course I was embarrassed to have cried during sex, but in my mind, Anders and I had crossed a threshold together, and the night had taken on an important, almost cathartic quality. I was finally ready to move on from Paul. The next morning, Anders kissed me good-bye, with no sign of a problem. I returned home and told Jess that I finally felt like I was completely over Paul, and that I was ready to take things to the next level with Anders. The only problem was—Anders apparently didn't feel the same because he *never* called me again. Of course I never called him again, either. But it was pretty clear who was blowing off whom. It always is.

I still cringe when I think about that night and wonder what would have happened had I not cried in the middle of sex. Not that I think Anders and I were meant to be together or anything crazy like that. I just think that I screwed up what could have turned into a more significant relationship—or at least a lasting friendship.

With all of this in mind, I decide that I'm certainly not about to make the same mistake with Richard. I never want to cry during sex again (unless it is *that* good—Ben once moved me to tears). I want the lines to stay clear. I know I'll think about Ben for a long time to come, but I'd strongly prefer if those thoughts did not transpire in the sack with another man. I don't want to taint my fragile start with Richard. Not that there is anything particularly fragile about my relationship with Richard—it's just that by definition, all starts are fragile.

Then, just as I think I'm moving beyond the rough patch, I get something in the mail that messes with my head all over again. I recognize Annie's handwriting immediately and feel a stab of guilt for not returning her recent calls or accepting her invitations for lunch. Annie and Ray are the only friends caught in the divorce crossfire, the only couple who is impossible for either Ben or me to fully claim. Everyone else is either more my friend or more his friend—and we have an unspoken deal where I stay away from his friends and he steers clear of mine. It's a respect thing. I am thinking all of this as I open the envelope, expecting a note of some sort. Annie is big on sending notes for no reason and often laments that the age of e-mail is eviscerating the art of letter-writing. But the correspondence is not a note; it is an invitation to Raymond Jr.'s baptism.

"Shit," I say aloud because I know Ben is opening the same invitation tonight, and the last thing I want to do is see him. Yet—at the same time—seeing Ben is what I want most. I hate myself and him all over again.

I slide the invitation back into the envelope and calmly consider my options. I could call Annie and tell her the truth. We are close enough friends that I should be able to confide in her. I would probably take this path if she were inviting me to, say, a random party. But because it is her firstborn's baptism, a very sacred event, I just don't feel right about the truth option. I know it would come across as incredibly self-involved. After all, such a move *would* be self-involved.

I consider lying. Making up an excuse. Telling her that I'm out of town that weekend. That I already have my nonrefundable airline tickets in hand. But then I would have to make up a whole, grand lie about a trip to Vegas or L.A. or New Orleans and always remember that I allegedly went on a jaunt on this random weekend in August. It would be just my luck to forget about my cover mid-weekend and answer the phone and have it be Annie asking Jess for her rum runner recipe. It seems to be the cruel law that people who don't lie like champs are precisely the ones to get busted on the rare occasion when they opt to deceive. Besides, in combination with all my recent excuses to Annie, she will strongly suspect that I'm lying. I would if the tables were turned.

I berate myself for not accepting at least one of her invitations to lunch or drinks over the past month. For not stopping in to see Raymond Jr. If I had made even a minimal effort, then blowing off the baptism would be less egregious.

I suddenly wonder exactly why I'm going out of my way to avoid Annie and Ray. I guess it doesn't exactly take a degree in psychiatry to decipher the reasons. In part it's the baby factor. The last thing I want to be around is a baby. I don't want to be reminded of what Ben chose over me. But I also don't want to be around anyone or anything that reminds me of Ben, period, and I'm afraid that Annie will offer up unsolicited details of Ben's new life. Details I most certainly don't want to hear. Unless those details include that he's single and miserable. And there's no way that that's the case. After all, I saw him yucking it up with Tucker. He may not be in love with her, or even *with* her at all, but by no means did he appear to be a broken man.

Of course I could always tell Annie that I don't want to

Emily Giffin

hear anything about Ben, but I don't want to come across as the big relationship loser, and I would appear to be emotionally unstable if I ruled out conversation about the most significant thing to happen to me, ever. Then Annie would pass this along to Ray who, as a man, would not have the good sense and tact to keep it to himself, and would instead tell Ben what a very pitiful case I am. Moreover, if Annie obliges my request to avoid mention of Ben, I inevitably will read all sorts of things into her ensuing silence. I will wind up thinking that, yes, I *told* Annie that I didn't want to discuss Ben, but if the report were favorable to me (unfavorable for Ben) she'd somehow find a way to sneak it into the conversation, as in, *I know you didn't want to hear anything about Ben, but he asks about you every time we see him and he seems desperately lonely without you.*

In any event, this invitation forces my hand.

I know exactly what Jess will say—and so I laugh when she comes home from work, glances at the invitation and says it. "You have to go. You have to take Richard. And you have to look hot." Her eyes are lit up for the first time since her conversation with Trey—who has not called back to change his mind, or even say hello.

I tell her that there's no way I am inviting Richard.

"Why not? I'm sure Annie wouldn't mind."

"I wouldn't do that to Ben. Or Richard, for that matter," I say. "Besides, it looks so *obvious*. Pathetically so."

"I disagree. I think it looks the opposite of pathetic. I think it looks like Richard is your boyfriend. People bring boyfriends to events like this."

"He's not my boyfriend, and you know it."

"He sort of is."

"No," I say. "He's really not."

"Then what is he?"

"He's this guy I like. A guy I've slept with *once*."

"So sleep with him a few more times and then take him."

I laugh and shake my head.

She says, "Fine. But you're going to be *really* sorry you didn't listen to me if Ben brings someone."

I stop cold and look at her. "You think he'd do that?"

"He might."

"No way. Never."

"Never say never," Jess says.

It's been her mantra for years, and I think I'm finally beginning to agree with her. There are no absolutes in relationships. You can't take anything for granted. You can count on absolutely nothing but the unexpected. You only get in trouble when you start thinking that you're some kind of exception to the rule.

I pick up the phone and dial Annie's number.

She answers with a cheerful, "Hey, stranger!"

Before I can talk myself out of it, I say, "Hey, Annie. I got your invitation, and I wouldn't miss it . . . Mind if I bring someone?"

seventeen

I feel a little guilty about using Richard to get at Ben. Or using Richard to make myself look good in front of Ben. Or using Richard at all. But Jess points out that I'm not really using him because legitimately liking someone negates the concept of *using*. She asks me whether I'd bring Richard to her theoretical baby's baptism. I answer yes as quickly as possible because I don't want her to dwell on the baby she's *not* going to have with Trey—and because I know exactly where she's going with her reasoning.

Sure enough, she smiles as if she's just proven a complicated theorem and says, "Well, then. You should have a perfectly clear conscience."

I shake my head and laugh as she slaps me a high five. It sure comes in handy to have a master rationalizer as your best friend.

So a few days later, I'm over at Richard's apartment, and we're making dinner. Or more accurately, I'm watching him make dinner and accepting small, uncomplicated assignments, like "wash lettuce" and "dice onion." I'm okay with the lettuce-washing; I take my time spreading the leaves on sheets of paper towel and then dabbing them dry before putting them into a big wooden salad bowl. Yet when I start slicing the onion in the wrong direction, Richard laughs and says, "Seriously, Parr, how can you not know how to cut an onion?"

"I know," I say, feeling a little chagrined. "I've learned a bunch of times—and then can never remember. It's the same with tomatoes."

He gently takes the knife from my hand and says, "Allow me."

I play helpless—which I guess isn't too much of an act—and watch his perfect slicing technique and fast, effortless chopping.

"Is it weird that that totally turns me on?" I ask. I've always had a thing for people with unexpected talents, and I wouldn't have pegged Richard as being particularly adept in the kitchen.

He laughs as I admire the crinkly lines around his eyes. He must have just showered before I arrived because his hair is still damp in the back and his cologne is a bit stronger than usual. He is barefoot, wearing dark jeans and a crisp white shirt with the sleeves rolled up to his elbows. I watch him scrape the onion with the backside of the blade, transferring it from cutting board to his frying pan of olive oil. It makes a satisfying sizzling sound as he smugly says, "Voilà!" Then he wipes his hands on a dish towel, opens a bottle of wine with a professional corkscrew—another thing I can't do—and pours two glasses. He hands me one, and we clink glasses without making a toast. I'm a fan of the no-toast, unless you have something really worthwhile to say. The *here's to tonight* or *here's to the chef* or *here's to us* brand of toasting has a way of diluting the moment. Or worse, creating an awkward lull, sort of like the question, "What should we talk about now?" Besides, if a man really looks in your eyes at the second your glasses meet—as Richard just did—it can be far more enticing than words.

I smile as Richard steps toward me, leans down and kisses me. He is a good head taller than Ben, which makes kissing while standing more difficult. Most girls prefer tall men, but I've always liked the intimacy that comes with compatible heights. It makes for more intimate slow dancing. Among other things. Not that I would change a thing about Richard. I kiss him back and taste wine. I decide that the first kiss of the night is always the best. Maybe Richard is thinking the same thing because we linger for a moment before he turns toward the stove and stirs his onions.

"Now. Don't distract me," he says. "This is serious business."

I study his back and the way his neck looks bent over the stove and decide that it's as good a time as any to ask about the baptism. I will be casual, just float it out there. No need to beat around the bush with Richard. That's the beauty of our relationship. Or whatever it is that we have going on. No pretense necessary. So I blurt out the bald facts: *Good friends had baby; baptism next weekend; Ben will be there; will you come?*

He spins around, grinning. "So you want to make your ex-husband jealous?"

I start to stammer a denial but he interrupts and says, "No problem. I'm in. And don't worry." He holds up his wooden spoon like a sword. "I'll do you proud."

"That's not why I want you to come," I say. "I just . . . thought it would be nice for you to meet my friends."

"Right," Richard says, smirking. "A baptism is the typical, mainstream way to meet friends. As opposed to, say . . . a drink or brunch? Or God, really going out on a limb and having dinner?"

I can feel myself blushing. I should have known Richard would tease me. I must appear really embarrassed because he lets me off the hook. He puts his spoon down, lifts my chin with his thumb and kisses me again—but this time it's more of a "buck up, little camper" sort of kiss, as opposed to an "I can't wait to see you naked" kiss.

When we separate, he is grinning again. "Should I do that for your ex? Perhaps we could sit in the pew in front of him and just start making out in church?"

My face feels hot as I say, "The ceremony is in Central Park by the Shakespeare Garden. And anyway . . . it was a bad idea. Forget I asked."

I really don't want him to forget it, though. I want him to go with me. Because of Ben, yes. But more because I just want him there with me. Just as I told Jess. I consider telling him some of this but can't figure out how to say it without sounding unduly serious.

"Hey, Parr," he says with a troublemaker's grin, "I'm not gonna forget it. I wouldn't miss this one for anything."

I wake up the morning of the baptism to the sound of a hard rain—the sort of downpour that usually waits until midday. My first thought is that my hair looks awful in any sort of humidity. My second thought is that I'm going to have trouble getting a cab and that the only time I really hate the subway is when it rains. My third thought is that Annie's plan to have the baptism in Central Park is now off, and the rain plan is to hold the ceremony in her living room. Her *tiny* living room. Inviting Richard suddenly seems like a very bad idea. It's one thing to bring a guest to an outside, public venue. It seems very much another to bring one to a small Manhattan apartment.

It's too late to change my game plan, though, so I shower, dry my hair, and put on the outfit that Jess has laid out for me: one of her own, vintage black Diane Von Furstenberg wrap dresses. (Dresses are one of the few things Jess and I can share.) Jess also bought me a new pair of shoes—an early birthday present—a pair of Manolos with an army-green heel and ankle straps made of black and green fabric. I stand in front of the mirror, carefully put on my makeup and spritz on my perfume.

Except for the fact that I am somewhat overdue for highlights, I am pleased with the finished result. I look good but not so good as to look desperate to impress. After all, I really don't feel the need to impress Ben, a man who has seen me at my absolute worst. Yet I also don't like the idea of showing up worse than he remembers me. I call Jess into my room to get her final approval.

"You look *awesome*," she says, beaming. "Somewhat conservative and understated but with loads of style. If Tucker comes, she's going to be insanely jealous. I mean, she might even develop a girl crush."

I laugh and say, "What about accessories?"

"I was just getting to that. I think you should go simple. You don't want to look like a trend whore in her twenties. Just put on your blue opal ring and your pearls. That's it."

I nod and say, "What purse should I bring?"

"I'll get you my Dior clutch. It's perfect. And don't forget your big tortoiseshell sunglasses."

"But it's raining," I say.

"It might stop. Be prepared."

I take a deep breath, exhale, and say, "Jess, thank you. I love my shoes. I love *you*."

She laughs and says, "Just try to have fun. Smile a lot. Touch Richard on the arm as much as possible. Hell, touch Ben on the arm as much as possible."

She leaves to retrieve her clutch just as Richard calls.

"Okay. I got my crotchless chaps on," he says. "Is that okay with you?"

I laugh and say, "By definition, aren't chaps crotchless?"

"You have a good point. Wear a hat, and no one will notice."

He then informs me that he's going to swing by and pick me up in a cab. Problem solved on the transportation front. I think of how I always handled logistics with Ben. I was the designated airline ticket holder, for example. He would inevitably lose them. Or at least he would panic and *think* that he had lost them. I can see him now, wide-eyed, furiously patting his pockets and scrambling in his bag, convinced that they were gone. We had once joked that it was a good thing that we didn't have kids. Because Ben would surely leave the baby on the subway.

Richard interrupts my thoughts with an offer of Starbucks for the ride. "I'm picking one up for myself," he says. "This is the earliest social engagement I've ever had."

I envision a disastrous spilling scenario—it would be just my luck—and tell him *no, thanks.* Fifteen minutes and a final pep talk from Jess later, I am out the door. Richard has already arrived in a cab with his iced coffee.

He leans across the seat and opens my door. I slide in and say, "Hey! Where are your crotchless chaps?"

"Changed my mind," he says, kissing my cheek. "Hmmm. You smell nice . . . Let me guess—the ex-hubby's favorite perfume?"

I smile and tell him the truth. "His second favorite."

"Ahh. Strategic. If you pick his favorite, you'll appear to be pandering. Still thinking about him. If you pick his least favorite, you'll look spiteful . . . which would also indicate that you are still thinking about him."

I laugh, because his analysis is spot-on. It's so nice to be with a man who has no instinct for jealousy. As a result, I feel I can tell Richard anything.

"Guilty as charged," I say.

"So," Richard says, smirking. "Anything off the limits of discussion today?"

I tell him he should probably stay off the topic of divorce and babies. "Which includes, of course, getting a divorce *because* of babies. Other than that, go for it."

We head uptown to Annie and Ray's, hitting almost no traffic and arriving exactly on time. Richard pays for our cab, and we dart out of the backseat, umbrellaless, into the lobby where he tosses his empty coffee cup into a trash can. Annie and Ray buzz us up, and we climb the stairs, finding the door open a crack.

"Hello?" I say as I wipe my feet on their sisal mat. My heart is pounding at the thought of Ben being on the other side.

"Come in! Come in!" I hear Annie trill.

I push open the door and put my gift—an engraved silver cup—on a table in the front hall. I look in the living room, and see that we are among the first guests to arrive. I feel an odd mix of disappointment and relief when I see no sign of Ben. For the first time it occurs to me that perhaps he's not coming. Maybe he's avoiding me. Maybe he's out of town. Maybe he's vacationing with Tucker. Maybe I should have just asked Annie.

"Claudia, honey!" Annie squeals. She is holding Raymond Jr. at her hip, but hugs me with her free hand. I can't believe how much he's changed in just a few months. He has moved beyond the tiny, chicken-legged newborn stage and is now in the alert, chunky, Gerber-baby stage. Babies are such a tangible reminder of the quick passage of time, but I resist the urge to comment on how much he's grown. I don't want to highlight what a neglectful friend I've been.

"Hey, Annie!" I say, kissing my friend's cheek before I turn my attention back to her son. He is wearing a cream linen jumper with a Peter Pan collar that is probably more expensive than most of my outfits. Annie is like a European when it comes to clothing—she has very few items in her closet, but all of them are extremely high quality.

I raise my voice a few octaves and say, "Hi, there, Raymond!"

I always feel self-conscious, almost foolish, when I talk to babies or very young children to whom I'm not related. Raymond scowls and looks away, burying his face in his mother's shoulder with an accompanying death grip to her elbow. It's as if he knows the truth about me—that I ended my marriage to avoid one of him. Don't they say babies and dogs can sense things about people?

Annie glances eagerly in Richard's direction just as I say, "Annie, I'd like you to meet my friend Richard. Richard—this is Annie and Raymond."

Richard says, "It's so good to meet you, Annie." Then he pats Raymond on his bottom, making that rustling Pampers sound. "Hey, buddy! How you doin'?"

Raymond Jr. holds firm. He will not be tricked.

"Nice to meet *you*, Richard," Annie says, her eyes flickering with curiosity. I offered her no details over the phone, nor did she ask me any questions. I could tell it took all of her willpower to not delve beyond, "So? Things are good?" I told her that they were. Now I have my proof: a distinguished, older man.

Richard and Annie make small talk, which consists mostly of Annie asking Richard a series of questions. *What do you do? Oh, so you work together? How long have you been there? Where are you from?* He answers pleasantly, though minimally, and asks a few questions of his own as Ray joins us with a "Well, well, what have we here?" look on his face.

I can tell right away that Ray does not approve of my guest. Which could mean a variety of things. It could mean that he is sad that his dear friends are no longer together. It could mean that he is feeling protective of Ben. Or it could mean that he thinks I'm sort of a jerk for introducing any hint of controversy into his son's special day. I am starting to feel as if the latter is most likely.

I wonder if Annie gave Ray any advance warning. Surely she did. Then again, I'm sure she's had other things on her mind, like the all-encompassing care of a new baby. Perhaps she is so consumed with her son that she and her husband rarely find time to talk anymore.

I watch Ray introduce himself to Richard with what appears to be an aggressive handshake. Then he turns to me and says, "Good to see you, Claudia." There is something aloof in his expression, and I find myself thinking that our friends could be taking sides. Ben's side.

"Nice to see you, too," I say. "Congratulations on Raymond's big day."

Annie fills the ensuing lull with a beverage offer. Richard

glances over at the makeshift bar set up on the other side of the room and tells Annie thanks, but he'll just help himself. "Does anyone want anything?"

I spot a half-dozen bottles of champagne set up like trusty soldiers and nod. It is only eleven, but I am definitely ready for a drink. "Whatever you're having is fine," I tell Richard, knowing how couple-y my words are.

Ray's face suddenly lights up as he belts out an "Uncle Ben's in the house!"

I inhale sharply but keep my eyes straight ahead, fixed on Raymond Jr. I know it's not possible for a six-month-old to know what's going on, but I swear that baby of Annie's turns, sneers at me, and then smiles at Ben who I can feel standing directly beside me. Close enough for him to smell my perfume —because I am breathing in his natural scent—one that I didn't quite realize Ben had. Sort of like coming home after a long vacation and realizing that your apartment really *does* have a unique smell.

Ben leans in to kiss the top of Raymond's head. He makes no comments about how much the baby has grown. Clearly he's come around a time or two.

Then he turns to me and says, "Hi, Claudia."

I exhale and allow myself to make one second of eye contact. He looks exactly the same. He looks like Ben. My Ben.

"Hi," I say. My voice sounds funny, and I feel a sudden shot of weakness. Physical weakness where my knees feel as if they might give. I try to smile, but can't. I'm not sure what to do with my hands. I wish I already had my drink. Annie and Ray exchange a glance and then slip away to greet other guests.

"How are you?" I manage to say as my eyes fall on Ben's bare left ring finger.

"I'm fine. You?" he says.

I tell Ben I'm fine, too, as I watch Richard out of the corner of my eye. He turns, observes me with Ben, and then turns back toward the window, a flute of champagne in each hand. He sips from one. He must know that I'm talking to my ex-husband.

"It's good to see you," Ben says sincerely.

"You, too," I say. It is.

"I'm glad you came," he says. "I wasn't sure if you would."

I glance at Richard again who is still staring out the window.

"I wasn't sure *you'd* come," I say.

"Oh, well, I'm actually Raymond's . . . uh, godfather," he says earnestly.

"Oh. I didn't know," I say. "What an honor."

"Yeah," Ben says. "It is pretty cool."

I smile as I feel an insane rush of what feels pretty close to high school jealousy. Like the feeling I had when my best friend Pam was elected to the homecoming court. We were so connected at the hip—we even looked alike. People always asked if we were sisters, even twins. So why was she chosen over me? I feel the same way now as I wonder why Annie and Ray gave Ben the nod—and not me? Is it because I don't want children? Is it because they're taking Ben's side? Is it because I've been a bad friend? Or maybe they were just more hard up for a godfather than a godmother. After all, neither Ray nor Annie has a brother.

At this point, Richard moves away from the window to make small talk with a man I don't recognize. I think, *Good, I have another minute.* Even though I'm not sure what to say next.

And then it comes out. My stellar question: "So you didn't bring Tucker?"

I instantly regret my choice. First of all, he *obviously* didn't bring her because she's not here. Second, I look nosy and petty and jealous.

"No," Ben says, a half-smile on his face. "I did not."

It occurs to me that the only possible advantage to my question would be if it actually cleared up the status of Ben's affairs, but his answer gives me nothing. So I am merely left with that foot-in-the-mouth feeling.

At this point, I see that Richard has finished up with his new friend. He looks over at me again, brows raised, as if to say, *No pressure, but should I join you?* I nod. Any other response would be rude, even to go-with-the-flow Richard. Then, just as Richard is walking across the room to join us, Ben says, "I see that you came alone, too."

One beat later Richard is next to me, handing me my champagne. It is an unmistakable gesture, but Ben looks confused, as if he's trying to place Richard. Which he can't do because they've never met.

I have no real choice but to say, "Ben, this is Richard Margo. Richard, Ben Davenport."

"Hi, Ben. Nice to meet you," Richard says.

I watch a cloud pass over Ben's face as he processes the name. I know that he does not forget my "Top Five Office List." He knows *exactly* who Richard is, and he's not happy about it. Sure enough, Ben does not extend his hand. Instead he flinches, his expression becoming very blank. Several seconds pass before he offers a very chilly, "How do you do." He cuts his eyes back at me. He knows that I know the significance of his *how do you do.*

It is what Ben's mother, Lucinda, said to her ex-husband's second wife, a woman who had everything to do with the breakup of her marriage. For years, Lucinda had agonized over what she would say to wife number two when she finally had the misfortune of meeting her. She refused to be rude. Yet she refused to tell a lie with a standard salutation like, *it's a pleasure to meet you.* Ben remembers his mother being downright triumphant when she realized that a curt *how do you do* fit the bill. Ben told me the story right before I met her. Told me that I should worry if I got a *how do you do.* But otherwise, I could assume she liked me.

Of course Richard is oblivious to this tale as he says, "Not too bad. You?"

Ben answers Richard with what my niece Zoe could interpret as sarcasm. "Super," he says, flashing a fake smile. Then he excuses himself and makes a beeline for his godson. As he scoops up the baby from Annie's arms, he turns and glares at me. The significance of *that* is not lost on me, either.

A miserable hour of mingling later, the ceremony, led by a female, Birkenstock-wearing minister named Sky, begins. I am not surprised by the hippie feel to the service, given the fact that we are in a living room rather than a church—and given Annie and Ray's religious background. They both grew up Catholic but each separately denounced the church in their early twenties for a variety of reasons, most of them political. They then went through their agnostic stage, which lasted for some time. Annie says they're becoming more spiritual since having Raymond Jr. and have begun to attend a Unitarian church on Second Avenue.

In any event, the minister spends a good amount of time talking about lofty concepts such as the inherent worth and dignity of every person; justice and compassion in human relations; the search for truth; and respect for the inter-dependent web of all existence of which we are a part. Along the way, she stops and asks the godparents if they will fully support and guide Raymond Jr. in the pursuit of these goals. My eyes are fixed on Ben as he nods solemnly and repeats, "I will," in unison with Annie's sister. Watching him, I can't help but think of our exchange of vows in the Carib-bean. How seriously Ben took them. And how seriously he's now taking his role of godfather. Then, when I think I can finally turn and escape to the buffet, Annie announces that the godparents would each like to read a prepared message for Raymond Jr.

Annie's sister speaks first, reciting a Langston Hughes poem called "Dream." Then it is Ben's turn. He clears his throat and gazes lovingly at the baby. I feel Richard's hand on my back as I look down at my new shoes and listen to Ben say in a loud, clear voice, "Raymond, I am so happy and proud to be your godfather. My wish and prayer for you is that you will be a person of character and integrity . . . That you will be strong yet gentle . . . That you will be honest yet forgiv-ing . . . That you will be righteous but not self-righteous . . . That you will always follow your heart and do good and beau-tiful things in the world. Amen."

I feel a wave of devastating sadness as I consider what a wonderful father Ben will be. How lucky his son or daughter will be. How glad and grateful another woman will someday be that I felt the way I did about having children. *Don't look at him,* I tell myself. But I do anyway. I can't help it. And maybe it's my imagination, but as I study Ben's face, I am pretty sure he is just as sad as I am.

"I should never have brought Richard to that party," I say to Jess after I've returned home and given her the full rundown.

"I'm sorry," Jess says. "But if it helps, I still think you did the right thing."

"How do you figure?" I say, unbuckling the ankle straps of my beautiful Manolos that I'm almost positive Ben failed to notice.

"Because," she says, "you showed him you moved on."

"But he hates me now."

"He doesn't *hate* you."

"You didn't see the look he gave me. He hates me."

"So he hates you. So what?"

"I don't want him to hate me."

"Yeah, you do. You want him to care enough about you to hate you. If he had sat there at the party yucking it up with Richard, you'd be feeling worse right now."

I grant her the point, but then say, "I feel like such a jerk for doing that to him."

"Claudia, you brought your boyfriend to a party. Big fucking deal. You know Ben's dating, too."

I twist my opal ring around my finger and sigh. "I don't like hurting his feelings. I feel as if I did it . . . deliberately. I don't think he would have done that to me."

"Look. It's not like you left him for Richard. *He* left *you*. He left you *hoping* that he'll meet another woman so that he can get her pregnant and have a family. Keep that straight in your head."

I nod. She's right.

"So no more feeling guilty," she says. "Okay?"

I nod again, thinking that that is way easier said than done. And I'm beginning to see that I might be feeling guilty for more than bringing a man to a party.

eighteen

Jess is three days late getting her period and is vacillating between panic and jubilation. I know all about Jess's pregnancy "scares." She's probably had about a hundred since I've known her. In fact, one of the first conversations we ever had was in the bathroom on our freshman hall. She emerged from a stall, pumping her fist, announcing, "I got my period!" I laughed and told her congratulations, feeling in awe of a girl who would be so open with a virtual stranger.

Jess has mostly been on the pill since that incident at Princeton, but she consistently forgets to take it. She'll look down at her packet of pills and exclaim, "Shit! What's today? Wednesday?" and notice that the last white pill to be poked through foil is marked "Sunday." At this point, she typically swallows three down at once. I always tell her the same thing: *Take the thing at the same time every day. Put it by your toothbrush. Leave a note on your mirror.*

But she doesn't. Or won't. Instead, she carries the pills around in her purse, forgetting to switch them with her choice of handbag. Then there are the times when she fails to fill the prescription altogether. Or the times when she is, in her words, "giving her body a break."

I think subconsciously—or maybe even consciously—Jess enjoys the drama. There is no other explanation for why such an intelligent woman would behave so haphazardly. She must thrive on our conversations about what she (we) will do if, this time, she really is pregnant. Will she have it? Will she get an abortion? Will she have it and put it up for adoption? The answer changes according to the guy, the time in her life, the wind.

Although I must say, this time seems different. This time Jess really wants the baby. Or maybe she just wants Trey. She continues to dance around a full-on confession, but all facts indicate that Jess *tried* to get pregnant. She apparently "forgot" to tell Trey that she hadn't renewed her pill prescription. And she's "pretty sure" that she had sex with him on day fifteen of her twenty-nine-day cycle.

I can tell that she believes that Trey will be with her if she's pregnant with his baby. I, on the other hand, am absolutely certain that Trey is going nowhere. He will not leave his wife. Nor will he even *tell* his wife. In fact, knowing Jess's luck (although it's hard to use the word *luck* when someone is utterly self-destructive), it would turn out that Trey's wife is pregnant also. I can just imagine the two babies being born in the same month. Maybe even on the same day. They will grow up on separate coasts with no knowledge of the other. Or at least Trey's legitimate son will have no knowledge of his father's illegitimate daughter. Jess likely will tell her daughter the truth about everything at a suitable age (an age we will debate for years). Then the two offspring will attend the same college and meet in their freshman composition class. He will fall in love with her, at which time she will be forced to tell him the truth about their father.

None of it would surprise me. Nothing *ever* surprises me when it comes to Jess.

On the third night of Jess's missed period, we go get sushi at Koi, a restaurant on Second Avenue near her apartment, even though it is Friday night, and we both had planned to go to separate parties. I'm too tired, and Jess says she has no interest in partying when she can't drink.

"C'mon, Jess. Do you *really* think you're pregnant?" I say, as I break apart my chopsticks.

Jess rattles off her symptoms. She says she's been exhausted and bloated. She says her boobs feel heavy and sore. She says she can just tell. She knows.

I look at her, thinking I've heard it all before. I say, "First, you *know* that those are also premenstrual symptoms. Second, you are a hypochondriac who *wants* to be pregnant. You're going to feel things."

"I'm not a hypochondriac," Jess says indignantly.

"Yeah, you are," I say. "How about the time we went camping and you just *knew* that you had Lyme disease? You actually joined an online support group for victims!"

"Yeah. I had all the symptoms," she says. "That was so weird."

"You *thought* you had all the symptoms."

She dabs her napkin to her lips and says, "Well. I think we should get a test after dinner."

I sigh and say, "How many dollars do you think you've spent on those tests?"

"I'm telling you. This time feels different."

"Okay," I say. "So tell me. What will you do if you're pregnant and Trey still won't leave his wife?"

"He will."

"But what if he doesn't?"

"I'd still have the baby," she says as she dips a California roll in soy sauce. She has already announced that she is staying away from raw fish. Just in case. "I'd just be a single mother. Lots of people do it."

"Would you keep working full-time?"

"Of course. I love my job."

"So you'd get a nanny?"

"Or two," she says.

I almost say, "What's the point of having a kid then?" but something stops me. Something that tells me that the *last* thing I should be doing is judging another woman's decision with respect to the subject of children.

On our walk home, Jess ducks into a bodega and buys a pregnancy test. She scans the back of the box and informs me that she will wait until the morning because results are more accurate then. I look at her skeptically, knowing that there is literally no way that she will resist testing tonight. In fact, I'm putting the over-under at about an hour upon our return.

I start to think that I might be wrong when I hear Jess on the phone, spewing investment-banking jargon. Something about discount rates and exit multiples. She might as well be speaking Portuguese as far as I'm concerned. Then I hear her say, "Look, Schroder. This isn't rocket science. If you want rocket science go work for NASA. Now. Just get me the presentation by tomorrow morning and get it to me in a fucking font big enough for that geriatric board of directors to read!"

I smile and tell myself that there's no way Jess is pregnant. Despite all her wishes for a baby, I just can't fathom it. At least not right now.

But minutes later, she bursts into my room, plastic stick in hand. I sit on my bed and try to catch my breath.

"Look. A cross," she says, presenting me the plastic stick. Her hands are trembling.

"You're pregnant?" I ask, still in disbelief. Never mind the scientific results before me.

"I'm going to have a baby," Jess says, looking teary. The happy kind of teary. The standing on the Olympic podium, mouthing words to "The Star-spangled Banner" kind of teary.

"Wow," I say, sitting on the edge of my bed. "I can't *believe* it."

"Neither can I," Jess whispers.

"Did you call Trey?"

"Yeah. He didn't answer."

"Did you leave a message?"

"Uh-huh. I said it was important . . ." Her voice trails off.

"How do you feel?" I ask.

"Scared," she says. "Overwhelmed . . . But happy."

I hug her as I whisper congratulations. We separate, staring at each other, then down at the stick, then back at each other.

"What are *you* thinking?" she asks after a minute more of silence.

I shake my head, feeling a wave of jumbled, crazy emotion. Mostly I am afraid for my best friend. I know how hopeful she is, how badly she wants things to work out with Trey, and how devastated she will be when reality sets in over the next nine months. I also can't help but feel a twinge of anger at Jess for doing this to herself, for going about motherhood this way. I resent her for making bad decisions in her life, and can't help but consider how those ill-advised decisions will impact me and my life. I didn't want a baby with Ben, my *husband*, so I certainly don't want one with a friend. But how awful would I be to move out when my friend is pregnant and needs me?

How awful would I be to intentionally distance myself at such a critical juncture?

Then, buried beneath all of the obvious reactions is this other strange pang. This worry that if I do move out and separate myself from Jess and her baby, I will be sidelined. Left out of something extraordinary. That Jess's life will become so much *more* than my life. It is almost as if I'm *jealous* of her. Which is insane because obviously I do *not* want a baby. *I do not*.

I start wondering what I always wonder when I have irrational, uncontrollable emotions of any kind: *Is it normal to feel this way? Do other people feel wistful over something they don't want in the first place?* I hope that the answer is yes, as there is always something comforting about knowing that you are not alone. That other people feel the way you do. That you are a bit screwed up, but still *normal*.

Jess reclines on my bed, staring up at the ceiling, as I scramble to come up with an analogy, something that will make sense of the way I'm feeling. My mind lands on my first love, Charlie, whom I occasionally run in to when I'm back in Huntington. Charlie is a firefighter in my hometown—which means he spends his weekdays rescuing stray dogs and cats and teaching fire safety at our old elementary school. He spends his weekends watching Jets games and chain-smoking Camel Lights with his high school buddies and playing in the backyard with his four kids. I would wager that Charlie doesn't own a passport and hasn't read a book since graduation. In short, his life is nothing like mine—and life with Charlie would never have been enough for me. But when I see him, I still feel a small burst of longing remembering the way it felt to be sixteen, emerging from a movie theater on a warm summer night and then parking in Charlie's car while we made out and listened to his cassette mix of love songs. And yet I do not confuse these feelings for actually wanting to be with Charlie.

I don't want a baby, either, but I feel a pang anyway. A very small pang, but still one that makes me blurt out to Jess, "If I had known this were going to happen . . ."

Jess's eyes widen. She says my name slowly, as a question.

"What?" I say innocently.

"Are you having second thoughts?"

"About what?" I say.

"About Ben? About having a baby? About having Ben's baby?" she says, looking concerned, suspicious, and hopeful all at once.

"No," I say emphatically. "Don't be ridiculous. No second thoughts here."

"Well, I guess that's a good thing," Jess says slowly. "Because if you *were* having second thoughts, your life would be, like, ten times more fucked up than mine is right about now."

I look at her and say again, "No second thoughts here."

The next morning I stay in bed, reading *Wuthering Heights* for about the fiftieth time. It is my favorite book of all time. And I think I love it even *more* now that my own relationship has ended. In a perverse way, I almost enjoy feeling as tormented as Cathy was over Heathcliff.

I find my favorite lines and read aloud to myself: "My great thought in living is himself. If all else perished, and *he* remained, I should still continue to be . . . He's always, always in my mind—not as a pleasure . . . but as my own being."

I sigh and flip to another clutch passage: "Because misery

and degradation, and death, and nothing that God or Satan could inflict would have parted us, *you*, of your own will, did it. I have not broken your heart—*you* have broken it; and in breaking it, you have broken mine."

Then, just as I'm getting all riled up in the satisfying, melodramatic throes of passion and despair, I think of how, early in our relationship, Ben read the book at my insistence. His first words when he finished the book were: "Well. That Heathcliff is a real laugh a minute, huh?" I smile, remembering how I laughed then.

And in that instant, my cell phone rings. I irrationally expect it to be Ben calling, but when I look down at the screen on my phone, I see that it's just Daphne. I answer, and she asks me what's new. It's not until that second that I process how bad it will be when she finds out about Jess. I take the path of least resistance and tell her nothing is new at all. Jess can share the news herself. I'm not going to unless I absolutely have to.

"What's going on with you?" I deflect.

"Oh, not much," she says.

"Did Tony's results come in?" I ask.

"Yeah," she says. "They did."

"And?"

"He's fine. No problems at all," she says, her voice sounding strangely high-pitched and happy. It occurs to me that maybe she is pregnant, but I don't dare ask. Instead I keep the conversation safe and say, "So what else is going on?"

"Oh, you know, just getting back in the swing of the school year . . . Working on some new bulletin boards and stuff."

"That's good," I say. "Your bulletin boards are amazing."

"Aww. Thanks, Claudia," she says.

There is a long pause and then Daphne says, "So, Claudia, do you think you can come over for dinner tomorrow? Around seven? I want to make you my lasagna."

"Is Maura coming?" I ask.

"No."

"Mom or Dad?"

"No. Just you. I thought it would be fun!" she says.

"Sure, Daph," I say, concluding that she's probably not pregnant. If she were, she'd likely invite us all over. But the way my life is going, I'm pretty sure that some baby talk will be involved.

The next evening I take the train to Huntington. As I step down from the platform, I see Daphne waving at me from her bright yellow Mini-Cooper. I walk toward her and can see something in her face that looks unnatural and exaggerated. Like a beginning actress *pretending* to be happy.

When I get to the car, I say, "Hey, Daph!" recognizing the false cheer in my own voice. I realize that it's mighty difficult to act normal when someone else is behaving oddly.

We make small talk on the drive back to her house, discussing her kids at school. She also tells me, in terms that go way beyond effusive, how much she adored Amy Dickerson's novel. She says she selected it for her book club even though they usually stick with chick lit.

"The girls are going to *love* it," she says. "It's just so . . . thought-provoking."

I glance at Daphne, thinking that it is quite possibly the first time Daphne has ever referred to her thoughts as being *provoked*. My sister is not at all dumb, but she is far from introspective.

218

When we get to her house, Daphne clicks open the garage door. I see Tony's black minivan parked inside and mentally rule out marital problems. At least anything imminent. Then again, this strange brand of chipperness would not really make sense in the context of divorce. Something else is going on.

"Home again, home again, jiggity jig!" Daphne says with a nervous laugh. It is what my father says every single time he pulls into our garage. Daphne picked the habit up. Maybe I would, too, if I had a garage to pull into.

I follow Daphne into the kitchen, say hello to her two yapping Yorkies, Anna and Gary, and survey a hearty spread of crab puffs made from English muffins and a lot of butter. Daphne is not a fancy cook—she just does the basics exceptionally well. Tony is sitting at the counter watching a baseball game, but when he sees us, he stands, walks over to me and kisses me on the cheek. "It's *wonderful* to see you, Claudia!" he says, sounding as stilted as my sister.

"It's *wonderful* to see you, too, Tony," I say.

Daphne turns down the volume on the TV and says sweetly, "Could you please turn the music back on, honey?"

He obliges, as I say, "Wow, Daph. Crab puffs. What's the special occasion?"

She gives me an innocent expression. "No special occasion. I—we—just wanted to have you over. That's all. Right, Tone?"

"Uh-huh," Tony says. "That's right."

I can feel myself grinning. "Uh-huh."

"What?" Daphne says innocently.

I laugh. "Something is going on here."

Daphne and Tony exchange an unmistakable glance.

"Would you like a glass of wine?" Daphne says. "We have white and red."

"Uh-huh. And let me guess what you have in the fridge. Chocolate mousse for dessert?"

Her eyes grow wide. "How did you know?"

"Because I know that *you know* that chocolate mousse is my favorite . . . So, Daphne, just tell me what's going on here. I mean—do you need to borrow money?"

I instantly regret my joke. My sister has never asked to borrow money from me, but things are frequently tight for her and Tony and maybe they *do* need some money for fertility treatments. Just in case, I add, "It's not like I have anything to spend my salary on now that I'm alone!"

Tony laughs. "Well, yeah, actually I could use some cash. Do you have an extra five grand lying around? I'd love a new set of golf clubs. Or a motorcycle," he says, making the revving hand motion of a biker.

"You're not getting a motorcycle! They're too dangerous," Daphne says, lapsing into her normal self for one second. Then she says to me, "Don't be silly. We don't need any money. But thank you. *Thank* you for offering. You are such a *generous, caring* sister."

I laugh and say in a hillbilly accent, "Okay. Listen, missus, I want my sister back. What did you do with my sister?"

Daphne gives me her best Stepford Wife expression and says, "I have no idea what you mean by that." Then she turns, wipes her hands on her apron, and busies herself with a Screwpull wine opener, Ben's Christmas gift to Tony years ago when we first began our Secret Santa name draw. I can't believe it stuck around longer than he did. I sit at the counter next to Tony and help myself to a crab puff. It is sheer perfection.

"Okay," I say. "Have it your way. I'm just happy to be getting the star treatment. These crab puffs are *divine*."

Daphne slowly pours three glasses of red wine, and when she finally turns back around, tears are streaming down her face.

Before I can ask her what's wrong, she says, "We don't want your money, Claudia . . . But we *do* want something from you."

I swallow my bite of crab puff and feel a knot in my stomach. For some crazy reason, I think that Daphne needs a kidney. Of course I will give her one of mine.

"Are you sick?" I ask, feeling weak with fear. The thought of one of my sisters dying young is simply too horrible to bear.

"No," Daphne says, her voice cracking. "I'm fine . . . But my eggs . . ."

"Your eggs?" I say, even though I know exactly what she is saying and exactly what she is about to ask me. I look at Tony. He is welling up, too. He covers Daphne's hand with one of his.

"I had my tests last week . . . and our doctor told us that my eggs are no good," she says, sobbing now. "They are, like, total *shit*."

"Daph . . . I'm so sorry," I say, standing to hug her.

She holds up her hand to stop me and then continues, "So Tony and I . . . were wondering if . . . if we might have one of yours?"

nineteen

"So why didn't they ask your other sister?" Richard asks me after I've told him the whole story about Daphne's worst fears coming true. About all of the tests. About the somber meeting with their doctor and his news that even in vitro with Daphne's eggs would be a waste of time and money. I hadn't planned on telling Richard the story, but I feel like I need to tell someone, and I don't want to discuss the topic with Jess. She's sensitive enough about her aging eggs as it is. Besides, Richard and I have just had sex, and I am feeling that surge of closeness, that urge to confide in a man who has just made me come. Twice.

Richard runs his hand through my hair and says, "Doesn't Maura seem to be the more logical choice since she's already had kids?"

I nod and say, "They had a few reasons for picking me . . . First, I'm younger. Better eggs, I guess. Second, I think they think it'd be too weird—you know, if they used Maura's eggs, then the kids would be cousins *and* siblings. Or at least half siblings."

"That would be sort of weird," Richard says.

"And the final unspoken reason," I say, "is that Maura would never agree to it."

"Why not?"

"She can be . . . a bit selfish," I say, instantly regretting the comment. I feel disloyal—and I don't want Richard's opinion of Maura to be colored before he even meets her.

"Selfish how? Like stingy with her time? Like she won't go pick a friend up at the airport kind of selfish?" he asks, pushing a piece of hair behind my ear.

"No . . . Maybe self-centered is more accurate. She means well, but I think she gets her sense of empathy from my mother," I say. "My mother will bitch for ages about the fact that Chanel discontinued a certain shade of lipstick, but then she'll expect a cancer patient to just . . . buck up and think positively . . ."

"Yeah. I know the type," Richard says. "But for the record, I don't think it would be all that selfish to turn this request down. I mean, that's a *lot* to ask."

"You think?" I ask.

"Well. Yeah," Richard says. "Sisters or not. It's *huge*."

I was hoping he'd say just this because I agree—it *is* a lot to ask. Still, I wonder if Richard is just saying so for my benefit.

"So what did you tell her?" he asks.

"Nothing yet. I told them I needed to think about it."

"Were they okay with that?"

"Yeah. They seemed to be. Daphne said she understood. Tony thanked me for even considering it. Then we dropped the subject and enjoyed Daphne's lasagna. Or at least I pretended to enjoy it, when all I could feel was the knot in my stomach."

"So would you and Tony have to get it on?" Richard says as he playfully grabs my left breast.

"Very funny," I say, pushing his hand away.

"Well? Would you?"

223

I roll my eyes and say, "Don't be stupid . . . There would be a surgery. An egg-removal sort of deal. Just like with in vitro."

"You'd have to have *surgery*?" Richard says, wincing.

I am thinking that men are such babies about pain, but I say, "That's the least of it."

"What's the most of it?" he says.

I think for a moment and then answer hesitantly, "If I have a baby out there in the world, I think I'd think of it as *mine*."

Richard blinks and then reaches past me for his glass of wine resting on the nightstand. "You'd *think* of it as yours? Or you'd *want* it to be yours?"

"Is there really a difference?" I say, thinking that in that sense, my eggs and my ex-husband might have a little something in common.

We fall asleep shortly after that, but then wake up sometime in the middle of the night, starting a full-blown conversation. It is a phenomenon that only occurs in the beginning of a relationship, when sleep seems to matter little. We are talking about Steven Gaines's radio show in the Hamptons— and how we should try to get one of my authors on—when Richard blurts out a question about my thirty-fifth birthday. I have not told him a thing about my upcoming birthday, which is now only two weeks away. I try to remember if there was a time in recent years when people at work went out for drinks for my birthday. I don't think it's happened since my thirtieth. I'm not big on birthdays—although I don't dread them, either. I'm just sort of indifferent to it. I mean, *everyone* has one, *once* a year, so I fail to see what all the annual fuss is about, at least once you pass your twenty-first birthday.

"How did you know about my birthday?" I ask. "Did Michael tell you?"

"No. Michael has yet to acknowledge to me that he even knows about us."

"How'd you know, then?"

"I might have sneaked a peek at your driver's license," Richard says.

"You're very resourceful," I say.

Richard rolls toward me. "I can be resourceful . . . when I want something," he says. I can feel him looking into my eyes, in the dark.

"And what exactly do you want?" I ask, my heart racing, although I'm not sure why.

Richard doesn't answer my question, but he finds my lips and kisses me. I kiss him back, considering in what way Richard wants me. In the same lustful way I want him? Is that all I really want? Or are we more about companionship—about filling a void and passing time? Could we be falling in love? Would I ever want to be with Richard in the way I was with Ben? Would I ever want to try marriage again with anyone?

As if he is reading my mind, Richard stops kissing me abruptly and says, "Can I take you away for your birthday?"

"Yeah," I say. "I would like that very much."

"Anywhere particular you'd like to go?"

"Anywhere with you would be just fine," I say in such a firm tone that I'm almost convinced that it is true.

In the morning, I return to Jess's apartment to get ready for work. Jess is sitting in the family room, wearing silky black underwear (Jess owns no cotton pairs) and applying lotion to her legs. The room smells of vanilla. Her hair is still wet, and spiky with gel. She looks happy and is singing Liz Phair's

"Perfect World": "I wanna be cool, tall, vulnerable, and luscious."

I think—*Well, you are* all *of those things.* Then I say, "Did the jackass call you back?"

I am, of course, referring to Trey. He is officially known as "the jackass" now. First he was "Jackass," a proper noun, but we decided he wasn't even worthy of that much and demoted him to a generic, random jackass. According to his assistant Daria, he is in Tokyo. We can tell she's lying for him. We already know that lying for her boss is part of her job description. "Tell him phones work in Asia," Jess said the last time she spoke to Daria. Apparently Daria had snorted and said, "Will do," before hanging up abruptly. Jess said it wasn't altogether clear who Daria was disdainful of—her or her boss. I said maybe Daria was sleeping with him, too. Jess didn't think it was all that funny. I made note of this: hold the jokes for a bit longer.

"Nope. No word," Jess says with a shrug. "Fuck him."

I study her face, for a sign of false bravado. There is nothing. I can tell she is starting to mean it. In fact, she is *so* strong that I begin to think that there is only one explanation: Jess wants the baby *more* than she wants Trey. Sort of the opposite of Ben and me. Could my best friend and I be more different?

"Fuck him," she says again.

I laugh and say, "That's how you got in this mess."

"Yeah. It *is* a bit of a mess," she says. "And yet . . . it feels *right.*"

Then she informs me she has scheduled her first prenatal visit for the following Thursday at two o'clock.

"That's exciting," I say, nearly meaning it.

"Will you come with me?" she asks hesitantly. "The nurse

told me that they check for the fetal heart sounds with a Doppler ultrasound. I'd like to share the moment with some-one . . . With *you*."

"Sure . . . I'll come," I say, feeling touched that she wants me there. And I want to be there with her, but I still have reservations. First, fall is our busiest season, and I can just see myself stuck in a waiting room for hours. Second, and most important, it seems to set a bad precedent. Will Jess then expect me to go to every appointment thereafter? And what about the nitty-gritty moments of childbirth? I imagine her asking me to cut the umbilical cord or photograph the emerging blood crown.

I marvel at the irony of me—a woman who does not want a baby—being asked to be an egg donor and a surrogate parent all in one month's time.

Later that afternoon, I get a call from a big-time agent, known in the business by her first name only: Coral. I don't know if Coral is her given name or a nickname of some kind, but what I do know is that she has one of the biggest egos in the business—and rightfully so, I guess. She has some *hugely* famous clients, and virtually everything Coral represents becomes a bestseller. As a result, all editors salivate at the mere *idea* of a meeting with her, and you know you're some-body if she's calling you.

About a year ago, Coral phoned me for the first time regarding a manuscript called *No Nude Beaches*. I felt as if I had really arrived as she rambled on and on about how much I was going to love this edgy but sentimental coming-of-age story about three women traveling through Europe together after their college graduation. Coral was right—I did love it—

but unfortunately so did everyone else, and I ended up losing it in an agonizing five-round auction when Elgin capped the advance I could offer at five hundred thousand. It was a heart-breaking blow, especially when the book skyrocketed to number three on the *Times* list—which is virtually unheard-of for a first-time novelist. I remember passing the book in the window display at the Union Square Barnes & Noble one evening on the way to dinner. I was so distraught, I couldn't even point it out to Ben, but he must have seen it, too, because he said, "Don't sweat it. Coral will call you again."

So of course I think of Ben when Rosemary buzzes me and says excitedly, "Claudia, Coral is on the phone!"

My heart races as I pick up the phone and say hello.

"Claudia, darling," Coral says. "Congratulations on the Dickerson novel. It's *brill*-iant!"

"Thank you, Coral. I really appreciate that. We're really pleased with how it's doing . . . So how are you?" I say, feeling pretty certain that Coral is not just calling to make small talk. She must have something for me.

"I'm well, dear . . . Listen. I'd love to catch up over lunch . . . And I *might* just have something for you to read. Something that would be *perfect* for you and your list."

"Lunch sounds great," I say, feeling thrilled but wishing that Coral would just messenger—or e-mail me—the manuscript, as most other agents do. Then again, maybe she's going to offer me an exclusive and she wants to give it a proper one-on-one showcase. I tell myself to play it cool as I say, "As for the project, thank you for thinking of me, Coral. I'd be delighted to take a look."

"Fabulous," she says. "Let's meet next Thursday at Eleven Madison Park . . . at, say, one o'clock? One-thirty?"

I glance at my calendar, see "Jess's Appointment" written in capital letters, and think, *Fuck. Baby conflict.*

"Hmm," I say. "Looks like I have something that day, Coral. I can do any other day next week."

"Sorry, dear. I'm booked solid for the next few weeks," she says, sounding miffed.

I think, *Nobody puts Coral in a corner,* and roll my eyes. I start to fold, but don't. Instead I bristle at her tactics. I am way too busy—and senior—for such games. I hear myself say, "Well, I'm sorry, Coral. But Thursday's a no-go for me."

I cross my fingers that she will throw out another date, or even better, simply offer to send the manuscript. But she only says, "A pity. Maybe next time."

I hang up and tell myself that if Coral calling you makes you somebody, then dissing her *really* makes you somebody. Then I tell myself nothing is as important as friendship. Or babies. Or friends having babies. But I can't help feeling a hint of resentment that my career is already being impacted by a baby that's not even mine.

The next morning Jess comes into my room just as I'm waking up and says, "Claudia. I'm bleeding." Her voice is calm, but her face is pinched and pale.

"Where?" I ask, picturing a cutting mishap in the kitchen.

"I got my period," Jess whispers. "I'm not pregnant any-more."

The word *miscarriage* flashes in my mind, but I shake my head and say, "Spotting is common early on." I sound as if I'm quoting a medical textbook so I add anecdotal evidence, "Maura spotted with all three of her pregnancies."

"Is *gushing* common?" Jess asks, her voice trembling.

"Claudia. I'm *definitely* no longer pregnant."

I look at my best friend, feeling afraid to speak, afraid that I'll say the wrong thing. I've heard that one-half of all women have a miscarriage at some point in their lives, but this is my first experience with it. I tell her how sorry I am. I reassure her that she will get through this. That *we* will get through this. I tell her what I always tell Daphne when her period comes— that she *will* be a mother someday. It will happen someday. I believe this.

But meanwhile, as I hear myself talking, there is a very small part of me that feels shamefully relieved by the turn of events. I am relieved not to have to go through the ordeal with Jess. I am relieved to have more time with her before she becomes a mother. But most of all, I am relieved for my best friend. I know she is grieving a loss now, but I hope that she will someday look back and think that this happened for a reason. That this was for the best. I want her to have a baby with a man much greater than Trey. A man she deserves. A man more like Ben.

twenty

I hope that my thirty-fifth birthday will stop the tide of baby talk, and the people in my life will give me that much as a gift. Instead, in the days leading up to the big benchmark, Daphne leaves messages on my voice mail, like, "Sure would be great to get those eggs soon. We could avoid amnio if we get them now!"

She, of course, is referring to the fact that most doctors recommend amniocentesis for mothers older than thirty-five, and although she pretends to be joking, I can tell she's serious. Even though I'm very freaked out by the whole concept of giving her one of my eggs, I am leaning toward telling her yes. Mostly because I just want to end my sister's pain, but also because I don't see that I have any real choice in the matter. I just can't fathom how I would tell her no.

I make the mistake of running the dilemma by Jess. The worst of her grief subsided after her doctor's visit when he confirmed that miscarriages are terribly common. He also checked her hormones and determined that everything was normal. He said there was no reason to anticipate future problems. Still, Jess's hypochondria commingles with Daphne's news and propels her into a frenzied state of high alert. She begins this crazy chatter about freezing her eggs and spends huge chunks of time at work forwarding me links on cutting-edge reproductive technology.

231

At one point, I e-mail her back and say that I have never heard so much conversation about eggs in my life, including Easter or Sunday brunch. As soon as I hit send, I worry that the joke was in bad taste or will offend her, but she shoots me back a good-natured "lol," takes the not-so-subtle hint and shifts her attention to my birthday plans. I make it very clear to her (and my sisters) that I don't want a party, surprise or otherwise. I tell her I'd just like a nice dinner out with a small group. I give her the usual names, minus Ben, plus Richard.

When Jess asks where I'd like to go, I tell her Babbo, even though it was one of my favorite spots with Ben. I am over worrying about where Ben and I went together. I want to reclaim my city. So Jess sends an e-mail out to Maura and Scott, Daphne and Tony, Annie and Ray, Richard and Michael (who, other than an elevator ride one morning, have yet to be together in my company). Everyone e-mails back that they can make it, except Ray. His excuse is that they can't find a babysitter. I don't believe him—there are plenty of baby-sitters in Manhattan—but am secretly happy that he won't be in attendance. I'd rather have Annie as a solo friend. I do not want to make the awkward "couple friends" transition.

Meanwhile, Richard is planning our three-day getaway to an undisclosed location. I don't even know whether we are going to a warm or cool climate as he has employed Jess to pack my suitcase for me. I press Jess to give me the scoop, but she holds firm in the same paternalistic way that she refuses to tell me whether a movie has a happy or sad ending. I like to be prepared when I watch a movie, in a proper frame of mind. I was so pissed after we watched *Out of Africa* together, a movie she had seen before.

"You should have told me he dies," I told Jess.

"It would have ruined it!" she said.

"But if I *want* to know, it's not ruining anything," I retorted.

Jess didn't see it my way. People who like surprises want you to like surprises, too.

So all Jess will tell me about the trip is that Richard is taking me "somewhere *really* good."

"Have I been there?" I ask.

She says no. Then she says that if I had to give up Ben, at least I had replaced him with someone like Richard.

"Nobody's *replacing* Ben," I say.

Jess gives me a look that tells me she's not so sure. "He sounds hot. I love his deep voice." Then she tries to imitate him, saying, "And Jess, uhhh, please pack her vibrator!"

"Grow up," I say.

"You," she says, her favorite comeback since college.

Only one of us wants to be a mother, I think.

The night of our group dinner, Richard offers to pick Jess and me up. I tell him thanks, but we'll just meet him there. He says fine and then takes my first drink order over the phone, which I think is a nice touch.

A few hours later, Jess and I are decked out in little black dresses. I am wearing my birthday shoes again. We take a cab downtown and are dropped off at the corner of Sixth Avenue and Waverly Place. It is a cool September night, and I regret not bringing a wrap as we walk the half block to Babbo.

"It's colder than I thought," I say, shivering.

"Are you *nervous*?" Jess asks in a teasing tone. She knows

that I always get cold when I'm nervous. "About Richard meeting everyone?"

"Maybe a little," I admit. "I want you, Maura, and Daphne to like him."

As soon as I say it, I wonder why I really care whether they approve. Maybe it's just a point of pride. And I don't want anyone missing Ben too much.

"Well, I love his voice already. Besides, if you like him, I'll like him," Jess says.

I am thinking that the reverse is far from true, but refrain from bringing up the jackass. It's been nearly a week since we've spoken of him, and I don't want to jinx the new trend. As far as I know, he still has *yet* to call her.

"Thanks, Jess," I say as another worry tugs at the corner of my mind, something I can't quite pinpoint. Maybe I just feel unsettled because I imagined my thirty-fifth birthday differently. I imagined Ben and I being somewhere alone together, dinner for two. Or at the very least, I pictured Ben in the scene.

But as Jess and I make our way into the humming carriage house, and I see my family and friends gathered at the bar, in party clothes and high spirits, my angst dissipates and I think, *Your loss, Ben.*

"Hey, guys!" I say, kissing everyone hello.

I save Richard for last, kissing him on the mouth, which feels funny to do in front of Michael, who I catch smirking at me and shaking his head.

"I can't believe you just kissed my boss," he says to me under his breath. And then, "You better get me a raise."

Richard hands me my vodka-tonic, which does not go unnoticed by my sisters and Annie.

I smile and say, "He called ahead." It is the sort of chivalrous gesture that makes other women envious, especially women who are married to men like Scott, who is, not surprisingly, on his cell phone. I ask if everyone has met. They have; Michael handled the introductions. We all make small talk until our table on the second floor is ready.

We go upstairs, and I sit between Richard and Michael. Jess sits across from me and takes charge of the wine list and conversation, two things she's very good at. After she's run her selection by everyone, and we all approve, she says, "So, Richard, I *like* you." Then she looks around the table and says, "What does everyone think of Claudia's new boyfriend?"

Michael says, "He's a helluva boss. Very fair."

Everyone laughs.

Daphne and Maura flash Richard identical smiles that say, *We don't yet know whether we like you for our sister, but we certainly think you're appealing.* Maura, especially, seems on board with my new boyfriend. She likes her men slick, smart, and sexy—and Richard is all three. It occurs to me that Scott is all three, too, and that maybe slick, smart, and sexy don't hold up as well in the matrimonial setting. But that's a moot point. After all, *I am only having fun.* And the dinner is just that. Fun and festive. Everyone is in good spirits, and the conversation rolls along smoothly, lots of funny stories, good laughs, fine wine and food.

We discuss Annie's upcoming project filming women in Afghanistan, and how hard it will be for her to be away from Raymond Jr. We chat about Maura's kids, what they are up to. And Daphne tells anecdotes about her kids at school. She has a particularly amusing tale about a note she intercepted during math class. Of course she read it. Everyone knows that teachers *always* read notes, even when they claim not to—but this just confirms that hunch.

"The funny thing," Daphne says, "is that this girl, Annabel, is the biggest teacher's pet, Goody Two-shoes you can imagine and yet there she is in the note, talking dirty to this bad boy named Josh."

Michael asks, "Fifth-grade dirty or straight-up, universal dirty?"

Richard laughs and says, "You're *dirty* for wanting to know."

Michael says, "C'mon. I wanna relive my youth here."

Daphne says, "Well, first she talks about wanting him to give her a 'titty twister' . . . and then she informs him that her AOL screen name is Bigghettobooty."

We all crack up.

"Does she have a big booty?" Annie asks.

"No!" Daphne says. "That's the most ludicrous part. She's a little wisp of a girl. A blue-eyed, wholesome-looking thing."

"But apparently, still bootylicious," Michael says.

We all laugh again, and I find myself thinking how lucky I am to have such good friends and family to help fill the void that Ben left behind.

But then, sometime between dinner and dessert, we're back to babies—*again*—when Jess announces that she is contemplating a visit to a Scandinavian sperm bank in midtown.

"A Scandinavian sperm bank?" Daphne says.

"Yeah. All the sperm come from Danish donors . . . Their slogan is, 'Congratulations, it's a Viking!'" Jess says, laughing. "They have this one ad that features a baby who is boasting about his ancestors beating Columbus to North America.

The caption reads, 'You'd better build a strong crib.' Isn't that hilarious?"

Richard, Maura, and Michael look amused; Tony and Daphne appear intrigued but skeptical; and Annie looks downright disapproving. Incidentally, Scott has missed the whole conversation as he has stepped away from the table to take *another* call. I'm not sure how I feel about the topic other than slight annoyance at Jess for bringing it up at all.

Richard and Michael start amusing themselves with some one-liners about the Danes—stuff about herring and Hagar the Horrible and Hamlet.

I can tell Annie's strident, women's studies side is about to emerge when she says, "Jess, are you *seriously* considering this?"

Jess nods. "Sure. Why not? I mean, these Danish donors are *gorgeous*. They all have the classic Scandinavian look. Tall, athletic, small nose, blue eyes, fair skin . . ."

"So, what, you're after some kind of *designer* baby?" Annie says.

"A designer baby!" Jess says, intentionally ignoring Annie's derisive tone. "That's *so* cute. Yeah. I guess that's what I'm after."

Annie continues, "Doesn't this strike you as unethical?"

"Unethical? How do you figure?" Jess says. I can tell Annie is getting on her nerves, as she often did in college.

Annie says, "Because of the stereotype that blue eyes, light skin, and height are somehow more valued. I mean, it commercializes people."

"Yeah! That's *bull*shit," Michael says, laughing. "Why aren't you checking out black sperm banks?"

Annie ignores Michael's joke and says to Jess, "I mean,

you're essentially supporting genetic engineering. *Eugenics.*"

"What's eugenics?" Daphne says.

Annie says, "It's a social philosophy that advocates selective breeding. Basically improving human traits through social intervention."

"And what's the problem with that?" Jess says.

"Yeah," Richard says. "If it can create more intelligent people, I'm all for it. Dumb folks cause a lot of problems in the world . . ."

"I totally agree," Michael says. "Idiots are always fucking things up for the rest of us."

Annie refuses to be sidetracked by jokes. "Eugenics can lead to state-sponsored discrimination . . . Even genocide."

"Oh, don't be so melodramatic," Jess says. "Because I think a little Danish baby would be cute, you're comparing me to the Nazis?"

"How much does it cost?" Daphne interjects. Tony looks at her, puzzled, as if to say, *Ain't nothing wrong with my seed, woman!*

"I'm not sure . . . It's probably pretty expensive." Jess shrugs. Money is not her issue. Then she turns back to Annie and says, "Besides, what's the difference between you picking Ray to be the father of your child and me picking Henrik the Dane to be the father of mine? It's a personal choice. It mirrors natural selection."

"Well, first of all, I didn't *pick* Ray to be the father of my child," Annie says. "I picked Ray to be my *husband*. We decided on children much later."

Now I'm annoyed at Annie, too. Her response hits a little too close to home. I cross my arms and feel myself become tense.

"Well, some people are just blessed to find a husband they love and have babies the old-fashioned way," Jess says.

"Yeah!" Daphne says. "I don't see the problem in using science to have a baby."

"I agree," Maura says, and then shoots me a worried look as if to say, *We must protect our sister here.*

Annie says, "Well, I just think this Viking sperm stuff is *creepy.*"

I find myself wondering if Annie would also think inter-familial egg donation was creepy. I bet she would. Then again, I might have to agree. It *is* sort of creepy.

"Look. I'll solve this problem once and for all," Michael says just as things are really starting to break down.

Jess looks at him and says, "How?"

Michael raises his eyebrow suggestively. "C'mon. Wouldn't you rather have a caramel baby with hazel eyes?" Then he looks at Annie and says, "And I know you'd approve of those melting-pot implications?"

Everyone laughs, including Annie, as I think, *Good ol' Michael.* You gotta love a friend who can manufacture a quality come-on during an ethical debate on eugenics.

Maura says to Jess, "I think you should take him up on that one."

Michael points at Maura and mouths, *Thanks.*

I look at Michael and say, "Thank *you.*"

I can tell Michael knows what I'm driving at—that I appreciate him changing the subject—because he winks and says, "No problem."

Annie and Jess exchange conciliatory remarks as if to acknowledge that they can have a lively disagreement and still remain friends. Even Daphne's sad expression fades as I

Emily Giffin

watch Tony put his arm around her and whisper something in her ear. She smiles. So I smile. Then I feel myself relaxing again as we turn to topics other than sperm and eggs and the orchestrated meetings between the two.

twenty-one

Later that night, after I've thanked everyone and told Richard I will see him in the morning, Jess calls me into her room and gleefully shows me the Viking baby Web site. I come very close to telling her how I wished she hadn't brought up babies at my birthday dinner, but decide against it. I know she means no harm. She can't help having an obsessive personality, a one-track mind.

She clicks on a link that brings up photos of various blond, blue-eyed donors. One of them is shown kicking a soccer ball and grinning. His name is Ian Janssen. I instantly remember that Tucker's last name is Jansen, and as I hone in on the second *s* in Ian's Janssen, it hits me that I might have spelled Tucker's name wrong during my initial Google search. I make a mental note to run another search with the extra *s*. Then I tell myself, *You will do no such thing! Do not turn into a psycho!*

I wonder what part of me will prevail in that battle—the well-adjusted, forward-looking me or the wistful, brooding, backward-looking me. Unfortunately, it's too close to call.

The next morning, just as Richard arrives in a black Lincoln Town Car, Jess hands me my luggage—her own oversized, cherry-red Tod's duffel that I love. She says, "Have fun. I know you will!"

On my way down in the elevator, I unzip the bag, peek

241

inside, and see my passport. Now I am *really* excited. Although maybe the passport is just a decoy.

When I get in the car, Richard kisses me on the cheek. He looks happy.

I say, "Jess told me where we're going."

He says, "You expect me to fall for that?"

"Yes?" I say as I remove my sunglasses from their case and slide them on.

"No."

"Fly-fishing in Colorado?"

He laughs. "You don't strike me as an outdoorsy girl."

"I'm not," I say, thinking of all the times growing up that my mother told me to get my nose out of my book and go get some fresh air.

"Good," Richard says. "Because I don't like camping. The woods itch." Then he changes expression and says, "So how annoyed were you last night? With all the baby talk?"

I consider playing it off but instead I say, "Pretty annoyed."

"I don't blame you," he says.

I give him a grateful smile and then say, "So, c'mon, where are we going?"

"I can't tell you that," he says. "But I can tell you this— I've been there a couple of times before, and I've *yet* to see a single baby on the premises."

I look at him and smile, thinking, *That was the perfect thing to say.*

An hour later we are at JFK, checking in at the first class American Airlines international counter.

"Milan?" I say, after we have our boarding passes. "I *love* Milan."

"Good to know," Richard says, "but we're not going to Milan."

Richard keeps his secret for the entire flight as we drink champagne, eat, watch a chick flick starring Kirsten Dunst, and sleep. Only after we have landed in Milan the following morning, cleared customs, and picked up our rental car, does Richard hand me a postcard of the Villa d'Este on Lake Como. I instantly recognize it, as it's a place I've been wanting to go since I was about fifteen and saw a coffee-table book filled with Helmut Newton's racy photographs taken on the villa's premises.

And I can't help but think of Ben, as Lake Como was the spot we had planned to go for our five-year anniversary. We had been "saving" it. It seemed too special for any random trip. I have revised my philosophy on saving things. There is no point. It's like my great-grandmother putting plastic on her new couch—one she didn't have a prayer of wearing out.

Of course Jess knew about these anniversary plans. So despite the fact that Richard has been to the Villa d'Este, I am highly suspicious that she had a hand in his choice. I only wonder if she was candid with Richard or manipulated him into the choice. She is fully capable of either. I decide it would be bad form to ask the question, so I just smile and say, "We're going to the Villa d'Este?"

He nods, looking pleased with himself. Then he says, "Jess said you've never been to Lake Como."

"I haven't," I say.

"I needed to fix that. It is heaven on earth. As Shelley put it, 'This lake exceeds anything I ever beheld in beauty.' "

I am a sucker for men spouting off poetry, and I can feel myself blushing as I say, "This is way too generous."

243

"Well, it's not unselfish. After all, I am going with you," he says. Then he points to a third-floor window facing the water and says, "And I intend to fuck you right in that room."

I look at him, thinking that if Ben had said he was going to fuck me somewhere, it would have sounded crass, unloving. With Richard, it is sexy. I wonder why that is, but don't come up with an answer.

Minutes later, we are driving through Italian hills. Everything is so beautiful that I don't know where to look.

"Don't you just love knowing you're in Italy?" I ask Richard.

He nods and says, "It beats the hell out of Jersey."

The ride is surprisingly short—under an hour—and we quickly come up on the little town of Cernobbio. Just beyond the town is our glamorous hotel. Richard pulls up to the main building, and a small, tidy man with a moustache opens my door before I can. As he welcomes us with a slight bow, I have the sudden thought that my expectations are too high—that Lake Como will not live up to them. But within seconds, I am relieved to find that some things really *are* that good. The grounds and gardens are magnificent; the vistas of blue mountains and misty water are breathtaking. Everything has a dreamy quality. I say this to Richard and then think that *dreamy* is a word I have never used, unless mocking someone or imitating Marcia Brady.

We walk to the front desk, as Richard says a robust American hello to everyone. I like that we are at one of the finest hotels in the world and yet he remains the same—friendly, unpretentious, borderline brash. In contrast, my demeanor changes in fancy hotels and restaurants. I can't help talking in a hushed voice and making my posture perfect.

As we check in, Richard glances up at the high ceiling and says, "Check it out."

I look up primly and then whisper, *"Ohhh.* Beautiful."

I suddenly miss Ben, as I always do when I see beautiful buildings or recall the romantic architectural language he taught me, terms like *belvedere turrets, fleur-de-lis ornaments, gingerbread bargeboard, Mary Hart arches, fretwork spandrels, voussoir vaults,* and *swan's neck molding.* I think of how much he would love this hotel and all of its exquisite detail. Maybe he can come here on his honeymoon. Try for a baby during his stay.

We are shown to our room by a young, gorgeous woman— the kind you can't stop staring at and so you certainly can't blame your boyfriend for staring, too. Which I catch Richard doing as she gracefully points out the minibar, the automatic blinds, and the safe. Then she welcomes us one final time, smiles and leaves.

When the door clicks after her, I say, "Well, she was a dog."

Richard smirks and says, "Was she? I didn't notice."

I'm not jealous at all, but I still give him a look as if I am.

He gives me a carnal look back.

I say, "Oh, yeah?"

He says, "Come here, you."

After we have sex, we nap for a couple of hours. It is an intense sleep—the kind you can only have when you are jet-lagged or sick. When we wake up, Richard says, "You think it's too cold for the pool?"

"Borderline," I say. "But let's do it."

I change in the bathroom, wondering how it is that I want privacy to change around a man I've slept with at least twenty times. Of course it took me three years to pee in front of Ben—and in the very beginning I had to run water or make him sing loudly—so I guess my modesty makes sense now. I dig into my bag and happily discover that Jess packed my most flattering bathing suit—the red bikini I last wore in St. John with Ben. It occurs to me that I never handwashed it upon our return. So it still has traces of the Caribbean on it. And maybe even a trace of Ben. I put my face up to it and inhale, but it just smells like a bathing suit I forgot to wash. No Ben. But maybe that's just because Richard's cologne is still lingering in my nose.

Richard and I spend the afternoon lounging on wooden chaises by the nicest pool I have ever seen—a rectangle of aqua blue floating right in the navy lake. The crowd is well-heeled and older, and Richard was right—there are no babies. We sip lemonade as I do a little work. I usually make a point not to work on vacations, but can't avoid it this weekend. I have a manuscript due back to an author the day I return. At one point, I laugh and tap the pages with my pen.

"That good?" Richard asks.

I nod.

He smirks and says, "You have such an eye for talent."

I can tell he's jokingly referring to himself. So I rest my hand on his bare chest, bat my eyelashes, and say, "Yes. I sure do."

He leans over and kisses me as I think, *I do not miss Ben. This is where I want to be.* Then again, there's got to be something really wrong with a person who could sit in this spot overlooking Lake Como and want to be anywhere else. The true test of a relationship would be: *Am I happy at this Motel 6 in Little Rock?*

After lunch by the pool, we play tennis on a clay court, high on a hill overlooking the property and lake. I tell Richard it almost seems like a waste to play tennis when we should be focused solely on the scenery.

He says, "Quit stalling. And prepare to be schooled."

I say, "As if."

I turn out to be right. My years of tennis lessons paid off. I am far better than Richard. He skips the serve altogether—just bounces and hits. I laugh and say, "You don't know how to serve?"

He shouts, "I'm a baseball player, honey."

I return the ball hard. He swings and misses. The ball hits chalk.

"In," I say. "Love-fifteen."

He says, "Did you just say you love me?"

I think, *Not yet,* but I say, "Uh-huh."

"Good," he shouts. "Ti *amo,* anche."

I don't know Italian but I can pretty much guess what he's just said.

That evening we have dinner on the veranda. The temperatures have dropped, but Jess packed my blue pashmina wrap. Richard is wearing a sport coat—yet he still looks more cowboy handsome than businessman handsome. We have one of our favorite discussions: who knows about us at work?

Usually Richard makes educated guesses based on elevator and lunch sightings. Tonight he says, "*Everyone* knows."

"*Nooo* . . . You think?" I say, pretending to be dismayed. I have only told Jacqueline—whom I swore to secrecy—but I secretly want everyone to know. I am proud to be dating Richard.

He nods. "*Everyone* knows."

"Nobody has said anything to me," I say.

"Nobody has said anything to me, either."

"So what makes you so sure that people know?"

He says, "I don't know . . . I guess because people generally don't comment on something they perceive to be a fling."

I nod, take a bite of my gnocchi, and scrutinize his words: *something they perceive to be*. Does this mean we're actually having something more serious than a fling? Or does this mean we are indeed having a fling? I am still analyzing his sentence back in our room after we have sex again—the hard kind that almost hurts. Long after we have said good night and rolled away from each other to sleep, I'm still not sure of Richard's intended meaning. I tell myself that it doesn't matter. It is what it is. We are what we are.

The next day is as blissful as the first, and Richard and I prove ourselves experts at lounging, eating, drinking, and having sex. In the late afternoon, we take a two-hour boat ride on the lake, passing George Clooney's house and Versace's villa; merely seeing these landmarks somehow makes me feel rich and famous, too. We stop in the picturesque village of Bellagio, known as the "pearl of the lake," where I buy a leather tote and Richard picks up a pair of handmade sandals. On our return trip, Richard strikes up conversation with several other hotel guests. He is one of those people who makes friends everywhere he goes. I decide that it is one of his best traits.

I wake up on our third and final day in Italy—which is my actual birthday—and think, *I am thirty-five. I am in striking distance of forty.* It is the first time in my life I have felt old, and it is not a good feeling.

I turn over in bed and see that Richard is already up and outside on the terrace, reading the paper and sipping coffee. He is wearing a white terrycloth robe, and for some reason I think of Richard Gere in *Pretty Woman*. Both Richards look good in white robes.

I get up and go to the bathroom where I brush my teeth and hair. Then I step outside in my own blue silk robe. Richard folds his paper in half, puts it on the table, and stands to kiss my cheek. "Good morning!" he says brightly.

"Good morning," I say, looking at the mist over the lake. "Beautiful day."

"It is," Richard says. "Great day for a birthday."

I sit, and we smile at each other.

"Coffee?" he says.

I nod, and he pours coffee from a small pitcher into my thimble-sized china cup. Then he points to the basket resting on a silver tray and says, "Continental breakfast. Are you hungry?"

"Not really," I say. "Not yet."

"Have a pastry anyway," he says forcefully. "You need your nourishment."

I shrug and then unfold the cloth napkin to discover a small unwrapped box tucked between a muffin and a croissant. It is clearly a ring box. I feel uneasy. Maybe because the last time I got a ring, I told Ben I would marry him. Maybe because the trip already feels like way too much of a gift.

"Well, looky there," Richard says.

"You shouldn't have," I say, meaning it.

He waves me off and says, "Open it."

I pluck the box out of the bread and lift the lid. Inside sits a substantial dinner ring with green and pink stones set in gold. It is the sort of interesting cocktail ring I would admire on another woman, but would never think to buy for myself.

"Wow," I say, sliding it on my right ring finger. It fits perfectly—thanks to Jess, I'm sure. "It's gorgeous."

"You're gorgeous," he says, grabbing my hand and kissing it in old-Hollywood style.

I thank Richard—which I hope encompasses the ring and the compliment. But I can't help feeling annoyed at both. They are both overkill. *Gorgeous* is simply not an adjective that applies to me. I'm attractive enough. I can even be pretty when all the pieces come together just right. But I'm not gorgeous—and I don't believe that Richard thinks I am. For the first time, I look at him and see insincerity. I can't help wondering how many women Richard has called gorgeous. I feel certain that the number is triple digits high.

"You really shouldn't have," I say again. Because I have nothing else to say.

"I *wanted* to," he says. And then, "It's no big deal."

I look at him and feel the full truth of his statement. It's really *not* a big deal to Richard. The ring. The Villa d'Este. The sex. Me. None of it is a big deal at all. I guess I knew this all along. I knew that all of this was just a matter of Richard living large. It was the sort of lifestyle I thought I wanted, too.

Still, at some point along the way, maybe on this birthday trip, I think I hoped for something more. Maybe I even hoped that I could find in Richard what I had with Ben. But it is suddenly very clear: Richard is not falling in love with me, and I'm not falling in love with Richard. We are not creating anything permanent or special. We are only having fun together.

It *is* a fling—just like he said last night—a fling with an ending yet to be determined. I feel relieved to have it defined. Relieved to know that we are both feeling the same way. But I also feel a sense of profound disappointment. In myself and in the way my life is turning out. My ring catches the sunlight as I think, *Maybe I am more like Richard than Ben. I am here because I am more like Richard than Ben.*

twenty-two

On the flight back to New York that night all I can do is ponder my relationship with Richard. I decide that giving a girl a ring when you're not in a serious relationship is sort of like giving a guy a blow job when you have no real feelings for him. It makes everything feel a little bit cheap. It cheapens the giver *and* the recipient. I don't *want* to feel this way about Richard's ring (or my blow jobs). I want to be enlightened and modern and independent and sexually liberated. I tell myself that Richard and I feel the same about each other. Nobody is using anyone—or perhaps we are both using each other equally. There is no deceit, no false pretenses. Richard is a grown man with plenty of experience, and he can decide for himself how he wants to spend his money. And I can decide for myself who I want to be intimate with. But despite my masterful rationalizing, the relationship just doesn't feel right to me anymore. Every time I look down at my new ring, I feel queasy.

By the time we land in New York and take a radio car back to the city, my mood has rubbed off on Richard, and our conversations have become noticeably strained. He has already asked me twice if something is wrong—which is far from our typical light dynamic. I tell him no both times because you can't very well tell someone who is not serious about you that you are not serious about him but that you feel somehow unsettled anyway. It's like calling an ex-boyfriend and announcing that you're over him. Or telling a boss who just fired you that you had wanted to quit for weeks. It's just . . . *weird*.

Besides, the last thing I want to appear is ungrateful. I *am* grateful. I loved our trip as much as you can possibly love a trip when you don't love the person you're with. When we pull up to Jess's apartment, I kiss Richard and thank him one final time.

He says, "I'm going to miss you tonight."

"I'll miss you, too," I say.

It is the first lie I've ever told him.

I only miss one person right about now, and his name isn't Richard.

"Well?" Jess says when I open the door. She is wearing an oversized man's undershirt and a pair of Daisy Dukes from our college days. The hem is unraveling in long strands. "How was it?"

"It was incredible," I say. "The place is breathtaking . . . and you packed perfectly. The lacy underwear came in handy . . ."

"But?" she says. A best friend can always sense a *but* coming.

"But I don't think I want to keep seeing Richard."

Jess's eyes widen and she says, "Why not? What happened?"

"I don't know," I say. "I really don't know. It was all great and fine, and then he gave me this." I hold up my ring.

She grabs my hand, identifying the gems as a pink tourmaline flanked by two peridots. Then she admits to giving

Richard my ring size, but insists that he picked it out himself. She had no input. Then she says, "Wait. I don't get it. Do you not like it or what?"

"I like it," I say.

"So what's the problem?"

"I don't know . . . The relationship—just makes me feel . . . *unmoored*."

"Un*moored*? What the hell does that mean? You read too many books."

I didn't expect Jess to understand, but I try to make her anyway. I say that Richard just feels like killing time, and killing time doesn't feel good when you're thirty-five.

"Shit," she says, wincing. "I forgot today was the *actual* day. I have your card somewhere—and another small gift . . . Happy birthday. How's it feel?"

"Not so great," I say.

"Why not?" she says.

"I feel old."

"So what? You don't want kids."

I think of the last time she told me that my age was irrelevant simply because I didn't want children. This time I say something. "I know I don't want kids . . . But that doesn't mean I don't want *anything*."

Jess looks hurt when she says, "You have me."

"I know I do, Jess," I say. "And I love you to death . . . But you know friends aren't the same thing."

She doesn't try to dispute this. Instead she says, "Well, you have Richard, too."

"Richard's not enough, either," I say. "I want more. I want what I had with Ben."

Jess inhales as though she is about to impart some wisdom

I am pretty sure she does not possess. Then she stops and just says, "Don't we all, my friend? . . . Don't we all?"

Later that night, my cell phone rings and awakens me from a fairly sound sleep. I answer with a disoriented hello.

"I expected voice mail."

It is a man's voice—and at first I think it is Richard, and then register that it is Ben.

I sit up and snap to attention. No part of me expected a call from Ben, on my birthday or otherwise. I say his name, which feels intimate because I am in bed, in the dark. I look at the clock. It is only nine.

He says, "Happy thirty-five."

"Thank you," I say. My heart is racing, and I am smiling. No, I am full-on grinning. Ben has just made me happier than any ring—or any other person—could ever make me.

"How was your day?" he asks.

"It was fine," I say. And then bravely add, "Better now."

"So," he says. "What did you do?"

I hesitate and then say, "Not too much."

I feel guilty for lying to him (Lake Como could never be construed as "not too much"). And I feel guilty because I went to Lake Como without him. I tell myself that I don't owe him the truth, and I am allowed to go anywhere with anyone I choose. But I still feel guilty.

"Annie says your boyfriend took you somewhere?" Ben says, and I can suddenly tell that he's been drinking. The boldness of the question gives something away, but beyond that, his speech is slightly slurred, all the words running together. And just as I am very good at guessing what time it is in the morning by the light coming through the window, I can pretty much guess that Ben's had five beers, six tops. What I can't tell, however, is whether he drank them alone or with Tucker.

"Oh, she did, did she?" I say, wondering whether Annie thought she was helping me out—or whether she was sabotaging me—when she passed this information along. Then I consider saying that Richard is not my boyfriend, but I'm not so sure I want Ben to have this information. It depends on whether he's with someone, which of course, I don't know. Apparently Annie's gossip only flows in one direction. Regardless of her intent, I feel on the verge of writing her off.

"So where'd you go with ol' Richard?" Ben says. "And I do mean *old*."

"Are you drunk?" I deflect. I do not want to tell him where I was.

"Maybe," he says. "I had to celebrate my ex-wife's birthday, after all."

"With Tucker?" I say, proving that, unlike Ben, I don't need five or six beers to ask immature, incendiary questions.

Ben says, "That depends on where you went with Richard?"

"Well, you either were with her on my birthday, or you weren't," I say.

"I was, in fact," he says.

"Fantastic," I say, marveling at how one person can take me from happy to agitated in seconds. In fact, I am suddenly angry enough to consider revising my stance on Richard. Maybe I'll have sex with him a few more times. In any event, I am going to wear my ring tomorrow to work.

Ben says nothing, so I say, "How did you and your girl celebrate my big day?"

"That's for me and Tucker to know," Ben says. "Just like, apparently, it's for you and *old* Richard to know the secret spot of your special celebration."

The "me and Tucker" is a knife in my chest. The pain is so sharp, in fact, that I blurt out, "Richard took me to Lake Como. The Villa d'Este to be exact. It was magnificent."

I hear a click and realize my drunk ex-husband just hung up on me, beating me to it by seconds.

The next morning I roll into work, turn on my computer, and promptly Google Tucker Janssen, complete with two ss. She is all I've thought about since about four A.M., first in the form of a disturbingly graphic dream, and then in my wide-awake, paranoid, and thoroughly pissed-off state. I am dismayed when I get six hits, but not nearly as upset as I am when I click on the first listing and pull up her grinning mug and an article in her hometown (Naperville, Illinois—I knew she was Midwestern) newspaper. The caption reads: HOMETOWN GIRL TURNED HARVARD MED STUDENT SAVES DYING MAN. The article is four years old—which means she's no longer a medical student. She's a full-fledged, *practicing* doctor. I scan the article and read her quote: "I've actually known CPR since junior high, so I didn't really apply any new skills. But the incident did lead to my decision to practice emergency medicine."

My heart drops as I grab the phone and hit my speed-dial button for Jess at work.

She answers on speaker phone with a jovial hello.

"Take me off speaker," I say with the urgency I feel.

I hear a rustle of her picking up the phone and then, "What's going on?"

"She's a *doctor*, Jess."

"What?" Jess says.

"I re-Googled her. She's an ER doctor."

"Tucker?" Jess says.

"Yes," I say, blinking back tears.

I hear Jess clicking away on her keyboard. Then she says, "Where are you seeing this?"

"Put two *s*s in Janssen," I say. "Like your sperm donor, Ian."

I hear more clicking and then, "Ohhh. Yeah. Here it is . . . Yeah, this is pretty unfortunate . . ."

I wait for something more, some pep talk about how being an editor is just as noble as practicing emergency medicine. She might be saving lives, but I'm enriching healthy lives.

Jess comes up with something else. Something better. "This doesn't prove jack. It doesn't prove they're dating. And it certainly doesn't prove that she's any good in bed."

"I need to know, Jess," I say, thinking of my conversation with Ben last night. "I need to know what's going on there."

"Okay," Jess says. "Did you try Googling their names together? In a joint search? It always pulls up married or engaged couples."

"Jesus! You think they could be *engaged*?"

"No. Calm down. I'm just saying . . . hold on . . . gimme a sec here to run this thing . . ." There is more clicking, then silence. Then I hear Jess whisper, "Well, *fuck* me."

"What?" I say. "What did you get?"

"I got a hit," she says.

"With Benjamin or Ben?" I say.

"Ben," she says. "You're not going to like it."

My hands shake as I type Ben Davenport in quotes next to Tucker Janssen, two *s*s. Sure enough, I get a hit, too. The

Chicago marathon results. Their time is the same: 3:42:55. Impressive, especially for a woman. So she's a doctor and an athlete. But by far the worst part about this discovery is that their time is the same. Which means that they held hands across the finish line, something Ben always told me we would do together. So now I have a complete picture: I know they trained together, flew to Chicago together, visited her family in her apple-pie hometown together, gutted out a marathon together, and finished together, hand in hand. This is *vastly* more significant than the Villa d'Este. Jess knows it too, which I gauge by her uncharacteristic silence. It takes an awful lot to defeat Jess, especially when it comes to my honor. But she is defeated now.

"And to think," I say. "This is just what we can pull up on Google."

"Yeah," Jess says sadly. "We'd better not run another search with the word *baby,* huh?"

twenty-three

That afternoon, my father comes into the city to have lunch with me at the Mayrose Diner. He offered to take me somewhere nicer, but on the heels of the Villa d'Este, I'm in more of a laminated-menu mood than a cloth-napkin mood. We sit in our booth and make small talk about Italy. I tell him he needs to add Lake Como to his list of things to see before he dies.

"I don't have such a list," he says, transferring his onion, lettuce, and tomato from the side of his plate to his burger.

"You need to have one," I say.

He gives me a look as if he's considering this. That's when I tell him about my Google search. His face twists up in sympathy. "I'm sorry, kiddo," he says.

"Yeah," I say. "A bummer, isn't it?"

"I guess it's time to really let Ben go," he says. "You don't want to become as bitter as your old man."

I reach out and pat his hand. "Dad, you aren't bitter," I say. But as soon as the words are out, I realize that his happy routine could be just that. Maybe he still misses my mother. It strikes me that she is the sort of person who, if you are unfortunate enough to fall for, you might never be able to stop loving.

He nods and says, "In some ways I am . . . But it's too late for me to change. You, on the other hand, have your whole life ahead of you . . . So what about this fellow Richard? Sounds pretty serious if he's taking you to Italy?"

I shake my head. It feels a bit funny to admit to my father that I went to Italy with a man I'm not serious about, but I still say, "I don't think that's going to work out actually."

"Why's that? Does he want kids, too?"

I'm not sure whether this is a joke or not, but I laugh and then dab at my lips with my napkin. "No. He doesn't, actually. In that sense, he's perfect for me."

My dad tries again. "So what's the problem?"

"I don't love him," I say. "I'm never going to care about him in that way . . . I would have thought that was okay. But I end up feeling a little bit empty around him."

My dad puts down his burger and says, "Don't you wish we could pick the people we love?"

"Yeah," I say. "Or just make the people we love want the same things we want."

"Yeah," he says. "That would be pretty good, too."

Jess calls me back that afternoon and says, "Let's go out tonight."

"I can't," I say. "I have to go to the gym and run a couple of nine-minute miles, thank you very much."

"You're not going to the gym tonight."

"I've heard exercise makes you feel better," I say, thinking that I've never really found that to be the case. More often, I find it to be frustrating when several consecutive workouts yield no visible results.

Jess says, "You need a few drinks."

I am tempted, but a few drinks with Jess almost never means a few drinks. Especially when one of us is dealing with any sort of upsetting professional, personal, or familial episode. It usually means a few drinks and then a long dinner and then a few more drinks. And then, if the tragedy is great enough, there is dancing at the cheesiest bridge-and-tunnel club Jess can dig up for us. It actually can be very therapeutic so I'm tempted to cave, but I consider the hangover that I will have tomorrow and make the thirty-five-year-old determination that it's not worth it.

I say, "I wish I could . . . But I'm too far behind in my reading. I accomplished almost nothing in Italy."

"Oh, c'mon. You're always behind in your reading," Jess says.

"Yes, but I'm *perilously* behind now," I say.

She says, "Tough. We're going out. Meet me at Temple Bar at seven sharp."

Then she hangs up before I can respond.

Temple Bar was one of the first bars Jess and I ever went to upon our move to New York. We got the recommendation from one of Jess's family friends, a girl named Caroline who had been living in the city for several years by the time we arrived. She gave Jess a list entitled "Cool Places to Be Seen in Manhattan," which we consulted before going out at night, putting asterisks next to our favorite spots. Temple Bar earned two asterisks. Even though the drinks were out of our usual happy-hour price range and we had to take an expensive cab ride to get to NoHo, it was always worth it. We felt cool when we were there—like we were making it in Manhattan.

One day, Jess's new boyfriend, a funny lawyer named Stu, came across the list in our kitchen. He and Jess had one of those relationships marked by merciless teasing; it was almost as if neither had evolved past the playground, hair-pulling stage. In any event, he took great pleasure in the find.

"Cool places to be *seen*?" Stu said, waving the list in the air, as she chased him around the apartment. "This thing is too *queer* for words. Who wrote this?"

Jess played dumb and said, "Oh, that ol' thing? Some friend of the family came up with that . . . Our dads work together. I barely know her. Tell him, Claudia."

"We barely know her," I echoed.

"Well, the only thing more queer than writing such a list is anyone who would actually *save* it," he said, cracking up as he made the L-sign for *loser* on his forehead. "And then make check marks and notes all over it!"

Jess's face reddened as she said, "Well, you're the *loser* who has accompanied me to half of those places!"

She promptly crumpled up the paper and tossed the list in the trash, but by that point Temple Bar had been firmly established as our favorite hangout.

A lot has changed since then. As a thirty-five-year-old senior editor and a nearly-as-old managing director at a top Wall Street firm, Jess and I no longer hang out much in that Village-NoHo area. Nor do we enjoy lounges like we once did, vastly preferring restaurants where people will dare to be seen in a color other than black. But, like a song that is inextricably tied to a certain time in your life, Temple Bar evokes much nostalgia from our early twenties.

So whenever I see that lizard sign adorning the entrance on Lafayette Street and then step into the romantically lit, red-velvet, deco interior, I have a wave of being twenty-three and so poor I had to nurse one drink all night (I made *nineteen* thousand a year when I started out at Elgin). I also remember the way I felt—both wildly intimidated and impressed by the city, both filled with a sense of doom and full of hope. Most of all, I recall our many twenty-something mishaps, almost always caused by a member of the opposite sex.

That much is actually *still* true, I think, as I find Jess in a corner table with a cosmopolitan. She hardly ever drinks cosmopolitans anymore, but the beverage remains part of the Temple Bar ritual (a ritual she established way before *Sex and the City* ever aired). She hands me my personal Temple Bar favorite, a martini with a kiss of vermouth, and says, "How are you?"

"I'm okay," I say.

"Really?"

I nod, but then say, "No. Not really."

"Okay. Look. I was thinking. This marathon thing is just *not* your style anyway," Jess says.

I think, *If that's the best you came up with all day, I'm really in big trouble,* but I say, "I've always wanted to run a marathon."

"Yeah. Yeah. Yeah. You *say* that," Jess says. "You say that in the same way I fancy myself the sort of girl who would enjoy snowboarding and bungee jumping and white-water rafting. I *wish* I liked adventure sports. But you know what? I don't. They're scary. They're *not* fun. So no, thanks . . . And you might *think* you want to run a marathon, but c'mon, do you really want to run twenty-six-plus miles? Do you really want to get up at the butt crack of dawn and train? *No.* You don't. So let the dream die, already."

"I guess so," I say. "I don't know . . . I know that this shouldn't bother me as much as it does. Nothing has really changed since I went to Italy with Richard . . . or talked to Ben . . . or saw those Internet results. I'm in the exact same place I always was—or have been since I got a divorce. So I'm really not sure why I feel so much worse now . . ."

"Well, suspecting that Ben is in a relationship was one thing. Confirmation is another. It's hard. I get that."

"I know. But I really thought I was moving on," I say, recalling my dad's pep talk at lunch. "Richard or no Richard, I thought I was okay with my decision."

"You *are* okay, Claudia. You *did* make the right decision," she says. "It's just that moving on sometimes consists of some minor setbacks along the way. You had to have your rebound guy in Richard. You had to worry about Ben's rebound girl. Which is probably all Tucker is in the long run. But regardless of whether she is or isn't, you *are* moving on."

"Just like you're moving on and forgetting Trey?" I say hopefully.

"Exactly!" she says, grinning. "He's actually coming into town next week. He left me a message. But I haven't called him back."

I shoot her a dubious look.

"I swear I haven't. And I'm not going to. I'm done with him. You need to be done with Ben, too."

I nod and say okay.

"So here's to fresh starts," she says, raising her glass.

"To fresh starts," I say, thinking that this time I almost, very nearly, mean it.

We then proceed to get really drunk together, and it feels just like old times, when a few cocktails at a trendy lounge could fix just about anything.

I don't mention Ben and Tucker for another few days, until one of my authors, Ethan Ainsley, stops by to say hello. Ethan recently moved from London to New York which made me happy because he is one of my few authors who has a perfect score on my four-point checklist, namely: (1) I like him; (2) I like his writing; (3) his books sell; and (4) he's reliable. More typically, I like the author and the writing but the books aren't as commercially successful as I'd hoped. Or I like the writing and the books sell well, but the author is pompous and unreliable.

So when Ethan appears smiling in my doorway, I smile back and tell him to come in, have a seat.

"Look what I got this morning," I say, handing him a mock-up of his next book jacket that the art director just gave me. "What do you think?"

Ethan looks down at the stark navy cover adorned only with a small, white pillow and breaks into a huge smile. "I *love* it," he says. "It's so simple . . . but perfect."

"I know," I say. "I think it's really good."

"Those guys in the art department are brilliant," he says. "Let's just cross our fingers that people judge my book by *this* cover."

I smile and say, "So what's doing? Just in the neighborhood?"

"Yeah. I was over at Paragon picking up ski gear . . . We're taking the boys on a little ski trip."

"That sounds fun," I say.

"Yeah. Should be a good time," he says.

"How is your family?"

"Good. John and Thomas just started kindergarten . . . and, in bigger news, they have a little sister on the way!" Ethan says, beaming.

"Ethan! That's awesome news!" I say, feeling genuinely happy for him. "Darcy really wanted a girl, didn't she?"

I suddenly realize that I might be confusing his wife with a character named Ellen in his first book. It's something I often do when it comes to Ethan's books, because in one of our early conversations, right after I bought his manuscript, he admitted how much his novel mirrored his own life and marriage. Specifically, he confided that like the hero in his book, he fell in love with a girl, despite her baggage, despite her flaws, despite his own fervent wishes to be free, unencumbered, and blissfully alone. All that went out the window. Because he just *had* to be with her. Needless to say, I was fascinated when I met Ethan's wife at his first book signing last year, and after only a five-minute conversation with her, I could see why he had fallen so hard for her. She was charming, unaffected, and drop-dead gorgeous.

Ethan says, "Well, Darcy insisted that she didn't care, but she was giddy at our ultrasound. I think she was feeling a bit outnumbered at home . . . And I secretly wanted a girl, too."

"Well, that's really good news," I say, thinking that I can be happy for someone when the news of conception is normal, straightforward, and unfettered by drama and controversy. "Congratulations!"

"Thanks," he says. "So, what about you? How are you doing?"

Ethan knows about my divorce. I recently gave him the abbreviated version ("I don't want a baby; he does") of why we split.

So I say, "Oh, I'm fine . . . Just keeping busy . . . you know." I consider telling him that I was briefly dating someone, but reconsider when I remember that Richard has done some work on his books. Incidentally, other than a couple of e-mails, I've yet to talk to Richard since our return. I'm starting to wonder if he came to the same conclusion about us.

Ethan hesitates and then asks, "Have you talked to your ex at all?"

The question shouldn't catch me off guard—Ethan is candid that way. But it does, so I find myself blurting out the latest on Tucker and the marathon. I tell the story with a self-deprecating, humorous bent, but Ethan's face stays serious. When I finish, he says, "So how do you feel about all that?"

I shrug, trying to brush it off. "The doctor-jock combo is certainly annoying," I say with a smile.

"So just the standard postbreakup pang?" he asks.

"More or less."

"But you don't want him back, do you?"

I think of my talk with Jess at Temple Bar. Then I think of the reason Ben and I broke up—and how nothing has changed since then. I think that I certainly know what the answer should be. But I still shock myself when I say, "Well, yeah. Sure I want him back. In theory."

"So go get him back, then," Ethan says matter-of-factly.

"I can't," I say.

"Sure you can."

"It's too late. He has a girlfriend. And, you know, there's the whole baby issue."

"Both are surmountable obstacles."

"Not really . . . I mean, who knows about Tucker? But the baby issue certainly isn't surmountable."

"Yes it is."

I look at Ethan, processing what he is saying. He is, more or less, telling me to have a baby to get Ben back. It is just about the worst advice I've ever heard—akin to Jess's dishonest attempt at entrapping Trey.

I shake my head and say, "I can't have a baby just to get Ben back."

"Well, then," he says slowly. "I guess he's not your *soul* mate . . . So that should be a consolation when you're looking up their future marathon results."

"Why do you say that?" I ask, feeling oddly defensive. As much as I want to feel okay about Ben in the present, I don't like the implication that what we had wasn't, at one time, the real thing.

"Well, because," Ethan says, "you'd do anything to get a soul mate back, right? . . . I mean, that's the nature of soul mates. You know, Romeo and Juliet swallowed poison to be together . . . So if Ben were *really* the one for you, don't you think you'd go ahead and have his baby?"

twenty-four

I don't think Ethan intended to make a profound or lofty statement. Nor do I think he was trying to offer any relationship counsel. Rather he seemed simply to be throwing out his offhanded two cents about the nature of true love. Essentially, he was just saying what we've all heard a million times—*love conquers all.*

So I'm not really sure why his words affected me. Maybe it was the fact that he *wasn't* giving me preachy advice. Maybe it was the parallel to his book—the recognition of art imitating life imitating art. Maybe it was the clarity of hearing something from a relatively random messenger, a player uninvested in your life, someone outside your inner circle.

All I know for sure is that Ethan's words cut straight to my heart and made me see my relationship with Ben in the least complicated, most stripped-down terms. I saw the bare essence of our breakup. The hard truth of the matter. I realized, almost in an instant, that I no longer bought all the propaganda about relationships ending because of bad timing and incompatibility and outside influences, like wanting or not wanting a baby. A baby is *huge*—it doesn't get much bigger than that—but so is religion and age and geography and being married to other people and feuding houses and so many other seemingly insurmountable factors that couples encounter and defeat when love is true.

So, right there in my office, I decide that as simplistic and naïve as it may sound, I *do* believe that true love conquers all. Therefore, one of two things must also be true: either my relationship with Ben was not what I believed it to be, or our breakup was a big, horrible mistake.

It has to be one or the other.

I know where I'm coming out in the matter. I only hope Ben feels the same way.

Later that afternoon I call Daphne and ask her if I can come and spend the night.

"Sure!" she says. "Tony's going out with the guys, so it's perfect timing."

"Don't cook," I say. "We'll order a pizza, okay?"

"Papa John's?" she says hopefully.

Papa John's versus Domino's is a raging debate in her house, with a multiple-prong analysis—cheese, crust, sauce, delivery time, value for money.

"Perfect," I say, feeling a wave of affection for my sweet suburban sister.

I return to Jess's apartment and quickly pack an overnight bag. As I'm retrieving my toothbrush from the bathroom I hear the unmistakable, distinct sounds of my best friend having sex with an equally expressive, not-so-gentle man. There are few things as unsettling as hearing a close friend having sex (only slightly less disturbing than hearing your parents doing it). But what makes the symphony of groans *more* offensive is that I recall that Trey is in town. I am filled with something close to rage—at him for toying with her—but more at

Jess for being *so* stupid. She damn well better be using a condom, I think, as I hurry out the door during a long, drawn-out moan.

About two hours later, I arrive at Daphne's and walk in her side door without knocking. She is sitting on the floor on a large throw pillow, grading tests in flannel pajamas and Snoopy slippers.

"Hey, there! Pizza just got here!" she says. "I got pepperoni. Hope that's okay?"

"Sure," I say.

I put down my bag and have a seat beside her, picking up a paper from the marked pile. It belongs to Annabel Partridge, who earned herself an A+ and a "Fine job" with three exclamation points *and* a smiley face.

"Wait," I say. "Isn't Annabel 'Bigghettobooty'?"

Daphne laughs and says, "Yup."

"Man. An A-plus with that sort of extracurricular activity . . . That really is an anomaly, huh?"

"Yeah," Daphne says, shaking her head. She flips to the bottom of the stack and produces Josh McCall's paper, covered with red marks, a big D, and a "You can do better" (with one exclamation point and a frowning face).

"Her guy?" I say.

"Uh-huh," she says, shaking her head and putting the stack of papers down. Then she clears her throat and says, "Look, Claudia, I know what you came here to tell me . . ."

"You do?" I say.

She nods and says, "You don't want to be our egg donor, do you?"

There is nothing accusatory or bitter in her words or

expression. To the contrary, she looks as if she feels sorry for *me*. That she understands my decision completely—and even, in some small way, agrees with me.

I lean over and hug her. "I'm sorry," I say. "I just—I just can't do it."

"We figured as much," she says. "It's okay, Claudia. It really is."

"Can I explain?" I say.

"You don't have to."

"I want to."

"Is it just too weird for you?" she says.

I exhale and rub my eyes. "I guess that's part of it."

"Like you feel like you'd be having a baby with Tony?" she says, trying to smile.

"Well, maybe," I say. "Maybe a little . . ."

"I know," she says. "I think Tony felt that way, too. I didn't see it until he asked me how I'd feel if the tables were turned and we were using my egg and his brother Johnny's sperm. I was like, 'That's *so* not a fair comparison. Claudia's beautiful and brilliant, and Johnny's a mean-spirited fuckup who had a really low SAT score' . . . but I still got his point . . . And I certainly don't want to do something that you—or Tony— might regret. This is too important."

"Thank you for saying that about me, Daphne," I say. "That's really nice. Thank you."

"Well, you are," she says. "And I don't think you're selfish for this decision. I don't."

"Okay," I say, feeling even worse because of how under- standing she's being. "I just . . . I feel like I'm really leaving you in the lurch. What are you guys going to do?"

"We have other options," she says. "We know we'll have a

baby. And we're going to have the baby we're *supposed* to have. Whatever baby we end up having will be the right baby. Our baby. And we know that we'll hold that child and think, 'If our journey had been easy, we wouldn't have *you*.' "

"That is so true," I say, feeling incredibly proud of my sister. I ask her if they're considering adoption.

"Yeah," she says. "We started researching some domestic adoption agencies this week . . . And my friend Beth just returned from China with the most beautiful little girl . . . and we're also looking into this really cool program called Snowflake. Have you heard of it?"

I shake my head.

She explains that it's a program where a couple can adopt an embryo remaining after the genetic parents have a baby through in-vitro fertilization. "It's sort of a controversial Christian organization," she says.

"Why is it controversial?"

"Oh, I don't know. I guess because these parents essentially believe that the embryos are children. Which is why they call it 'adoption' and not 'donation' . . . But Tony and I don't really care what they call it."

I say, "Well, that sounds like a great option . . . And then you could still experience pregnancy and childbirth."

"Yeah," she says. "For some reason, carrying the baby is more important to me than the DNA . . . So we're really optimistic and excited about moving forward, somehow."

"I'm glad, Daphne. Thank you for understanding." Then I hesitate, knowing that there is no taking back what I'm about to say next. But I want Daphne to be the first to know.

"What?" Daphne says.

"Well . . . I . . . I just wanted to tell you there's sort of another reason I didn't feel right about being your egg donor . . ."

"What's that?" she says.

"Well, I think . . . I think maybe I should have a baby of my own, after all."

She stares at me, her mouth dropping open. "You want a baby?"

"I want Ben."

"So, what? Are you guys getting back together?"

"I don't know," I say. "But it's all I want."

"And then you'd have a baby?" she says.

"If that's what it takes," I say. "I'll do whatever it takes to get Ben back."

twenty-five

I plan on going straight to work the next morning from Daphne's house, but I left my bra at home. I would go without one, but I'm wearing a tight sweater that is on the thin, almost sheer, side. Daphne jokingly offers up one of her bras but we both know that's not an option. Her boobs are significantly bigger than mine. So I head home to finish dressing, hoping that I don't run into Trey.

Fortunately, I don't.

I do, however, run into Michael, standing in front of the television with a remote in his hand, in all of his naked glory.

"Shit!" we yell in unison.

"What are you doing here?" I say, realizing how dumb the question is. I mean, he's certainly not here just lounging around in the buff, watching Sportscenter. I avert my eyes, but not before I catch an unwitting crotch-level shot of Michael that is sure to be emblazoned in my head forever. I combine the image with the sound effects from last night and think, *Wow, Michael. And I thought you were nothing but another pretty-faced publicist.*

At this point, Jess emerges from her bedroom, looking smug. "Have you two met?" She tosses a towel to Michael, who quickly wraps it around his waist.

"Yeah. We've met a few times," I say, smiling.

Michael smirks back at me and says, "We thought you were at Richard's."

"I was at Daphne's actually," I say, taking my coat off, remembering my bra situation one second too late.

"Nice *tubes*, Claudia," Michael says. "Guess it is show-and-tell at Elgin Press today. Or at least *show*. We can talk about it, though . . . If you want."

I put my jacket back on and say, "Forgot my bra. Sorry."

"No need to apologize," Michael says.

Jess gives him a playful, but strangely possessive, jab, which tells me that this might be a dash more than an isolated hookup. At least in Jess's eyes. My instinct is to leave the room and get the separate scoop from both parties later in the day, but then I figure that I might as well just ask the question now. So I say, "What's going on here anyway? How long have you two been creeping around like this?"

Jess slides her arm around and says, "Since you were in Italy, and I found my sperm bank."

Michael laughs and says, "Don't listen to her. We use condoms."

Condoms, plural, I think, as Jess laughs and says, "I'm talking him into it, though," she says, laughing.

"Seriously?" I say.

"Seriously," Jess says. "He has good genes, you know."

I look at Michael, a man who can't even commit to giving a woman a key to his apartment. He smiles and shrugs.

"But we're also in love," Jess says. "So it's all good."

"That's true," Michael says. "I love her."

I study their matching inscrutable expressions. They are thoroughly amused with themselves but also strangely serious.

Emily Giffin

I shake my head and say, "This is too fucking weird." Then I head to my room to get a bra.

That afternoon, I am trying to work, but mostly contemplating how I should get in touch with Ben, when there is a knock on my office door. I assume it is Michael who has yet to show his guilty face.

"Come in!" I say, leaning back and mentally preparing my one-liner.

The door opens and Richard appears, sporting my favorite literary look: tweed blazer, turtleneck, and glasses. I am happy to see him—and still quite attracted to him. But overriding this is a sense of awkwardness due to the fact that in the ten days since our return, this is our first face-to-face interaction.

"I didn't know you wore glasses," I say with a nervous laugh.

"Reading glasses," he says, taking them off and slipping them into his jacket pocket.

I smile and motion toward my guest chair. "Have a seat."

He closes the door to a crack and sits down.

"So, Parr? What's the deal?" he says. He gives me a little smirk that doesn't completely mask a dash of hurt pride. I am pretty sure that Richard is not accustomed to being blown off in any manner. "You didn't like Lake Como or what?"

I clear my throat and stammer, "I've just been busy . . . But no, I had a lovely time at Lake Como."

"Lovely, huh?" Richard says with an amused expression.

"You know what I mean. I had a great time," I say more sincerely. "*Thank* you."

"You already thanked me," he says. "No need to say it again."

We smile at each other for what feels like ten minutes, but

is probably only about thirty seconds. In that brief window, it becomes absolutely clear, if it wasn't already, that our affair is over. I know Richard has no deep feelings for me—and I'm almost as sure that he has at least one other woman in his rotation, and a few on the back burner. But I still feel compelled to give him an explanation. So I say, "Listen. I feel really pathetic telling you this, but—"

Richard interrupts and says, "Careful. Pathetic can be charming on the right woman."

I laugh and say, "Not in my case."

"Let me guess," he says. "You're still in love with your ex-husband?"

I look at him, wondering how he knew. I can't think of a single time I've brought Ben up since Raymond Jr.'s baptism. Then again, maybe that's precisely *how* he knew. I consider a full explanation, but instead I say offhandedly, "I told you it was pathetic."

Then I reach into my top desk drawer for my cocktail ring. I can't return the trip to Italy—and it would be way too uncomfortable and gauche to offer up money for my half of our travel expenses. But I can symbolically return the ring. I say, "I feel weird about keeping this." As I attempt to hand it back to him, I have an unexpected jolt of being in high school when I returned Charlie's letter jacket to him upon our departure for college.

Richard waves me off and says, "Oh, for God's *sake*, Parr. It was nothing. It wasn't even that expensive. Keep it."

"Are you sure?" I say.

He gives me an exasperated look.

I put the box back in my drawer and say, "Okay . . . . thank you. I really do *love* it."

"Well," he says, standing. "*That* was the point, ya know."

He stands as I feel a mix of relief and regret. I am relieved that the conversation was so painless, and that I have no sense that working together will be awkward moving forward—which is obviously the biggest fear with any office romance. But I feel regret because I like Richard and will miss hanging out with him. And frankly, I will also miss sleeping with him. The thought of being thirty-five, at my theoretical sexual prime, and abstinent is not one that I relish. I know that I'm at risk for being completely alone. Richard turns to leave and then looks back at me with a trace of a smile. "If you change your mind, you know where to find me. Just call me. No strings attached."

After he is gone I replay his words and decide that although he meant it as a selling point, there is something almost tragic about a no-strings-attached kind of life.

Of course there is also something really sad about the opposite sort of life, too—a life where people stay together *because* of strings, I think, as Maura phones me from the parking lot of Zoe's ballet practice and says, "Well. He's doing it again."

I know right away that she is talking about Scott. He is cheating on her again.

"Could you be wrong?" I say. "Remember that one time you were wrong—and he really was just working late?"

I hear her inhale and then say, "I hired someone to follow him. I have him on tape."

"Oh, *God*, Maura . . . I'm *so* sorry."

"Don't," she says. "You'll make me cry."

I try to switch out of sympathy mode and deal with facts instead. "Tell me what happened," I say.

Maura says that she started suspecting Scott of having an

affair based on the same tired patterns: working late, flowers sent to appease her, distracted behavior, ceaseless voice-mail checking. She says that the worst part has always been the wondering, so last week she opened the yellow pages and called the first PI listed, a guy named Lorenz whom she describes as a "*Sopranos* outcast type who cleans up well enough to look like a legitimate businessman." She says she paid him a one-thousand-dollar cash advance and in five days he had proof—a blurry video of Scott meeting his woman in a bar in Battery Park City. They had three drinks each and got cozy in a corner booth.

"How cozy?" I say.

"Daphne would call it *canoodling*," she says. Maura and I always tease Daphne for her celebrity-magazine jargon.

"Hmm," I say. "So what happened next?"

She tells me that Lorenz followed them onto the elevator at the hotel, taping the following furtive whispers behind him:

"Can you *please* stay overnight?"
(Inaudible).
"*Why?*"
"I can't, babe (inaudible) . . . I have a few hours."
"That's not long enough."
"Let's make the best of it."

Lorenz then trailed them to their room and listened at the door for a few minutes. The following morning he returned, slipped a maid fifty bucks to let him into the room. He took photos of two empty champagne bottles, a plate of half-eaten strawberries (so trite), and stuffed the sheets from the bed into his duffel bag.

"Why did he take the sheets?" I say.

"Semen samples. Classy, huh?"

I digest the sordid details and then say, "Who was she? Do you know?"

"I have no idea," she says. "But when I first saw the tape I thought it was Jane."

"Your best friend *Jane*?" I say, horrified.

"Yeah. But it turned out, it was just her body and hair double. I mean, this girl could be Jane's lost, slutty *twin*. And I've always suspected Scott of having a thing for Jane. So when I saw this video my heart literally *stopped* and I'm thinking to myself, Oh, *my* God, I am *so* going to kill Scott, and then Jane, and then myself. And the only thing that pulled me out of the moment was my next thought, one that made me almost smile. I thought to myself, Daphne is going to get three kids out of this deal."

"Wait," I say, as innocently and nonchalantly as possible. "Daphne gets the kids if you and Scott both die?"

Apparently I'm not subtle enough for Maura, who says ever so defensively, "Well, she's *married*, Claudia . . . And she *wants* kids."

"Oh, yeah. I understand," I say, but just as I did on the day of Raymond Jr.'s baptism, I have a twinge of envy and small stab of indignation. I hope that at the very least, I am the backup should Daphne die, too. I decide this probably isn't the right time to delve into guardianship matters. Instead I drop the subject and say, "So it wasn't Jane?"

"No. It wasn't Jane. And I know Jane would never do that. But stranger things have happened . . . I think the only people I fully trust in this world are you and Daphne. But I guess I'm lucky to have two, huh?"

A scene from *Hannah and Her Sisters* flashes into my head,

which is one of the most disturbing movies I've ever seen for that very reason. I simply can't fathom Daphne or Maura betraying me in such a way. Or Jess for that matter. But to Maura's point, the list is short.

Maura continues, "So I think that whole initial shock of thinking Scott was with Jane worked in my favor. I mean, I was so unbelievably *relieved* when I saw that girl's face and realized it wasn't Jane after all. It was almost like a small battle victory in the middle of a war you're losing badly . . . Besides, in a sense, there's no new information here. We already *knew* Scott was a disloyal asshole. So I'm just dealing with gradations of that right now. He's a slightly grander and more *consistent* asshole than I previously thought." She laughs.

I smile, impressed at my sister's ability to keep her sense of humor.

"Have you confronted him?" I say. "Does he know you know?"

"No . . . And let me tell you, it's really something watching him act all innocent around the house, like Joe Good Husband." She imitates him: " 'Say, Maura, want me to whip up some blueberry pancakes?' "

"Disgusting," I say, knowing that no matter what happens to my sister's marriage, I can no longer keep up the pretense of liking Scott.

"Yeah. It really is. But a small part of me also takes perverse pleasure in having the goods on him. It's like I got the last laugh, you know? It's like, 'Who's the fool now?' "

"So, what next?" I say.

"I haven't decided on strategy. I don't want to act impulsively. What do you think of giving him a chance to come clean and confess?"

"You mean, tell him that you suspect that something is going on and see if he fesses up?" I say.

"Yeah. Something like that. You know, without telling him I have proof."

"Sounds like a good idea," I say. "And if he confesses?"

She exhales into the phone and says, "I don't know. More counseling, I guess. Maybe we could apply to be on *Dr. Phil*."

I laugh. "You wouldn't, would you?"

She says, "No! I can't *fathom* why people would expose themselves like that. I mean, the worst part about this is probably the humiliation."

I think to myself that if the humiliation is the worst part about this then she really doesn't love Scott anymore. I ask her if she does.

"Oh, shit, I don't know," she says. "I'm so far beyond that analysis. I mean, I guess I love the man I *thought* he was. Or the man he used to be. And occasionally, I still have a faint glimmer of love for him when I see him with the kids. He's a great father, if you can be a great father when you're doing this to your family . . ."

She pauses as I think of our mother. Maura is likely thinking of her, too. I can't believe my sister has to go through all of this again.

She continues, "But no, I don't love him anymore in the way you're asking about. I don't love a man who can make my life feel so seedy when *I've* done nothing wrong." Her voice cracks for the first time, so I try to ward off her tears by speaking crisply, as a mother does to her child who has just fallen down and is considering whether to cry. "Okay. So what if he denies everything?"

My strategy works because Maura's voice sounds strong

again when she says, "I don't know. But I'm thinking I'll just pack up the kids and get the show on the road."

"You should tell *him* to leave. And with that video, you'd totally get the house."

"I don't know if I even want the house," Maura says. "Our life in that house is a *joke*."

We sit in silence for a long stretch until Maura says, "So Daphne told me about the egg donor stuff. And about Ben."

I have a split second of discomfort, wondering if Maura cares that Daphne and I confided in each other first. I wonder how old my sisters and I will be before we no longer compete at all in our circle of three. Then I say, "Yeah. It was hard to tell her no, but I had to."

"Because you want Ben back?"

"Among other reasons . . . But to be honest, that was the main issue . . . I think I made a mistake. I really miss him."

"Yeah," Maura says. "I'm not surprised. I thought you might change your mind."

Maura's *I told you so* is subtle but annoying. It occurs to me that I could do the same to her. I could tell her that I had my suspicions about Scott from the very beginning. That I thought he was way too charming and smooth to be believable. I think of their engagement when Scott hired an airplane to fly with the WILL YOU MARRY ME, MAURA? banner along the coast in East Hampton. I remember telling Jess that I didn't trust any man who turned a proposal—what should be a private, intimate expression of love—into something so public. I considered telling Maura the same—expressing my worries that she was marrying a shameless show-off, the sort of man who thrives on the chase, the hunt. But I don't think it would have changed anything. And what would be the point of telling her all of this now? Maura must know in her heart that she made a mistake marrying Scott. Just like I know that I made a mistake leaving Ben. So I say, "Yeah. I guess sometimes you have to find these things out for yourself . . ."

"Are you going to tell him how you feel?"

"Yeah," I say. "As soon as I can work up the nerve."

Maura sighs and says, "Isn't it strange that a baby was the only thing keeping you and Ben apart? And the kids seem to be the only thing keeping Scott and me together?"

"Yeah," I say. "I should have had a baby for the right guy."

"And I had babies with the wrong guy," she says, confirming my theory that women are *always*, at least subconsciously, aware of their big life mistakes. Sometimes it's just not worth looking too closely. Unless those mistakes can still be fixed.

"Well," I say, wondering if it's too late for my sister and me. "Aren't we just the pretty pair?"

"We sure are," Maura says with a fragile laugh. "We *sure* are."

twenty-six

Another two weeks pass as I agonize over how to get in touch with Ben. Should I drop in on him unannounced? Should I call his apartment? His cell? Office? Should I send an e-mail? Mail him a haiku?

Break up with Tucker
She is not the one for you!
I'll have your baby

Of course the haiku is a joke, but the point is, I'm *actually* writing them in my head, drafting e-mail messages on the back of takeout menus, and practicing heartfelt monologues in the shower. Yet the more I think about my next move, the more indecisive I become. I also grow increasingly paranoid that, in Jess's words, Tucker and Ben's relationship could be "rapidly solidifying." She should know, I think, as I watch her fall in love with Michael. It's almost a visible process—like watching a flower unfold its petals on time-lapse photography. I've seen Jess smitten many times before, but for the first time, her emotional intensity is not accompanied by drama and angst. There are no text-message battles. No storming out of bars. No cheating. No jealous rages over ex-boyfriends. Instead, everything between them seems normal and healthy and miraculously two-sided, which is confirmed every time

Emily Giffin

Michael stops by my office. He appears even happier than usual—and the conversation always works its way back to Jess. He asks me open-ended, endearing questions about her—things like, "What was she like in college?" He wants all the details and background you hunger for when you're smitten with someone.

Of course, I'm delighted with their romance as I get to spend time with two of my best friends at once. It's efficient and comfortable and satisfying.

One rainy Sunday in November, the three of us are lounging in the living room in our sweats, reading the paper, when Jess looks up at me and says, "You know, Claudia, you really need to call Ben *before* Thanksgiving."

"Why?" I say.

She says, "*Because*. Thanksgiving is one of those crossroads holidays. You don't want them taking that step together."

"What step?" I say.

"Spending the holidays together . . . If that's the direction they're headed in, you have to get in there and bust things up."

Michael lowers the Business Section and winks at me. "Yeah. She's right, Claudia. Going home with someone for Thanksgiving is a *major* step. It's *exponentially* more significant than merely meeting one's parents."

As I watch them exchange an adoring glance, I realize that a Thanksgiving invitation has not only been issued, but accepted. I look at Jess, surprised. She has not mentioned a single thing to me about her holiday plans. It occurs to me that, for the first time, she isn't discussing every small aspect of her relationship with me. There are no strategy sessions, no

288

speculation about what Michael is thinking, no analysis about what something he's done (or hasn't done) means (or doesn't mean). Maybe it's because she's never dated a friend of mine before, and she doesn't want to put me in an awkward position. But more likely it's because she's finally in the kind of sincere relationship where you follow your own gut about things rather than polling your friends at every turn.

"Wait," I say with feigned bewilderment. "Are you guys spending Thanksgiving together? In Birmingham?"

Jess glows and her voice turns creamy. "Yes. Michael's coming home with me."

I look at Michael and say, "Oh, really? Mighty big step for the likes of you."

He says, "Tell me about it. I'm risking my life going down there."

Jess rolls her eyes and says, "Would you stop saying that!" She turns to me. "He acts like he's going back in time to the nineteen fifties when he crosses the Mason-Dixon Line."

Michael laughs. "I just don't want to get lynched when I show up with a blonde."

Jess frowns. She is very proud of her Southern roots, even though she has no desire to live in Alabama again. "Are you about through?" she says to him.

Michael takes her hand. "Sorry, babe . . . You know I can't wait to meet your family and see your old stomping grounds."

Jess looks fully appeased. Michael leans over and kisses her. Both of their mouths open slightly as if I'm not in the room. I look down at my paper, picturing Ben doing the same thing to Tucker. Jess and Michael are right, I think. I have to get to Ben before the holidays.

*

The next morning, I arrive at work determined to contact Ben before the end of the day. I decide that e-mail works best given our last contentious phone conversation. I spend the next half hour at my desk, drafting my salutation. I change *Dear Ben* to *Hello Ben* to *Hi Ben* to just plain *Ben*. I type a colon, then backspace and replace it with a comma and then opt for my personal favorite—the no-nonsense dash. Incidentally, the semicolon is one of my favorite punctuation marks, too, which Ben once pointed out to me during one of our early e-mail exchanges. He wrote something like, "Think you have enough semicolons in there? You sure love that little guy." I wrote back, "I do love the semicolon; I love you, too." It was the first time I had written the words out to him. So perhaps a carefully placed semicolon will soften him, remind him how we once were. As I contemplate sentence two, my phone rings. It is Maura. I answer, grateful for the interruption.

"Hey," I say. "What's going on?"

"He denied it," she says.

"Did he *really?*" I say. I don't know why I'm so surprised. Why would a born and accomplished liar suddenly buck up and tell the truth?

"Yeah," Maura says wearily. "And he did so strenuously . . . and with such *detail*. He was so good that I almost started to *believe* him. Which is crazy considering that I've *seen* the tape and *heard* the audio. I mean, he's *scary* good."

I say, "Did you tell him you have proof?"

"Not yet," she says. "But I'm going to confront him this weekend. I'm going to tell him that I want a divorce . . . That I'm tired of living a lie. I can't stay with him just for the kids . . . Besides, I don't even think it's good for them to grow up like this. Kids can always sense when something's wrong. We did."

"I know," I say, remembering how wistful I felt after sleep-overs with friends who had parents who seemed to truly love each other. I could usually convince myself that my family was fine until I had evidence of what happy really looked like.

She continues, "I mean, I really don't think I have a choice here . . . I think I have to just put my head down and get through this."

"I'm *so* sorry, Maura. I wish I could change things for you."

"I know," she says. "Thanks."

"Do you want the name of my attorney? She's a shark," I say. "She'll get you whatever you want."

"I'm hoping that we can avoid that whole scene. I want to use our family attorney as a mediator—as long as Scott is rea-sonable. I'm going to tell him that I want to sell the house and split everything. And, of course, I want custody of the kids . . . That could be the biggest sticking point."

"Are you *sure* this is what you want?" I say, feeling a wave of intense grief as I think of those three kids being shuttled back and forth between two houses. Of Maura saying good-bye to her children on Christmas morning when they leave to open presents at their daddy's. I wonder if there is even a small possibility that Scott could still change. If Maura could, some-how, give him one *more* chance. Or perhaps I'm just thinking of my own haste in getting a divorce and how much self-righteous anger played a part in my quick decision. Was I too concerned with being right and punishing Ben for reneging on our deal? Is Maura doing the same thing now? I clear my throat and gently say, "Do you think this is a little quick? Have you really thought this through?"

"It's been a long time coming, Claudia," Maura says. "Enough is enough."

"What are you going to tell the kids?" I say.

"I don't know yet," she says. "The boys are too young. I guess that's a good thing."

"Yeah," I say, thinking that they will likely have few, if any, memories of their parents together.

"So. Daphne's going to take the boys on Friday night, and I was hoping you could take Zoe for the weekend?"

"Absolutely," I say.

"Thank you," she says.

We are both quiet for a moment. Then she clears her throat and says briskly, "So this is it. T-minus-five days as Mr. and Mrs. Stepford."

There is something about Maura's situation that makes me feel even more desperate to talk to Ben. So as soon as I hang up with my sister, I bang out the rest of the e-mail. I write:

Ben—
Hope you're well. I'm sorry for how our last conversation ended; I hate fighting with you. I was wondering if we could get together sometime soon? I have something I want to talk to you about. Let me know . . .
Claudia

I take a deep breath and hit send before I can change my mind. Then I put my head in my hands and pray Ben puts me out of my misery soon. Ten minutes pass and nothing comes. I go to the bathroom and get a cup of coffee, remembering what I always used to tell Jess. "A watched phone doesn't ring." I return to an empty in-box. A moment later, my e-mail notifier dings. But the message is not from Ben. Nor is the next or the next. I turn my volume down on my computer and position my chair away from my screen. I allow myself only one check per half hour. Still nothing.

As the day wears on, I go from being nervous to downright ornery. I feel irrationally annoyed at every friend who chooses today, of all days, to say hello or pass along a joke. And when Jess forwards me a playful exchange between Michael and her with the subject line *Isn't he cute?*, I feel my first stab of envy over their relationship. I'm not at all bitter, but definitely a bit begrudging. *It's not fair,* I think, and then instantly dislike myself for having one of the single most maladjusted and counterproductive thoughts a woman in a crisis can have. *Life's not fair,* I tell myself. Everyone over the age of ten knows that. Then, I feel my heart twist as I have an even sadder, more sobering thought: *You have no one to blame but yourself.*

twenty–seven

Four excruciating days pass with no word from Ben. I picture an array of depressing scenarios: Ben so gloriously indifferent that he lets my e-mail get buried in his in-box, forgetting to write me back altogether; Ben scoffing at the screen and delet-ing my e-mail in disgust; Ben forwarding my e-mail to Tucker and the two of them sharing a good chuckle about how desper-ate I sound. I consider calling Annie and asking her if she's talked to him, if she knows anything about his life. After all, she was certainly pretty free with the details of *my* relationship with Richard. But I just don't want to go down that road. I don't want anything to get lost in translation. Plus, I don't entirely trust that Annie has my best interest at heart. I know I'm her friend, but she's Ben's friend, too—and by now she could even be close to Tucker.

Jess agrees. "Just deal with him directly," she says.

"What if I never hear back from him?" I say.

"You will . . . He's probably out of the office, working on an off-site project or something. Either that or he wants to make you sweat. And if he's making you sweat, he still cares."

"You're right," I say, but in my head, I'm steeling myself for the possibility that my window of opportunity has closed for good. That I might never talk to Ben again.

On Friday afternoon, after a long lunch with one of my

favorite agents, I hunker down to read a few unsolicited manuscripts, otherwise known as slush because most are sloppy, uninspired muck. They are so dreadful, in fact, that most houses and editors won't even accept them. It's just not worth the time or limited editorial resources. To this point, in thirteen years of reading slush, I've only brought *one* manuscript to editorial meeting, and it was shot down in about six minutes flat.

Ben once asked me why I bothered with those kinds of odds. "You don't buy lottery tickets or gamble," he said, "so why do you read slush?"

I explained to him that it wasn't entirely rational. I told him that part of it stemmed from my deeply rooted neurosis that developed in my junior days, a sense of wanting to be thorough, cover all my bases. You never knew where the next great novel could be lurking. But beyond that, I told him that I just liked the *idea* of slush.

"How so?" he asked me as he skimmed a particularly brutal query letter over my shoulder. "You like the idea of boring storylines and scads of grammatical errors?"

"It's hard to explain," I told him. "It's just that slush is so *democratic*. I like the *idea* of giving a shot to the struggling writer. I like the idea of the underdog overcoming the odds and achieving greatness."

"Well, it's a good thing for me you feel that way," Ben said, kissing me. "Because I sort of came from the slush pile of blind dates."

I laughed and told him that was very true. "Just look what I would have missed if I had blown off that date."

From that day on, whenever Ben wore mismatched socks, or burned toast, or did anything haphazard, I'd call him my slushy husband. It was one of our many inside jokes.

So it is very fitting that Ben finally e-mails me as I am perusing a few slush manuscripts that Rosemary screened for me as the most promising of the dismal lot. I glance up when my notifier dings, and am shocked to finally see his name in my in-box. My heart races, and I sit there, my mouth slightly agape, paralyzed with fear. Something about his bolded *Benjamin Davenport* looks so ominous. Or maybe it's the *no subject* that follows. I am suddenly convinced that his words will be terse and grim: *I don't see any point in getting together; I have nothing to say to you.*

A full hour passes before I work up the nerve to open his e-mail. I read his three sentences twice, searching for meaning: *Next week is hectic. How about after Thanksgiving? Does Monday work for you?*

Nothing. I can glean *nothing* from his e-mail, but it certainly doesn't seem promising that he bypassed my name or any sort of soft closing. And I simply can't believe I had to wait *four* days for *three* ambiguous sentences. But by and large, I feel relieved. It's better than what it could have been. I still have a dash of hope as I send my response: *Sure. Pete's Tavern at 12?*

As New York's oldest pub in continuous operation, Pete's is a bit of a tourist trap, but Ben and I never minded. We spent many a late night cozied up at the bar, so as soon as I hit send I worry what he'll think of my sentimental choice of venue. But his response comes nearly instantaneously. *See you then. Have a good Thanksgiving.*

Highly doubtful, I think as I scratch a big red *reject* across one writer's treasured manuscript.

*

Later that night, as I'm returning home from work, I spot Maura and Zoe scurrying along the sidewalk toward Jess's apartment. Maura is holding Zoe by one hand and carrying her Dora the Explorer sleeping bag and monogrammed canvas L.L. Bean bag in the other. Both of Zoe's pink Keds are untied, the laces dragging behind her on the damp pavement. When she finally sees me, she squeals, "Aunt Claudia!" as if I'm famous. Zoe does wonders for my self-esteem.

"Hey, Zoe!" I call out. "Are you coming to spend the weekend with me?"

"Uh-huh!" she yells back. "And Mommy said I can stay up as late as I want and eat whatever I want."

I look at Maura to make sure this is accurate. My sister shrugs wearily. She looks drawn and forlorn—like she doesn't have the energy to fight about bedtime and sugar cereals. I wonder if this is the beginning of the divorced-parents "pay off your kids" phenomenon. All kids know that the only fringe benefit of having parents who split up is that you can play on mom and dad's guilt, exhaustion, and competitive spirit to extract maximum benefits from both camps. I remember how my own Christmas presents doubled in number and value after my mother left.

Zoe lets go of Maura's hand and scrambles toward me. I bend down to double-knot her laces. Then I kiss her cold, rosy cheek and whisper in her ear, "Guess what I got you?"

"What?" Zoe says excitedly.

"Pop-Tarts!"

Strawberry Pop-Tarts are Zoe's favorite food—but she's only allowed to have them on special occasions. Until now, Maura's been all about organic foods.

"What flavor?" Zoe asks excitedly.

"Strawberry. With frosting and sprinkles," I say. *"Duh!"*

Zoe beams. It's so nice to be able to please someone so easily. I just wish I could fix Maura's problems, too. I stand and put my arms around my sister. I can feel her ribs and the sharpness of her shoulder blades through her Burberry trench coat. "You're so bony, Maura," I say. "I'm worried about you . . ."

Maura sighs and touches her cheekbone. "I know. I look haggard, don't I?"

"You don't look haggard," I say. "Just . . . too thin. You need to take care of yourself—"

"It's funny," Maura says. "Until this week I always believed that you could never be too rich or too thin . . . Now, I'm not so sure . . . I'd rather be poor, fat, and happy . . ."

Zoe interrupts and says, "Is Jess home, too? Can I try on her shoes?"

"Why, of course! All one hundred pairs!" I say, thinking that if I'm a B-list celebrity in Zoe's eyes, Jess is Madonna. Even a six-year-old can sniff out gradations of beauty and style.

Maura glances at her Cartier watch and sighs. "Okay. The boys are at Daphne's . . . Scott's expecting me at eight . . . I better get home."

"Good luck," I say. Then I touch her arm and tell her I love her. It's something Maura and I rarely say to each other, although we never question it.

"I love you, too, Claudia. Thank *you*," Maura says. Then she kneels in front of her daughter and brushes her hair away from her face. "And I love you, pumpkin."

"I love you, Mommy," Zoe says, hugging her mother around the neck.

"Be good for Aunt Claudia," she says.

"I will, Mommy."

Maura smiles at her daughter. Then she stands and faces me.

"Call me when you can," I say.

She nods, turns, and walks swiftly toward her silver Range Rover, her high-heeled boots clicking on the sidewalk. I watch her for a few seconds, feeling overwhelmed by worry. Her weekend ahead makes my upcoming lunch date at Pete's Tavern seem like a trivial encounter. I guess that's the impact three innocent children have in the equation.

When I look down at Zoe, I see that she, too, looks concerned. She is squinting as she watches her mother start the car and pull away from the curb. Maura waves and gives us a little honk. Zoe waves back and mouths, "Bye, Mommy."

I've never seen my niece look so sad and wonder if it's because she senses that something is wrong—or if it's only that she's still a little young to be away from home for two nights. I tousle her hair and say, "Ready to get out of the cold, Zoe Doughy?"

She nods and says, "Aunt Claudia?" Her voice rises into a high-pitched question.

"Yeah, honey?" I say, nervous of what she might ask.

Sure enough, she asks one of her trademark questions: "Why is Mommy so sad?"

So I give her one of my stellar answers: "Mommies get sad sometimes. That's all . . ."

Zoe sighs and then says, "She said the *s-h* word in the car yesterday. And then she cried."

"Mommies say bad words sometimes. And they get upset sometimes," I say. "But she'll be fine. *Everything* will be fine."

"Do you promise?" she says, her blue eyes big with worry.

I panic, wondering what the right answer is. Is it right for me to make such a promise? What constitutes *fine*? I certainly don't want to lie to Zoe. I have a sudden memory of one troubling *Family Feud* episode I watched when I was about seven. The final, bonus-round question was "Top five lies your parents told you." I remember racking my brain, trying to come up with something, while the Johnson family ripped off answers with ease. *Survey Says . . . Santa Claus! Easter Bunny! Tooth Fairy!* It was a devastating moment. In part because I had discovered a sad truth about my favorite trio, but also because I had just received a handwritten letter from the North Pole—a letter I now knew to be bogus. I ripped it off my bulletin board and confronted my parents about their lies.

Still, I think carefully about Zoe's question and decide that things *will* be fine. So I say, "Yes, Zoe. I promise you."

She gives me a hopeful smile. Then she slides her small hand into mine and says, "Can we go eat Pop-Tarts now? For dinner?"

"Great idea," I say. "Pop-Tarts for dinner. And Pop-Tarts for dessert!"

"And for appetizers?" she says.

"Yup. For appetizers, too," I say, smiling. "What could be better than that?"

As Zoe and I are finishing our elegant three-course meal of strawberry Pop-Tarts, Jess returns home from work. She and Zoe hug and kiss hello as I discreetly ask her if Michael will be coming over later. She shakes her head and says she wants to hang with us. I am happy about this as I wasn't sure how to explain an unwed sleepover to Zoe. To this point, Zoe turns to Jess and says, "Who's Michael? Your boyfriend?"

"Yeah," Jess says, smiling. "He is."

Zoe fires back with, "Do you love him?"

Jess looks at me and laughs.

"She cuts to the chase," I say.

"What's that mean?" Zoe says.

"You ask very good questions," I say.

"Oh," Zoe says, and then returns her expectant gaze to Jess.

"Yeah," Jess says. "I do love him."

"Why?" Zoe says.

"Well. He's smart. And nice. And funny. And very, very handsome."

Zoe's pale brow furrows as she processes this data. Then she asks the question we all have wondered. "Are you going to marry him?"

Jess finally looks stumped. "Hmm. Well, Zoe, I don't know. We'll see."

"When will we see?"

"I don't know. It's hard to tell."

"Why is it hard to tell?"

"Well, because sometimes you love someone but they might not be the right person for you. That takes some time to figure out," Jess explains, much better than I could have.

"I hope you marry your boyfriend," Zoe says. "That would be *really* romantic."

"That *would* be romantic," Jess says. "Let's make a wish for a happy ending."

Zoe closes her eyes and makes a silent wish. When she opens them, she is solemn. "Uncle Ben and Aunt Claudia got a dee-vorce," she says as if I'm not in the room.

"I know," Jess says, without looking at me.

"But she loved Uncle Ben," Zoe says and then looks at me. "Right, Aunt Claudia?"

"Right," I say. Then I go out on a questionable limb and say, "And I always will."

Zoe brightens. "So maybe you'll marry him *again*?"

There it is, I think. My one great hope unearthed and put out there by a child. I consider my responses. I consider saying that it's a possibility. That I want that very much. That I miss Ben with my whole heart and believe that I made a huge mistake in not considering having a baby with him. That I was too stubborn and rigid and vindictive and proud for my own good. That I hope I'm not too late.

But I am afraid to say any of this out loud. I don't want to jinx myself. Instead I just offer up a vague and halfhearted, "Well, Zoe, I wouldn't hold your breath on that one."

Always literal, Zoe inhales dramatically and holds her breath, her cheeks puffing out and her face turning red.

"*Breathe!*" I say, laughing.

She shakes her head, a smile straining at the corners of her mouth.

"Zoe! *Breathe!*" I say again, tickling her until she releases the air in fits of laughter. When she finally gains her composure, she says, "Aunt Claudia?"

"Yeah, Zoe?"

"If you do marry Uncle Ben again, I hope you do it soon. You know why?"

I watch her anxiously, concentrating on an itch in the small of my back. *Surely* the child doesn't know about aging eggs. *Surely* she doesn't know that I am going to have to offer Ben a child for the mere *hope* of getting him back. I finally say,

"Why's that, Zoe?"

" 'Cause. If you wait too long, I'll be too *old* to be your flower girl."

I smile with relief. "Hmm. That's a really good point, Zoe. You are getting up there in years."

"So don't wait too long," she says. "And don't 'lope this time."

"E-lope," I say.

"E-lope," she repeats.

"Ohh, right. Hmm. Well. We'll see about all that," I say, wondering how long Zoe can keep up her barrage of questions. If I'm not careful, she might have me talking about my e-mail exchange with Ben, our lunch date, and my earnest hope that my ex-husband hasn't fallen madly in love with a girl named Tucker.

I brace myself for her next inquiry, which turns out to be blessedly innocuous: "Can we try on shoes now?" she asks me.

"Absolutely," I say, relieved that I don't have to tell my niece about Tucker, the fast-running, pretty-haired, fertile doctor who can't possibly love Ben like I do.

twenty-eight

The next morning I awaken to the sight of Zoe in her lavender polka-dot nightgown, standing on her tiptoes with her nose and palms pressed against my bedroom window. I study her earnest profile and the way a patch of her hair is spiked with static electricity.

I finally break her concentration and say, "What's so interesting out there, Zoe?"

She turns, runs over to the bed, and says, "It's snowing, Aunt Claudia!"

"Really?" I say.

"Yeah! Come look," she says.

I follow her over to the window, remembering how thrilling snowfalls were as a child. Now snow simply signals inconvenience, particularly in a city that quickly turns into a dirty, slushy, slow-moving mess. But I forget all of this as I look outside with my niece. I even feel a twinge of disappointment when I see only a few scattered flurries and no accumulation on the ground.

"It doesn't look like it's going to stick," I say. "Just your standard November tease."

Zoe looks crestfallen, and I think of how my sisters and I felt when our hopes soared on a snowy morning, only to have them dashed by the man on the radio announcing in the most chipper tone, "All schools open!" Or even worse, when he'd give you a string of schools that *had* closed, but then announce that yours was the exception, without so much as a one- or two-hour delay as a consolation. One of the happiest days of my childhood was when my mother informed us that she was overriding one such poor decision. "I'm not taking any chances with you riding that bus. I hereby declare a snow day!" There were some fringe benefits that came with having a non-rule-following mother.

"If it sticks, can we go sledding in the park?" Zoe asks.

"Sure," I say, as I think of how emotions seem so magnified when you're a child. Joy is more all-encompassing, disappointments more crushing, hope more palpable. "You want to do a snow dance to help it along?"

Zoe lights up again and says, "What's a snow dance?"

I leap up onto my mattress and make up an exaggerated tribal dance which she imitates. Our legs and arms flail in the air until we are out of breath. Then I say, "Okay! Let's get moving! We have a busy day ahead of us!"

"What are we doing, Aunt Claudia?" Zoe asks.

I highlight our itinerary, which includes a matinee, a trip to FAO Schwarz, and a horse-and-carriage ride in Central Park.

Zoe looks gleeful. "Well, I better go put on my dress then."

I smile and say, "Yes. You'd better. And I think today calls for a touch of makeup, don't you?"

Zoe smiles even wider. She is a true girly-girl and is always clamoring for things like pierced ears, shaved legs, and makeup. Maura would kill me if I put holes in Zoe's ears or gave her one of my razors, but a little rouge and lip gloss is another story. She walks primly toward the bathroom and says in a voice more mature than her years, "Why, Aunt Claudia. That is an *excellent* idea."

A few hours later, after an inspired performance of *The Lion King,* Zoe and I exit the New Amsterdam Theater on Forty-second Street. The sun is out, and there is no trace of snow, but the day still feels wintry and festive. The city is already decorated with white lights and wreaths, and the streets bustle with holiday-season tourists. Zoe puts on her fluffy pink beret and matching gloves as I quickly hail a cab and ask him to take us to the Plaza, just across the street from FAO Schwarz. The whole way uptown, we sing "Hakuna Matata" in rounds. It is one catchy tune. In all of our merriment, I nearly forget the underlying reason for Zoe's visit. I wonder if she will someday know the full truth about our weekend. If she will look back on our time together, and her memories will be more bitter than sweet.

We are dropped off in the driveway in front of the Plaza. I pay the cabbie and hold the door open for Zoe. She spills out of the cab, forgetting to be ladylike in her corduroy jumper and fancy coat. Then she points to a blue-faced mime holding freakishly still near the fountain in front of the hotel.

"Can I go see him?" she asks.

"Sure," I tell her, remembering how Ben used to say, "How is that considered a talent? Who actually would bother to practice something like that?" Clearly many others disagree with Ben's assessment of mimes because there is a fairly sizable crowd gawking and videotaping.

Zoe scampers off toward the mime, while I stay near the hotel stairs and retrieve my cell phone from my purse. I want to see if Maura has called with any sort of update. There is one new message, but it is only Daphne. I keep my eye on Zoe as I listen to Daphne tell me that she just made a lemon Bundt cake, and the boys are licking the beaters. Daphne goes on to say that she hasn't heard a word from Maura. "Cross your fingers for some good news," she concludes.

I consider that Daphne's version of good news is likely not the same as mine. Short of abuse, Daphne believes couples with children should stay together. I think it's more about being happy. Not Christmas-photo-card happy, but truly, deep-down-in-your-bones happy.

I skip Daphne's message and listen to a very old one from Ben that I haven't had the heart to delete since our divorce. It is the only recording I have of him. There is nothing special about it—he is only relaying the phone number for our optometrist—but the mere sound of his voice washes over me, and I feel my heart flutter. I wish I could talk to him sooner than next Monday. My promise is ready on my tongue: *I will have a baby for you, Ben. I will do anything to get you back.*

I hit save, flip my phone shut, and look up to see Zoe, still mesmerized by the mime. She is now holding her beret in her hand and the sun is shining on her hair, making it look redder than usual. For one glorious moment, I am filled with a sense of well-being and peace.

And then everything changes in an instant.

I see the boy first, a scrawny skateboarder wearing baggy shorts, Converse high-tops, and an orange helmet. I wonder how he managed to get out of the house without a coat on a day like this. He is no older than twelve and has an adolescent awkwardness about him despite his fluid, confident stunts. He is clearly showing off, but pretending to be oblivious to his few admirers who have tired of the mime. He must be a loner, I think; boys his age usually travel in packs. I watch him surf several stairs and land effortlessly before picking up speed. That's when I see Zoe running back over to me, directly in his path. I freeze, knowing what's about to happen, but feeling powerless to stop it. Sort of like watching a scary scene in a movie with a menacing soundtrack. Sure enough, the boy careens toward Zoe, grunting, "Yo! Yo! Watch out!" I can see his body strain to change direction, and I pray for his skills to prevail. But as he pivots, he slips off the board and crashes into her. Zoe is thrown backward like a small doll, making a sickening thud on the sidewalk. The boy is sprawled on the sidewalk next to her, looking more embarrassed than injured.

I hear myself scream, can feel my heart pounding in my ears. Everything seems to move in slow motion as I weave past the crowd and kneel over Zoe. Her skin looks gray, her eyelids are closed, and blood is streaming down the left side of her face onto her white rabbit-fur collar. Fear and terror fill me as I check to see if she's breathing. She is. Still, I think, *What if she dies?* I fiercely tell myself not to be crazy; children do not *die* from skateboard collisions. It was only a minor accident. But then I think: *Concussion; head-and-neck injury; brain damage; paraplegia.* I think of other freak accidents, like the young boy I once saw on *60 Minutes* who was paralyzed playing a casual game of ice hockey. I have a fleeting image of Zoe going to her senior prom in a wheelchair.

Get a grip, I tell myself. *Spring into action and stop being so dramatic!* Yet all I can do is call Zoe's name and gently shake her shoulders. She does not respond. My mind swirls with first-aid principles I learned long ago, in Girl Scouts and my high-school health class: *Never move a person suspected of head or neck injury; check her pupils; exert pressure to stop the blood; call 911; yell for help.*

I can feel the stares and concerned hush around me as I find a Kleenex in my purse. As I press it against Zoe's head, her eyes flutter and open. I say her name in a rush of gratitude. She whimpers and touches her face. When she sees the blood covering her pink-gloved hand, she shrieks. Then she turns to the side and throws up. Somewhere, in a remote place in my brain, I remember that vomiting is a sign of a concussion, but I can't recall how serious a concussion is. And I have no idea how to treat one.

Zoe sits up and begins to wail for Maura and Scott. "Mommy! Daddy! I want my mom-*meee!*"

The skateboarder limps over to us and mumbles an apology. "Sorry," he says. "She got in my way." He looks afraid that he might get in trouble. I want to blame him, yell at him for skateboarding in a crowd, but I just say, "It's okay." He slinks off with his board tucked under his arm, moving on with his afternoon.

As I turn my attention back to Zoe, an older man emerges from nowhere, crouching over us. He is well dressed and has a low, soothing voice. He gently asks me if I am her mother.

"I'm her aunt," I say guiltily.

This happened on my watch.

"I hailed you a cab," he says, pointing a few yards away to a cab in the driveway in front of the hotel. "He's going to take you to the NYU Medical Center. She probably just needs a few stitches."

Zoe wails at the mention of stitches and then frantically protests as the man tries to lift her from the pavement.

"Let him carry you, honey," I say.

She does. A few seconds later, I slide into the cab. The man hands me Zoe, along with a soft, white handkerchief with his monogrammed initials: *WRG.* "You'll be fine, honey," he says. I'm not sure if he's talking to me or Zoe, but I want to kiss this kind, silver-haired stranger whose first name starts with a *W.* The man gives the driver the hospital address and closes the door. As we zip down Fifth, Zoe curls up on the seat next to me and sobs. I hold the handkerchief against the cut on her hairline, which is matted and sticky with blood. At some point, I realize that I left her beret on the sidewalk and feel another stab of guilt. First I let *this* happen; then I lose her favorite hat. I can only imagine what Maura will think when I tell her what happened: *I know you love Ben, but are you sure you're up to being a mother?* I call her now—both at home and on her cell—and am relieved when I get voice mail. I'm not ready to make this confession—nor do I want to upset my sister who is already dealing with so much. I try to comfort Zoe by repeating the man's words. I tell her that she's going to be fine, just fine. "I want my Mommy" is all she can say back.

By the time we arrive at the hospital, Zoe's bleeding has slowed, and I am no longer worried about paralysis or permanent brain damage. Still, her name is called almost immediately after we register at the front desk. Which is in striking contrast to my trip to the ER with Ben when he broke his ankle playing flag football and we sat in the waiting room for seven hours. Or the time I ate bad sushi and literally thought I might die from stomach pains but still had to wait for what seemed like every gang member in New York and a fleet of Hell's Angels to be seen before me.

So I feel an enormous sense of relief when Zoe is given priority, and we are led to an examining room. A nurse helps her change into a gown and then takes her vitals. One beat later a sunny resident whips through our curtain partition and introduces himself as Dr. Steve. Dr. Steve is a mix between Doogie Howser and George Clooney's character on *ER*. He is painfully youthful but still confident and charismatic. I can tell right away that Zoe likes him, and he is able to calm her down as he gathers information about her accident and symptoms while masterfully mixing in other questions about her school and hobbies. After a brief physical examination, he looks at Zoe and says, "Okay, Zoe, you had a pretty bad spill, so here's what we're going to do . . . We're going to order up a little X-ray of your head and give you a few little stitches right behind your ear."

Zoe freaks at the mention of stitches (they need to come up with a new name—what kid would be okay with the thought of her skin being sewn together with a needle?), but Dr. Steve flashes his dimples and convinces her that not only do his stitches not hurt, but also he will use *pink* thread that dissolves like *magic* in a few days. Zoe is sold.

"What are the X-rays for?" I ask, still a bit fearful that there could be some sort of serious head injury.

"Just a precautionary measure," Dr. Steve says, turning his dimples loose on me. "I'd be very surprised if she had anything other than a superficial injury."

I nod and thank him. Dr. Steve leaves to order Zoe's X-rays and collect his pink thread while I find a piece of paper in my purse and initiate a rousing game of hangman.

Two hours and minimal drama later, Zoe's X-rays confirm Dr. Steve's prognosis, and she is as good as new with five pink stitches and a major crush on her doctor. He hands her a lollipop—the good kind with a Tootsie Roll inside—and says,

"So, Zoe, I like you and all, but I really hope I never see you again in here."

She smiles, becoming uncharacteristically shy.

"So what do you say, Zoe? Do you promise to stay out of the path of speeding skateboarders?"

Zoe says she'll try, and he high-fives her.

I wonder if Dr. Steve took a class in bedside manner with young children or if all of this just comes naturally to him. Maybe it's something that requires practice. Maybe I could find a how-to book on the subject: *How to Deal with Medical Emergencies and Children in Crisis.*

Then I think of Ben. If I am lucky enough to get him back, I won't have to be perfect. We can figure things out *together.* I envision our little girl, running to us with a menacing splinter. He will man the tweezers, and I will be at his side, ready with a Garfield Band-Aid. We will be a good team. We were once. We will be again.

And then, just as Zoe and I are headed toward the exit with our discharge papers and backup lollipops in hand, I hear a vaguely familiar voice behind me, saying, "Claudia? Is that you?"

My stomach drops as I place the voice. Then I turn slowly and look straight into Tucker Janssen's big, green eyes.

twenty-nine

"Hi, Tucker," I say, taking in her perfectly pressed white doctor's coat, blue scrubs, and shiny stethoscope. And of course, her long, blond mane pulled into her trademark ponytail. She is prettier than I remembered. But maybe it's the difference between seeing someone after a run and seeing someone with a bit of makeup. I shudder to think what she might look like fully dressed for dinner. My heart sinks, and I eye the exit door, hoping that our conversation will be short. Despite the very significant thing we have in common, I have nothing to say to her.

"Hi, Claudia," she says, looking completely at ease.

I remind myself that I'm not supposed to know that she's a doctor. So I go through the song and dance of feigning surprise. "Are you a doctor?" I say.

"Yeah," she says with false modesty. "I'm a pediatric surgeon."

"Oh," I say. "That's nice."

"What are you doing here?" she asks, glancing down at Zoe. "Is everything okay?"

Her concern seems genuine, but is still highly irritating. I know it's irrational, but I feel as if she is judging me. Assessing the magnitude of my negligence. Concluding that I would, indeed, make an unfit, inept mother.

I say, "My niece had a little spill, that's all. But she's fine now."

"Poor thing," Tucker croons.

Zoe, who has returned to her outgoing self, chimes in, "I got five stitches!"

I panic, wondering what else Zoe will say. I pray that Tucker won't mention Ben because then the floodgates will open. I can just hear Zoe: *How do you know Uncle Ben? Aunt Claudia dee-vorced him because she didn't want kids. But Aunt Claudia says she'll always love him. And if they get married again I get to be a flower girl!*

Sure enough, Zoe's comment gives Tucker license to interact with my niece. As if sharing a grave secret, she stoops, winks, and says, "The pink kind?"

Zoe beams. "Uh-huh. The pink kind."

Tucker tousles Zoe's hair and gives her a doting smile. Then she stands and says to me, "She's adorable."

"Thanks," I say, although I'm not sure it's appropriate to accept compliments on behalf of someone else's child, even if she is my niece. I shift my weight from one foot to the other. Then my mind goes blank as I look toward the exit again. I desperately don't want to segue into other topics, like, say, marathons or Ben. I wonder if Tucker knows about my plans to see her boyfriend. I surmise that she does, as I recall how Ben told me when his ex, Nicole, sent him a birthday present about a year after we began dating. Struggling to sound nonchalant, I remember saying, "Oh. That's nice . . . What did she give you?"

"A book of poetry," he said matter-of-factly, as if it meant nothing to him at all.

Meanwhile, I couldn't think of a more menacingly meaningful gift than a book, let alone a book of *poetry*, and it took all my willpower not to ask which book, what poems. Instead I just mumbled a cool and oh-so-secure, "Well, that was thoughtful of her."

Ben said, "Yeah. Whatever. No biggie. Just wanted to tell you in the interest of full disclosure."

That's how Ben is—direct and honest. So I'm sure he was very forthright about our lunch date.

Sure enough, Tucker says, "So. How are you doing these days, Claudia?"

Her words are innocent enough, but there is a shade of condescension and pity in her voice. She is also, ever so subtly, laying claim to her man. She is behaving *exactly* as I would have behaved had I run across Nicole in my early days with Ben. She is pleasant and dignified, but still demonstrating who is in charge.

"Fine. And you?" I say tersely and formally. I am not about to be intimidated. I was *married* to Ben. Marathon or no marathon, she hasn't *earned* the right to be so territorial.

"I'm great," she throws out comfortably. She might as well add, *And so not threatened by you.*

My discomfort shifts to resentment as I process her *great*. There is no doubt about it: *great* surpasses *fine*. The bitch just *has* to outdo me. Any benefit of the doubt I've ever given her flies out the hospital door. I want to slap her or throw cold water in her face. Do one of those things that people only do in sitcoms.

And that's all *before* her hand darts up to shift that godforsaken ponytail from her left to right shoulder, and I see her ring.

Her *diamond* ring.

Her diamond ring on her *left* ring finger.

I can't say for sure if she flashed it on purpose, but I do know with certainty that she saw me looking at it. So I have no choice but to acknowledge it now. I take a deep breath and recruit every bit of will I have in me to point in the general direction of her hand and say, "Congratulations."

She smiles triumphantly and glances down at her hand before dipping it into her jacket pocket. Then she blushes and says, "Thank you, Claudia. It . . . happened quickly."

"Yes . . . Well . . . congratulations," I say again, feeling so dizzy with devastation that I can barely see straight, let alone move.

Tucker starts to inquire about my Thanksgiving plans, but I interrupt and say we really must go home now. Then I take Zoe's hand and lead her outside where we climb into a taxi. I give the cabbie our address. As I watch the city blocks blur by my window, I am gripped with the knowledge that this day will forever remain the worst of my *entire* life. There will be no such thing as perspective. Time will not heal this. I will be marked by that moment in the hospital forever. It will become a part of who I am. In fact, it already has. I try to concentrate on breathing in and out, telling myself not to cry, but I am losing the fight. I can feel the grief rising uncontrollably in my throat. Then, somewhere between that East Side hospital and my best friend's apartment, I fall apart, right in front of my six-year-old niece.

"What's wrong, Aunt Claudia?" Zoe asks, her own voice shaky with fear. She has never seen me cry before. "Why are you sad?"

"Because my heart hurts," I say, wiping my tears away with the back of my hand.

"Why? Why does your heart hurt?" she asks me, now on the verge of tears herself.

I can't answer her—so she keeps asking the question. Over and over.

Finally I say, "Because I love Uncle Ben."

"Why does that make you sad?" she says, her small hand darting out to take mine.

"Because, Zoe," I say, too defeated to spin the truth or try to protect her. "Because Ben is going to marry someone else."

"That *girl* doctor?" Zoe says, her eyes wide with horror.

Through fresh tears, I nod and whisper yes.

I spend the rest of the afternoon trying to explain to Zoe one of the very saddest notions in love and life: sometimes the timing is wrong—and sometimes you realize the heart of the matter way too late in the game. I tell her that it was a big mistake to divorce Ben. I wanted my life to look a certain way, and when Ben didn't fit into that plan, I gave up on him. And now, the person I care about most is gone. Ben belongs to someone else now. Ben belongs to Tucker. *The girl doctor.*

Maybe Zoe truly grasps what I'm telling her, but at the very least she pretends to understand, her expression becoming almost comically philosophical. I feel a bit ashamed for dumping so much on a child with a head injury and parents on the brink of disaster. But I can't help myself. There is something soothing about her company and her innocent commentary.

"Just be happy, Aunt Claudia," she says at one point. As if it's the easiest thing in the world to do.

I smile and say, "I'll try."

But inside I'm thinking, *Never. I'll never be truly happy again.*

Jess and Michael return home a short time later. As I introduce Zoe and Michael and they shake hands, I can see Jess registering my red-rimmed eyes.

"What's wrong?" she mouths over Zoe's head, wrongly assuming that I've actually shielded my niece today.

I say, "Imagine the worst."

Jess thinks for a beat and then pretty much nails it. "Ben and Tucker got married?"

"Close," I say.

"Eng*aged*?" she says, aghast.

I give her a grim nod.

Her mouth falls open and Michael busts out with a "Get the fuck outta here."

Jess glares at him and points at Zoe. I know Maura will get the curse-word report, although in the scheme of the day, one little F-word falling through the cracks doesn't seem all that destructive.

"Sorry," Michael says to me with a grimace.

"I've heard it before," Zoe says, crossing her arms. She is definitely relishing her role in this adult drama.

"Did he call you?" Jess asks. "Did Annie tell you?"

"No," I say, letting loose a bitter laugh. "We actually ran into Tucker in the ER."

"The *ER*?" Jess says. She and Michael look floored as Zoe and I regale them with the gory details of her accident and hospital visit. After Jess and Michael inspect Zoe's stitches and give her a few props for being brave, Jess gets right to the point: *What did the ring look like? Have they set a date? Do I think Tucker could be pregnant?*

I shrug three times in succession, and at her last question, I say, "It's a moot point anyway."

"Oh, no, it's *not* a moot point," Jess says. "It ain't over till it's *over*."

"Heard that, sister," Michael says, putting his arm around Jess.

I stare back at the blissful couple in the throes of early passion—a couple who can't fathom feeling differently than they do at this moment in time.

"Oh, it's *over*, guys," I say, glancing at my sidekick for confirmation. "Right, Zoe?"

She nods somberly and says, "Yeah. The timing was *all* wrong."

After Jess and Michael leave for dinner, Zoe and I curl up on the couch watching the original *Parent Trap* with Hayley Mills. It was one of my favorite movies as a child, and like the satisfying child she is, Zoe tells me more than once that she prefers this "old-fashioned" version to the one with Lindsay Lohan.

When the phone rings, I glance at the caller ID. It is Maura. My heart seizes with the thought of *more* family drama. And aside from any report that she has for me, I positively dread telling her about Zoe's accident.

"It's your mom," I say as I hit the pause button on the remote control and answer the phone.

"Hey, Maura," I say gingerly. I'm going to have to ask cryptic questions with Zoe right next to me.

"I wanna talk to *Mommy*!" Zoe says, her voice becoming babyish and whiny.

"One sec, Zoe," I say, and then ask Maura how she's doing.

"I'm fine," Maura says, sounding stronger than I expected.

"What's going on? How are you?" I say.

"I'm fine, but I can't really talk now. He's in the kitchen," she says in a low voice.

"Can you give me an overview?" I say while Zoe continues to clamor for the phone.

"Well, in a nutshell, he's crazy sorry. Like begging and crying sorry. He keeps saying that he doesn't know *why* he does what he does. He says he needs help. He wants to see my therapist, Cheryl, something he was never willing to do before. He says he'll do *anything* to keep our family together," she whispers. "I've *never* seen this side of him. It's not like before. I guess it's because . . . *I'm* different this time. I haven't cried once."

I glance at Zoe and choose my words carefully. "Is he trying to say he has some sort of . . . addiction?"

"Well, he hasn't said that *exactly* . . . I just think he's . . . a very unhappy person."

That might be true, I think, but it doesn't give him the license to run around all of Manhattan and make everyone in his family miserable, too. But it's not up to me to make judgments—or decisions for my sister—so I just say, "How do you feel?"

"I don't know," she says. "But I know I have the upper hand for a change . . . And that sure feels good."

There is a long pause and then she asks how Zoe is.

"She's sitting right here, patiently waiting to talk to you. I'll put her on." Then I inhale sharply and say, "But first I need to tell you something—"

Maura interrupts. "Oh, God, what happened?"

I am amazed at her mother's intuition as I reassure her that Zoe is fine. Then I give her the least melodramatic version of the accident. I leave out the part about Tucker and finish by saying, "I'm *truly* sorry I let that happen."

"Don't be silly," Maura says, but her voice is shaking a bit. "Accidents happen. It's not your fault . . . Lemme talk to her."

"Sure," I say, handing the phone to Zoe, who promptly and predictably bursts into tears when she hears her mother's voice. I guess it's a natural reflex when you talk to the person you love most in the world. Which means I better not go through with my lunch with Ben. I can just see myself blubbering in our booth.

After Zoe gives Maura her rendition of the accident, and the ride to the hospital, and Dr. Steve and her stitches, she launches into Ben and Tucker's engagement. I don't have the energy to stop her or intervene. Besides, her report is fairly accurate, right down to the "blond ponytail" and the "big, sparkly diamond ring."

When I finally take the phone back, Maura says, "Is that true?"

"Afraid so," I say. "Her imagination isn't *that* good."

"God. I'm *so* sorry," she says.

"I know," I say. "So am I."

In light of the accident, Maura decides that Zoe should return home tonight. "She needs to be here with us," Maura says. The *us* is not lost on me, nor is the fact that Maura and Scott arrive together. I wonder if this means that Maura is going to give Scott "one more chance." Or whether it's her way of showing Zoe that *both* her parents love her very much even though they no longer love each other.

What I am sure of, though, is that Maura looks much better than she did at Zoe's drop-off a mere twenty-four hours ago. She looks strong—with perfect posture and good color in her cheeks. In contrast, Scott has a gray pallor and a scared, mealymouthed manner.

It occurs to me that things could very easily have gone the other way. Scott could have responded with a cavalier, "All right, you got me. Now let's get a divorce." Or worse, he could have said, "I'm in love with this woman, and we want to get married."

At the very least, Maura gets to choose now. And being the decision maker is always empowering. I am happy for my sister for having at least that much. I wish I did.

I kiss Zoe good-bye at least four times and tell her I think we need to have another sleepover soon so we can go to FAO Schwarz and have our carriage ride. "And maybe it will even snow the next time," I say, missing her before she's even gone.

"Can I come back soon, Mommy?" Zoe asks, looking up at Maura.

"Of course," Maura says.

As Scott scoops up Zoe in his arms, Maura takes my hand, squeezes it and quietly says, "Take care of yourself."

"You, too," I say.

When the door closes behind Zoe and her parents, I say aloud to myself, with as much sarcasm as I can muster, *"Today is the first day of the rest of your life."* It's a cliché I've always disliked—as much for the obvious truth of it as the pressure it creates to have a productive, fantastic day. So naturally, I decide to do the opposite. I throw in the towel and crawl into bed, not even bothering to take a shower first and wash the hospital and Tucker germs off my skin.

thirty

Over the next three days I vacillate between numb disbelief and gut-wrenching misery. Work is slow, as it always is before holidays, so I spend most of my time editing at home—and much of that time in bed. Jess informs me that excessive sleep is a sign of depression—as if that is some kind of revelation. She gives me turbocharged, Richard Simmons–esque pep talks. I shrug her off, telling her that I'll be fine. Even though I'm not at all convinced that I will be.

My lowest point comes in the middle of the night when I wake up after dreaming the final scene in *The Graduate*. Everything is just like the movie, only I am Dustin Hoffman and Ben does not leave a very pregnant Tucker at the altar. Instead, he and his whole family just look at me like I'm crazy until Ray and Annie each grab one of my arms and cart me out of the church and stick me on that bus, all alone. I wake up, sweaty and teary and so full of fury that I scare myself.

The next morning, I find Jess in her room, doing last-minute packing for her trip to Alabama with Michael. Against my better judgment, I tell her about my nightmare.

She says, "Well. Fortunately, you will be reclaiming Ben prior to their *wedding* day."

I give her a blank look, and she says, "Like on Monday?"

I shake my head and say, "There isn't going to be any *reclaiming* . . . And I'm not going to go through with seeing Ben on Monday."

"*What?*" she says.

"I'm canceling," I say emphatically.

"Oh, no you're *not*," she says even more emphatically.

"There's no point," I say with a listless shrug.

"There is *too* a point," she says. "Look, Claudia. The fact that they got engaged doesn't really change the analysis here."

"Yeah, it does," I say.

"No, it doesn't!" she says. "If Ben can get a divorce from the love of his life, he can most certainly break off an engagement."

"How do we know that *she's* not the love of his life?"

"Because *you* are," she says. "And you only get *one* of those."

"Since when do you subscribe to that notion?" I say.

"Since I've finally experienced true love."

"Well. I got news for you, Jess. Ben loves her," I say. "He wouldn't propose if he didn't love her. He wants a baby, but not that badly."

"Fine. Maybe he does love her in some narrow way. But he loves you more and you know it . . . He doesn't have full information. He *needs* full information. Once he knows that you want children, he'll have to break up with her."

"I don't *want* children."

"Yes you do."

"No I don't," I say. "I would have been *theoretically* willing to have his."

"Same difference."

"Not really."

She zips up her red Tod's bag with authority and says, "Well. I say we let Ben be the judge of that. Shall we?"

Meanwhile, my own Thanksgiving plans are up in the air until the eleventh hour. Maura almost always hosts a dinner at her house, but for obvious reasons, this year is the exception. Daphne is the logical backup choice because my father, understandably, refuses to go to Dwight and Mom's house, but when we tell my mother the plan, she gets on her soapbox about "you girls never coming over here." And then shoots off on another tangent about how we've never really accepted Dwight. I am in no mood for her nonsense so I quickly squelch her spirit and say, "Listen here, Vera. We're going to Daphne's. You can't even cook."

"We can have food brought in," she says.

"Mom. Drop it. The decision is made."

"Says who?" she says in the voice of a small child.

"Says me," I say. "So join us or don't. Entirely up to you."

I hang up and decide that the only true beauty of hitting rock bottom is that nothing can really faze or rile you. Not even your mother.

A few minutes later she calls me back with a conciliatory, "Claudia?"

"Yes?" I say.

"I've decided."

"And?"

"I'll come," she says meekly.

"Good girl," I say.

Thanksgiving morning is bleak and gray and drizzly, but also unseasonably warm, a depressing holiday combination. It takes every bit of will I have to get out of bed, shower, and dress. One of my mother's life principles flashes in my head—*if you dress up and look pretty, you will feel better*. And although I basically agree with this, I discard the advice and settle on an ancient J. Crew rollneck sweater and a pair of Levi's with threadbare knees. I tell myself that at least it beats sweats and sneakers, which I resist only because I can just envision "wearing sweats and sneakers on Thanksgiving" listed in a *Suicide Warning Signs* pamphlet.

I can't find a cab so I have to walk to Penn Station and barely make my noon train. I am stuck in a seat facing backward, which always gives me motion sickness. Then, about halfway to Huntington, I realize that I left my fancy twenty-eight-dollar pumpkin pie from Balthazar on the kitchen counter. I say *shit* aloud. An old woman across the aisle from me turns and gives me a disapproving stare. I mouth *sorry*, although I'm thinking, *Mind your own business, lady*. Then I spend the next twenty minutes worrying that I will turn into the kind of disgruntled person who dislikes old people. Or worse, I will become a bitter old person who hates the young.

When my father picks me up at the train station, I tell him that we need to swing by the grocery store to pick up a pie.

"Screw the pie," my dad says, which I translate to mean, *I heard about Ben's engagement*.

"No. Really, Dad," I say. "I promised Daphne I'd bring a pumpkin pie."

Translation: *I'm a total loser. All I have left is my word.*

My dad shrugs and a few moments later we pull into the Waldbaum's parking lot. I run inside, grab two skimpy pumpkin pies, already reduced to half price, and head for the express "twelve items or less" lane.

Fewer, I say to myself, thinking of how amused Ben was when I corrected grammar on public signage. *Twelve items or fewer, dammit.* I truly hope that Tucker is a math-science girl in the strictest sense of things and screws up her pronouns on a daily basis. She is Harvard-educated, so I know her mistakes aren't overt, as in, *Me and Daddy are going to the store,* but with some luck, she might be prone to making other sorts of mistakes—the kind intelligent people make while believing that they are being intelligent. Like failing to use the objective case for all parts of the compound object following a preposition, as in: *Do you want to come with Daddy and I?*

The beauty of this is that Ben will be forced to think of me every single time. Then, one day, he might break down and share with Tucker the trick I taught him so long ago: *Try each part of the object in a separate sentence. "Do you want to come with Daddy?" "Do you want to come with me?" Hence: "Do you want to come with Daddy and me?"* Maybe her eyes will narrow and a cloud will pass over her face. "Did your ex-wife teach you that one?" she'll say with disdain born from jealousy and failure to measure up. Because she might be able to put people back together again, but she will never be able to diagram a sentence as I can.

Then, as I'm paying for my two sorry pies and some Cool Whip, I see Charlie, my high school boyfriend, get in line behind me. I usually like running into Charlie, and other high school friends, but my divorce has changed that. It's just not the sort of update you feel like inserting in small talk, but at the same time, it's rather impossible to avoid mentioning. Besides, I've about reached my quota for chance meetings this week and don't have it in me to be friendly. I keep my head low and slip the checkout girl a twenty.

Just as I think I'm going to escape, Charlie says, "Claudia? Is that you?"

It occurs to me to pretend that I didn't hear him and just keep walking, but I like Charlie and don't want to come across as an urban snob—something he once accused me of being—so I turn, smile, and give him my best impersonation of a happy, well-adjusted adult. "Hey, Charlie!" I say. "Happy Thanksgiving!"

"You, too, Claudia!" he says, pushing forward his last-minute items: a gallon of whole milk, three cans of cranberry sauce, and a box of tampons. "How ya doin'?"

"Fine!" I say brightly as I look down and see Charlie's son shaking a pack of orange Tic Tacs. He looks exactly like Charlie's kindergarten photo, which was framed in his foyer the whole time we were dating. The little boy looks up at his father and says, "Can we get these, Dad?"

I anticipate a, *No. Put it back,* which is the standard parental grocery-store retort, but Charlie says, "Sure. Why not?" and tosses the Tic Tacs on the belt.

I smile, remembering what I liked most about my first boyfriend—his knee-jerk response was always, "Why not?" He was uncomplicated and upbeat and easy. At one point, I might have thought these traits made him a simpleton, but now I think they just translate to happiness. After all, he is the one with a family. He is the one buying hygiene products for his spouse. And I'm the one who is divorced, with my father waiting for me in the car outside.

"So what's doin'?" Charlie says with a big smile.

"Not much," I say and try to deflect with a question about his son. "Is this your oldest?"

"No!" Charlie says. "This is my youngest, Jake . . . Jake, this is Claudia."

Jake and I shake hands, and I pray that we're winding up, but then Charlie asks, "How's Ben?"

"Actually, we got a divorce," I say.

"I'm sorry."

"Don't be," I say. "He's getting remarried."

Then I laugh at my own joke. Charlie does, too, but it is the awkward sort of pity-laugh, not a ha-ha laugh. We exchange a few more pleasantries, both of us promising to tell our families hello. All the while, I can tell he's thinking, *I knew it. I knew she was in for a sad life when she told me after our prom that she didn't want kids*.

Daphne has everything under control when my father and I arrive at her house. But by under control, I don't mean Maura's version of polished perfection. On the contrary, Daphne's house is in a state of noisy disarray. The kitchen is a mess, and Tony's football game is competing with Daphne's favorite Enrique Iglesias CD and their frantic Yorkies. Still, everything smells good and feels comfortable. Daphne is standing at the stove, all four burners ablaze. She is wearing her GOT CARBS? apron and looks relaxed. My father joins Tony in the family room, and I put my pies and Cool Whip in the refrigerator and say, "Hope you have dessert backup."

"Of course I do," Daphne says, smiling proudly and pointing to a freshly rolled-out pie crust on the counter.

"So," I say, settling onto a bar stool. "Have you heard from Maura? Is *he* coming?"

Daphne knows I'm referring to Scott. She sets about peeling a Granny Smith apple and tells me that as of this morning, Maura hadn't decided whether to let him come or stay home alone. She was pleased to know that Scott's parents and sister's family had already booked a trip to Disney World for the holiday—so if she chose to exclude him, he'd have no backup plan.

A moment later we hear my mother and Dwight at the front door.

"Hell-*ooo*?" my mother trills as she sails into the kitchen, heavily perfumed, wearing a flowing St. John ensemble with navy pumps. Her outfit conjures the phrase "dressy casual," which is her favorite dress-code designation for her own parties. Despite her allergies to dogs, she gathers up Daphne's Yorkies and allows them to lick her mouth. "He-wo, Gary! He-wo, Anna!" she croons as I think that baby talk to dogs is only slightly more annoying than baby talk to babies.

Dwight is also dressy casual. He is sporting tasseled loafers, Ray Bans, and a jacket with shiny, gold buttons. He takes off his glasses and presents three bottles of merlot to Daphne. Then he rubs his hands together vigorously enough to start a fire. "Soo, ladies, what's shakin'?" he says, surveying the simmering pots. "Smells good in here, Daph!"

Then, as I watch him strut around the kitchen, I think of how Ben used to imitate his walk and say, "Ever notice the way Dwight's pelvis enters a room about five minutes before he does?" I always liked when he made fun of Dwight, yet the thought that Ben might share such observations about my family (even my mother's husband) with his bride-to-be has the strangest effect of creating loyalty where none existed before. Dwight isn't a bad guy, I think, as I kiss him hello for what very well could be the first time ever. I wait for my mother to put down the dogs, wash her hands, and use her inhaler. Then I give her a hug.

"So good of you to dress up," she whispers in my ear.

I smile and say, "Yes. But you'll be happy to know that should there be an accident and I am disrobed by a paramedic, I am wearing my best underwear."

She smiles as if to say, *I taught you well.*

The doorbell rings, and we all glance at each other nervously, a question hanging in the air: *Will Scott show up with his family?*

Even my mother is subdued.

"You get the door," Daphne says as she nervously reties her apron.

I head to the door. When I open it, I am genuinely surprised to see Scott. I really thought Maura was leaning toward banishment. Hillary Clinton's quote about Bill pops into my head: "He's a hard dog to keep on the porch." Clearly the same can be said of Scott. Although here he is, back on the porch with Maura.

"Hi, guys," I say, bending down to hug the kids first. Zoe points to her stitches—or more accurately, the spot where they once were. "They disappeared," she says. "Just like Dr. Steve said they would!"

I laugh and hug her again.

When I stand, I look right into Scott's eyes. For once, they don't look smug or beady. Instead, he is more chagrined and contrite than he was on Saturday night. And Maura looks even peppier. I think to myself, *Carefree, confident, popular girl is on a date with ever-grateful, second-tier wannabe.* It is role reversal for them, and I am filled with a sense of nostalgia, remembering that was how my sister *used* to be, in the days before Scott. I wonder what happened first. Did Scott's behavior change Maura into a victim and put her in a constant state of anxiety? Or did her priorities somehow get skewed, so that she could allow someone like Scott in her life?

I give him a chilly hello and then kiss my sister. More tense hellos are exchanged in the kitchen. Then we all move into the family room to watch the football game that only Tony really cares about. I keep my mind off Ben by observing Scott and Maura. He is pandering to her every need—refilling her wine glass, rubbing her shoulders, handling the kids when they act up—and I find myself thinking of one of Annie's theories on relationships that she calls the "benevolent dictator" theory. She says that in an ideal relationship, the balance of power is equal. But if someone has to have *more* power, that someone needs to be the woman. Her reasoning is that when most men wield the power, they abuse it and succumb to their innately self-serving, self-indulgent instincts. Women who have power, on the other hand, tend to rule in the interest of the family unit rather than their own self-interest. Which is why matriarchal societies are peaceful, harmonious ones. And why societies ruled by males are ultimately destroyed in war.

Of course when Annie first shared this theory with me in college, I tried to debunk it with tales of my own parents. I told her my mother held all the power—and was all about self-interest—while my father was the well-intentioned good guy. Yet, upon looking around, I had to begrudgingly admit that Annie *was* onto something and that my family seemed to be the exception to the rule. My friends with divorced parents almost all had passive martyrs for mothers; and the ones with parents in strong marriages all seemed to have forceful mothers and doting husbands.

I watch Maura now, imagining her coronation as benevolent dictator. The ruler who could have cruelly left Scott at home with a Swanson frozen dinner after usurping him from the throne. Instead, she brought him along to our family feast.

332

She showed him a drop of grace and at least short-term clemency. Some might say this makes her a fool or a coward. I might have said the same thing last week. But as I watch her today, I think it has more to do with strength of spirit, of wanting to do what is best for her children and struggling to find that answer. Still, children or no children, I also know that she's reached the end of the line. If Scott is lucky enough to survive this incident, I am certain that she will not tolerate another betrayal, even a small hint of one. This is his final, *final* chance at redemption. I can tell Scott knows it, too.

I just wonder if sheer force of will to forgive can be enough to set things right for my sister and her family. Because after all, power is one thing. Love is a different creature altogether.

When the turkey is done, we are told to migrate to the dining room, despite Tony's request that we watch the end of the game and eat on TV trays. Daphne doesn't dignify this with a response. Instead she ignores him and says, "Everyone grab a beverage and c'mon!"

Dwight leads the charge, a glass of wine in one hand and a can of diet Dr Pepper in the other. As he rounds the corner, he booms, "Whoa! Look out! Assigned seating!"

Sure enough, Daphne has set the table with little place cards made out of brown construction paper and pilgrim stickers. She has placed smaller ones at a card table for Zoe, Patrick, and William.

Maura eagerly circles the table, inspecting the names, as people do at a wedding reception. She quickly plucks Scott's up and switches it with Dwight's so that she is no longer seated next to her husband. Meanwhile, Scott frowns and the rest of us pretend not to notice as we take our seats.

Tony says the blessing, and afterward, Daphne insists on adhering to our family tradition—we all must name something we are grateful for. I personally think that that is a mighty dangerous activity considering the tenuous circumstances that comprise our lives on this particular Thursday. But I'm not about to rock the boat. Instead, my mind races with generic possibilities for my own offering.

Daphne gives a final instruction, "Remember. No repeats." Then she says, "Dwight, you can start."

Dwight smiles and says, "Okeydokey. I'm grateful for the food on this table that Daphne prepared for us. Everything looks great!".

"Dammit, Dwight," I say. "You took mine."

Dwight laughs and says, "I'm also grateful that I got to go first!"

Zoe clamors to go next. She says she is grateful that her head is better and that she had so much fun with Aunt Claudia last weekend. I smile at her. Zoe then says she will go for Patrick and William. She says that her brothers are grateful for all of their toys and books.

My mother picks up at the adult table where Dwight left off. She looks at the ceiling, as if pondering her bounty of blessings. She is always good for an unexpected, attention-grabbing song of thanksgiving. One year it was: *"I'm grateful that Ross Perot did so well in this year's election."* Another year: *"I'm grateful that my husband Dwight now knows that gifts from Kohl's and other retail stores of that ilk, though well intentioned, are not acceptable."*

This year she goes the self-aggrandizing route and says, "I'm thankful for the creative energy our Lord has bestowed upon me as I have embarked on my exciting new career in photography."

I try not to crack up and am assisted in this effort by the fact that Scott is up. His eyes remain closed, as if still in prayer. Last year I remember he was grateful that the stock market was finally rebounding and the economy getting back on track. This year, he clears his throat and says, "I'm grateful to be here at this table."

His simple statement is the most genuine and humble utterance I've ever heard from him, and I can't help feeling moved. I am a long ways from forgiving him, but I realize that empathy might be the first step. And I *do* feel nearly sorry for him. Maura, on the other hand, looks completely unfazed when she quickly comes back with, "I'm thankful for my beautiful children, my supportive parents, and my *loyal* sisters."

Ouch, I think.

"What about Daddy?" Zoe says. The child misses *nothing*.

"Oh, yes, Zoe, thank you," Maura says. "I'm grateful that you have a daddy who loves you and your brothers."

This seems to appease her, so we move on to my dad. After he gives his standard thanks for the health of everyone at the table, it is my turn.

I know I have a lot to be grateful for, but all I can think of is Ben. Of how my life feels so *depleted* without him. I think for another minute, surveying the faces around the table. Ben and I used to be our own little family, but now the people in this room are the only family I have. The only family I likely will *ever* have. So I say, "I am thankful for the love in this room. For knowing that despite any trouble we might find ourselves in, we will be here for one another in the end."

Everyone is quiet for a moment. Even William and Patrick look somber.

"Okay," I say. "Daph?"

We all look at my sister. She and Tony clasp hands and smile at each other, and I instantly know that they have big news. That we will all have something *real* to be happy about.

Sure enough, my sister smiles angelically and says, "Tony and I want to do one together this year." Then she looks around the table and says, "We are grateful that God is finally blessing us with a child."

My mother gasps. "Dear God! You're pregnant! It's a miracle!"

"No, Mother," Daphne says quickly. "I'm not pregnant . . . But you're right, it *is* a miracle."

Her voice breaks as if she is about to cry so Tony continues for her. "We're adopting a baby. A baby boy. He's due on December twenty-second."

For one moment, we are all stunned and then our collective shock converts to the purest form of joy, the kind that translates to simultaneous laughter and tears. Daphne regains composure, telling us to eat before the food gets cold.

"As if we can eat! Tell us the details," Maura says as she stands and hugs Daphne, then kisses Tony.

We all follow suit, standing in line to congratulate the proud parents-to-be. Even Scott seems to forget that he is in the doghouse as he high-fives Tony.

Then as we all sit back down and share our Thanksgiving meal, Daphne tells us about her fateful meeting with her son's birth mother in an Easy Spirit store at the mall in Huntington. We all laugh at her introduction because it is *just* like Daphne to befriend strangers.

"Easy *Spirit?*" Maura says and then mockingly spouts off the company motto, " 'Looks like a pump, feels like a sneaker!' "

Daphne smiles and says to Maura, "I know, you're appalled by my fashion sensibilities, but those shoes are *so* comfortable . . . And I'm not trying to impress fifth-graders with my footwear."

My father throws his hands up in mock exasperation and says, "Enough of the shoes! Tell us what happened!"

"Okay," Daphne says. "So I'm trying on these shoes and this really cute, young pregnant girl sits down next to me. I notice that she's not wearing a wedding band, and I start wondering if her hand is just swollen from being pregnant and her rings won't fit or if she's not married and got pregnant accidentally. And I'm sort of thinking that it was an accident because, you know, she looks *soo* young. Then I have to admit, I have this pang of bitterness, like, how is *that* fair? How can some people have a baby so easily and get pregnant when they don't try at all and don't even really want a baby?"

"Daphne!" Maura and I say in tandem. Daphne is known in our family for being the slowest, most circuitous storyteller of all time.

Daphne laughs and streamlines her tale. She says that she and the girl—whose name is Amber—got to talking about how comfortable Easy Spirits are. Amber told Daphne that she waitresses at night and her feet hurt all the time. Daphne told Amber that she's a teacher and she sure knows about achy feet. It turns out that Amber is in college getting her degree in education. Daphne asked her what college. Amber said Hofstra, which is where Daphne went to school. They then discussed professors they both know and courses Amber is taking and where she'd like to someday student-teach.

So then Daphne asked about her baby, and after a few minutes of polite chatter about the gender and due date, Amber came right out and told Daphne the rest of her story—that she got pregnant accidentally (the condom broke) and her boyfriend—now ex-boyfriend—wanted her to have an abortion. And so did her parents. But Amber said she just couldn't do that. But she also knows in her heart that she isn't ready to be a mother and that it wouldn't be fair to the baby to try. She wants a better life for her son. So she decided to give the baby up for adoption. She researched agencies and finally registered with one in Westchester, the kind that facilitates open adoptions. She said she had met several couples, but just hadn't found the right match yet. She said that everyone had been supernice, but the vibe was always off. Now the baby was coming soon so she was running out of time.

Daphne pauses for a second to sip from her water glass. Then she says, "At this point, I just burst into tears with this guy named Bo helping me into a pair of chocolate-brown loafers . . . Then, I find myself confiding in Amber, telling her all about our struggles. And when I finish, we just sort of look at each other. Straight into each other's eyes. And it's like, in that instant, we both just *knew* that we were meant to meet . . . So we end up buying the same pair of shoes, and going to the food court to talk more. That night she came over for dinner and met Tony, and they hit it off, too. Right, Tony?"

Tony nods. "Yeah. I really like her . . . She has a good head on her shoulders."

"And a great, big heart," Daphne adds.

"What does she look like?" Maura asks.

Daphne says, "She's cute. She has straight brown hair and dark eyes and a sweet smile. She's tall . . . at least five ten."

"The tall part is pretty cool," Tony says. Tony is on the

short side and frequently laments his height with respect to athletics. Daphne says he had the ball-handling skills and three-point shot to play college basketball. If only he had been a little taller.

"Do you know anything about the . . . father?" I ask.

"Yeah. We saw a picture of the *birth* father," Daphne says, subtly correcting me, letting all of us know that Tony will be the *only* father, not the pimply teenager who impregnated Amber, then dumped her and encouraged her to abort. I will not make that mistake again. She continues, "He looks like your normal, average guy. He goes to Hofstra, too . . ."

"And he's six *three*," Tony says, laughing.

"So what exactly is an open adoption?" I ask.

Daphne tells us that Amber will be a part of their son's life. She says, "We want him to know his birth mother."

"So it's a done deal?" my father asks.

Daphne nods and says that she and Tony have already sorted out most of the paperwork and paid their fees. Then she says, "It's crazy . . . and all happening so fast . . . We have so much to do in the next few weeks!"

My mother looks worried as she asks what I am thinking but would never have said aloud, "How do you know Amber won't change her mind and try to get the baby back?"

Daphne's answer is patient but persuasive, as if she herself once had the same concerns but has now come to see the light. She says, "Actually, Mother, birth parents in open adoptions are less likely to change their minds. They are at greater peace with their decision because they can see for themselves that the baby is happy . . . And one can argue that in some ways, open adoptions are better for the child, too, because he won't have to spend a lifetime wondering about his birth mother."

Emily Giffin

My mother looks unconvinced. "Will there be any . . . *boundaries*?"

Tony says, "This agency is really great, Vera. They help you set up an individualized plan and guidelines for visits, letters, and phone calls. We're working on those details . . . But it's clear that we want the same thing as Amber. She wants to see him a few times a year—not be over here every day or anything like that. She wants to go on and have her own life."

"Yes, but what will you tell your son?" my mother asks. "Won't this whole thing . . . confuse him?"

I am struck by the irony of such an unorthodox mother being so thrown off kilter by an untraditional arrangement. I can tell by Maura's expression that she is thinking the same thing. But Daphne remains patient. She says, "Think about it, Mother. If an aunt or uncle or grandmother is a part of a child's life, is he confused?"

"No—" my mother says.

Tony cuts her off. "Well, those people are blood related, too . . . But there's no confusion, you know?"

My mother nods.

"Your parents are your parents. Kids *know* who their parents are . . . And the whole point of an open adoption is that the birth mother supports that. *She* chose *us*. Amber wouldn't want to ruin her own plan by interfering in our son's life."

Daphne finishes by saying, "A child's birth family is a part of who he is . . . Whether we knew Amber or not, that would be the case. And we want our son to know her. We think this will be best for everyone . . . I know it might sound weird in theory, but once you meet Amber, you'll see that this is right for everyone involved."

I know what Daphne means about this statement. About

340

how something can feel one way in theory and a very different way when you apply it to your own life and the people who comprise your life. I think of several examples of this phenomenon right here at the table . . . Maybe in theory my sisters and I—and even my father—should hate my mother, but we don't. We tolerate, even love her, in spite of herself . . . Maybe in theory, a woman should leave a man who cheats on her. But in Maura's case, this might not be the right answer . . . Maybe in theory I didn't want children. Maybe I still don't. But as I watch my sister and Tony gaze at each other, I think of what it would feel like to be back with Ben and expecting a baby. *Our* baby. And for the very first time in my entire life, I actually *almost* want one.

thirty-one

Daphne tries to convince me to spend Thanksgiving night at her house, but I tell her I have too much work to do. The truth is I just want to be alone to continue my pity-fest in solitude. So over the next three days I do just that. I wallow in *what if* and *what could have been* and *what will never be*.

At some point every day, I shower and brush my teeth but that is the extent of my grooming. I order food in—the greasier the better. I drown in wine, opening bottles before dark. I listen to sad songs, or happy ones that remind me of Ben and, therefore, might as well be sad songs. I read old journals. I comb through all of our photo albums and boxes stuffed full of playbills and ticket stubs and casual notes we left on the kitchen counter for each other. Things as simple as: *Be back in an hour. Love, Ben.* I relive all of our memories, dwelling the longest and hardest on small, intimate, seemingly inconsequential moments. The sort of moments I thought Ben and I would never run out of.

I don't answer the phone and don't leave the apartment at all until Sunday afternoon. The local news and the view outside my window let me know that it's chilly and damp, but I still forgo gloves or a scarf or a hat, wearing only a sherpa-lined jean jacket. As the heavy, prewar apartment door swings behind me, I inhale the cold. It hurts and feels good at once. I have no destination in mind so I just wander the virtually empty city streets until I find myself on a bench in Washington Square Park. At a nearby table, two old men play chess. They look like brothers, but perhaps I just think *all* old men look alike. In any event, they are the mirror image of each other, both with the same thick, mottled hands, drab-brown messenger caps, and black orthopedic shoes pointing out and away from their folding chairs. I know only the basics of chess—how each piece is allowed to move—but I pretend to contemplate their strategy. I frown and nod as if to say, "Ahh. *Nice* one. You've got him now!" They ignore their audience of one, which makes me feel as invisible as air and even more desolate. An hour seems to pass before one man finally chalks up a silent victory, not even uttering the word *checkmate*.

I stand and walk home in the windy dark, and all I can think of is Ben and Tucker, laughing together somewhere warm and bright, basking in their engagement.

That night I pick up the phone to call Ben and cancel our lunch. I have prepared my "something came up at work" excuse. Maybe I will even use one of Jess's banker expressions: *gotta put out a fire.* I remember Ben once teasing Jess, saying, "That's insulting to the good men and women of fire departments everywhere." And then, "Don't be dissin' Charlie like that," referring to my high school boyfriend.

In mid-dial, though, I hang up, deciding to wait until the morning to make my final call. I can't risk that he is with Tucker tonight. The thought of her hovering in the background—sitting close enough to Ben to hear my voice on the line—is just too much to bear. It would add insult to injury—if you can call what I am experiencing a mere injury.

A few aimless hours later, I am in bed, trying to sleep. Just as I am drifting off, I hear Jess and Michael return from their trip, laughing the hearty laugh of new lovers. They are still in the blissful early stage of a relationship when clever, inside jokes abound. I put a pillow over my head and tell myself that Tucker can't possibly be funny on top of everything else. Life's not equitable, but I have found that God does his best to divvy up humor and good hair. This must be my final conscious thought because I wake up remembering a dream about Tucker. In it, I re-Google her and discover that she is doing a Saturday night stand-up gig in the Village. According to the online four-star reviews, her shtick includes uproarious one-liners about motherhood and good-natured barbs directed at her doting husband.

It is still completely dark outside so I expect it to be two or three, but I look at the clock and see that it is five on the nose. If it were four-something, I'd stay in bed, but five is late enough to surrender to the day.

I get up and take a long, hot shower. Then I get dressed as if I weren't going to cancel my lunch with Ben. I liken it to shaving your legs before a first date even though you *know* that pants removal is not on the agenda. After all, what if I can't reach Ben on the phone? I can't very well stand him up. Or what if the very small part of me that wants to see Ben, no matter what the circumstances, wins out over all reason?

So I put on my nicest suit and highest heels. I give myself an impeccable blowout, and apply my makeup with great care. I put on red lipstick because red lipstick always makes you feel more confident. As a finishing touch, I slide Richard's ring on my left hand. I know I look pretty—which Michael and Jess's expressions confirm when I step out of my room.

"Damn, girl," Michael says as he glances up from his bowl of Raisin Bran. "Lookin' good."

Jess hugs me and says, "Yeah. At least you're going out strong."

Her comment is not lost on me. Despite her big talk of trying to bust up Ben's engagement, even she seems to be throwing in the towel. I wonder what changed over Thanksgiving. Maybe it was spending that time together with Michael and imagining Ben doing the same thing with Tucker's family.

"Thanks, Jess," I say.

She gives me a wistful look and says, "Be strong."

Michael nods and echoes her instruction. They are in accord on every front. I wonder if, over time, they will even start to look alike. It would be quite a feat for a biracial couple, but I'm not putting anything past these two.

I head into work and tell myself that I will call Ben around ten. But as it turns out, my morning *is* crazy, and I really *am* putting out fires. So by eleven, I've yet to call him. I recognize that calling to cancel inside an hour is bad form—and that I need to be a big girl and a good sport. I need to show up on time and look him in the eye and congratulate him on his engagement. It is the right thing to do.

So forty-five minutes later, I am cabbing it to Pete's Tavern on Irving and Eighteenth, practicing what I will say: *Congratulations on your engagement, Ben. I am happy for you and Tucker and wish you the best.* But when I walk in the pub, already decorated for the holidays with white branches, red lights, and Santas galore, I see Ben reading a newspaper, and all of those rehearsed lines fly from my mind.

We are early enough to beat the worst of the lunch crowd,

so Ben was able to secure the most famous booth in New York, the one where O. Henry supposedly wrote "The Gift of the Magi." As I walk the few steps over to my ex-husband, I am reminded of the line from O. Henry's story about life consisting of "sobs, sniffles, and smiles, with sniffles predominating." He sure was right about that.

Ben looks up from his paper and we make eye contact, both of us nodding politely. He folds his paper and pushes it aside as I take off my jacket and will myself to sit and say hello. My hands are shaky, and my voice does not sound like my own.

"Hello," Ben says, in a tone I can't pinpoint. He sounds happy and sad at once. He looks changed—yet utterly the same. His hair is a bit longer than I've ever seen it—but purposely longer—not in-need-of-a-haircut longer. I don't want to like his new look, but I do. He is wearing his hunter-green hooded sweatshirt, one that predated even me. I can conjure the feel of the soft-brushed cotton and have the strongest urge to reach out and touch his sleeve. It suddenly occurs to me that he didn't come from work—Ben's wardrobe is casual, but not this casual. He is drinking coffee, and his cup is already half empty. So I say, "How long have you been here?"

"Awhile," Ben says.

"We did say noon, right?" I say.

"We did. Yes."

"Did you come from work?"

"No," Ben says. "No work today."

I start to say that we could have met somewhere else, so that he didn't have to travel all the way from the Upper West Side, but I stop myself when I realize that Tucker might live in this Gramercy neighborhood. Instead I nod and say, "Just taking the day off?"

"Yeah," he says as he unzips his sweatshirt a few inches, low enough to reveal an ancient REM concert T-shirt. I know that he bought it the night he almost caught Michael Stipe's harmonica. I also know that there is a hole in the left sleeve, one that I used to poke my finger through.

Our waitress arrives a moment later and asks if we're ready to order. We tell her we are—although I haven't begun to think of food. Ben orders the smoked turkey breast sandwich.

"I'll have the same," I say because it requires less effort than anything else.

"Something to drink?" she asks.

"A Coke, please," I say, although the last thing I should have right now is caffeine.

She nods, takes our menus, and briskly walks away as I think, *Now what?*

Ben fills the silence and says, "Look. I know why you wanted to see me today, Claudia."

"You do?" I say, thinking that *I'm* not even sure why I wanted to see him today. To congratulate him on his engagement? Or to talk him *out* of his engagement? I look at him expectantly, hoping he'll just say it for me.

"Yeah," he says, running his hand through his hair as he looks down at the table. "And I think it's really big of you."

"You do?" I say, realizing that it's the former. That he thinks I came here today to give him my blessing in person. That he thinks his ex-wife is mature and gracious. I tell myself that I must live up to the billing.

Ben nods. Then he unzips his sweatshirt the whole way and takes it off. My eyes dart to the familiar hole. I manage a small smile and say, "Well . . . thanks."

I know I need to say more—say the actual words he is

Emily Giffin

expecting from me—but I can't get them out. I simply can't make myself give him my blessing and my final good-bye.

Instead I muster up a weak, "I want you to be happy."

He can take it or leave it. It's the best I can do.

A long silence follows, one in which Ben fiddles with a packet of Equal, and I refold my jacket on the seat next to me. We look up at each other at the same second, and I'm shocked to see grief on Ben's face.

"I want you to be happy, too, Claudia. I do . . . But I just can't let you do this."

I try to process his words, but they make no sense. "Do what?" I say.

"Marry Richard," he says, pointing to the ring on my left hand.

"What?" I say, totally confused now.

His voice is low and his words come rapidly. "I know you came here to tell me you're engaged to Richard. And I know you think you found in him something we didn't have. A promise of the kind of life you want . . . the kind of life you deserve . . . I also know that I'm too late. *Way* too late. That vows have been broken and bridges have been burned. But I just want to tell you, Claudia . . . I *must* tell you that I love you with my whole heart and I'd do anything to get you back. I don't need a baby. I don't even want one if it's not with you . . . I don't want anyone or anything but you."

I am stunned and speechless. I simply cannot believe what I'm hearing. It is *my* speech—the words I thought about saying to Ben, so many times, at least until I saw Tucker's ring. It is too much to process at once so I start out with a simple question. I look at him and say, "What about Tucker?"

348

"What about her?" Ben says, looking as dumbfounded as I feel.

"Aren't you marrying her?" I say.

He laughs and says no.

"But I saw her ring," I say.

"Claudia. She's engaged to some guy named Steve," he says. "A doctor at her hospital . . . Why in the *world* did you think the ring was from *me*?"

"But you . . . ran the marathon together," I say, feeling foolish with my flimsy Internet evidence.

"Well. That's what you do with running partners," Ben says. "You run marathons together."

I feel a surge of relief so great that it is more like joy. It is as if I've been living with a terminal illness and have just discovered that the diagnosis was all wrong. That I'm going to live a long life after all. Something escapes my throat, but I'm not sure whether I'm laughing or crying. I think it is both.

I say, "Well. I'm not marrying Richard, Ben. I'm not even *dating* Richard anymore."

"You're not?" he says. "But Annie told me he gave you a ring."

"He did," I say, twisting it off my finger and dropping it into my purse. Then I swipe at my tears and say, "But it wasn't an *engagement* ring . . . It was . . . *nothing*."

Ben breaks into a smile as he says, "So wait . . . you're *single*?"

"Yeah," I say. "Are you?"

He nods, still smiling. Then his expression becomes grave as he reaches out for my hands. I give them to him. A feeling of warmth and well-being fills me up and renders me speechless. I desperately want to tell him that I have come to the same conclusion about us. That I would do anything to get him back, even if that means having a baby. That I nearly might even *want* a baby with him. That all I want to do is share my life with him, in whatever form that takes.

And I will tell him all of that. Soon. But right now I just squeeze his hands and look into the eyes of the only man I've ever truly loved.

We are quiet for a long time until I finally say, "I can't *believe* you're single."

"Yeah," Ben says. "But I'm thinking of asking someone out."

"Oh, really?" I say, smiling. "Who might that be?"

"My ex-wife," Ben says. "Do you think she'll say yes?"

"I think she might," I say. "I think she might do *anything* for you."

thirty-two

It is Christmas Eve and nearly dark, possibly my favorite hour of the year.

Ben and I are in the car, crossing the Triborough Bridge on our way to Daphne and Tony's house. We are about to meet their son, Lucas, who arrived three days ago, right on schedule, the most divine Christmas present imaginable.

The radio is on low and Nat King Cole is singing "I'll Be Home for Christmas." Ben's hands are gripping the steering wheel, at ten and two o'clock, perfect driver's ed form. He is usually a more laidback driver, even in heavy traffic, and it occurs to me that he could be nervous about seeing my family again. I ask him the question, admitting that I am a bit anxious about our visit with his family tomorrow afternoon.

As if busted, Ben shifts to the single hand at six o'clock position and says, "Maybe a little nervous . . . but I'm mostly just excited to see everyone."

I smile and say, "Even my crazy mother?"

"Even crazy ol' Vera," he says, shaking his head. "I love *everything* that is part of you."

I lean over and kiss his cheek. We have only been back together for a month, and the little things still thrill me. Things such as the feel of his rough whiskers a mere few hours after he shaved. Being in a car with him. Listening to Christmas music. Everything with Ben feels new and sacred and exalted. I suspect that it will for a very long time. Maybe forever.

A half hour later, we are exiting the Long Island Expressway and approaching Huntington. It is now completely dark. Ben points out the sliver of a moon, and the multitude of stars not visible in Manhattan. The stars are the best part about the suburbs, I muse aloud. Ben says he agrees—but then adds, "Not reason enough to move out of the city, though."

He is full of such subtle, conciliatory comments since our reunion lunch. We both are, although we are still dancing around the real crux of our divorce. We don't speak of such serious matters at all, other than when we tell our friends and family the story of that fateful day at Pete's Tavern. We will likely be asked to tell it again tonight. I'm sure we will roll our eyes and say, *"Again?"* while secretly relishing every part of the story—*our* story. The sickening hours leading up to our meeting, our slow-dawning realization, our euphoric cab ride back to my old apartment after lunch. I am sure tonight we will add a new detail, as we do every time. Perhaps I will imbue it with the literary significance that was never lost on me: *There we were in O. Henry's booth, playing out our own version of the "Gift of the Magi." Each of us willing to give up something for the other, for love.* It seems a fitting twist for Christmastime.

Zoe is waiting for us at the door when we arrive. She flings it open and yells, "Uncle Ben!" as she runs out into the driveway without her coat or shoes.

Ben swings her up in his arms and says, "Zo-bot! It's good to see you again, girl!"

"I missed you *soo* much, Uncle Ben!" she says, looking at him adoringly.

"I missed you too, sweetie," he says.

"I knew you'd come back!" Zoe says, and it strikes me that she will one day learn that not all endings are happy. With luck, her parents won't be such an example. So far they seem to be forging ahead with a very fragile peace.

"Well, you're a wise little girl," Ben says, putting her down on the front porch. "Now let's get inside. You're going to freeze to death."

Zoe beams and takes his hand, "Yeah! C'mon inside and see Baby Lucas!"

"Hey, Zoe, what am I? Chopped liver?" I say, pretending that I actually mind playing second fiddle to Ben.

Zoe smiles over her shoulder. "Hi, Aunt Claudia! You can come with us, too!"

By now, everyone in my family, except Daphne and Lucas, are gathered in the foyer, wearing huge, silly grins.

"Hi, everyone," Ben says with a sheepish smile.

My dad emerges as the patriarch and official family spokesperson. "Welcome back, buddy!" he says, extending his right hand.

"It's good to be back, Larry," Ben says, and the two shake hands as my mom snaps a picture. She snaps another as my father says to himself, "Aw, what the heck," and then gives Ben the sort of embrace you would expect when a man has just returned from a long tour of duty in a faraway war.

The others line up for their turn. First Maura, Scott, and the boys. Then Dwight. Then Tony.

"Congratulations," Ben says to him.

"You too, man," Tony says.

Meanwhile, my mother is photographing every embrace, snapping away. I let her—because I don't want to stifle her spirit and because I have a feeling I'll want to relive this night for years to come.

My mother ceremoniously hands her camera to Dwight, saving herself for last.

"Ben, darling," she says, pausing for dramatic effect, "what took you so long?"

Ben laughs and says, "I don't know, Vera. I was a fool."

"Yes, you were," my mother says with tears in her eyes. Then she points to me. "And so was this daughter of mine."

"Okay. Okay. *Enough!*" I say, laughing at my family's over-the-top enthusiasm. "We have a baby to meet!"

"Yes! Come in here," Daphne calls out from the family room.

We round the corner, and there is my sister, in the soft glow of the fire, holding her newborn son.

"Ben, Claudia, this is your nephew Lucas," Daphne says. "Lucas, meet Aunt Claudia and Uncle Ben! . . . That is what he should call you. Right, Ben?"

Ben takes my hand and says, "Yeah, Daph. That's what he should call me."

"Well, come get a better look at him," Daphne says proudly, as she unfolds the blue blanket from Lucas's face.

It is a moment I've been wondering about ever since Thanksgiving. Will I feel differently than I did when Maura gave birth to her three children? I am worried that I will. But as soon as I gaze down at Lucas, I am relieved to realize that I feel *exactly* the same. Filled with pride and wonder and gratitude and anticipation of so much to come.

"He's exquisite," I say.

Too good to be real. And yet, he is real.

"I know," Daphne says. "I can't *believe* it."

"Aunt Daphne, can I please hold baby Lucas?" Zoe asks—which is William and Patrick's cue to chime in with their own request to hold the baby.

"Not now," Maura gently tells her kids. "Lucas needs his mommy right now."

Daphne gives Maura a grateful glance. I can tell she is not ready to pass around her child. She has waited way too long for this night.

We all have.

Much later that night Ben and I are back in our old apartment. It is finally starting to feel like home again—which is a good thing because Michael is moving in with Jess in January. They're calling it a "trial run" but I know better. Sometimes it's easier to take things in small steps.

Like Ben and I are doing now. I have moved about half of my clothes back in with Ben, and am rifling through our dresser drawers now, looking for my red flannel pajamas.

Ben laughs, and I say, "What?"

"I knew the lingerie get-back-together stage wouldn't last forever."

"It's Christmas Eve!" I say. "Time to be cozy. Not sexy."

"Well, I got news for you," Ben says.

"What's that?" I say, smiling.

"You're *both*," he says.

I smile as I head to the bathroom to brush my teeth. Then I hesitate for a long moment before taking my pill. I return to the bedroom where Ben is waiting for me in his own green flannel pajama bottoms. We turn out the lights and get under the covers. Our kisses are cozy at first, like our pajamas, but quickly become urgent and hungry.

"How can I love you this much?" Ben says at one point.

It is one of those things you just can't answer. Like trying to explain magic or miracles or faith.

"I don't know," I breathe, thinking that there are a *lot* of things I don't know. I don't know whether I will ever overcome my fears of motherhood. Whether I will someday *be* a mother. Whether I am capable of being a good one.

But for now, it is Christmas, and I am with Ben, and that is all that seems to matter. So I hold on to him tightly and whisper his name. As a wish and a promise for things to come.